T0354963

FEAR'S DRIVE

DECLARATION OF WAR

CAMERON A. PERSON

Archway Publishing books may be ordered through booksellers or by contacting:

Archway Publishing
1663 Liberty Drive
Bloomington, IN 47403
www.archwaypublishing.com
844-669-3957

ISBN: 978-1-6657-4104-0 (sc)
ISBN: 978-1-6657-4105-7 (e)

Library of Congress Control Number: 2023905396

Print information available on the last page.

Archway Publishing rev. date: 03/29/2023

For everyone who helped me along the way.

PROLOGUE

"Fear." The worn older man's hoarse voice boomed out across the barren valley, its natural bass seeming to shake the debris around him. "Every species has experienced this natural instinct of self-preservation. Its origin dates back to even our earliest evolutionary ancestors, from the humans of our current era trailing backward through primates to the first tetrapod to make the revolutionary leap from water onto land, all the way back to the first single-celled organism that decided to seamlessly split down the middle to create an exact copy of itself in what can be considered the first fearful reaction of isolation. In all recorded history, very few beings have been exempted from this phenomenon, and those slim few are the great men and women who have shaped history so far."

His voice paused as he let out a chuckle that could send shivers down the spines of even the mightiest opposition.

"Yes, every now and then there arise those among the mindless, fear-driven masses with the strength of will to rise above that unnecessary burden and evolve in ways no normal living being could ever imagine."

As he spoke, he began toying with a black liquid-like substance secreting from the inside of his coat sleeve. "These incredible people arise far and few between. But when they do, they give the evolutionary process an unprecedented leap forward. Like the great strides that brought the age of the primitive Neanderthal to a close and dawned the age of the superior-minded *Homo Sapiens*."

His tone shifted. "However, in the endless pursuit of dreaded perfection, one cannot just sit idly by and wait for those great people or great strides to come their way. Sometimes, one must take it into his or her own hands to rise and push the species forward, even if that means making the hardest of decisions."

"This world is a garden, one that was meant to be inhabited only by ascended beings deserving of its radiance. Why should parasites who seek to do nothing but damage and pollute this beautiful planet that has done nothing but support and nourish us since the dawn of time be allowed to roam free and continue their rampant destruction?"

He clutched his hand tight as he continued on, the black substance worming its way back into his coat sleeve.

"To be a driving force in evolution, tampering with the creation of people's so-called God ... makes one close to a God himself, does it not? What use does a God have with the primitive concept of fear when he's tasked with the purge of the parasitic scourge that's killing this planet?"

He waved his arms out expressively and gestured to the desecrated landscape around him.

He cracked another chilling smile. "We created FEAR to be that driving force, separating the strong from the weak, the good from the evil, the remedies ... from the parasites, and to attempt to start a new and better direction for the world around us."

"My organization believes in my cause. They believe in me and the new age I will create. And who am I to betray that faith? I will admit, though, I'd never considered we'd face this level of opposition."

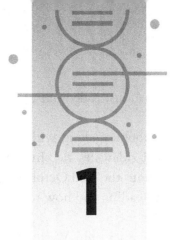

1

JUST OUT OF VIEW

The streets echoed with the buzzing of energetic city life; the car horns, diversified voices, and rumblings of construction, along with the handful of other screeches and screams, were the norm for the people calling New York home. The noise never ceased, for this was "the City That Never Sleeps."

To some this may have been miserable, but for most, they couldn't imagine anything else.

The city's plethora of noises were more prominent this particular morning, specifically from the cars littering the streets, as their drivers repeatedly honked and exclaimed in irritation at the man gallivanting over the hoods of their stationary vehicles.

He raced down the gridlocked street, sliding across one car after another without even a glance in either direction.

His name was Sam Newman, a young man born and raised in the concrete jungle of New York and one of the few who didn't mind all the racket. It drowned out all the static and invasive thoughts that paraded through his mind on a daily basis.

Coming to a halt a ways up the street, he took a quick look in the glass reflection of a nearby storefront, running his hand through the thick strands of auburn hair lying on his face. It was handsomely messy as usual, as if he had just rolled out of bed with a fully done head of hair.

With his backpack bobbing along with him as he weaved his way down the crowded sidewalk, he shivered, watching as his visible breath dissipated into the cold October air. He raced fluidly, knowing where he was heading and how to get there like the back of his hand.

Whipping around a corner onto West 37th Street, he reached a certain alley that lay a bit outside his usual route. Stopping to light up his second-to-last smoke, he savored a couple quick puffs before continuing with his daily task. With the cigarette placed tightly between his lips, he knelt at the entrance of the alley, quickly pulling out a small piece of Tupperware from the front pocket of his backpack.

Taking the lid off the container and revealing the heaping portion of dog food, Sam called out to the figure he could see curled up underneath the makeshift shelter a distance into the alley. "Here, boy!" he called.

Out popped a fluffy, albeit slightly dirty, yet still otherwise beautiful golden retriever. The surprisingly well-fed pup came barreling out of the alley, tackling Sam as it proceeded to aggressively lick at his face and knock his cigarette to the ground.

"It hasn't even been twelve hours yet, boy." Sam laughed, propping himself up as he started to pet the ecstatic dog. "Ah, hell. I know. I missed you too, buddy." He wrapped his arms around the dog as it dug its head into his shoulder to give him a hug.

Relighting his unfinished smoke, Sam sat with the dog as it chowed away at its fresh food and water. To that day, he still didn't know the dog's name, having gotten by so far with simple terms like "pup" or "buddy." Though he'd tried to name him a few times, the dog never answered to anything he could come up with.

The closest he'd ever got was when the dog glanced his direction at the name Ruckus, but even then, he still wouldn't respond to it.

He always figured it was because the dog's previous owner had already named him.

And asking him was clearly out of the question.

Sam had never actually spoken to the dog's owner, only seen him every few days as he passed by the very alley he now stood in, seemingly the old man's home. He could always be found sitting out along the street with his cup placed in front of him, and the dog always sat close by. He usually held a sign that read, "I tried to take on the world. It won."

It had been like that for at least a year or so, and Sam couldn't help but feel sad every time he saw the old man. His sign, while simply put, held no lies, just the bare truth of a man who had plummeted down the economic ladder. Though he wasn't exactly in any better position, given the threat of eviction he'd been facing in the last few months or so, he always tried to give the spare change or bills he had on him as he passed.

Then one day Sam had passed by the alleyway, and strangely enough, he hadn't seen either the man or the dog anywhere in sight. He thought nothing of it, figuring they had finally moved to another area of the city and began to continue on.

Stopping in his tracks just as quick as he started, he turned his head and listened, faintly hearing the echo of the dog aggressively barking from somewhere within. It was an odd occurrence, given that, in all the time he'd seen them, he'd never once heard the dog bark.

Down the dark alley he went, following the growing sound of barking and what now seemed to be an old man's weak pleas for help. He dashed forward, whipping around another corner to find a group of spindly men surrounding the dog's owner as he lay face down on the ground.

That was the last thing he remembered.

When he had come to, he found himself alone and knelt down in the alley with no sign of the men from before. Wiping the blood he felt from his lip, he turned to face the motionless body of the old man lying on the ground a few feet away, with the dog nuzzled up to him as it let out gut-wrenching whines.

He had gotten there too late; the man had lost too much blood from the stab wound on his abdomen.

The police said it seemed like a mugging gone wrong.

That was that—the man he'd never spoken to was gone from this world without a trace, leaving the dog to fend for itself in this unruly city. Sam had tried to bring him home, but his studio had strict rules regarding pets.

When that was a dead end, he'd reluctantly called animal control.

He had some slight apprehensions about leaving the dog on its own in an unfamiliar place, but he knew the streets of New York were no place for a stray dog.

The traffic alone was one of the biggest dangers.

When a week or so had passed, and he still hadn't heard back from the shelter, he called and asked if they had managed to find him yet. The shelter attendant said that, in the numerous visits they'd done to the alley, the dog had escaped twice, scared off the dispatched handlers three times, and the remaining few times, they simply couldn't find him. They finally abruptly ended the conversation by telling Sam that, unfortunately, they wouldn't be making any more visits to the dog, given how much resistance it seemed to give and the large volume of calls they had to respond to.

Sam went ballistic at their disregard for the dog, pleading for them to try again until they eventually just hung up on him.

So he decided to care for the lone pup in the meantime while he put out feelers for anyone who would be able to take him in. It took a few tries to get the dog to come out to him initially, but once he had, all it took was one call.

Aside from having built a makeshift shelter out of a few spare materials he turned up, he made it a routine to stop by the alley at least once a day to feed the puppy.

It'd been about three months since he'd started, but still no one had answered any of his online ads to take the dog.

Sam ran his hand along the animal's back as it chowed away at the foul-smelling kibble, taking another drag from his cigarette as he did so. He lightly rubbed the scar across his left cheek as he habitually did, exhaling the smoke as he took out his phone to check his messages. His boss had just sent him a reminder that one of the pieces of mail in his bag was on deadline for three thirty that afternoon.

He double-checked which one he was talking about, reading the recipient as one Dylan McMaster.

Something about the name struck a chord in his mind, but no matter. He glanced at the time on his phone and read the bold 3:18 p.m.

"Ten minutes," he muttered to himself while putting out his cigarette.

Looking down at the remaining few embers scattered in the ash, he turned over to the dog at his side, who simultaneously turned to look right back at him.

"I guess it's that time again, buddy," he told him.

The dog let out a soft whine as it stuck its head in his chest, as if asking him to stay just a little longer.

"Aw, come on, boy. Don't make me feel any worse than I do. I gotta work if you wanna keep eating that kibble you love so much." His stomach suddenly growled, stopping his sentence. "Whew, I gotta get to work if I wanna be able to eat this week too." He laughed.

He slung his bag back over his shoulder, stood up, dusted off the back of his pants, and then knelt over to pet the dog one more time. "I'll stop by later on tonight on my way home, buddy. You sit tight till then." He snickered. "Not like you'd go anywhere else even if I asked ya to."

With a wave, Sam exited the alley. The content pup eagerly awaited his next visit.

● ● ●

A number of blocks away in one of the Diamond District's tallest skyscrapers, numerous employees averted their gazes from the apparent origin of some very prolific screaming.

It didn't faze people much, as most everyone was employed by the man doing the belligerent complaining. In this work environment, it was either learn to work through the constant beratement and condescension, or you just weren't cut out for the job.

The building belonged to John Moriano, CEO of Moriano Incorporated, one of New York's longest-running conglomerates.

He was a portly man, so much so everyone would gather in the break rooms placing quiet bets on whether the buttons on his suit would pop off that day. If the man had hair on his head at any point, it was decades ago, and now it felt as if the sheer thought of hair on him was unnatural.

The yelling echoed out from within his office, and everyone who knew who was on the other end of Moriano's rage simply snickered as they passed by.

Inside the office was a young man sitting silently opposite Moriano, his mind worlds away, finding himself in a trance as he stared at the bulging vein on his boss's beet red forehead.

His name was Dylan McMaster, a thin yet well exercised young man, clad in a form-fitting, charcoal gray suit. Sweat dribbled down his forehead and under his heavy eye bags as he stared at the screaming man before him, his mind so distracted he couldn't even make out what mindless rabble was being thrown at him.

Dylan was now a two-year resident at the company and was still facing heavy opposition from his fellow employees, given just how quickly he'd passed over them in the company's strict hierarchy. He had earned it though, having graduated from high school an entire year early; he would have even been valedictorian if he hadn't rejected the position due to his severe social anxiety.

With his associate's degree in hand, he'd headed straight for college, from which he'd graduated top of his class with two master's degrees in only four years.

It was a feat that had led to many significant job offers coming in.

In terms of workplace weaknesses, the only one he really had was his attitude, which regularly put him at odds with those around him.

While he could take medication to quell the anxiety he regularly faced, all it did was make him feel more comfortable calling out people's mistakes.

"A double-edged sword," he'd often say.

His lack of filter had only isolated him from those he worked with. And right now, they all felt a little giddy hearing how he had finally veered away from his "wonder child" persona.

"*I cannot fathom your incompetence, McMaster!*" Moriano screamed, finally breaking Dylan free from his trance. Moriano scoffed. "Giving the CEO of New York's largest conglomerate the wrong proceeding date. This union was going to be a great day; Moriano Incorporated and Reliance Industries were finally going to merge after years of being each other's top competitors. It would have made us the largest company in the entire East Coast. But because of your blunder, we now are woefully unprepared to plead our case. We have none of the legal documents, let alone our simple quarterly reports prepared for this, because you told him to come in a week early!"

Dylan was already feeling guilty enough about his oversight without the pieces of spit flying at him, as he could've sworn he'd given their competitor the right date and time. He unfortunately knew, though, he hadn't been 100 percent in a while, as events in recent weeks had left him immensely distracted. So it wasn't that hard to believe he had made a mistake somewhere along the line.

He began his feeble reply. "Sir … I swear it was an honest mistake. It won't happen again."

Moriano fumed as he tried to restrain himself. "A mistake. A *mistake*?! You bet your dead-eyed, scrawny ass it won't happen again, because if Reliance rethinks his decision because of your 'mistake,' I promise you it'll be your last one at this company." Moriano stared deadpan into Dylan's eyes as he clenched his teeth in anger.

"Everything will still go as planned, sir, I promise. I'll call him now," Dylan quickly replied, panic apparent in his voice. He couldn't afford to lose his position on this deal.

However, what Moriano didn't know was that Dylan knew the man they were set to meet today on a personal level. They'd actually gone to high school together.

After the both of them had graduated at different times, they had admittedly seen each other far less often than they should have, both heading off into different directions regarding their futures. Nonetheless, they had managed to keep in contact with one another as best possible through calls and texts and maybe the occasional bar outing if they both had the time.

Dylan pulled his phone from his pocket, sliding his finger across his shattered touch screen as he looked for Victor's number, hitting the dial button the moment he found it.

A few blocks away, a well-dressed and finely groomed man rushed down the crowded sidewalk after hopping out his town car, his beige overcoat flapping in the wind. The traffic that day had left him and his good friend driving him stationary, and after seeing a strange man leap across their car and sprint down the roadway, he finally told his driver to head home when he could and that he'd be following the acrobat's lead and going it on foot.

His thin, jet-black hair bobbed with each stride he took, and you'd never guess he'd shaved the night before by the half inch stubble covering his chin.

His name was Victor Reliance, the youngest CEO in the state, and of New York's largest company to boot, Reliance Industries. The family-led company had been left to him years ago by his late parents, Edgar and Vanessa Reliance.

He'd been on his way to an important business venture he'd been setting up with an old friend's company when they'd been met by the heavy traffic.

His phone began to ring out from his pocket.

He answered out of breath, "Hey, Dylan … I'm on my … way. What's up?" He paused as he waited for his friend to answer, momentarily catching his breath.

"Mr. Reliance? This is Dylan McMaster of Moriano Incorporated … There is absolutely no excuse for the mistake on my part, but I accidentally gave you the wrong date for the merger proceedings. I know it's unprofessional, but I hope you won't rethink your decision because of this," Dylan did his best to speak calmly, but he couldn't help feeling a sense of uneasiness as Moriano breathed down his neck.

Besides his confusion as to why Dylan had called him "Mr. Reliance," Victor sighed in irritation, given the fact he'd told his ride to go home.

But unlike the CEO he was arranged to meet with today, he wasn't too upset. Even if it wasn't a friend of his he was planning this deal with, he knew getting irritated at the intermediary was the wrong call. He knew both in business and in life, mistakes would be made, and how the company's leader decided to respond would determine what kind of outcome would come about. You couldn't expect respect if you wouldn't give it; it was a lesson his father had taught him early on in life.

He felt his young age gave him an insight into the coming few years of business that older leaders couldn't seem to grasp, as if they, too, were rooted in how things were done in the past. As if they believed their power and social standing alone demanded that others grovel at their feet.

He'd done things differently so far, though, having made a goal with himself years ago to never turn out like some of the men of power both his father and he had interacted with.

Victor laughed. "Don't worry, man. Things happen. I'm only a few blocks away. What do you say I come by anyway, and we can just iron out a few of the fine details before the actual proceeding? Get the ball rolling, ya know?"

Dylan was instantly relieved. With Moriano staring holes through him, the last thing he needed was for Victor to back out of the whole thing.

"Hello?" Victor asked.

Dylan realized he had taken a second to respond and quickly blurted, "Yes, of course, sir. We'll be here."

● ● ●

Sam stood outside of his destination, looking it up and down in discontent as he stared at the giant Moriano Inc. sign plastered at the top of the building.

He let out an intense sigh of disapproval. One of the things he hated most in this life was the blatant ego of the human species. It was one thing if your name could have a double meaning like the rich boy Reliance's, but naming a company after yourself for no other viable reason than to see your name in big flashing lights was undeniably self-centered in his eyes.

Shrugging off his disappointment, he opened the thick, glass-panel front door that lay before him.

Sam was a decently built guy, often hiding his surprising physique under the simple baggy clothes he usually wore. To an outside view, he may have come across as thuggish or unapproachable. The first thing most people noticed about him was the sharp ferocity his consistently furrowed brow gave him. Yet when he brushed his thick auburn hair back off his face and wiped the scowl of irritation from his expression, his bright smile and piercing blue eyes could put most people at ease.

He walked into the building and took out the envelope from his bag, quickly rereading the recipient's familiar name, Dylan McMaster.

"There's no way," he thought to himself before walking over to the front desk and asking where he could find him.

The office manager looked at her computer. "Mr. McMaster is on the twenty-fifth floor in the middle of a meeting, but if you talk to our receptionist up there she should be able to hold the envelope for you."

He thanked her and headed toward the elevator. But to his dismay; he found an "Out of Order" sign taped to the doors. His head hung low as he grunted and slunk to the door for the stairs, opening it to look up at what appeared to be a seemingly endless spiral staircase.

While he had grown up in the city, he had mostly lived in the rural areas, where the buildings rarely topped four or five stories. So every time he ventured into the heart of the big city, he always felt a little out of place.

Once again, he groaned and began his ascent of the seemingly endless spiral.

The door swung open as Sam slumped through, gasping for breath. Though he had a pretty decent stamina, a continuous jog up twenty-five floors was too much for anybody.

"Fuck stairs. Multimillion dollar company ... can't even be bothered to repair an elevator."

As he regained his breath and looked around, he saw the receptionist the clerk had spoken of. He made his initial thought of the woman relatively quickly, remarking to himself about the slight look of fear written on her expression.

He realized why pretty quickly as he finally heard the man yelling through the doors behind her, which was mostly profanity to boot.

As he approached the receptionist, he held up the envelope, pointing to the name on the front.

After squinting to see what it was he held, she pointed to the doors behind her with a face that seemed to say, "Good luck." It seemed like she had no intention of handing the letter over for him.

He smiled and grabbed the handle, letting himself in.

John Moriano instantly ceased his incessant rambling and just stared at Sam, a very gross stare if one had to describe it. In front of Moriano sat Dylan, who had just turned to face the newcomer.

A look of confusion washed over Sam's face as something clicked in his head.

Dylan began, "Can I—"

"What the hell do you want? Get the hell out of here before I call security!" Moriano interrupted.

The friendly look in Sam's eyes instantly disappeared.

"Well?" Moriano continued. "Did you hear me!? Are you deaf or just stupid!?"

As he started to speak, Sam's voice shifted to a considerably darker tone. "Talk to me like that again. I *fuckin'* dare you." He caught himself and focused on refraining from saying anything more. After clearing his throat, he looked away from the dumbfounded CEO and over toward Dylan. "I take it you're McMaster?" Sam asked in his usual tone.

Dylan's confused look deepened. "Uuum, yeah … Do I know you?" He glanced back at Moriano, who seemed absolutely stunned that someone had actually spoken back to him. He couldn't help but be in a slight sense of awe of this random stranger, the only person he'd ever seen be able to shut Moriano up.

Sam's pace quickened. "Nah I don't think so. I just need a signature."

Dylan signed the clipboard Sam extended toward him, taking the letter as he watched the man leave without a word.

As he watched the door shut once more, Dylan couldn't help but think about how familiar the guy was, but the thoughts quickly left his mind as he turned and faced the infuriated boss he had admittedly forgotten about.

Leaving only one thought lingering in his head. *Shit.*

● ● ●

Blocks away in one of New York's most stunning attractions, crowds roared as they passed by the critically acclaimed Broadway theater. Each and every one of them came from entirely different walks of life, each one led here by the many paths they'd each woven for themselves.

A man rudely brushed his way through the crowd of smiling faces, a youthful exuberance and a prideful aura about him. He wore an expensive black leather jacket with a bright red stripe along the arms and shoulders. He sported an ominously black mask of seeming Japanese origin, resting upon his slick black hair that was so greased up it seemed wet, and accenting all of it was the large bag slung over his shoulder.

Finally making his way past the crowd, he headed into an alleyway just off the main strip of the area.

Once he felt he had walked far enough he was sure no one could see, he took the bag off his shoulder, careful to set it down ever so gently.

Unzipping it, he stuck his hands in and pulled out a large black machine of sorts. It was rectangular in shape, covered in strange gold wiring, and had a large orb structure built into the center that housed a strange blue stone.

"And now," he slowly told himself.

He pressed a sequence of buttons on the front of the machine; it began to hum, growing louder and louder with each coming second. Standing back up, he started a slow run down the other direction of the alley, using his lead foot to push off with such strength that the ground beneath him crumbled.

With a gust of wind, he shot out of sight quicker than the eye could see.

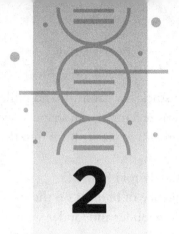

2

RAGING LIGHT

D ylan slunk down the long beige hallway, slowly maneuvering his way through the sea of coworkers floundering about, all silently mocking him with their icy gazes. It seemed obvious word on what had happened had already made its way throughout the office, simultaneously shattering his reputation as the wonder child and making him feel even further isolated from the peers he was supposed to be able to collaborate with.

As he reached his tightly cramped office, his mind fluttered with a million thoughts.

Moriano had officially removed him from the merger project, despite his being able to quell the situation with Victor. It was still better than having been fired, but the financial stability that would have come from a deal like that was hard to let go of. He'd have to call Victor later that night to complain about the whole thing.

Yet, that still wasn't even the forefront issue on his mind. For the last few months, he'd been in a rough patch with his high school sweetheart, Ashley, given how they'd seemed to drift from each other recently.

As he rose quickly through the ranks at his new job, her acting career had begun to take off in recent months. She'd already starred in a number of Broadway productions. Their careers had simply continued to take them down different paths.

While he'd been working with the goal of setting them up for a good future together, he could feel her slipping farther and farther away as her popularity rose at work.

It had come to a boiling point the week before, when he'd tried to plan a romantic dinner out to make up for the time they'd been missing out on—only for her to leave him sitting in the restaurant alone for the night, not bothering to call for six hours due to a last-second decision to spend the night partying. She claimed she'd forgotten, despite talking of it earlier that very same day. He'd been quite angry, so much so he'd spent the last week at a hotel to cool down. Yet, love was love, and he couldn't deny the heaps and bounds of it he had for her.

She just always seemed to have something more important happening—whether it be with her model friends or her production directors or whatever hunk costar she was working with at the time. She always assured him there was nothing going on. "We're just friends, my God!" as she'd put it.

He never truly thought she would actually cheat on him, but the thought kept creeping its way into his mind whenever he had a free moment to himself. He couldn't help but worry that her new lifestyle was beginning to change her.

Dylan sat in his chair clenching his fists, before suddenly remembering the letter he'd received earlier. He thought back to the man who'd given it to him as he reached into his pocket.

"I swear I knew that guy. Where the hell from?" he muttered to himself.

Cutting the thought short, he started opening the envelope and took out a folded piece of paper. The front of the folded paper had a pink lipstick stain, and beneath that read, "Ashley."

It made sense; he knew she hated phones. While she did use the one she had, she had always believed that taking the time to write out a formal letter showed more character than simply tapping a few keys on a screen.

Not knowing what was to come, he unfolded the letter.

● ● ●

The roar of the crowd around the Broadway theater blended together in a symphony of diversity—friends from all over the world meeting one another, families visiting from out of state, lovers out on romantic dates for the day. All of them were painfully unaware of the seemingly harmless machine just out of their views.

The black box's humming continued, growing louder and stronger with each passing minute.

Everyone stumbled as the ground sharply rumbled with no warning, causing the crowd to fall silent for a few moments and finally revealing the humming to them all. A father of two jerked around as the sound of a loud click echoed out from the alley behind them. He told his sons to stay with their mother as he carefully went to investigate.

Turning the corner, he was greeted by a bright white light beginning to illuminate its surroundings. Despite its alluring glow, his deepest, most primal survival instincts lying dormant in the recesses of his brain jolted to life, telling him whatever that was, it wasn't good.

He sprinted back to his family, the frantic fear on his face sending chilling jolts through their chests.

"Run!" he violently screamed.

The rest of the crowd had already become wary of the ominous hums and growing rumblings echoing around their surroundings, doing their best to remain as collected as they could. Yet once they all noticed the great white light filling the sky, and the panicked family running from the scene terrified, all logic and reason went out the window.

That was all it took to cause a mass panic in the streets.

The brighter the ensuing light grew, the louder and harder the rumbling got. Families fought to stay near each other as the masses trampled down the busy streets, forcing numerous innocents to the ground and underneath the oncoming stampede of scared civilians. Various crunches and cracks filled the ears of the ones fortunate enough to stay topside.

Electronic-like noises began to sound into the air, piercing everyone's ears and dyeing the sides of their cheeks red from their burst eardrums.

● ● ●

Suddenly, everything stopped.

No more rumbling.

No more noises.

Just bright white light continuously filling the sky.

Everyone calmed for a moment as all turned their gazes upwards. Then, as the people closest to the machine heard another faint click, the limits of what can be defined as absolute chaos tested themselves.

As if Pandora's box had been opened, releasing the slumbering cosmic energies of the universe from their primordial shackles, an explosive wave of otherworldly energy burst forth from the spherical core of the machine.

The energy rushed forth, its raging light blanketing everything in its path from its epicenter outward.

It swallowed up a terrified Sam leading a group of sprinting bystanders a few blocks away on to Dylan and the workforce of Moriano Inc., all struggling to cram themselves through the doorway after they'd noticed the light in the sky. The out-of-order elevator had forced everyone into the stairwells, and Dylan would never forget the cracking sounds he heard as people disappeared below the crowd. It made its way even onto Victor as he tried herding groups of people out of the shops along the streets.

A wake of destruction, despite being limited to a finite area, utterly ravished the landscape. That was it. Times Square was gone. Chunks of the Diamond District and Midtown were gone as well, leaving only a crater that, in later years, would become a national monument to the lost instead.

Even if the destruction was held within a certain area, the enigmatic energy continued onward for miles, killing power for nearly the entire northeastern section of the country.

Authorities say that the radiological force had made its way almost fifty miles before dissipating.

● ● ●

A great distance away from the ensuing chaos, a sophisticated, well-dressed older man gazed upon his creation from his safeguarded viewing facility amid the great blue sea. The graying on the sides of his hair and beard added to his distinguished look as he took a sip of a vintage, aged whiskey, swishing the alcohol around his mouth to savor the taste, along with the pride of his achievement.

Various flooded-together cries for help could even be heard from where he stood without the help of their various cameras set up around the city, numerous of them turning off one by one as the blast radius grew.

The sight thrilled him on an instinctual level, sending shivers of excitement down his spine as old memories began to stir.

He cackled, grinning ear to ear as he spoke in his deep, hoarse voice. "Those of you who survive, rest now. For when you wake, we have a great deal of work to do."

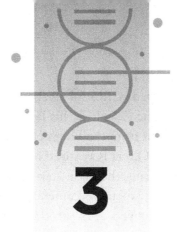

3

CALAMITY'S AFTERMATH

New York's surviving populace was reeling.

They had been ravaged and violated by an attack both unforeseen and unexplained, with numerous tens of thousands of innocent civilians caught in its wake. Buildings were toppled, land was devastated, and countless lives were lost. As the city did its best to heal, the remaining news stations still up and running throughout the city did their best to keep the survivors in the loop.

"It is still unknown exactly how many lives were tragically lost last week, as evacuation and rescue efforts are still underway."

"This is *New York Morning News*, with follow-up on the unknown explosion that swallowed up Times Square last week."

"No news on whether this was a terrorist attack has been released to the public yet, but authorities' tight lips seem to speak louder than words."

"The sheer force of this explosion has sent low-grade tidal waves to our neighboring cities across the water, heavily flooding sections of land that weren't a safe enough distance from the bay."

"This was no ordinary explosion. We *all* saw the cloud of white smoke … light, whatever it was! We have the right to know what this was!"

"The brilliant-minded CEO of Reliance Industries is still presumed to be among the casualties, his last known location being revealed to be only blocks from the blast's epicenter."

Channel 12 reporter Olivia Ray stood outside the massive crater that had been formed during the blast, staring into the red blinking light on the ridiculously expensive camera planted in front of her. "Our hearts, souls, and prayers are with the families and friends of the departed after this unfathomable event. The 'Day of Light' will go down as New York's most tragic occurrence. Back to you, Eric," she finished.

Her cameraman Ryan clicked off the camera. "And we're clear," he told her, beginning to carefully dismantle the complex machine piece by expensive piece.

"Thank God," she muttered. "I can't stand to be around here much longer. This place really gives me the creeps."

"You and me both," he admitted, loading the camera into the van as he began to voice his looming question. "So, have you made any theories yet? About what happened?"

"Your guess is as good as mine until any more information comes to light. Even the cops are stumped right now," she answered with a huff.

"You mean David's stumped?" He shot her a look, disbelief written on his expression. "Please tell me you haven't been talking to him again."

"Stop. You know that's not what I want, but he's still my best source on the entire force. No one else was willing to give me an inside scoop, not that there really is one in this case. Nobody knows anything right now." She decided to brush off the accusation, knowing he only wanted the best for her. "It scares me, Ryan, knowing that someone … or something can do all this, and no one has the faintest idea of who, how, or why."

She turned her gaze out into the crater, feeling her body shiver from the sight.

● ● ●

As damaged as the city and its inhabitants' psyches were, time still went on, and after a few months had passed, the city officially cordoned off the crater site.

The CDC dubbed it a "hazardous zone."

The designation wasn't for the sole reason of the dangerous environmental factors, but because low-grade amounts of an undiscovered form of radiation had been discovered by the CDC in the remnants of the area. Residents were told it wasn't enough to declare the rest of the city dangerous, but it was enough to cause legal troubles for anyone who decided not to abide.

After making that decision, military presence in the city nearly stopped altogether, with none the wiser on why they'd leave so soon after such a grievous event.

Conspiracy theorists had a field day coming up with the possibilities of what had caused all of this, as anyone who knew or saw anything that happened right before was dead or presumed dead.

Due to the sky erupting white that day, locals had started calling the day of the explosion the Day of Light. And despite the fact the crater had been scorched black, what had once been Midtown was now Light Valley.

The rescue efforts yielded little results. Of the near million people caught in the blast, little over 4,500 people were found and recovered.

Though the number of rescued civilians gave a faint sense of relief to a slim few, compared to the amount of people still missing, no one felt as though they could celebrate the return of their once thought lost family members.

Though numerous support groups were started to help the families through the losses of their loved ones, far too many people found themselves without any real mental help in this trying time. Properties that offered some kind of care were flooded with the millions who had lost something, spilling out into the streets from the sheer number.

No one knew the why or the how. All that was known was that, one fateful afternoon, everyone's worlds had changed in a split second.

Of all the lives changed by this calamity, three particular lives had yet to experience it for themselves. One, however, was about to get his first taste.

In a distant secluded spot, four months after the Day of Light, Dylan opened his eyes.

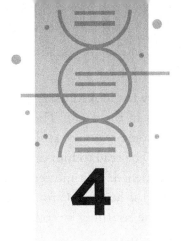

4

GLIMPSE OF THE
NEW WORLD

The heat had never particularly bothered Dylan, as he'd dealt with his fair share of New York's warmer weather—from warm sunny days to scorching heat waves that lasted weeks.

Despite that, something about the heat that woke him this morning had him drenched in sweat. It was as if the source of the great heat was right nearby.

He looked up into a flickering overhead light that seemed to boil his eyes, wiping beads of sweat from his brow as he did so. Slowly, the fog of his mind began to clear. He carefully sat himself up as he tried to make sense of his spinning head.

Looking around the space he found himself in, he quickly noticed it looked to be a hospital room of some kind—judging by the hospital gown he was wearing and the IV drip he saw in his arm.

The room was solid egg white, with nothing but the dim overhead lighting for illumination. There were no windows anywhere along the walls of the room, which left him with a strange tightness lingering in his chest. It felt as if the walls were slowly moving inward as he started to feel his head shift from spinning to aching from the stress.

Above the door was what looked to be a thermometer, reading an abnormal 103 degrees in the room. Then there was the strange clock next to it that, for some reason, was showing some very weird numbers. "128:21:59:07?" he read to himself.

"What the fuck happened?" he muttered while still sitting in the bed, grasping his head as he peered around the room. He did his best to try and think of the last thing he could remember—running, screaming, white light.

He'd been in the middle of reading through Ashley's letter when he'd looked up to see some kind of bright light filling the sky a distance away. The whole building had then been thrown into a panicked frenzy, everyone clamoring over each other as violence began to break out, every individual fighting his or her way through the crowd to get out of the building first.

After that, however, he drew a blank. The next thing he knew he was waking up here, confused and hot.

"Nurse?" he called out, feeling a faint layer of phlegm in his throat, as if he hadn't spoken in quite a while.

After a few moments of no reply, he attempted to find the usual assistance button you could find, with no such luck. His gut plummeted as everything continued to get stranger and stranger.

In the corner of the room, he spotted a chair with clothes folded on it. They were covered in dirt and small tears all over the fabric. He easily noticed they were the clothes he last remembered wearing.

With a gut-wrenching uneasiness bearing down on him, he recklessly yanked the IV drip out of his arm and bolted up toward the tattered clothes. Rifling through the stack, he found a crumpled piece of paper among them, immediately realizing it was Ashley's letter.

Its contents all came flooding back into his memory:

> Dylan,
> I know how you hate letters. "Relic of the past" as you'd usually say. But I've been doing a lot of thinking. I'm sorry. I've been distant … and I've lied.

But I want to fix things, really fix things. I don't want to lose my best friend. Please come home soon so we can talk about things.

—Ashley

He was positively ecstatic—talking, that was all he'd wanted to do for months. To finally be able to come to a mutual point of understanding where they both would just be honest with how they were feeling about what had been happening.

Grinning ear to ear, he knew he needed to head straight home to see her.

Finishing the last button on his shirt, he paused for a moment as another wave of confusion suddenly washed over him.

What had he actually been in the hospital for?

He definitely wasn't in pain. His mind had cleared up relatively quickly, and he didn't see any wounds, aside from the fresh scar he could feel across his lip. Not only was there this new scar, but it seemed he'd somehow grown out his beard since the last thing he remembered.

Then there was the pulsing ache in his head.

As he thought deeper, he was interrupted by the sound of yelling outside the room. *"Anyone here? Fuck! Is this place really empty?!"*

The scream made Dylan jump and face the door, momentarily glancing at the thermostat that had jumped up to 106.

Reaching for the knob, he quietly turned it, barely opening the door to peer through the crack. As that crack slowly widened, a wave of heat burst its way into the room, causing the temperature to jump a few more degrees.

Dylan wiped the sweat from the side of his face, an intense worry apparent on his expression.

At the end of the hallway he saw a familiar figure, a messy, brown-haired guy in a black, unzipped sweatshirt, coupled with an irritated scowl on his face as he looked around the long hallways. It was the man who had just delivered the letter to him … earlier today?

Yesterday? Dylan wasn't quite sure at this point. He almost didn't even recognize him underneath his own fresh beard.

He walked out of the door, cautiously calling out to him, "*Hey, you're here too?*"

Sam instantly jolted around, grabbing his chest as he threw his head back in relief. "Jesus bro, you scared me ... McMaster? What the hell are you doing here?"

"So we *do* know each other?" Dylan questioned. He hadn't shaken the feeling he'd recognized him before too.

"Well, I guess there's no use hiding it now. I know I may look a bit different, but ... Midtown High, class of 2014. Though you did graduate a year early, so I guess you'd be class of 2013, huh?" Sam replied, strolling forward and closing the gap between the two.

Upon reaching him, Sam extended out his hand. "I'm Sam, Sam Newman," he proclaimed with a smile. His irritation had seemed to dissipate a bit, leaving only his warm expression.

Yet Dylan strangely felt as if his expression didn't match how he actually felt. Nevertheless, Dylan's sinking feeling seemed to fade upon finding another soul wherever it was they were.

"Sam? Wait, Sam?!" He looked him up and down in disbelief, "Holy hell man, you grew up! I used to be like a foot taller than you." Dylan laughed as he pointed out the inch or so height difference between them in Sam's favor.

He reached out to return Sam's gesture and shake his hand, only making contact for a brief moment before yanking it back and exclaiming in pain.

"Whoa, what the hell happened?!" Sam questioned.

"That didn't burn?" Dylan half-shouted as he began rubbing his hand to quell the stinging.

Through their bantering, the two of them heard approaching footsteps coming from around the corner of the hall. Both cautious about the sketchy, ill-lit place they had found themselves in, they half rushed to look at the origin of the sound, careful not to make too much noise. Down the hall, they both saw a man walking in their direction, still clad in a hospital dress.

His hair was jet black, with a thick and untamed beard to match that put both of theirs to shame. As he scanned the hallways around himself, he finally made eye contact with Dylan.

"*Victor!?*" he exclaimed.

"What the hell? *Dylan!?*" the man shouted before making his way over. "Where are we? What happened? Where are my clothes?" He rattled out as many questions as he could without biting his tongue.

Both Sam and Dylan did their best to understand the words racing from his mouth despite the distraction, as they kept noticing the hospital ventilation blow Victor's gown upward, giving more and more of an unnecessary peek beneath.

Gross, Sam couldn't help but think to himself.

Dylan raised his hands in an effort to calm the man as he finally finished his rushed questioning, "Take it easy, man. I think we know about as much as you do. Why don't you slow down and tell me what you remember."

"I ... I don't even really know," he admitted. "I was on my way to Moriano when ... it all just goes blank."

Victor glanced over at Sam. "Who's this?"

"Sam Newman," he replied, raising his hand with his introduction. An irked look washed over his face as he let the words loose from his lips.

"No way." Victor's face slightly lit up, looking deeper at Sam for a moment as he pondered the name. "Sam ... as in from Midtown? Holy shit, it is you! Dude it's so good to see you. Where the fuck have you been!?"

"How fuckin crazy is this?" he turned and asked Dylan. "I mean we haven't seen you since before graduation." He excitedly gestured toward Sam, who had seemed to check out of the conversation as he aggressively patted his pockets.

"You good, man?" Dylan questioned.

"At the present moment? No, not really. My smokes are gone, and my nerves are shot to hell. That last one woulda come in real handy right now." Sam couldn't quell the uneasiness growing in his voice.

Turning to face Sam, Victor asked, confusingly, "What's got you all jumpy?"

Feeling his pulse begin to race with the ideas of what may be happening, Sam felt a slight throb in his head, a subtle downward shift in his tone becoming apparent. "This isn't completely weird to you guys? Where the fuck is everybody!?"

Victor felt his body start to warm, droplets of sweat forming on his forehead. He wiped the moist feeling off of his strangely soaked brow. "Yeah I noticed that. I must've been walking like ten minutes before I even found you two."

"The room you woke up in, where is it? We should get your clothes and go," Sam half ordered, glancing around the intersection of corridors they stood in.

His pulse had started to quicken even more. What the hell was this place? At first glance, it looked like a hospital; yet there were no nurses, no labelings on the walls, no noise.

It was silent besides the three of them.

Sam loved movies, all kinds of movies. He loved analyzing them and guessing what would happen next before it actually did, and the current scenario was the perfect setup for a horror movie, and he wasn't taking that chance.

Dylan could see Sam was beginning to panic. "You look like you're about to jump out of your shoes, man. What are you thinking?"

Sam began, "Something isn't right. We all wake up in this, what? Empty hospital? What hospital do you know that doesn't have *anyone* in it? Not to mention the fact that, for some odd coincidence, we all used to go to school together. This is way too weird to be mere coincidence … Now"—he turned away from Dylan and towards Victor now, both seeming to be a little jumpy themselves now after seeing this pushier version of their old friend—"where is the room you woke up in?"

● ● ●

Tucked neatly into the corner of the hallway, a camera zoomed in for a closer look at the three men with a microphone loosely picking up their conversation.

On the other end of the stream of data coming from the camera sat a young man in a room full of less than a dozen capable men and women. Each of them was stationed on his or her own personal computer, monitoring camera feeds and screening for anything useful to their organization.

Streams of footage were coming in from everywhere—traffic lights, bridge cameras, Grand Central Station, every camera this collection of individuals could hack themselves into.

The young man watched his screen as Victor reentered his room, leaving Sam and Dylan waiting outside. Clicking the "urgent" button on his headset mic, he began his report.

"Subjects one through three are active and on the move. Should we mobilize the reentry squad!?"

Just as he finished, a large hand firmly gripped his shoulder, the owner of which spoke with a deeply hoarse voice. "While your mindfulness of protocols is commendable, young man, I'm afraid we'll be taking a different course of action with these three."

"Sir, are you sure?" the young man questioned.

"I understand the apprehension about letting subjects leave on their own, but this is a good opportunity to let them get a glimpse of their new world. This is a good day. Our cause gains three powerful new allies. I'd like their individual handlers tasked with surveillance. And have them highlight the way out for them while they're at it."

● ● ●

Sam, Dylan, and Victor, all three now fully dressed, continued silently down the empty hallways full of confusion, passing numerous wide open doors to rooms just like theirs as they did.

The only sounds were the ominous creaks of the creepy structure they found themselves in, accompanied by the occasional growl of their stomachs. Each of them could hardly focus from the hunger that was beginning to set in.

In an instant, a crackle of electricity rang out, and all the lights shut off around them, leaving them stranded in the pitch black.

"Holy shit," Victor whispered.

"What the hell is going on?!" Dylan shouted just after him.

Sam shuddered, overcome with a strange sensation that made the hairs on the back of his neck stand up. A warmth spread throughout him as he thought to himself it felt like they were being watched.

With another surge of electricity, a single light flickered on at the end of the hallway to their right.

The trio stood motionless, unsure of whether or not to follow the mysterious light beckoning them forth. But what other choice did they have? With no other options available to them, they all took their first step forward, cautiously growing closer to the light as it flickered in and out.

As they finally reached the aged bulb, they turned around to see what they could find, only greeted by the four dark hallways surrounding them. To make matters worse, the light above their heads burnt out in a quick flash.

Yet, just as fast as the first went out, another bulb lit up down the hallway behind them.

"Yup, we're gonna die," Victor muttered.

Hallway after hallway, flickering light after flickering light, they continued on, wondering if they were simply walking to their unfortunate demise. Their every thought was filled with what they may possibly find around the next corner.

Coming to a stop underneath the newest light presented to them, they waited until the light burnt out like all the rest, each under the impression another would light up any second afterward.

After a few moments and still no new clue as to what direction to go now, the panic settled back into the trio.

They each stumbled back, feeling their back come against the walls of the hallway before sliding down and taking a seat. It seemed like there was no way out of this hell. They'd gone down at least a dozen turns and still hadn't found any sign of an exit.

Just how big was this place?

Victor broke the silence. "Hey, is that another light?" He pointed down a long, darkened hallway to their left.

A single sliver of light shined down at the end of the corridor a few dozen yards away, illuminating what seemed to be a single rusty ladder leading upward. Each of them carefully took one step after another as they made their way down the hallway, all of them wondering if this was finally the exit.

Finally reaching the sliver of light, Sam peered upward, unable to make out what was above them through the blinding light. Just before beginning their ascent, he glanced over to the side of the ladder, faintly seeing some sort of crest brandished on the wall—a sword and shield with a crown laid on top, with what seemed to be running gears intermingled throughout it. The strange logo only added to the suspense of the strange situation.

A man on a mission, Sam grabbed the first rung of the ladder and led the three of them toward the hope of salvation above them.

Upon reaching the top, he reached out for what appeared to be a cracked-open manhole cover. He froze. Had they been underground? This nightmare kept getting weirder. Just where would they find themselves after going through?

Sam slowly placed his right hand on the metal disk, its cold touch sending chills through his body. There was something strange about the feeling of cold, though, its usual sensation nowhere to be found.

Somehow, somewhere in his mind, he knew that going through this hole was a bad idea on numerous levels.

With one swift motion, he shoved the cover out of its slot and up into the air, watching it land a number of feet away.

A gust of cold air washed over the three of them, letting a loud howling sound echo out as the wind made its way downward through the long tunnel.

Sam was stunned. For something that was supposed to weigh at least fifty pounds, that was as easy as throwing a pillow.

Though the light from outside the hole momentarily blinded them, determination pushed them all forward, each of them slowly picking himself up from the ground as they all fought to catch their bearings.

As their eyes adjusted and their surroundings became clearer, all they could see was black and gray. The gray slowly cleared up into distinct concrete shapes and rubbled buildings, and the black turned into scorch marks covering everything as far as their eyes could see.

They found themselves surrounded by pure destruction and carnage.

"Where the hell are we?!" Dylan exclaimed. Last he remembered, he'd been in Midtown. How in the world had he ended up wherever this was? Just as he finished his thought, he heard numerous dings ring out from Victor's pocket and watched him reach in and pull out his phone.

Unlocking the shattered screen of his personally manufactured device, Victor's heart sank as he saw the date posted on his home page, February 20, 2020, 2:37 p.m.

Months of messages, voice mails, and various notifications filled his feed faster than he could read through them all.

How could that possibly be? It was the fourteenth of October; or at least that's what he remembered it being. Confused, he questioned the two men who had checked out in sheer awe of the scene.

"What's the date?!" he half burst out.

"Well … I mean yesterday was the fourteenth?" Sam answered, his voice devoid of feeling, as though he couldn't muster the energy to be concerned, given how caught up he was in the gruesome scene surrounding them.

"Of what month?" Victor pushed, hoping what he saw was some kind of fluke.

"Victor, it was obviously October. Are you OK?" Dylan hesitantly asked, carefully setting his hand on Victor's shoulder so as to not to set him over the edge, or himself for that matter.

He showed them the screen of his phone, reading the horrifying February 20, 2020. Everyone's stomach did backflips in response.

Whipping out his own phone, Sam started tapping on its power button over and over. "Dead," he finally let out.

Darting his head around the area, he tried to scope out some kind of landmark.

His eyes slowly went wide as he noticed where the bay lay around them, and if he had to take a guess based on that. "Guys, I think … I think this is Times Square."

Realizing the gravity of the situation, they all looked around. Sure enough, in the distance they could see other buildings. Oddly, they seemed to form a perfect circle around all the senseless destruction.

Victor's face went pale at the thought that Reliance industries was supposed to be nearby, and it was nowhere in sight. He could feel his chest tighten at the thought of whether or not Hartley had managed to avoid whatever had happened.

A thought occurred to Dylan amid their collective confusion. When he'd woken up, he'd seen a weird clock that read, "128:21:59:07."

Now after seeing the harrowing date plastered on the screen, the numbers finally made sense.

One-hundred-twenty-eight days.

Twenty-one hours.

Fifty-nine minutes.

Seven seconds.

Whatever was going on, someone or something was keeping track of how long they had been in those rooms.

"We've been down there for over four months?" Dylan forced the question out with fear in his voice.

In unison, Sam, Dylan, and Victor all turned toward the gaping hole behind them, the pitch black within almost seeming alive.

Though none expressly said it, they all had a similar feeling that nothing would ever be the same now. They seemed to feel that they should never have come out of that hole and that there was no going back anymore.

They had no idea just how right they were.

5

OUT OF THE LOOP

The trio gasped in disbelief of the barren wasteland they had found themselves smack in the center of, left with the depressing realization they were right where the heart of their city had once stood.

No one could even muster any words. They were too busy making sure they remembered to breathe, the sheer shock of the sight leaving them quite literally quaking in their boots.

Sam's eyes suddenly went wide, his head darting from side to side as he tried to gauge where exactly they were. He shot to his side, breaking into a full sprint as he weaved around the various debris.

"Sam!?" Victor screamed before both he and Dylan, feeling confused, broke into a sprint after their frantic friend.

Despite their best efforts, Sam continued to get farther and farther ahead, beginning to hurdle and bound his way straight over the rubble.

"Jesus, he's fast," Dylan let out as he and Victor slowly climbed over the city remnants.

Just as they left the area, three ominous figures rose up from out of the hole in the ground, who proceeded to follow after the unsuspecting trio.

After a number of minutes, Sam came to a halt at an eerily familiar landscape, feeling his blood begin to boil as he looked at the wasteland that even reached this far out. He slowly took another step, hearing the scrape of metal along the ground.

Kneeling down, he wiped the dust and debris off what seemed to be a street sign. His heart sunk as he read the bold lettering, "W 37th St."

With tears welling in his eyes and a burning sensation engulfing his chest, Sam burst forward, screaming out with everything he had. "*Buddy*!?" he cried out, tears already streaming down his terror-stricken face.

As he ran down the familiar remnants of the roadway, he pictured the buildings that used to be here, the small shops on the side of the road that always pressured him to buy, the collage of faces he'd see on any given day.

"*Puppy!*" he screamed out once more, never having cursed himself more for not knowing the poor dog's name.

He saw where the alley should have been just up ahead, but all he could see was fallen rubble littering the ground.

"*Noo!*" he sobbed, skidding to his knees as he finally reached the debris, shoving his hands in with everything he had as he pulled piece after piece away from the pile.

The farther in he went, the larger the pieces of rubble continued to grow, until he couldn't even seem to budge anything anymore.

"*Fuuuck!*" he roared, so infuriated by his own lack of strength he began to slam his fists into the sides of his head in complete and utter rage. Screaming out into the empty distance with every ounce of air in his lungs until his vision seemed to blacken, he pounded his fists into the solid concrete again and again, over and over until the sound of his flesh colliding with stone drowned out all other noise in his head.

He was too far gone to even notice the blood spilling out from his knuckles, their random sprays and spurts creating an abstract scene of sorts around him, the streaks of blood drenching the stone and telling a tale of a broken young man's rage.

Two hands forcefully grabbed Sam's shoulders, yanking him back from the wall of stone as he continued to thrash his fists around.

"*Sam!*" Victor screamed, attempting to hold his arms still for a moment. It was as if Sam had been possessed, taking everything Victor had just to simply hold him still. "*Saam!?*" he shouted once more, finally seeing some kind of reaction in him.

Slowly but surely, Sam's movements decreased to a halt, his eyes seeming to light back up from whatever trance he had been in. Looking around with confusion apparent in his expression, he finally noticed Victor and Dylan standing beside him, Victor's hands planted firmly on his arms.

Their expressions conveyed that they were utterly perplexed, a part of them simply confused and the other part filled with fear—fear of the man who stood before them, fear of what he may be capable of, fear of just how little they knew about him.

It was a look Sam was all too familiar with.

He immediately knew what had happened without even needing to ask, aggressively jerking his arms out of Victor's grip. "I'm OK now," he softly called.

"What happened!?" Dylan questioned, shaken up by the complete 180 of personality Sam had just shown them. In the time he'd known Sam, he'd been such a timid, soft-spoken person, never seeming to show any ounce of emotion on his face besides a select few occasions.

"I … this is where my dog was," Sam admitted, taking one last look at where the alley once stood, seeing the bloodstained walls before him. He gritted his teeth and shoved that burning feeling of rage deep within himself, turning away to go anywhere else but here. "Let's go," he muttered, silently beginning to make his way forward, blood still dripping from the tips of his fingers.

Victor and Dylan stood in shock of what had just happened for a few moments, looking around the bloodied mess of an area.

Victor began to slowly follow after Sam, turning back to check on Dylan before continuing. "You coming?" he asked.

Dylan's eyes were spanning the area where they had found Sam, a wave of utter confusion taking hold of him. "Did Sam … really do all of this?" He motioned out to the clearly recently moved pieces of rubble, showing the enormous sizes of some of them.

It was baffling that Sam had even been able to budge most of the smaller pieces.

Sharing a look, they both turned to look at the numerous bloody fist marks Sam had left in one focal area of the largest stone. Both continued after Sam before noticing the indentations in the stone where Sam's knuckles had started to chip it away.

The three figures stepped out from behind a pile of rubble, waiting for their targets to get a little farther away before they continued after them. As they strolled past the scene of Sam's outburst, the forefront of the three chuckled beneath his eerie black mask. Amusement over the bloody abstract painting filled his head, his excitement over the newest prospects growing right alongside it.

● ● ●

The following few hours blurred by—spent climbing, crawling, and shimmying over and across the rubble that once had been a piece of their homes. It was a true-and-blue wasteland. The rotting smell of death filled their nostrils, and the unbearable feeling of sadness weighed on their already heavily taxed minds.

How were they still alive? Why were they still alive? What made them so special that they got to live and experience this hell?

They could see bloody limbs sticking out of the rubble all around them, the various sizes of the arms and legs giving away the victims' ages. The amount of children he saw made Sam puke three times in as many hours.

The traumatic ordeal had already left a hefty toll on their minds, each of them beginning to feel a hollow sensation inside, like a piece of them they hadn't even truly known was a piece of them had been stolen.

They all just wanted to get home, lay down, and hopefully just wake up tomorrow from a horrible nightmare.

Dylan's mind kept thinking back to Ashley's letter as they slowly trekked their way to freedom, attempting to think of a lighter subject in the wake of whatever this was. He wasn't sure why he had woken up where he had. All he knew was he wanted to go home. He wanted to see the woman he knew he undoubtedly loved and just hold her.

In his eyes, all their issues, big or small, were a thing of the past. He was ready to just be over it all.

His mind went to the ring he'd bought a year or so ago but had never had the chance to use, as their problems had started not too long after that. Yet the past was the past. He was finally going to do it. He was going to ask her to marry him.

Victor, on the other hand, couldn't keep himself focused on one thing for very long, bouncing between thoughts of his next meal and his lifelong friend, Hartley. Food, though, seemed to be the forefront issue on his mind.

He was starved, potentially had been for four months at that. He knew that wouldn't be the case if Hartley had anything to say about it. The fifty-six-year-old man, who still seemed as spry as he'd been in his twenties, had been with Victor since before his parents had passed when he was young. Victor knew Hartley was single-handedly the only reason he had made it to where he was in life; without his help, he'd forget to tie his own shoes.

As far as Victor was concerned, Hartley had been with him long and through enough that he considered him as close to a father as he would ever have.

Victor's excitement rose at the thought of sitting down to one of Hartley's home-cooked meals with him again.

And then there was Sam, who'd been unusually quiet even for him. He simply walked ahead of the group, eyes trained ahead of him as he did his best to keep his mind blank. He was fearful of what may happen to him if he focused on everything that had happened.

With no one waiting for him at home, he started to panic at the thought of being left alone with his own damaged mind.

He just wanted to forget this whole ordeal and to push away the negative feelings this unequivocally terrible day was putting him through.

As they walked toward the place or person they longed for most, the distant skyline steadily grew closer until they finally began to hear the familiar sounds of their home. Finally, they were filled with some semblance of hope in this trying time.

"*Look*! It's Central Park," Dylan exclaimed, increasing his pace to a half sprint and almost passing Sam.

"Wait," Sam loudly whispered, throwing his arm out to stop Dylan from going any further.

Dylan and Victor quickly stopped in their tracks behind Sam. "What's wrong?" Dylan asked. "We're almost there." His chest felt ready to burst from excitement.

Pointing forward, Sam motioned toward the strangely cautiously dressed men up ahead, all of them clad in bright yellow hazmat suits. They were pacing around the perimeter of the rubble as they waved some kind of machinery around, its high-pitched whining echoing out across the barren land.

The three of them dove to duck down below a patch of rubble, peeking around as they watched the group of men slowly moving closer to them.

"What the hell is going on?" Victor whispered. "Are we safe here? They're wearing Hazmat suits!?"

They all threw their hands up in front of their mouths, now having been presented with the possibility of breathing anything toxic in.

"Should we ask them for help?" Victor suggested. "Maybe they can tell us what's going on and possibly get us home? Maybe they can even tell us why we woke up down there."

"I don't know if that's a good idea. I get the feeling we're not really supposed to be here." Sam looked back onto the group of men, who had begun to finally veer away from them.

He wondered what it was they could have been looking for out here in this wasteland.

"Here's our chance," he told them, before starting to rush forward, slowly increasing his speed as he ran so as not to attract unwanted attention.

Following his lead, Victor and Dylan raced behind him. "Just a little further!" Dylan whispered excitedly.

All three of them were so caught up in the moment that none of them realized how casually they all seemed to soar across the concrete chunks, occasionally even leaping at least seven or eight feet through the air with ease.

They could see and hear the roadway at this point, noticing a quaint little one-way road straight ahead of them cluttered with the usual evening traffic. Gaining speed gradually with his excitement, Sam stopped paying attention to his footing, tripping not even ten feet from the edge of the crater.

It wasn't until then that Sam actually realized how fast he had been going. He barreled through the air, skidding across the top of a passing Kia Forte and landing on the concrete sidewalk just past it.

The car screeched to an abrupt halt as a young woman practically jumped out. She started to run to Sam but found herself cut off as a crowd slowly formed around him, helping him to his feet.

They each exclaimed in unison about the tumble he'd just taken.

"*Are you OK!?*"

"*Bro, holy shit, you flew!*"

"*Somebody call an ambulance!*"

"*No!* No ambulance," Sam interjected, yanking his arms back from the strangers. Realizing they were only concerned for his well-being, he breathed in and out. "I'm sorry. That was uncalled for. But I assure you. I'm OK." He raised his arms to show the people and himself. "See? Not a scratch on me."

He noticed he had a huge group of people staring at him all around the roadway, including a trio of strangely dressed men a block or two away. The forefront of the men wore some kind of black mask that covered his face, but Sam could feel his intense gaze nonetheless—almost like some kind of warmth coming from their general direction.

"Well, that's all well and good. But what about my car?" Sam heard a female voice call from behind him with a huff, turning around to see a young brunette woman with prolific anger in her oddly piercing gray eyes. She was pointing behind herself to what had once been a nice recently purchased Kia but now had a shattered windshield and a concavely dented hood. "I'm very glad you're OK and whatnot, seeing as how I couldn't afford a lawsuit like that. But how do you expect to pay for this? Because I sure can't!?"

Sam panicked for a second; he hadn't even really realized he'd hit a car, let alone damaged it like that. That's when a thought occurred to him. He had done that damage to the car and landed on solid concrete, yet he was strangely unscathed. He was hardly even sore.

As he stood there, an odd feeling he couldn't put a name to welled up in his chest. Sam hardly noticed when Victor and Dylan managed to catch up to him.

"*Sam*! Shit, that was a nasty fall. Are you OK?" Victor exclaimed, reaching out to grab Sam's shoulder.

"Yeah, I'm OK, but I have other problems," Sam said, brushing Victor's hand off him as he motioned toward the angry lady and the destroyed windshield beside him.

Turning in that direction, Victor made eye contact with the woman, who appeared to be overtaken with a mixed expression of curiosity and confusion. She blinked a few times, shaking her head as if she couldn't believe what she was seeing.

"Are you ... Victor Reliance?" she asked as her look of confusion seemed to shift to excitement.

Hesitantly, Victor confirmed her suspicions. "Yes ... I am, but I really don't have time—"

Before he could even finish his sentence, the woman seemed to blow a gasket. "*Oh my God*! Where have you been? Do you know what happened on the Day of Light? Why are you miraculously appearing four months later? Who are these two men?" She prattled on without taking a breath, nearly gasping for air once she finished.

Victor was shocked. While the woman seemed familiar to some degree, he wasn't sure if he'd ever met her. Yet here she was questioning him like some kind of cop or paparazzo. "Slow down a second, miss. I don't even know your name. Let's start there," he remarked, quickly realizing the irony of him stopping someone's barrage of questions.

She palmed her forehead. "I'm sorry. Where are my manners?" Reaching into her leather coat pocket and pulling out a small recording device, she clicked the bright red button and pointed it toward Victor, Sam, and Dylan.

"My name is Olivia Ray with Channel 12 news, here with the presumed dead Victor Reliance, missing since the infamous Day of Light. Any comment on where you've been for the last four months, or anything on what went down right before the bombing?"

Day of light? Explosion? The three of them knew they'd been gone for a while. But a bombing? The image of the wasteland was beginning to make sense.

"What are you talking about? What bombing?!" Sam burst out, surprising even himself.

"You're kidding, right?" Olivia laughed. "Four months ago, the last time Mr. Reliance was seen, an explosion of white light cratered nearly two miles all around Times Square. No one has seen or heard from Mr. Reliance since then. Wait, didn't you just come out from the crater site? Were you caved in somewhere? Were the three of you caved in together? Are there other survivors? How did you get out? What did you eat?"

Sam, Dylan, and Victor were already worried about what they would discover had happened in the last few months, but an explosion? This lady's belligerent questioning wasn't making it any better either.

"Yes, we came out of there. We woke up in this—" Dylan began before Sam placed his hand on his chest, stopping him from saying anything else. The look on his face obviously emphasized he wanted him to stop.

Confused, Dylan followed Sam's lead and shut up.

Olivia just stared at Dylan, having just noticed him for the first time. The instant she met his strangely deep brown eyes, noticing the subtle ring of hazel along his pupil, she felt her heart flutter. *Now's not the time*, she thought to herself.

As she shook those thoughts loose from her head, she cleared her throat. "Whatever he was about to say, I'm glad he didn't. I *need* a camera crew here," Olivia told herself and whoever else was listening. She turned back to her car to grab her phone and call Ryan. Luckily enough, he lived not too far from there. So he'd be able to get there faster than if she called into the station.

"You guys just stay put while I …" She turned to look back at the strange trio, but all she saw was a small group of bystanders beginning to point down a nearby alleyway in unison.

"Damn it," she muttered, her head hung low in disappointment.

● ● ●

Sam led his newfound friends down the alley across the street, careful not to be seen by the nosy reporter they'd just met.

"Hey, Sam?" Dylan began.

"Yeah, what's up?" Sam answered, eyes still facing forward as he led them into another alleyway.

"Why'd you stop me from telling her what happened? I mean … maybe she could have helped us fill in the blanks?" Dylan asked, his head hurting from the events of the last few hours.

"I feel like he's right. She seemed harmless. I will admit she knew how to talk. I mean, don't get me wrong, I hate reporters. But being this far out of the loop is kinda scary," Victor replied with a light laugh.

"Maybe, maybe not. From my experience, reporters are just more trouble than they're worth. We can figure things out as we go. Not to mention all the press coverage we'd get for 'coming back to life.' I don't know about you guys, but I'm good," Sam finished while glancing back to face them.

When he turned, something caught his eye a distance behind Dylan. Three strange men stood outside the alley they'd entered, the same three men Sam had seen just after exiting the crater. Their gazes were like daggers as they locked their eyes onto Sam, Dylan, and Victor.

"Let's get moving," he said as he motioned in front of himself, clearly picking up his pace. He wanted to be sure the men were following them before he made a call on what to do.

After turning down three more alleyways, Victor and Dylan began questioning why they were continuing to take alleys and not streets—or why they'd just gone in a full circle for that matter.

Sam continued to assure them this was a better idea.

Every alley they turned down, he could still see the three men standing there. There was no mistaking it now. The trio was following them, but why was the question.

Sam felt as though he already knew the answer.

It didn't take a rocket scientist to piece things together—that them being gone for four months, the odd hospital they'd woken up in, the explosion they'd heard about, and these men following them were all connected in some way.

He just didn't know how.

Whoever these guys were, they were good. Sam was usually pretty adept at losing a tail. But yet there the trio was, still hot on their trail.

"Guys, listen close. Look at me and don't panic," Sam whispered while coming to an abrupt halt. Dylan and Victor could hear a slight difference in his voice, almost as if someone else was talking.

Dylan's heart dropped. He looked over at Victor, whose face had gone pale. The events of waking up to now had left them severely wound up, and Sam's strangely scary warning did not help.

"I'm pretty sure we're being followed," Sam whispered to them while still looking toward the men who'd also come to a halt. He couldn't seem to hide his anxiety as he looked upon the forefront of the men. His strange black mask gave off an ominous aura that Sam could swear he could actually feel. "You see those guys back there?" Sam questioned while slyly pointing them out.

The other two jerked their heads around to get a look.

"Jesus! Not so fuckin' obvious. Scream out, 'Come grab us,' why don'tcha," Sam lectured, letting out a huff of disbelief.

The masked man gave a light wave as they turned their gazes toward him.

"I see them," Dylan whispered back, noticing he'd begun to sweat a little. It had started to get hot again just like back in the hospital.

"They've been behind us since we got out of the crater—just watching." Looking around and spotting a fenced-off alley, Sam continued, "Let's cut down here."

● ● ●

Down the street at the beginning of the alley, the three figures stood and studied the three men beginning to climb over a tall chain-link fence.

The first of the three figures started to stroll forward, continuing his pursuit. He had an air of arrogance and mystery to him, emphasized by the strange mask resembling a demon laid upon his face, his greased-back hair sticking out from underneath. The clothes he wore gave away the fact that he was well off, judging by the $10,000 frosted Rolex on his wrist and the pointless black leather racing jacket he wore.

He'd never even touched a motorcycle in his life.

He slightly snickered beneath his mask. "Seems Sam hasn't lost his touch. Still near impossible to follow the guy. Dylan and Victor could learn a thing or two from him." He focused on the scene past the fencing, his piercing black eyes fixed on the men disappearing into the crowded street.

The second of the men followed close behind, his suit jacket flapping in the cold February wind. He tugged on his silver beard, as he always did when he was deep in thought. "All three subjects seem to be showing positive signs of awakening. Should we make the report?" he asked through his phlegm-lined throat, unable to stop glancing back at the menacing figure behind himself.

The last of the men rubbed the old wounds along his arms, almost like a tick. His shirtless body was covered in thick, protruding scars from everything you could think of—knives, bullets, fire, even scratches and bite marks here and there. It looked as though this man had been to hell and back—and gone back for seconds.

His body was trembling with anticipation. He'd been told his next target was suspected to be a bigger challenge than any of his previous. "Why not just grab them now?" he said in a raspy voice, his throat so scarred he couldn't speak properly.

"You know our orders, big guy. Just watch from a distance and let them discover themselves. I'm sure we're in for a good show. For now, we hang back and relax. Your turn will come, so long as you remember who makes the rules around here," the masked man offered. "Come on. We can't let them get too far."

In an instant, all three of them burst forward, disappearing and leaving behind nothing but small sparks of electricity in the air and crumbled stone on the ground.

● ● ●

After carefully following Sam's instructions, they all stopped outside an apartment building in Lenox Hill, watching the evening sun slowly begin to disappear over the horizon. Dylan lit up once he realized they were only a few blocks from his apartment now. He'd had enough crazy for one day. He just wanted to go back home to Ashley.

He was sure she was worried sick. It'd been four months. He wouldn't be surprised if she thought he was dead. Hell, maybe he was dead, and all of this was simply a dream.

He sighed in relief as he felt the slight sting of his fingers pinching his arm, proving to himself in some small form that this was real, that he was indeed still alive, and this urge to hold the woman he loved was all the more proof he needed.

Not counting his missing number of months, it had been a month or so before that that they'd even touched each other.

"OK, guys, stop." He let the words fall out, pulling himself to a halt.

Sam and Victor stopped to listen.

"We have to be far enough away from those guys by now, right?"

Glancing around in every direction he could and only seeing the slowly dispersing crowd along the busy street, Sam nodded. "Yeah, we should be OK. I don't see them anymore," he said while still taking a few more looks.

"All right, look, I really appreciate the help, guys. I honestly don't know if I would have found my way here without your help, but I need to get home. We've been missing for months and I need to tell people I'm alive. I need to see Ashley," he finished, looking down the street in the direction of his place.

"Whose Ashley?" Sam asked with a look of curiosity.

"My girlfriend. We're … well, we were having problems before this all started, but this feels like a second chance. Right? I mean we should be dead, but I'm standing right here. I have to fix things." Dylan thought of all their petty squabbles, all their huffs and puffs for truly pointless reasons, and he couldn't see any point to them. It was like being "dead" for four months had hit the reset button, and he was sure gonna take that opportunity.

Sam placed his hand on Dylan's shoulder, giving him a warm smile and an encouraging nod. "You do what you gotta do, man. My dad used to say that love was fickle, and that it loves to throw curveballs to test the two of ya—knowing that, if you can work through it together, you'll be all the better for it. It's a little cheesy, but my old man loved my mom more than I've seen anyone love anything."

Dylan felt hope pour into him through Sam's hand, his simple gesture successfully wiping the fear from Dylan's mind. He noticed, though, that for as much as Sam appeared to feign happiness, there was a strange tinge of sadness in his eyes that he'd sworn he'd seen before. He swore he could feel … loss, resonating from within him. "Loved?" he asked.

Sam quickly adjusted his mannerisms, embarrassed by the quick, momentary break of his shell. He cleared his throat before continuing. "Yeah, they passed when I was young. It's OK. It's not a big deal. My point is, if you love her, go get her, man."

"Thank you. I appreciate that. OK, I can do this. How do I look?" Dylan asked, putting his arms up, looking himself up and down. His clothes were covered in tiny tears and dust; hell, all their clothes were.

"I'd suggest a quick shower and a change of clothes before anything." Victor laughed.

"Yeah, I think we could all use that. You'll be fine though. Just go home, get cleaned up, and do whatcha gotta do," Sam assured him. "I'm probably gonna head home too. I need to sleep."

"Should we … I don't know, meet up in a few days after we've all settled back in?" Victor questioned, knowing full well that he intended to investigate every second of what they'd experienced. "I have Dylan's number, but I'd need yours, Sam."

He strangely felt that, even if they didn't want to, they'd end up meeting again.

Sam gave the both of them his number, all three then lightly laughing about how crazy their day had been. After they said their goodbyes, each of them headed off in his own direction, toward his own individual goals.

Each was painfully unaware of just how much life can change in only four months.

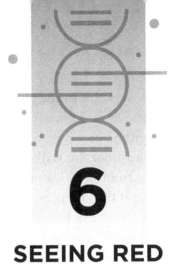

6

SEEING RED

February 20, 2020, 6:01 p.m.

Dylan raced down his darkening street, feeling drops of rain begin to pound against the top of his head. He could finally see his apartment building a few blocks away now. He nearly slipped and fell as he slid across the heavy rain, coming to a stop out front at the entrance to his building.

He was ecstatic to finally be home.

He imagined how he and Ashley's reunion would go—him walking in, alive, her bursting up and running to him. The two of them would hold each other, finding some semblance of light in this dark-feeling time. That's all he wanted right now—to be held by the woman he loved. That and to finally use the ring he had bought; it was upstairs in his sock drawer, just waiting to be grabbed.

He went through the front doors and started up the stairs to their nice studio apartment on the third floor. It wasn't much, but it worked for just the two of them, and he had always planned to buy a house once they were married and had a family.

He even had a secret savings account for that specific purpose. He'd started it years ago right after meeting her. Even at his first job as a cashier at the local convenience store, he would put half of each of his paychecks in every week, all in the pursuit of building a life for him and the person who he had known even then he wanted to spend the rest of his life with.

As he reached the third floor, he walked down the hallway to apartment 306. Pausing in front of it, his mind raced as his anxiety started to bubble up. What if this didn't go well? What if she'd met someone else? What if she didn't live here anymore?

"Fuck it," he told himself, hearing Sam's words from before. "Love throws things your way to make you better for it," Dylan told himself, feeling the strange sense of strength he'd garnered earlier from Sam's words flowing into him.

After using his key to twist the rusted lock, he grabbed the knob, proceeding to twist and push it forward. Upon entering the studio, he immediately noticed it was quiet, too quiet. Ashley always had some song or another from her favorite shows playing around the apartment. Yet, there was nothing.

He walked to the bedroom area, expecting her to be sleeping behind the makeshift wall they'd built around it so they wouldn't have to show their guests their personal space.

Turning around the wall, he found nothing. Walking around the whole apartment now, he noticed the odd amount of dust accumulated on everything—almost as if no one had been here in months.

His anxiety started bubbling up again. "*Ashley!*" he called out. He knew no one was here, but again he called out. "*Ashley?*"

He tried thinking of where she could be. Her family was religious, so they often went to St. Patrick's Cathedral for Mass, but it wasn't Sunday. Maybe she could be at her parents' house; she often went there for family dinners.

He decided to check there first, telling himself she had to be there for sure.

He walked back to the bedroom and grabbed a change of clothes, deciding on a nice blue button-up and a pair of black dress pants before taking them over to the shower area.

● ● ●

After showering what actually felt like four months of grime off his skin, Dylan looked into the mirror, pushing his still wet hair up and back before getting to work with his electric razor.

With a clean shaven face, he got dressed quickly before opening up his sock drawer, moving a few pairs out of the way to look down at the ring holder. He picked it up and opened the container. The rock was decent sized, not Rockefeller sized but big enough to tell he'd saved up a long time for it.

Stuffing it in his pocket, he set off for Ashley's parents' house, locking the front door behind himself as he left.

He hadn't seen the Montgomerys since New Year's 2018. Elliot and Maria were plenty nice people, but their religious nature made them very judgmental of other lifestyle choices—particularly his own. He had grown apart from God when he was much younger and showed no desire to revisit the subject. He always found some excuse to get out of all of their religious traditions, even so far as to start working Sunday mornings to get out of morning church.

Elliot and Maria loved Dylan. They'd just slip little hints of advice into their interactions much too often, as if suggesting that any issue could be solved with a prayer.

Elliot was ex-military, having served two tours in Korea when he was young. He'd often have the whole family gathered around listening to his old war stories. However, more often than not, it would end up being a story he'd told a hundred times.

Maria, on the other hand, was a very frail, gray-haired woman who loved little else besides her family, God, and her dream of traveling the world in her lifetime.

They'd used their savings to buy a cozy house in Midland Beach of Staten Island, smack in the middle of the suburbs—one of the things Dylan hated most.

In the city, it was obvious everyone was crammed together, more often than not easily able to hear through their neighbors' walls. Yet everybody, for the most part, minded their own business. There were far more things to do and see in the city than to care about what your neighbors were arguing about. In the suburbs, though, everyone found any reason to make anything their business too.

When he was young, he and his family had lived in a small town in Maine. But when disaster had struck, and his parents had tragically passed from a gas leak in their home, he and his sister, Paige, had been sent to live with their grandparents in Georgia.

Dylan already wasn't a fan of the town he and his family lived in, yet somehow his grandparents' neighborhood seemed to make it pale in comparison when it came to how boring a place could be.

It was bad enough he was dealing with the loss of his parents before every neighbor found any excuse they could to walk up and make a conversation, almost as if they had nothing better to do than pry into other people's lives. If they weren't digging into his family's tragic accident, they were grating his ears with the obnoxiously annoying comments about how much he and his sister had grown since last they'd seen them. Evidently, that was the only thing older folks knew how to talk about with young children.

The only way he ever got through the transition was his sister. Paige was always coming up with games to play or finding cool spots along the river near their grandparents' property. She kept Dylan's mind occupied in the face of boredom-laced grief. But for her, playing with her older brother was and always would be simply her favorite thing in the world.

Simpler times, Dylan thought to himself.

• • •

As the cab pulled up in front of the house, Dylan paid the driver and ran through the scenario in his head a hundred times. Ideally, he'd knock, and the person he wanted to see most in the world would pull open the door. He'd propose and then spend the rest of his life with her.

As he walked up the steps and under the same warm porch light he'd stood beneath the night he'd picked Ashley up for their first date, his lips curled into a smile, growing wider as he ascended. When he finally reached the door, he took a slow deep breath and brought his hand up to knock.

The silence after the knock was excruciating. It felt like it would go on forever until the door suddenly opened with a loud squeak.

It was Maria. And for as frail as she had always seemed, he remembered her always having an air of enthusiasm and energy to her. But this woman standing before Dylan appeared defeated, like all life had just been sucked out of her, leaving only a shell of a person.

"Can I help you?" she softly asked, her eyes low and not meeting Dylan's. She didn't seem to recognize him.

"Maria ... it's me, Dylan," he said, confused. Normally, whenever he came over, she always talked his ear off the moment she saw him.

"I don't appreciate jokes like that, young man. I oughta—" She cut herself off, finally meeting Dylan's gaze.

Her eyes instantly filled with tears before she dove into Dylan's arms and hugged him harder than he'd been hugged in a very long time. He hugged her back, feeling the love emanating from her.

She sobbed into his chest for a number of minutes until she couldn't anymore, finally pulling away, "How are you alive? No one heard anything since the explosion. We all thought ..." Her words trailed into a sob.

Dylan could feel tears welling in his own eyes as he felt the sadness in her voice. "I know, it's been a confusing day for me, and an even crazier few months for everyone else I imagine. I ... I woke up in the hospital this morning." He found himself lying instead of going into detail about his strange experience. "As soon as I could, I raced over here. I got a second chance. I'm ready. I'm gonna ask Ashley to marry me," he finished, glee apparent on his face.

Maria just stared at him for a few moments, expressionless, almost like she was processing what he had just said. Then almost out of nowhere, her eyes finally closed, tears raining down her wrinkled cheeks once more.

She fell back onto Dylan's chest, sending his heart plummeting into his stomach. "Maria, what's going on?" He forced the words out.

Without pulling her head from his chest, she tried to talk through her cries. "Ashley … she … she's dead. She died on the Day of Light," she choked out through her tears.

Dylan's heart stopped, his brain seeming to shut down along with it from the sheer stress of this day. He was sure he'd heard her wrong. There was no way Ashley was dead. "What the hell are you talking about?!" he blurted, his breath beginning to grow faster and faster.

"When you left home, she turned into a wreck. And on that day, she went to St. Patrick's to think. She always felt safe at the church. But … but then, there was the explosion." She gripped his shirt so tightly her knuckles turned bright white, her tears beginning to soak through his shirt.

Dylan still couldn't hear his heart beating in his chest as Maria's cries dulled into white noise around him. All he could hear was a low rumbling that seemed to stem from the base of his skull, like the distant rumble of a pissed-off stampede barreling through and eviscerating everything in its path. He could almost feel something forming in his chest, visualizing it as a small ball of red.

He forced it down. He didn't want to add to the stress that was clearly already killing Maria.

She led him inside, neither of them noticing the cracks in the wooden porch where Dylan had just stood.

Upon seeing Dylan, Elliot teared up and yanked him into a bear hug without a word, just the soft trembles of a man who'd nearly lost everything. Dylan could feel the older man's tears on his shoulder. He was stunned; he had never once seen the war vet cry besides the quick wave of tears he'd hidden the day of Ashley's graduation.

They all sat down, Dylan unable to stop staring at the pictures of him and Ashley hung around the house.

That red ball in his chest felt like it grew a little bigger.

He learned that, on the Day of Light, Ashley had been praying at St. Patrick's, which had lain right in the path of the destruction. After the bomb had gone off, the news and emergency services said they were still finding survivors for the first few days. Given such, Elliot and Maria held onto hope for as long they could, for both Ashley and Dylan.

When February rolled around, and there hadn't been a new survivor found since November, they had to come to terms with reality. They both had to be dead.

They had begun setting up funeral services for the both of them; it was set for the twenty-first of that very month, tomorrow. Obviously, there would have to be some last-minute changes to the plans, given that Dylan now stood here before them.

At dinner, they half begged him to stay with them till after the funeral, as it had been deathly quiet around there since Ashely couldn't pop in and liven the place up like she used to.

They offered him Ashley's old room; they had loosely kept it the same after she'd moved out on the chance she ever needed a place to stay for a while.

He reluctantly agreed, telling himself he was doing it for the incredibly kind and brokenhearted people who had taken him in as one of their own when he was young. But the honest truth was that he knew only silence awaited him at home, and the thought of feeling any more alone than he did right now scared the hell out of him.

Right down to the still growing red orb.

Dylan hadn't realized how hungry he was till food had been placed in front of him. He'd scarfed down nearly three servings of Maria's signature Alfredo pasta. Yet, no matter how much he shoveled into himself, the pit in his stomach wouldn't subside.

Nonetheless, he needed to rest. And after spending a few hours talking to his would-be parents-in-law about some of the blanks he still had for the last few months, including the fact he'd turned twenty-five during the time he'd been gone, Dylan adjourned to his temporary room.

Closing the door behind himself, he looked around.

The room hadn't changed much since the first time he was in it—the same old posters on the wall, the same desk with the same now ten-year-old computer, the same view of the water through the window behind the bed. He could still picture Ashley sitting on the bed practicing her lines for the school's production of *Hamlet* that year.

Taking a seat on the bed, he thought back to his first time in this room. He had been seventeen, a senior in high school and set to graduate a year earlier than most kids his own age. He had been dating Ashley for about a month at that point, and she had finally talked her parents into letting him come over under the guise of them being study buddies.

He remembered taking his first steps into her room, her sitting on the bed waving him in with a smile.

"Relax, I'm not gonna bite you." She laughed.

He did his best to be smooth. "I wish you would?"

She just laughed. The thing that drove him to Ashley the most was her way of making his heart flutter. No other girl ever affected him that way.

Pulling himself out of his thoughts for a moment, he noticed it was past eleven o'clock at that point, and he knew he should get some sleep.

It was hard to believe it had been four months since he'd first opened Ashley's letter. He'd only been awake for about twelve hours, but he felt as though he had an entirely new life now. With a lump in his throat, he lay back on the bed. Feeling a lump in his back pocket, he reached in and pulled out the ring holder.

As he gazed at the ring, all he could think of was Ashley's smile.

The growing ball of red, once maybe the size of a marble, was now nearly as large as a baseball, making it all the more difficult for him to shove it back down once more.

Placing the ring holder on the dresser, he kicked off his shoes and unbuttoned his button-up. He lay in the bed and covered up before turning over to face a framed photo of himself and Ashely on vacation in Hawaii, feeling tears well up in his eyes.

He closed them, doing his best to hold in everything he felt at that moment. But he could no longer hold back the seeming floodgates held behind his eyes. He lightly cried into Ashley's pillow, still smelling her familiar scent ingrained in the fibers, stifling his cries until he eventually drifted off to sleep.

● ● ●

The time before the funeral went by in a blur—lots of time spent looking at old photo albums with Maria, having to stop every now and then to console her. There was a lot of time spent sitting on the back porch. That was where he and Ashley had planned their first anniversary.

They'd vacationed in Hawaii for a month, Dylan taking time off of college, while Ashley took a much-needed break from readying herself to plunge into the acting world. They'd both burned so badly they'd had blisters for weeks.

As he'd sat on the porch, chest aching while he stared off into the distance thinking of better times, Elliot would occasionally come find Dylan and just silently sit with him for a while.

Dylan wanted to talk to somebody about the now heavy-feeling red ball in his chest. He was smart enough to know now that that ball was anger, and it was building up. The thought of what was gonna happen when it boiled over freaked him out. He had decided that Ashley's family was dealing with enough right now. They didn't have the time for this.

But who else did he have?

If he could, he'd call up his sister. Paige was always good at listening to her older brother's issues. That was off the table though, so he decided to do his best to just keep pushing all that emotion farther and farther down. But every time he did, he could feel it grow all the more.

By the time the funeral finally came around, the weight of the red ball had him nearly ready to burst.

● ● ●

Traditionally, when a member of the Montgomery family passed, they'd hold a service at St. Patrick's. But seeing as it was no longer standing, they decided to hold the service at Elliot and Maria's house.

The first members of the family to arrive were Elliot's brother and his wife—surprisingly enough, given they'd come all the way from Florida to attend. Dylan had never really met the two, but they seemed nice enough.

Over the next hour and a half, at least twenty people had all piled into the house. Each one pulled Dylan aside to give their personal condolences, each another painstaking reminder of what he'd lost.

They all sat around the living room, reminiscing on stories about Ashley. It should have been a day of remembering a beautiful person for all the wonderful things she'd done. But every, "I'm so sorry"; every funny story of the past; and every second spent knowing the woman he should have been marrying right now was gone just made him angrier.

It felt like the red ball in his chest had finally begun to crack from the sheer weight of itself.

He stood in the back of the room, listening to everyone's stories one by one, each one putting a new crack in the ball of anger.

Shaking with a pure hatred for the world he lived in, he clenched his teeth in an effort to hold his feelings at bay. When he finally let out a deep breath, a small strand of red smoke slowly leaked from the corner of his mouth, narrowly avoiding everyone's gaze, including his own.

Given the fact that Ashley's body had never been found, the family based the service around a large portrait of her that they had commissioned. Dylan couldn't help but feel as though her striking blue eyes followed him around the room; he'd noticed it out of the corner of his eye during every interaction he had that day.

After finishing the service, the family hung the portrait in the den of the Montgomerys' house, everyone helping to shift numerous old photos and decorations around as they made the portrait the focal point of the wall.

Maria placed her hand on the picture, as if trying to say one last goodbye before she went into Elliot's arms, beginning to blubber once more as she told him how much she loved him.

Dylan looked at the married couple, two people who had gone through everything the world had thrown at them. And at the end of it all, there they stood in one another's arms. Just like Sam had described, they'd stood through every curveball, every heartbreak, and every bad day, and not a single thing could tear them apart. That was what he and Ashley were supposed to have.

Did that mean he and Ashley weren't meant to be?

He clenched his fists and gritted his teeth in an effort to reign himself in, his head beginning to spin from the flood of emotions he held just beneath the surface.

Needing some air, he went onto the back porch. All he could think of was what Ashley was thinking—right before.

He hadn't really had a chance to actually stop and think about the explosion or anything that had happened for that matter. He'd been thrust into a new world he didn't recognize that he was forced to accept as his own.

The crater he'd been in was enormous, and he couldn't help but think about the amount of life that must have been lost in that big of an explosion.

"Who could have done such a fucked-up thing?" he muttered as he touched the scar along his lip.

He thought about what he would do, should he ever get five minutes alone with the person responsible. He found his head filled with angrily twisted thoughts as he gazed out onto the bay.

Upon seeing some of the family members beginning to grab their belongings and head for the door inside, he thought it was about time for him to head home as well.

Stepping back inside, he walked over to Elliot.

"Sir, I think it's about time I head out. I need to sleep in my own bed," he said softly. His chest continued to ache as the red ball continued to grow within him. It felt like it was ready to burst.

"Are … are you sure you can't stay one more night, son?" Elliot asked.

Dylan's chest tightened. He could tell Elliot had a buzz from his drink. He didn't normally call him son. As much as it hurt to leave after hearing that, he couldn't stay here anymore.

"I'm sure. I need some time to process everything. It's been an eventful few days for me. I'm sorry," Dylan apologized. He needed to get out. He felt like he was gonna pop at any moment.

Elliot finally let up, and Dylan went around saying his goodbyes, promising to meet Elliot and Maria for lunch soon.

He'd called himself a cab, asking it to pick him up from the street down the block, feeling the urge to take a walk through the cold night air.

As he headed down the darkening street, he thought about how robbed he felt. Some unknown terrorist had stolen the most important person from him, had stolen four whole months of his life, of numerous peoples' lives probably, and there was nobody to be held responsible.

Would these lingering questions ever be answered? Would he ever find out exactly what had happened? Would anyone?

When he reached the street where the cab was supposed to pick him up, he stopped and leaned against the streetlamp. He started to pound his head against the lamppost in tune with the pounding of his chest, trying to drown out the thoughts of hatred he was feeling. Each pounding was like the swing of a hammer on an anvil, and with each swing, the cracks in the red ball grew. The feeling in his chest and spine was strange, like the slow, steady rumble before an eruption.

He saw the cab approach and stood up, his body feeling heavy like something within him was weighing him down.

As he rode home, he thought of what he was gonna do now. The one week he spent living away from Ashley was the most confusing week of his life. He'd spent the last six years with her. How was he supposed to go another sixty without her?

As he walked up the stairs of his apartment building, he felt immensely heavier with each step he took. With every step, there was yet another fracture in the red ball that was already barely holding itself together. Upon reaching his front door, tears welling in his eyes and beginning to bubble over, heart pounding out of his chest as he shook in anger, he finally saw it.

Trails of red smoke rose from his hands and arms.

Panicking, he quickly grabbed his door handle and turned it, hearing a large crack in the metal.

He remembered he had locked it.

Stepping in and slamming the broken door behind him, he clutched his head as the pounding grew more and more intense. The red smoke had started coming off of his back and shoulders now, flowing out violently all around him. The more it leaked from himself, the angrier he continued to grow.

Sweat poured down his body, steadily soaking his clothes.

Falling to the ground, he slammed his fists against the ground again and again. Images of Ashley's face and memories of himself running alongside a crowd of screaming people flashed through his mind.

He saw himself turn around and see a large cloud of white light heading toward him.

Dylan lowered his head to the ground as he cried out, flashes of white and Ashley pounding through his skull, the rumble of his heartbeat drowning out all other noise. The red ball of anger in his chest could take no more. It was finally ready to burst.

As it burst, every emotion he'd suppressed in the last few days, every angry thought and horrid notion he'd had came viciously boiling over. The trails of red smoke enveloped him in a violent, swirling motion, his eyes unable to process anything he was seeing besides a wall of red.

Dylan roared. The smoke instantly expanded in an explosion of blood red fog around him, the shock wave generated by it throwing everything near him hurtling back.

The expansion had left a small crater around Dylan, accentuated by numerous scratches now dug into the hardwood flooring beneath his feet.

Releasing that emotion seemed to take Dylan out of his trance. He slowly opened his eyes and saw what he had done. He was in shock, at a complete loss for words as he felt something trickle down his lip. Reaching up and feeling something wet oozing from his nose, he looked down at the blood on his fingers as he felt his head go light.

He started to fall to his side, losing consciousness before even hitting the ground.

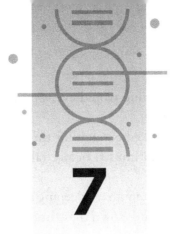

7

REFLEXIVE INFERNO

February 20, 2020, 5:45 p.m.

As Sam walked, time began to blur together.

He kept trying to think of everything that had happened, but the last coherent memory he could piece together from before today was screaming—endless screaming.

The images of the bodies they'd seen were burned into his eyes and weren't showing signs of waning anytime soon. All the exhausting emotions swirling in his chest were beginning to build up, and his skin was beginning to feel like a furnace as he made his way through the empty streets.

Why couldn't he remember anything else?

With frustration and an endless pit of hunger weighing him down, he walked until the sunset, continuing on into the shadier part of town as night descended around him.

Raindrops began to fall one by one, faster and faster, until Sam couldn't even see five feet in front of himself.

Standing in a vacant lot near the bay, drenched from head to toe, he stared into the night sky while wondering what came next. Would he just go back to work like everything was normal?

The feeling that nothing would ever be the same wouldn't stop gnawing at his brain.

He decided he'd walked enough for the night, quickly glancing at the street signs around himself before taking the next right turn to head home.

He'd think after four months of sleeping he'd never want to again. But at the moment, shutting down these lingering questions sounded better than anything.

He felt strange. He'd come home to an empty home most every day of his life, but the idea of the deafening silence awaiting him had him slightly apprehensive. He couldn't remember the last time the thought of being alone had scared him. It had become one of his greatest weapons in life, never needing anyone for anything.

Why was he suddenly feeling it now after all these years?

The rain had pounded against the back of Sam's skull, continuously drenching every crevice of his body as he made his way down alley after alley. Before long, the unfortunate souls calling this particular alley home had all set their eyes on him as he walked past their encampments. It wasn't often someone who had somewhere to go came through these parts.

Dubbed the "End of the Line" by the many people led here by one misfortune or another, this wasn't a place people chose to take a leisurely stroll through.

In Sam's case though, these alleys felt more like home than his actual apartment. During the more problematic years of his life, he'd lived here for a time, hiding away from the world and anyone who would do him harm—everything from the law and social services to shop owners he'd stolen from for scraps to eat. It had been a long time since he'd been here, but for some reason he'd just felt drawn to it tonight.

It was as if some force was pulling him in that direction.

"Going somewhere?" Sam heard a deep voice creepily whisper from somewhere behind him, yanking him out of his trance.

Darkness had engulfed everything around him, so he couldn't pinpoint exactly where the voice had come from right away. Sam's heart dropped. He knew these weren't safe parts whatsoever. He knew full well what some of these people were capable of.

Trails of steam rose up from his rain-soaked jacket as he thought more into some of the gruesome images of his childhood, things he hadn't thought about in years.

Just as he was getting swept away by the onset flood of memories, the voice in the alley called out to him again.

"I'm talking to you!"

A tall brute of a man emerged from the shadows, only partially illuminated by the distant streetlight a distance behind Sam.

All Sam could really make out about the character was the grime he was covered in, almost as if he hadn't left the alley in years. He quickly forgot about that, as the figure inched a little closer, revealing a pair of glowing, bloodred eyes amid the darkness.

Sam stumbled backward, falling to the ground. His heart pounded louder and louder until he actually couldn't hear the rain anymore, just the sound of his beating chest.

The brute continued to slowly creep forward. "You smell like … food," he snarled. "You'll be easy, right? It's been a few days since I've eaten." His deep voice revealed a hint of excitement with the word *food*.

"Stay … back," Sam forced himself to say.

He'd dealt with a wide variety of people in his life, having had to fight off more than his fair share of attackers in his twenty-four years. But the closer this person got, the heavier his presence started to weigh down on Sam. It was as if his sheer, soul-shattering will could crush someone to their knees without lifting a finger.

Sam could clearly feel the intent to kill radiating off of the man creeping forward, all of it directed at him. He was always good at noticing the small signals and cues as to what kind of a person someone was going to be, but this was completely different than anything he'd ever felt before. It was as if he could feel the man's soul leaking out, revealing him for what he truly was, a monster through and through. Sam knew this person was dangerous down to his core and that he absolutely needed to get as far away from him as possible.

Steam slowly began to fill the alleyway, and he was so focused on the danger at hand that Sam still hadn't processed that it all seemed to be originating from himself. Nor did he notice his clothes slowly drying themselves around him, despite the continuous downpour.

Bringing himself back to his feet, he ever so slightly crept backward. Just as he began to make a move, the brute instantly shifted, his now fully illuminated arm gripping the nearby dumpster with such monstrous strength that the metal crinkled like paper in its hand.

Then, before Sam could even try to wrap his head around what he'd just seen, the beast bellowed an ear-numbing roar—a roar so loud it shattered the windows around them both, leaving Sam frozen in place with fear.

The beast took another step forward, fully revealing itself amid the dim light of the city street, allowing Sam to now see it in its monstrous entirety.

The man, if this creature standing before him could even be called a man at all, was easily seven feet tall. His long, oily black hair stuck to his skin, which was sticky with putrid-smelling sweat. He was a behemoth, flush with thick, black-tinted veins all over his beastly, overdeveloped muscles. He kept moving closer, step by step, continuing to drag the dumpster behind him. Its high-pitched whine echoed out as it continued to scrape along the concrete.

As he closed in, Sam made a gut-wrenching realization. It wasn't grime or dirt that this thing was covered in but, rather, a combination of old and fresh blood.

Shoving his fear out of his mind to the best of his ability, Sam attempted to stand his ground. "*I said stay back, damn it!*" he yelled, trying to assert himself with what little power he believed he had.

As he yelled, what had been steam billowing out of him quickly turned to dark smoke, an intense heat radiating out from him as his clothes seemed to finish drying on his body. A plume of thick, gray smoke floated up in front of his eyes, finally making him notice that this brute wasn't the only strange thing in this alleyway.

That brief moment of distraction gave the brute exactly what it wanted. With another large roar, Sam heard the loud scrape of the dumpster, making him look back up to face his attacker.

The dumpster slammed into Sam head-on just as he'd finished bringing his head back up.

He'd never felt anything like it. The collision felt like he had been standing on tracks, rammed head-on by a speeding bullet train. He felt his thought process go haywire as the dumpster flung him back, unable to see out of his haze-filled eyes.

Both Sam and the dumpster flew back and out of the alleyway at inhuman speed. If he hadn't instinctively thrown his arms up to defend himself, he felt like his rib cage would have exploded.

He forcefully shoved the dumpster off to the side of himself, knowing he'd be crushed any second if he didn't.

Feeling a sudden crunch behind himself, Sam crashed into a parked car, caving in its side and shattering glass all over him and the road. With his head reeling, he scanned the area he found himself in, seeing nothing but crumpled metal and upholstery.

He slowly ripped himself from the collapsed car, taking notice of how surprisingly unharmed he was. Just like that morning when he'd skidded across the top of the reporter's car.

What the hell is happening? he asked himself.

All he knew in the moment, and the scariest part of all, was that some strange part of himself was getting excited.

A faint glow caught Sam's attention. Turning to look at his arm, he saw ripples of orange flickering in and out, its pulsing glow coming through his sleeves. He could feel heat radiating out from himself, watching as the lower sections of his sleeves started to burn away, revealing his glowing veins beneath, almost reminiscent of flames.

Deep in the back of his skull, a tingle of instinct burned throughout his spine. Every fiber of his being screamed at him to fight back, but he had no way of knowing how to act on it.

How could he fight against this monstrosity?

He just heard the same gravelly voice again and again in his head. *"Fight! Move! Live!"*

"Given that you're still breathing, that means I was right," the brute called out while taking another step forward, that single step turning into a short stride. Before long, he was in a full sprint toward Sam. The concrete crumbled as he slammed his foot down with each increasingly longer stride. As he approached, earth quaking beneath him, he leapt up into the air and swung his grotesquely massive arms back, gearing up for an attack.

The burning sensation in Sam's spine returned in full force. In an attempt to protect itself, his body let instinct take over. As quickly as the beast closed in, Sam threw his hands up.

The monster's fists landed, causing an explosive shock wave to radiate out and destroy what glass was left in this rundown neighborhood. Cars parked along the streets wailed out as its force set off their alarms, waking whatever tenants who hadn't already heard the disturbance.

At the center of the destruction stood Sam, hands clutched on the attacker's giant wrists. His breath was ragged from the strain of stopping such an immeasurable force. Yet Sam continued to hold his ground with the last of his strength.

The brute looked down onto his would-be victim with a hint of fear in his eyes. Not once in either of his lives had anyone been able to stop him. "That's ... not possible. I'm supposed to be the strongest," the beast mumbled, anger rising in his voice.

Sam looked up and stared him straight in the eye, feeling the burning sensation in his spine continue to burn hotter as a flicker of flame loosed itself from his eye. Within his body, all the way down into the core of his DNA, flames exploded into every fiber of his being. His veins roared with bright orange energy as he let the energy within himself take hold.

He began to let out a roar that resonated from the deepest, darkest depths of his soul—a part of himself that had not seen the light of day in years before today. A reflexive eruption of flames burst out of Sam's whole body, blanketing everything within reach.

The beast attempted to struggle, but Sam's tightening grip left him caught in the wake of the ensuing inferno. It screamed out as it fought to shake off Sam's hold, but to no avail, its consciousness was beginning to fade with each passing second.

Pure destructive power continued to freely flow out of Sam's body, melting the surrounding concrete and setting fire to all shrubbery nearby. It was as if a miniature sun had spontaneously appeared on earth.

As his roar died down, so too did the powerful flames that came with it. Condensing and shrinking back down into his body, and as the last of the light died out, all that was left was Sam standing over his attacker, letting out deep, wheezing breaths.

The beast lay unconsciousness at his feet, charred and bleeding—but still breathing.

That part lightened the load on Sam's heart. He may have needed to defend himself, but no one had the right to take another's life. "Guess ... you weren't the strongest." He forced the words out through labored breathing, his ribs starting to ache from the collision with the dumpster.

Now that the moment had passed, the adrenaline of the situation had run its course. As such, its effects started to dwindle. Falling to the ground, he finally gave himself a moment to process how absurd this all was.

Bombings? Missing time? Strange attackers? The possibility of erupting in flames? His mind was in a tailspin, trying to think of any way this could be possible. Yet nothing came to mind.

Suddenly, it dawned on him. He wasn't the only one who'd woken up in that bunker this morning. Dylan and Victor had both gone through the same ordeal he had, it stood to reason that they may have experienced something strange as well.

Before he could finish his thought, he was interrupted by the sound of approaching sirens, and after looking around, he wasn't surprised. The surrounding trees were still burning and showing no signs of stopping, not to mention the demolished car and melted state of the roadway.

"Huh, two cars in one day." He laughed, trying to lighten the tension in his chest.

Using what strength he had left, he pulled himself to his feet and headed in the opposite direction of the sirens. Every ache and creak of his body pushed for him to collapse, to find any comfortable spot and to sleep.

After running until he couldn't hear the sirens anymore, he slowed down to catch his breath, eventually finding a nice spot to rest in a nearby park.

At that point, he was so tired he didn't bother to walk the rest of the way home. He laid himself down on the nearest park bench, and instantly drifted off to sleep.

● ● ●

The next morning, Sam awoke to the sound of unfamiliar voices. "Is he dead?" one of them asked. "Look at his clothes. They're charred and burned!"

"You don't think … he had something to do with the fire a few blocks over last night, do you?" a different voice interjected, a female voice this time.

Sam had a feeling he shouldn't get caught up here until he knew what was going on with himself.

"Turn him over. Let's get a look at his face," a third and final voice suggested.

That was Sam's cue. He could never explain the events of last night without finding himself locked up for arson—or worse. With that, he sprung himself up, careful not to show his face as he began a full sprint away from the group. As he ran, everything zipped past, faster and faster until he could barely make out what it was he was passing.

The burning feeling from before was back. But this time, it seemed to respond to Sam more than before. Screeching to a stop somewhere in an alley along the bay, he looked down at his hand as he realized he could turn the feeling off and on with a thought. With a simple thought the burning feeling grew, and as it grew hotter, smoke began to rise off his hand until, eventually, it engulfed itself in flames.

Just then, all sensations of burning disappeared without a trace, replaced only with a gentle warm feeling.

Turning his head to face a distant trash can, he focused on that warm sensation, feeling it circulate throughout his hand until a blast of fire burst forth from his palm. Watching the flames tear through and reducing the trash can into a puddle of molten metal, Sam grinned ear to ear. For as scary as all this was, a growing part of him was still continuing to get excited.

It was like a story out of a comic book. What person hadn't dreamt of having powers at one point or another? He flipped around, feeling his flames shaping into a sphere within his hand, before whipping it at another can. "Whoa. That one was different," he remarked. It was getting easier to flip the switch for the flames within himself.

A million questions ran through his mind. This had been the most confusing span of time in his life, and that was saying something.

Turning off the flames, he just stared down at his hand. Why was this already so easy? Without any idea of how to answer his own question, he decided it was finally time to go home. There had been more than enough roadblocks on his way there, and he was ready to be back in his safe space.

He decided he'd give himself some time to unwind and possibly play around with his newfound abilities a bit more. But ultimately, he needed to get in touch with Dylan and Victor. He needed to know if he was alone in this, and something in his gut told him he wasn't. With a goal in mind, he set off on his long walk home, a sense of eagerness pulling him forward.

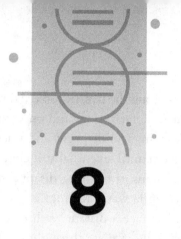

8

TIP OF A BLADE

February 20, 2020, 5:45 p.m.

As Victor left Sam and Dylan, he pulled out his phone and scrolled through his contacts till he found Hartley's name—or Harty as he usually called him. The nickname spanned all the way back to when Victor was young and still unable to properly pronounce Hartley; the name had just stuck as he got older.

He took a deep breath and hit the call button, anxiously waiting through a number of dial tones before finally hearing a faint click resonate over the line.

"Hello. Reliance residence. May I ask who's speaking?" he heard Hartley softly answer.

Hearing his voice made Victor's chest ache. He felt tears well up in his eyes from the relief his voice brought him. He didn't realize how long he had remained silent until Hartley repeated, "Hello? Is anybody there?".

"Harty … It's Victor. I'm alive … I guess that's really the only way to put it." Victor dryly chuckled. Given the situation, he didn't know what else to say.

The line stayed silent for a couple seconds, heavy breathing making its way through the speaker. "Quid est maximus dignissim in hac vita?" Hartley asked sharply in an interrogating manner, yet even through the phone, Victor could sense a feeling of hopefulness. It was one of the oldest phrases in his family taught to him and to every young Reliance as they paved their way through the world. The Latin phrase loosely translated to, "What is the greatest asset in this life?"

The answer was easy. It was one of the only things he could remember his father saying to him before he'd passed. "Desiderium melius tua omnis competitorem," Victor answered, which could be loosely translated to, "A desire to be better than your every competitor." He could have sworn he heard a small gasp on the other end of the line.

"Sir, I … Where are you?" Hartley's voice was trembling with shock.

"I'm near Gramercy Park. I've … I've had a long day. Can you meet me at Peter's Field? On 2nd Avenue?" Victor asked, finally beginning to feel his nerves dial back a bit. Hartley always had a way of doing that for him.

Hartley told him he'd be there as soon as he could and hung up.

Sighing in relief, Victor began his trek towards the park.

Victor walked through the darkening streets, his mind in a haze as he thought of the events of the day thus far. He kept thinking about the strange place they had all woken up in that morning, mentally making a note to go back there and find it again in the next few days or so if he could find the time.

He was simply too curious a person to let that strange occurrence go, not that everything else he had discovered wasn't strange, but any thorough investigation needed a strong starting point.

When he finally reached the street across from Peter's Field, he looked down on his dusty clothes, small tears all over them. He couldn't shake the feeling of the putrid stench seeming to coat him.

"I need a shower." he sighed.

Feeling his stomach begin to churn once more from his lack of food, he placed his hand on his abdomen, noticing something odd as he did. He saw that his watch face had been cracked at some point of the whole ordeal; the watch was an heirloom that had been in his family three generations before himself. But something else made his heart skip a beat after a second glance. Upon closer inspection, he could see a small black tendril of some sort coming out from under his watch.

Hesitantly, he grabbed his sleeve and slowly pulled it up. "Oh my God," he muttered quietly. The tendril went up to a larger concentration of the strange substance on his forearm. It looked oddly alive—shiny and black, with glowing blue streaks flowing through it almost like food coloring in water. The blue glow lit up the dark space around him as his pulse increased its pace.

Unable to believe what he was seeing, he pulled his sleeve back down to hide it. Sprinting across the street, he shielded his face from the oncoming rain and darted his head around, frantically searching for Hartley.

He'd know what to do. He always did.

"*Victor!*" He heard someone call from behind him.

As the sound of rain faded out, he turned around, knowing immediately whose voice it was he had heard. With tears in his eyes, he finally saw Hartley standing there a few feet away from him. They both stood there motionless, as if trying to figure out if everything had been a dream or not, the both of them unable to take much more heartache.

Hartley was ragged and out of breath. Unsure of where exactly to meet, he had frantically raced around the entire perimeter of the property as he searched.

Victor gazed upon his sunken, teary eyes and baggy clothes, immediately noticing he had lost some weight.

Hartley's tears poured down his cheeks, blending into the heavy rain on his skin. "You're ... you're here. How ... how are you alive?" he choked out.

Victor thought he looked like was gonna have a heart attack. That was when he made the decision to keep his strange new issue to himself for now. He half ran to Hartley, taking the old man into his arms and squeezing with everything he had.

"I missed you so much, kiddo," Hartley cried into Victor's shoulder.

• • •

As they rode through the torrential downpour, hastily making their way home, Hartley's burning questions couldn't be held back any longer. "I don't understand. If you're alive, why haven't you reached out to me?! Why would you stay hidden this long!?" There was an unmistakable hint of anger in his words, which Victor completely understood. Just as he had nearly no one else besides Hartley, the older man had no one else other than Victor as well.

"It's a long story. I honestly don't entirely understand it myself," Victor admitted. He'd barely had any time to process anything that had happened.

"Well I have time," Hartley said, pulling off the empty roadway and placing the car in park in one exceedingly quick motion. He aggressively turned his head toward Victor, his stern expression eerily reminding him of his late father.

Victor couldn't help but chuckle. Sometimes Victor forgot that his father had practically raised Hartley too. Taking the stern expression as there was no alternative, Victor sighed and began telling him everything he understood about what had happened.

He recalled how he had been heading toward Moriano Inc. when the ground had suddenly begun to rumble, and before he knew it, all he could hear were screams—horrible screams, and then nothing.

The next thing he knew, he was waking up to a blinding overhead light and an intense heat. His beard, which he was sure he'd shaved the night before, was longer than he'd let it get in years. Confused and undressed, he'd run out of the room searching for help—only to find nothing but the vacant space he had apparently been placed in. For a brief moment, he had thought maybe he was already dead.

"That's when I found Dylan and, strangely enough, Sam, from back in high school. Thankfully, they both seemed to be handling things better than I was at that point." Victor chuckled, knowing it would have been an entirely different situation had he not found them.

There was an oddly long pause before Hartley answered, "Sam?"

Victor felt as if the name had meant something to Hartley. "Yeah, remember? We went to school together for a time. I'd say that may be one of the weirdest parts of the whole thing—too weird to be a coincidence. I know you know Dylan. But do you remember Sam?" Victor prodded.

"I remember two friends of yours. They used to come by when you all were young," Hartley quickly remarked, oddly quick if Victor said so himself.

"I know I attended high school with them, but I don't remember any of my friends coming over before that, let alone them," a confused Victor responded. Confusion of another sort quickly washed over him. Why couldn't he remember any other friends besides them?

Or better yet, why was it so difficult to remember a time before he'd met them?

"Oh ... did I say that? I must be remembering wrong. Sorry, kiddo. Happens as I get older," Hartley corrected himself, giving Victor an unshakeable feeling there was more to it. He decided he would poke more at his story later on, beginning to feel the onset of a headache forming.

For now, he simply wanted to get home and rest. Yet there was one more thing he longed for at the moment.

• • •

As they pulled into the parking garage of his building, Victor wiped the remnants of his much-needed meal off the surface of his beard, relishing in the heavenly taste of such a simple fast food cheeseburger. He sighed in relief, knowing that, at the very least, food hadn't changed in the last four months; if anything, it tasted worlds better than before.

As he slammed the car door shut, the bag of his remaining burgers clutched in hand, something made his body shudder. His right arm felt cold, as if something slimy was moving on it, until the feeling strangely came to a halt. He gripped his arm, expecting to feel the familiar soft sensation of his flesh-and-blood arm, but his eyes widened as he felt something rock solid in its place.

Hartley had noticed the look in Victor's eyes. "Kiddo? You OK?" he asked as he made his way to Victor's side of the car.

"I'm fine. I'm fine. It's just a headache," Victor insisted, doing his best to hide what was going on.

Despite his uneasiness, a strange childlike curiosity was coming over him, one he couldn't begin to explain. He needed a moment alone to study what was happening.

He followed Hartley through the front doors of the Reliance Soho building—originally an apartment building nearly thirty years ago. But Victor's father had bought it out shortly before Vanessa had given birth, and he'd renovated the building into the home Victor would come to grow up in.

Already an eight-story building, there was plenty of room to renovate and build a life for the growing family, and the place had just enough extra for Edgar's workshop—where he'd often bring his work home and spend hours in.

The workshop had been Victor's favorite spot in the house for as long as he could remember. He'd often sneak in and watch his father fiddle with his machinery when he was young. It was what would one day spark Victor's eagerness to join the family business and pursue science for himself.

He looked around the main hall; while it didn't seem to look any different than when he had left it, he clutched his changed arm as he tried to come to grips with the fact that nothing would probably ever be the same from that point on.

Before heading up the stairs to the living area, Hartley turned to look at Victor, whose mind seemed to be scattered a million miles away. "You're being pretty quiet, kid. And I'm not a wall. I know something's up. Does it have something to do with your arm?" he asked, stretching his own out to point at Victor's hard grip on his forearm. "You've been gripping it since we got here."

Victor's heart quickened. What could he possibly say? That some weird goop was covering his arm, and it was rock solid? No, that was not the way to go. As he grew more anxious with the situation, the strange feeling of the substance moving across his arm came back, the cold slimy sensation growing closer and closer to his hand.

Hartley's hand landed on Victor's shoulder, pulling him from his trance once more. "All right, kid. That's enough for one day. You should get some sleep. We've all the time in the world to get to the bottom of this whole mess," he assured him as he pulled Victor in for one last hug. He relished in the warmth of the young man he no doubt considered his own son.

Feeling the warmth of Hartley's hug lifting his spirits, Victor held him right back with his remaining normal arm. He thought back to every time Hartley had pulled him in for one of his famous hugs. Even on the night all those years ago that Victor had lost his parents, Hartley had still managed to make him fall asleep in his arms.

New developments or not, it was good to be home where he felt safe.

Finally back in his own room, Victor made his way to the double-door closet beside his bed, standing before the full-length mirror attached to the oak-made door. Longing to wear anything other than what he had on, he started taking off the top half of his clothing.

Upon removing his button-up, he stopped dead in his tracks and stared into the mirror. The black substance had now covered his right arm in its entirety, the thin tendrils on his shoulder winding around his torso and leading to what seemed to be the source of it all, a golf ball-size hole smack-dab in the center of his chest.

He stumbled back, his heart nearly pounding out of his chest. He stared into the seemingly blinding, pulsing blue glow of the coating on his arm. He did his best to slow down and make sense of what it was, but he couldn't seem to form a coherent thought in his head.

"OK Vic, gotta calm down. Science doesn't scare. It analyzes and adapts," he muttered to himself, breathing deeply in and out to calm himself.

It was another one of his family's famous phrases, one he remembered hearing both his parents say over and over when he was young.

When his heart finally didn't sound like the rumble of train tracks, he stood himself up, holding out his black-and-blue-clad arm. Touching the substance once more, he confirmed it was indeed a solid structure. It felt tough as he knocked on it a few times.

A smile swept across Victor's face; his childlike curiosity was beginning to creep back into him.

● ● ●

The next morning, Hartley awoke to silence, a debilitating silence that made his heart skip a beat.

Bolting up, he questioned whether or not yesterday had even happened. He quickly threw on his robe and nearly jumped all the way to the door.

He hurried himself through the long corridors, coming to a stop in front of Victor's room. With a deep breath, he twisted the handle, pushing the door open as he prepared himself for the worst.

He found a strange sight for sure as he peered into the abnormally cluttered room. He'd kept the room spotless in the time Victor had been gone, yet the floor was covered in numerous empty food wrappers—burgers, chips, candy, instant noodles, you name it.

The mess was a welcome sight to his nerves, finally allowing him to calm a bit and observe his surroundings, the slight smell of bacon filling his nostrils as he did. He crept toward the kitchen, which had to have been the origin of the smell, slowly peeking around the corner of the doorway as he approached.

His heart lightened as he felt a ray of warmth wash over him; he looked at Victor, apron clad, seeming to be whipping up breakfast of some kind. Hartley almost didn't want to say anything, afraid he'd break the trance and reveal it all to be a dream.

"Morning," he heard Victor gleefully call out, slightly startling him. "Are you hungry?" he called again, turning to face Hartley this time.

"Absolutely." A smile crossed Hartley's face.

"Good. Everything is almost ready. Grab yourself a seat," Victor gleefully replied while turning back to the nearly finished pan full of scrambled eggs.

Giving them a final few stirs, he turned off the burner and walked over to the dining table where Hartley now sat. After dishing the two of their plates up a healthy portion of eggs, numerous strips of bacon, a few fatty links of sausage, and two overly buttered pieces of toast, Victor sat to join him. Yet before Hartley could even begin to eat, he couldn't help but notice the glove covering Victor's right hand.

"OK, kiddo, you gonna tell me what's going on with your arm now?" Hartley asked, placing his elbows on the table, hands crossed in front of his face. "There's no use hiding it," he added.

With a mouthful of the breakfast sandwich he'd just made, Victor wiped his hands and finished his bite without directly looking at Hartley. "I know. But I need to know you're not gonna freak out," Victor began, his head held low as he spoke.

Waiting a moment before saying anything, Hartley lightly replied, "OK."

As Victor's heart quickened at the thought of how Hartley would react, the blue glow that had died down the night before began to shine through his sleeve as it flowed throughout his arm once more.

A wave of memories and terror pounded through Hartley's wide eyes at the sight of the glow.

Removing the glove and taking off the right sleeve of his shirt, Victor revealed his predicament to his newly poker-faced friend. The substance had spread, covering not only his arm but also a growing section on the right side of his chest now.

Hartley stood up without a word, simply coming around the table for a closer look. He placed his hand on Victor's jet -black-and-blue arm. "How long has it been like this?" he asked with his eyes still trained on the eerie blue glow.

"Since last night. It's spread a lot since it first started, but—" Quickly stopping, he looked over toward the kitchen drawers to his left. He stood up and walked over. Opening the drawer, he pulled out the largest kitchen knife they had.

As he rested his black-clad forearm on the countertop and raised his other in the air, the knife clutched so hard his knuckles had turned white, he aimed the knife at the mysterious substance that coated him.

"But?" Hartley nervously asked.

Quickly looking over at Hartley, Victor finished what he had to say. "But there's a little more to it." As he finished his ominous statement, he turned away from Hartley, whose stomach plummeted at the sight of Victor plunging the knife at his own arm with all his strength.

All Hartley could manage to get his mouth to let out was a useless waste of breath. "*Victor!*"

He suddenly heard a sharp metallic crack, followed by a loud clang on the stained oak hardwood flooring behind him. Before he could register what had happened, Hartley had sprung up and over to Victor to check on what he was sure would be a severed limb.

Upon reaching him, he was shocked to find that Victor had the blade pressed firmly against his arm, yet the blade had been cleanly snapped in half.

Jerking his head around the other direction, Hartley discovered what had made the clang on the floor; it was the other half of the blade.

"I spent hours last night wondering what this was," Victor told him through his smile of childlike wonder. "When something hits me, I can't explain it. But there was this feeling of nostalgia almost."

Victor turned to look at Hartley with a face he'd only seen him have a few times in his life—a face that all but had the words *I'm thinking of doing something crazy* plastered all over it. His eyes were wide with a burning scientific curiosity.

"It's armor!" Victor exclaimed.

Hartley couldn't do anything but look at the young man. Somewhere buried deep within Victor's eyes, all he could see was a young boy, outfitted in his father's vastly oversized lab coat—running around the house yelling how he was gonna be a great scientist just like his dad someday.

Even in the face of the dangerously unknown, he still found a way to see the possibilities that lay beneath the surface.

A scientist through and through, Hartley thought to himself. *Your dad would've loved to see how you turned out.*

• • •

After finishing breakfast and talking about everything for a while longer, Victor decided to adjourn back to his lab for further testing, leaving Hartley to his own devices.

As he strolled down the long corridor, Hartley decided to head back to his own room as well.

Taking a seat on his neatly made bedspread, he looked over at his dresser and the locked drawer on the bottom. He grabbed the key ring he always kept on his hip, flipping through the many differently shaped keys, each one belonging to a variety of locks placed all over the property. After finding a slightly rusted silver key, he unlocked the drawer, pulling out a dusty old scrapbook.

Opening it, he was greeted by old family photos of the Reliance family. He gleamed as he looked upon the numerous photos of the family who had given him a home all those years ago. He looked upon multiple pages of the Reliances all posing for their regular family photos, all of which Hartley had carefully sorted into chronological order. Both he and Victor's father were sticklers for remembering the small moments. The farther into the worn album you delved, the older you could watch Victor grow.

Yet at some point, the photos featuring Edgar and Vanessa stopped altogether. His heart dropped at the thought, causing him to pat his eyes dry. Having lost the two of them was one of the hardest things Hartley had ever been through. And having believed he'd lost Victor too had left him lost in this vast, dreadful world, with no idea what purpose he really served.

He thanked whatever God there was that Victor had somehow come home to him.

Deciding to delve into the happier times some more, he made his way backward through the scrapbook, this time slower than before. After a few moments of fond memories, Hartley found himself stopping in his tracks, bringing his joyful memory lane to a halt.

He stared down at a photo that hadn't seen the light of day in years, simply gazing at it with an intense expression of worry. The photo showed a young Victor, early grade school by the look of it, and two other young boys posed with wide grins in front of the Reliance vacation home in East Hampton. One boy had a wild head of auburn hair and a warm smile that accentuated the gleeful aura about him, and the other sported combed-back chestnut hair and a familiar set of brown eyes. Each of their respective dominant arms were outstretched into the air, displaying the eerie sight of flames, armor and smoke coating their hands.

Hartley couldn't hide his fear, intense anxiety filling him as he continued to stare down at the once-thought well-buried memory.

He placed the album back into its usual spot, locking the dresser drawer before donning his usual night attire, pulling the covers out and lying back on his satin sheets. He blankly stared upward, thinking of everything that had happened, unable to shake the feeling he'd wake tomorrow and find it all a dream.

Leaving him alone once more.

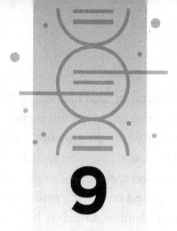

9

JUST THE BEGINNING

"**G**ood evening, New York. This is Eric Tolbert with Channel 12 news. Tonight, almost five months since devastation ravaged our homes, the sudden reappearance of tech mogul Victor Reliance. And we'll also get into strange occurrences happening around town, including but not limited to the blaze set near the homeless encampment known as the End of the Line late last night," Tolbert announced, just as rehearsed, the high-grade studio lighting glistening off the beads of sweat on his forehead.

With his hands folded in front of himself, he presented a powerful presence to the best of his ability, despite his apprehension over only having been promoted to anchor the month prior.

"Almost five months ago, a bomb of still yet unknown origin detonated in the middle of Times Square. The death toll continues to rise every day, as many of the once believed lucky few are still succumbing to their grievous wounds following their rescue. We've been told the cordoned-off area should still be treated as extremely dangerous and that no unauthorized personnel should be entering the crater sight until the CDC has told us otherwise. On scene outside the crater right now is our very own Olivia Ray, with updates on a few things New Yorkers are no doubt still wondering about. Olivia?" Tolbert finished, turning toward the directed camera.

On the other end of the stream, Olivia brushed her light strawberry blond hair past her ear as she heard her cue call. "Thank you, Eric. I'm here at the edge of the Light Valley crater site near Central Park—where just yesterday, missing CEO Victor Reliance was seen exiting the crater site with two other unidentified men." She motioned toward the busy street, where her car windshield had been totaled the other day.

"All three appeared to have been trapped for a long while but were gone before any authorities could ask them any questions about where they've all been. The other two alongside Reliance have still yet to be identified. We now go to eye witness testimonies of Reliance's sudden reappearance," she finished.

Everyone interviewed that day all had their fair share to say about Victor's new world debut.

"His friend came flying through the air! Busted this lady's ride and just took off."

"I bet they were caved in somewhere. But then again, it begs the question of how they suddenly got out?"

"Yo, how the hell did they survive that long with no food?"

Many people were ecstatic that three more people had survived the harrowing blast. Others, however, weren't so happy about it.

"You ask me, he shoulda died that day. Why's my sister crushed under that rubble but the rich guy gets to live? Not fair if you ask me," a young man angrily asserted to Olivia.

He knew all too well that money had nothing to do with it, but with that kind of tragedy and anger hanging on your shoulder, it's hard not to see the apparent unfairness at play.

"Authorities have attempted to reach Reliance in the hopes of finding any clues as to what transpired that day," Olivia announced, "to no avail so far, as Reliance has been holed up in his Soho building since his homecoming. None of us can blame him. No one knows what he may have experienced these past four months."

• • •

Olivia hopped into her car, taking a moment to look at the space where her windshield should be. She'd been told the repair shop had to special order her replacement, so for the moment, she had to deal with a clear sheet of plastic.

She let out a heavy sigh as she thought back to Sam's face. She was determined to find him and discuss the funds for repairs but had absolutely no way of knowing how without his name. Nor was she even sure if she'd win if she took it to court. She had hit him at the end of the day.

Starting the car up, she began her drive to her next broadcasting spot. She was told there had been a bizarre fire the previous night, the tenants nearby all stating they'd seen an altercation right before the blaze had started, but when authorities arrived there was no one around. Just the charred remnants of a blaze that had burned so hot it had taken three fire trucks and just as many hours to extinguish.

She hadn't actually seen the site herself yet. So going in, no one could have faulted her for expecting just a simple fire. She wasn't prepared for the scene she pulled up to.

A wave of journalistic excitement rose in her as she thought how lucky she was to be the first reporter on site. At first glance, it seemed like another bomb had gone off. There was a dumpster that had plowed through a brick wall; the nearby trees were burnt to cinders and still smoking on the ground; but strangest of all, a large portion of the road had actually been melted into liquid.

The liquid concrete was still bubbling from the heat.

Pulling her hair up into a ponytail, Olivia readied herself for another broadcast, quickly speaking with the nearby authorities and tenants to get their stories together.

• • •

"And three … two …" Mouthing the word *one*, Ryan signaled Olivia they were live.

"Hello again, New York. I am on site of the blaze reported last night in the End of the Line's network of alleyways. While its origin is still not known, local authorities have concluded it wasn't an incendiary device of any kind, further deepening this mystery. According to eyewitnesses, just before the fire began, arguing could be heard from the alleyway the ordeal took place in."

She turned and pointed into the alley, noticing how dark it was, despite the daylight shining all around.

"People heard a large crash, which was later determined to be the alleyway's dumpster barreling through the adjacent building's solid brick wall. Our witness testimonies state that whatever happened next can only be described as a force of nature. A plume of flames is said to have violently erupted from the alleyway, leaving the surrounding area charred and black—as well as a large section of concrete reduced to hot molten liquid. Authorities say that anything that could burn that hot is not easily accessible to the public, leaving us all with a familiar burning question. Who ... or what, is to be held responsible?"

Olivia quickly caught her breath as she got ready to finish up. "Multiple blocks away the next morning, citizens reported seeing an odd individual sleeping in the park. His clothes were burnt and falling off according to the group who found him. When the group attempted to roll the man over and see his face, he was reported to have run off.

"Leaving us right where we were, confused ... and afraid for our city. I'm Olivia Ray with Channel 12 news. Back to you in the studio, Eric."

Ryan gave her a thumbs up that they were clear, and Olivia finally relaxed herself. Her biggest issue with the job was the posture of it all. Having dealt with mild scoliosis her whole life, she struggled to keep her back from arching throughout the long broadcasts.

She turned back one more time to look at the site, with one hand rubbing the arch of her back. She couldn't help but notice that something felt strange about the whole thing. Not that random fires, or reappearing missing persons weren't strange on their own; but there was something deeper going on. She could feel it in her bones.

"Instinct," her father would have said. He would have told her to follow it too.

Her mind kept flashing back to Victor, Sam, and Dylan emerging from the crater site. Coincidentally, only a matter of hours before the blaze that took place a number of blocks away. It was a long shot of course, but her journalistic nature couldn't drop it without further investigation.

The one thing she knew for sure was that New York hadn't seen the last of its dark days.

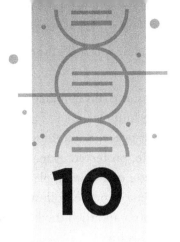

10

ANYBODY WOULD BE BETTER THAN ME

On the morning of the twenty-second, Sam stirred, struggling with recurring nightmares that kept him from restful sleep. He found himself laid upon strange white blocks, surrounded by an infinite void, and somehow even with his eyes closed, he could still see both himself and the black space around him from a third-person perspective.

His body rolled to the side, plummeting off the white blocks that had supported him only moments ago. As he fell faster and faster with his back to the ground, he instinctually shifted his weight around, flipping himself over to look at what came racing his way.

Below him lay a vast and deathly dark ocean, stretching out farther than he could see on every side.

Farther and farther down he fell, wind whistling in his ears from the wind as he grew closer and closer to the ocean at a dangerously fast speed, until finally, he slammed into the face of the water.

For a brief moment, he felt the sensation of fluid filling his lungs, of pressure gripping every inch of his body and crushing him as he sank deeper and deeper. Then it changed, the ocean around him shifting into a dark room, muffled words floating into his ears as he felt his head cradled against the soft embrace of someone's chest, their mere presence beckoning him closer.

For a moment, he felt peace. Something about the person's hold on him made him feel safe, protected even.

Images of the silhouette of a woman placing him in a dark closet abruptly ended his moment of peace, followed by a number of loud crashes just outside the room and then the horrific screams he would remember for the rest of his life.

The memory morphed around him once again, leaving him in another black space with some kind of object gripped between his hands that he couldn't see, the sound of a loud *snap* ringing repeatedly in his head. The scene changed before his eyes once more. Now he saw the image of a lone dog tucked underneath a wooden shelter, whining as a wave of white energy flooded over him.

Smoke filled his nostrils, abruptly pulling him out of his nightmarish state. He woke to his burning bed. "Shit!" he yelled, swatting at the flames.

For a moment he forgot, about the bomb, about his abilities, and about this apparent new world he lived in. Bringing on the heat in his spine, he focused on the flames in front of him. Slowly, the flames rose off of the bed and absorbed into his hand, and just like that, they were gone, replaced only by ashes.

Flexing his hand, he thought to himself, *This is gonna take some getting used to.*

Pausing for a moment, his mind raced with the still fresh images of his recurring nightmare as he placed his hands on his face and leaned forward. He quietly sobbed into his hands, doing his best to hold back the tears running down his arms and staining his sheets. But just like every time the pot of pitch-black emotions he held boiled over, there was no stopping it once it started.

"I'm so sorry, buddy," he whispered into his palms, unable to stop seeing the sweet little retriever sitting beside him as the puppy ate his favorite food, the look of contentment he'd give him just after he'd finished.

Why hadn't he just said fuck his studio's policies and taken the dog home? Why had he left the dog on its own every night? Would he really never feel the dog's warmth as it pressed its head into his chest for a hug?

"*Fuuck!*" he aggressively shouted.

Yet again, life had left him with the depressing realization that this world has nothing better to do than to plunge its inhabitants into a crude, unforgiving hell.

Wiping the tears from his eyes, he looked around his emptied studio apartment, eyeing the numerous black trash bags scattered around the floor that held most of possessions.

When he'd returned home the other night, he was greeted by a bright yellow "Eviction" notice taped to his front door.

The note had said the landlord had done all he could to keep any vacated units untouched as long as possible, in hopes some of his missing tenants would be found alive among the Light Valley crater site. But times had gotten tough since the bombings.

The city's economy had nearly flatlined after losing all the revenue sources that had been destroyed, and landlords and small business owners were forced to cut numerous costs to keep themselves afloat. That meant, unless he could find a way to raise enough money to pay his landlord back what he'd missed, as well as the next month's rent, he'd need to find another place to live sooner than he was prepared for.

The fact he needed a new job still remained.

Now fully awake, Sam threw his blanket off and sprung up to his dresser with considerably more energy than usual. He wasn't sure if it was his new developments or simply just anger building up in his chest. Physically, he felt great. Every ache from the previous day had completely faded, and his body felt strangely brimming with strength as he tensed all the muscles of his torso. As he made his way to his dresser, he passed the standing mirror placed nearby, quickly stopping to get a look.

He looked into the mirror at himself, quickly looking at numerous scars all along his chest and abdomen.

He didn't pay them much heed, as he'd seen them nearly every day of his life. And he quickly found himself distracted by something else. Not only did he feel great, he looked great. He'd always been in good shape, but he somehow seemed to have puffed up a bit through the night; he excitedly took in the new definition of his unusually fit physique.

He also couldn't help but feel like he'd made the right decision to leave a bit of facial hair on himself when he'd shaved after coming home. He'd left himself loose stubble siding around his goatee he'd left mostly untouched, and he felt as though it accentuated this new size his physique held, strangely making him feel older.

With tears still in his eyes, he gave a light laugh before brushing off the distraction, knowing he had other things he needed to worry about today. He needed to get in contact with the other two and try to get to the bottom of everything. He wasn't exactly looking to rekindle their past friendship, but there was no one else he could think to ask about all this.

He grabbed an easy pair of pants and a plain white T-shirt, throwing his usual dark hoodie on over it all. As he descended his stairs, he planned out his destinations for the day. First thing was first. He hadn't had a cigarette in four months apparently, the longest he'd gone since he'd started at fifteen.

He stepped out into the street, quickly wiping the remaining tears from his eyes before taking his first right to head to his usual corner store.

He wondered how the store's owner, Abraham, would react when he walked in. He and his wife had lived in the apartment above the shop since before Sam was even born, having opened it together in their twenties. Abe was a good man. When Sam was younger and living on the streets, he was the only one who didn't run him off when he caught Sam tucking food items under his shirt.

Apparently, Abe had come from a very similar background when he was young. So when he'd catch Sam up to his usual antics, he didn't look at him as a thief pillaging from his store but, instead, saw him as exactly what he was—a young man simply fighting to survive in this hellish world we all lived in, dealt a shitty set of cards by the cosmic hand of fate at play.

Sam wasn't a very touchy-feely kind of person, as events in his life had left him scarred, and he was very cautious about letting someone in close. While there wasn't a particularly strong relationship between the two, Abe was different from most people. He'd always leave the store's surplus items in a small crate behind the store, knowing Sam would make his way back there each night as he raided their dumpsters.

Eventually, a deal seemed to fall into place. As Abraham would leave food out back for Sam, Sam would hang around the neighborhood and act as bodyguard of sorts for the store. The particular area they lived in was plagued by crime—robbery, vandalism, auto theft, and even onto some nastier crimes Sam struggled not to view as death worthy. A number of the scars along Sam's torso came from the time he'd spent representing the store.

As he crossed the street, he wondered how much the folks running the store may have changed. He paused and stood in front of the entrance to the shop, but before he could continue, he saw a shocking sight on the inside of the building.

Abe was standing behind the counter with his wife, Anna, tucked behind him, both of their hands stretched into the air as they stared at a masked gunman standing on the other side of the counter. The man seemed angry, judging by his balled fist and the slight jerks of his hand and body as he seemed to scream something at them.

Sam's brow tightened. He felt heat rise within himself, throwing his hood on before grabbing the handle for the door. It was the perfect opportunity to do something with this tension stuck in his throat.

The bells above the door jingled as he pulled it open, slowly strolling in as the gunman twisted around to see what the noise was. The man pointed the gun at Sam, unable to meet his eyes due to the hood over his low-hanging head. *"Who the fuck are you?!"*

Sam stood before him, motionless besides the slight shake he felt in his muscles, like they were aching to put this man down. He didn't even know him, but the gruesome images ingrained in his mind were bringing something dark out of him. "Leave," he quietly ordered, his voice twisting itself into a growling rasp.

"The fuck did you say?" the gunman questioned. "Do you not see the gun pointed right at your head? You blind or just fuckin' stupid?!"

Sam gritted his teeth. What was this fascination people had with insulting his intelligence?

"I said leave now," he started, that same twisted rasp still hanging onto his words. He brought his head up to meet the man's eyes, revealing the smoke rising up and out his mouth with his every scalding breath, "Before I do something I'll regret."

Abe's jaw dropped at the sight of Sam's familiar face.

At the same moment, the gunman's eyes went wide at the harrowing sight of Sam's threat. Immediately, he cocked back the hammer of his nine millimeter.

Staring straight down the barrel of the gun, watching the man's finger inch toward the trigger, Sam's eyes strained themselves the most they could to figure out his next move, until time seemed to physically slow itself around him. Taking an outside step with his right foot, his body pivoted around the same direction and out of the line of fire, his lead hand clutched tight at his side before swinging upwards with all his might in one swift and powerful motion. The sensation pulsing through his body was eerily similar to what he felt when he'd run from the people who had found him on the bench.

In the single blink of an eye, the gunman's finger squeezed the trigger in response to the knuckles digging into his gut, their sheer might lifting him from the ground and up into the air. A combo of saliva and blood exploded from his mouth as his body rocketed into the ceiling, lodging itself between all the insulation and aluminum framing.

Sam's jaw dropped. He'd had no intention of hitting anywhere near that hard. He'd only wanted to incapacitate him. He didn't even know he was capable of that much raw strength. Was this another change that came with the flames?

The man groaned up above them, shifting slightly as he wormed around in his unconsciousness, lessening the strain Sam felt.

Dropping to his knees, Sam grasped his head in shock. He'd nearly killed that man. Overtaken by anger from an entirely different situation, he'd subjected him to the rage he held within. He hadn't struggled with control for years. Why was his grip suddenly loosening? Did it come with the influx of power he'd somehow gained? He needed to figure out what was happening. He wouldn't allow his control to completely slip.

Never again.

"Sam?" a trembling voice spoke up in front of him.

Lifting his head from his hands, he looked up to glance over at the counter, seeing a teary-eyed Abraham staring down at him.

"It is you," he continued, beginning to run around the counter to meet Sam. Dropping to his knees in front of him, he just looked at him, stuck in disbelief of both his friend coming back to life and of the smoke continuing to rise up off of him. "What happened to you, son?" he asked with tears in his eyes.

Fluid flooded Sam's eyes as he saw true worry on the man's face. Standing back up, he tried to calm himself, reaching out within himself to flip the switch off. Once the smoke stopped rising off his shoulders, he took a deep breath and patted his eyes dry. "It doesn't matter," he told them. "Are you two OK?"

Both Abe and Anna glanced upward at the man tangled in the shredded mess of their shop's ceiling. Wiping his own eyes now, Abe couldn't help but let out a chuckle. "Well, all things considered, I guess it could've been a lot worse."

Sam was in disbelief, his lips trembling as he spoke, "You're ... not scared?" This was the first time he'd used his ability in front of someone, and he'd be lying if he said he didn't expect some kind of angry mob to immediately follow.

"I watched you grow up for the most part, kid," Abe explained. "And I can't say it isn't a bit nerve-racking seeing what I just saw, but there's no way you could be a bad kid. Too much good in you, whether you see it now or not. Damn it's good to see you. I'd pull you in for a hug, but I know how you feel about that."

Sam laughed. "Thank you. It's good to see you guys too." He looked up at the man dangling above them once more. "I swear I'll pay for that." Then again, he had no idea how he would do that. Did he even have a job anymore?

"Not a chance," Anna interjected. "You think we'd make our savior pay for something like that. That's what homeowner's insurance is for."

"We'll have to file a police report first, though," Abe added. "It might not be too good an idea for you to be here when we do."

Sam's jaw tightened. How would the police deal with someone like him? "What'll you tell them?"

"The truth. Well, a version of it at least. We'll just tell them a hooded figure came through and stopped the robbery, tell them he took off right after," Anna assured him. "It's not like we have cameras they'd be able to check."

Sam smiled. He was thankful he'd met such kind people when he was young. He wondered how life might have gone if he'd swallowed his pride and actually asked them for help all those years ago. Would they have taken him in as their own? It didn't matter anymore. He was just thankful he had met them at all.

"Thank you," he quietly let out, maneuvering around so he could head to the door.

But as he grabbed the handle, Abe called out to him. "Wait!" He turned around to Anna, and she handed him something. "You can't forget your usual."

He tossed the items toward Sam, who turned around to catch them. He looked at the pack of smokes and the energy drink that now lay in his hand.

"I take it from what you just showed us, big things are coming this city's way, things no one is prepared for in the slightest. Can … can we still count on you if we ever need help?" Abe asked him.

Taking one of the cigarettes out of the pack, he placed it between his lips, quickly igniting a flame on the tip of his finger to light it. As he put the flame atop his finger out, he gave them a smile before heading out the door. "Always."

• • •

Sam approached the roadway, savoring the earthy taste of his favorite brand of cigarette as he planned his next stop.

He figured it was time to get in touch with the other two. Judging by how easily his grip on himself slipped back there, he needed to know what was going on. He wondered if the rich boy had experienced anything similar. And if he had, did he know what had caused it?

He pondered those thoughts more deeply as he took out his phone and searched for Victor's number. As he hit the dial button, he heard sirens approaching from behind, turning to see a police cruiser pulling up outside of Abe's shop.

"Shit, time to go," he muttered, making his way across the street down the block a bit.

"Hello?!" Victor yelled through the phone with no warning, slightly startling Sam.

He almost couldn't hear him over the noise in the background, like machinery clanging in a factory.

"Hey, this is Sam," he began. He instantly thought about how weird this all was, and he didn't wanna risk saying anything aloud over the phone. "I was wondering if you had some time to meet today. There were some things I thought we should discuss."

To his surprise, the machines in the background all clicked off in a row.

• • •

On the other end of the phone, Victor's mind raced. *Has Sam experienced something too?* He hadn't yet even considered that Sam and

Dylan could have been changed too; he'd been too caught up in his own bubble. "Yeah, for sure. Let me send you my address. And what do you say you meet me here in an hour or so?" Victor asked.

He'd been up for a day and a half toying around with his new ability. He'd yet to figure out how to retract the liquid back into his body, and his right side was still mostly covered at the moment. The most he'd figured out was the liquid's purpose, but since then, nothing.

The two agreed to meet and hung up.

Victor turned around in his chair, looking at the assortment of tools and machinery surrounding him. Dozens of snapped saw blades, broken hammers, and a prototype laser intended for diamond mining all scattered around his workspace.

None of them held up against the armor, not even a scratch.

The door across the room swung open, and in came Hartley with his routine round of afternoon tea for himself and coffee for Victor. Hartley set his tray down, eyeing the random equipment lying around as he put three creams and two sugars into Victor's just the way he liked.

After Victor had revealed his armor to Hartley, the two had sat down to a very long talk. They talked about everything that happened to Victor from the moment of the blast, all the way up to when Victor and Harvey were reunited, over and over, in order to go over what they knew.

Hartley seemed to take everything very calmly. Not once showing an ounce of confusion or fear on his face, he simply listened and absorbed the things he was hearing. "So what do you plan to do now?" was his only question.

It was a good one. What was he going to do? Unable to think of an answer at the moment, he'd completely brushed off the question. Sam calling woke him up a little bit. Victor had all but forgotten everything outside of his own personal bubble.

Not once since waking up had he even thought about his family's company, let alone about whether or not it was still standing. Victor couldn't imagine what his father would say. No matter whatever fell onto his plate, his father was always able to stay on top of every aspect of his life.

Turning to Hartley, Victor asked, "Harty, what's happened to Reliance?"

Having just finished preparing their respective beverages, Hartley took a seat. As if looking for the right words, he took a moment to respond. "Now that's a bit complicated to say the least. As of this moment, your board of directors are assuming control, and they've run everything smoothly, but —"

Victor's heart dropped. "But what?" he asked feebly.

"But the Midtown branch was lost the same day you were. Most of its productions have moved to the Brooklyn premises, but it was a relative setback. Furthermore, there's a potential new buyer who's expressed interest in the company. The board tells me he's come in many times and made a number of offers. They're tempted to take it." Hartley was resistant to reveal all of this. He'd planned on waiting till Victor had been home a while longer before saying anything.

Victor was shocked. "There's no way. This was Dad's company that he left to me. I won't let it be handed out to some random buyer! Either way, they can't. It specifically states in the company's policies that, in the event of my death ... or in this case my having gone missing for a number of months, at least a year has to pass before the board can even think of turning it all over to someone. I've already named you my successor should anything happen to me."

Hartley sighed, bracing himself for what he had to say next. "Traditionally, yes, the board would have to wait a set time of one year, unless —"

"Unless what, Hartley? Come on!" Hartley beating around the bush was starting to irritate him, causing a strange murky sensation to begin tickling the inside of his chest.

"What do you think, kiddo!?" Hartley asked him. "This wasn't a normal occurrence. You didn't pass away or get in a simple accident. The city was attacked, and you and thousands of others ... Well, let's just say that both the city and your board didn't have what it took to keep hoping."

"*But still!*" Victor continued. "That still doesn't change the fact that they overlooked my documented statement naming you as the company's successor. You can't tell me that was because of the bomb."

"Well ... no," Hartley softly said, dreading where the conversation was heading and what he'd have to tell Victor.

"*Then what!?*"

Hartley sighed. "Look, the board started to shut me out pretty soon after you disappeared, assuring me they were keeping everything well maintained. I tried to fight back because I knew it was what you wanted. But I mean, come on, kid, I don't know the first thing about running that place. And between the legality matters of your ... passing—documents, wills, billings—I just didn't know what to do other than to trust the board. I couldn't even take care of myself, let alone a nationwide business."

Taking a moment to let it all sink in, Victor took a good look at Hartley, seeing just how frail he'd seemed to become over the last few months. "Hartley," Victor started, "I can't imagine what you must have gone through on your own, and I know you never asked for the burden I left you. And I will spend the rest of my life trying to make it up to you. But I need you to tell me why the board went around my policy."

With a nervous tightening in his jaw, Hartley finally gave in. "Mr. Garretson of the board has been very open with me about what's been happening since your absence, and he's told me some of the other board members saw your disappearance as a blessing in disguise for their goal of transitioning back into the company's pharmaceutical roots. And if that wasn't bad enough, the company that's placed a few very substantial offers on the board's table is somehow connected to your uncle."

All noise around Victor seemed to drown out, slowly replaced by rage—pure black rage.

"Uncle Marcus is back?" He slowly let the question out.

Victor hadn't seen Marcus since before his father had died. There was a lot of bad blood between the two, given that Marcus hadn't called or visited once after Victor's parents had died; he hadn't even come for the funeral. He'd just sent his daughter, Victor's cousin, Avery, in his stead, without even giving her a reason for his absence for her to relay. Just sent his nine-year-old daughter to fly from wherever he was with a nanny to sit through a funeral for a man she'd barely known.

Victor had never displaced his anger toward Marcus onto her though; she'd been just as confused as him probably. Although it had been many years, and that was the last time he'd seen his cousin face-to-face since, he still remembered how much he appreciated her doing her best to cheer him up at the funeral's reception.

But Marcus … Not a word for over fifteen years. And now he shows up trying to take everything from him.

"*No! Absolutely not!*" Victor fumed at Hartley. "He doesn't get to just show up and take everything!"

Black rage crept into every part of his body as he stood himself up, struggling to move away from Hartley. Instinctively, he knew something was coming. Thinking about Marcus's return only aggravated him further as he groaned and fell to his knees. With waves of agony erupting within him, he let out his cries of frustration.

Hartley rushed toward him. "Victor! What's happening?!"

Victor motioned for him to stay back right before slamming his armored fist into the concrete flooring, cracking it from sheer strength. He could feel the armor coating his arm start to move, spreading further onto his chest.

He looked down onto his hand. As he watched, the armor formed claws at the tips of each of his fingers, and sharp spikes poked out of his whole lower arm, each spike starting to glow that bright neon blue. Just as the armor finished shifting, the pain stopped altogether.

Shifting back to sit on his butt, he took a few deep breaths in an effort to slow his rampaging heartbeat. He studied his now changed arm, chuckling at his inability to bring anything coherent to mind.

He placed one of the claws onto the ground and slowly pulled, slicing through the concrete with ease.

Sharp, he thought to himself with another laugh.

"Victor?" Hartley called out.

Turning to face him, Victor noticed his expression. The old man was finally showing fear in his now pale face.

"I'm OK, Harty. Just need a second," Victor said, doing his best to put his old friend at ease.

The strange tickling sensation in his body started receding, and with it, so too did the armor—slinking its way back up his arm and into the hole on his chest, which closed itself back up afterward.

"Whoa."

He was interrupted by a loud ring of the doorbell.

Hartley and Victor shared a look. "Expecting company?" Hartley asked.

Confused, Victor made his way to the front door. It hadn't even been thirty minutes since he'd finished his call with Sam. Who could be at the door? To his surprise, who should he find behind the door but Sam, sweat dripping down his forehead, a faint trail of steam flowing off of him as he took multiple deep breaths?

He'd been testing how fast he was now, using that new speed he'd discovered to race to Victor's in ten minutes, which would have taken over an hour at a normal pace. He soon realized, however, that his new speed came at a great cost to his stamina.

Victor abruptly spoke up. "How the hell did you get here so fast?!"

The only answer Sam could think of was, "I know a few shortcuts." What would he say? I ran here from the bay?

Inviting his guest in, Victor led Sam down a number of hallways. As they walked, Sam took a moment to look at all the photographs hung along the walls. Dozens of pictures of Victor and the people who Sam somewhat remembered as Victor's parents stared back at him. He looked upon every major moment in Victor's life, documented and framed. His parents stood in the background of every photo with huge smiles. And at the center of every photo was a young Victor with a smile Sam knew only came from true happiness; he vaguely remembered the feeling.

As he continued along, he noticed that, at some point, Victor's parents weren't in any more photos. Thinking back, Sam remembered hearing about the deaths of Edgar and Vanessa Reliance. There'd been a freak accident on a highway, and they both had been declared dead on arrival.

That must have been before middle school, judging by how old Victor looked. Yet in every photo after their passing, Victor still held that same smile across his face.

Thinking into it, Sam understood pretty quickly why Victor was still able to have a smile like that after losing them. In every picture, before and after their passing, there was another man, who was always ecstatic in every picture.

The man seemed to stand with Victor through everything. There were photos of Victor's first day of high school, his first car, his first date. The images captured everything up to what looked like Victor's first day as CEO of Reliance, the two of them standing in front of the building, smiles wide and bright.

Sam thought of his own upbringing, thinking how different he may have ended up if he would have let someone in when he was young.

"You OK? You're pretty quiet," Victor chimed in, glancing back at Sam over his shoulder. He wasn't a big fan of awkward silences.

"Yeah … just admiring your decor," Sam softly replied, a blank somber tone in his voice, like his mind was elsewhere.

Victor could almost feel sadness coming off of him, and for reasons he didn't quite understand, that, in and of itself, made him sad. Continuing forward, Victor motioned for Sam to follow, and the two made their way down the corridor.

Upon reaching a large metal door, Victor stopped.

"What do you keep in here? WMDs?" Sam joked.

"Something like that," Victor replied with a grin.

A look of shock quickly washed over Sam's expression. He could remember that grin from when they were young; it was always right before the boys did something just a little bit nuts. He thought how odd it was that, just before all this happened, he could barely remember either Victor or Dylan, but now memories seemed to be flooding through his mind the longer he was in contact with them. He wondered if they felt the same way.

As they entered the bunker-like room, a number of lights flicked on row by row, illuminating what Sam could only guess was millions of dollars' worth of equipment—stuff he couldn't even think of a name for.

"Holy shit," were the only words he could think of.

Victor let out a chuckle as he heard Sam. "I have a few projects going at the moment. Sorry about the mess," he said through his chuckle. Motioning his hand toward an empty chair for Sam, Victor sat on his own.

"So, you said you needed to talk?" Victor asked. He was anxious to see what Sam needed, but his mind kept being pulled away by the thought of Marcus.

Sam waited a moment, thinking of the best way to say everything "Have ... have you noticed anything strange since waking up?" He was unsure of whether or not he should just show Victor.

"Strange how?" Victor shot back.

Sam was pretty sure they'd experienced similar events, but he wanted to be positive. On the chance he was wrong, he didn't want to freak him out. Then again, Abe and Anna had seemed to take it OK. He stood up and shrugged his shoulders, deciding it was easier to just get it over with. Raising his hand up, he warned Victor, "Don't freak out," before his veins began to glow bright orange, flames quickly enveloping his arm.

Victor just stared, that same childlike grin plastering itself onto his face once more. As if in reaction to Sam's ability, that same murky feeling twitched within him, and Victor felt the hole in his chest open up, the armor pumping out of it and making a beeline for his right arm. With his arm now coated in the armor, he turned to Sam with his armored arm raised. "Maybe I have noticed a few odd things."

The two old friends spent some time talking about each of their respective experiences since the other day. They covered the highlights—from Victor's less-than-subtle way of telling Hartley to Sam's would-be mugger, who was more than just strong—and then moved onto what they had discovered themselves capable of afterward.

Victor had a hundred questions, his natural scientific curiosity was having a field day with all these new developments.

Sam spoke about how he'd felt like this new world they were living might be just a little easier to adapt to if they knew what they were dealing with, and the only way to do that was to exchange information. "Have you heard from Dylan?" he wondered. "I don't know for sure, but I think it's safe to say he'll have been affected too."

"Actually, no. I hadn't really done much before your call. I'll try and get a hold of him." Victor took his phone out of his pocket, already calling his number.

He waited through a number of rings before he got Dylan's voice mail. "Nothing," Victor said, shrugging his shoulders. "I know he lives up in Lenox Hill, but it's been forever since I've been over. I think I have his address written down somewhere … Just give me a minute."

With that, Victor kicked off the table while sitting in his swivel chair, launching himself across the room in front of a large computer monitor.

While Victor looked through the files on his system, Sam decided to look around and kill some time. "You care if I smoke in here?" he asked, waving his pack of smokes in the air.

Victor gave him a quick thumbs up, immediately continuing to click away on the computer.

Sam shrugged his shoulders, lighting up the tip of his finger and putting it to the cigarette tucked between his lips, taking that savory first puff. He approached the nearest table, picking up a broken saw blade. "And not even a scratch?" he said to himself as he exhaled his puff, still dumbfounded at the comic book-like abilities they'd found themselves with.

A part of him wondered which was stronger—his flames or Victor's armor.

Sam couldn't take his eyes off the large machinery surrounding him, he knew Victor was rich but this was a little ridiculous. "Got enough toys, rich boy?" Sam called out to Victor with a light chuckle.

Victor gave him a sarcastic laugh. "Found it," he then called out.

Walking back, Sam looked up at the screen, shocked to see that Dylan's address wasn't the only thing Victor had pulled up. He could see the names of Dylan's family, his cell and work numbers; basically anything you could pull up on someone, Victor had done it. "Holy shit, dude. I thought you said you were pulling up his address, not his whole life story," Sam joked.

"Yeah, I know. It's a habit of mine. My mind is always so caught up in work, I sometimes forget about everything else," Victor explained. "So I record everything everybody tells me about themselves. That way, if I ever start to lose touch with the world around me, I can ground myself again. Well not everybody, but the people I interact with most."

Sam grinned, happy to see Victor wasn't that different a person than he remembered. Being from the family and status he was, no one would be surprised if he ended up growing up to be a rich, judgmental snob. But even when they were young, Victor had been the kind of person to ask the rumor-swirling loner over to hang out.

Looking up at the info on the screen, something caught his eye. Both Dylan's parents were deceased as well—and his sister too. He thought back to school and his old memories of the trio, but he couldn't remember Dylan even having a sibling.

A dead relative wasn't something you could just ask about, let alone a whole family. Sam knew that from his own dark experiences. But the fact he didn't know such important things about someone he'd once called a friend made him feel sad.

Had these three ever truly been friends?

He remembered that Dylan didn't even know Sam's parents were gone. A mix of emotions plagued him, causing his head to ache slightly, and his unclear memories weren't helping. He then realized something that put a pit in his stomach. As strange as everything already was, the realization that all three of their parents were dead only deepened everything.

His eyes went wide with questions, almost forgetting where he was at the moment. Victor spun around, having just finished blacking out Dylan's private info. The squeaks of the wheels on his chair pulled Sam back to the matter at hand.

"Now here's the deal," Victor started. "I agree we all need to sit down and talk things out. But there's some things I need to take care of." Victor still couldn't forget about the situation with Marcus. "Do you mind grabbing him for me? If I don't take care of these things now, it'll just cause issues later on," he finished.

He worried that the longer he waited to confront the situation, the higher a chance Marcus would have of stealing everything, and he wouldn't allow that.

Seeing that Victor had something on his mind, Sam agreed to get Dylan on his own, writing the address down on a sticky note and sticking it in his pocket. Victor and Sam planned to meet once more after Sam had returned with Dylan, and the three of them would attempt to figure things out.

Sam's familiarity with the city always aided him in multiple aspects of his life. From his courier job, to his brief time as a taxi driver, all the way back to when he needed to know where was safe to sleep when he was young, the knowledge had come in handy. Given that, he knew that Dylan only lived about two hours away from Victor's Soho house.

Making his way down the crowded street, Sam noticed how bundled up the people crowding the city streets were. Everyone wore scarves, puffy coats, and even gloves and earmuffs in some cases. Then there was him in his thin hoodie, warm as could be. Quickly grasping the situation, he smirked. Would he never have to worry about being cold again? Rain, snow, wind? He wondered if his base heat was too hot to be affected by them?

Feeling a sudden urge to run, he ducked into the alleyway to his right, wary of running full speed in a large crowd. Before he broke into a sprint, he noticed a fire escape to his left leading up to the rooftop above. With a smile, he leapt up, grabbing the rungs of the ladder and pulling himself up.

With his strength, every pull upwards shot him up a level of the fire escape, making short work of getting up the side of the building. His whole body was giddy with excitement as he looked across the gap of the roofs.

Thinking back on his feats of strength just since waking up, he thought to himself, *I can make that.*

He walked himself to the end of the roof, turning around to point toward the direction of Dylan's apartment. Finally pushing off with his lead foot, he broke into a sprint, keeping his torso low to the ground and using the momentum it gave him to his advantage. Gaining all the speed he could in the short space, he approached the ledge and planted his feet, preparing for the jump.

That familiar heat feeling made its way down into his feet and erupted a quick yet forceful explosion of flames through the soles of his shoes, propelling him forward much farther than he'd intended. His feet left dissipating trails of flames following behind him as he soared through the air with ease.

Clearing his first target and landing on the next roof over, he rolled to shake off the fall, looking back to see if that had actually just happened.

Excitement rose up though his adrenaline-tightened chest, a smile sweeping across his face all the while. He instantly broke into another sprint, using his flames to propel him into the air once again as he bounded across the rooftops as fast as he could go.

Every time he launched upwards, he'd look down onto the roadways and see people pointing up at him. He knew no one was likely to actually see his face, but he still felt he should be a little more careful not to become the center of attention, so he adjusted his jump path to go more forward and less up—an action that drastically increased his speed.

Rooftop after rooftop, he blasted forth until he finally rolled to an abrupt stop. Knowing that Dylan lived less than a block away, he decided it was easier to walk from here.

He felt a strange sensation on the bottoms of his feet. Looking down, he found a charred mess that had been his shoes. *Damn,* he thought to himself.

After removing his shoes and awkwardly setting them neatly on the roof, planning to replace them after grabbing Dylan, he decided to do one more test. He looked over the edge of the roof, carefully checking to make sure the alleyway was clear of people.

After confirming it was, he took a deep breath in, stuck one foot off the ledge … and jumped forward.

Down he went. It was at least six stories, almost a sixty-foot drop. As soon as his foot left the safety of the roof, the possibility of death flooded into his mind—that there was every chance in the world he might just go splat.

He pushed all fear to the back of his mind, deciding to trust in these new abilities. He had no idea what he would end up being capable of in time. For the moment, however, all he seemed to be capable of was producing flames from one or two parts of his body at a time. He sent his flames down into his legs, coating his two bare feet in as much flame as he could muster. The ground steadily grew closer and closer, until he finally impacted into its seemingly solid embrace.

The ground caved inward in an explosion of orange, Sam immediately bursting out of the blast and rolling on the ground to a skidding stop. His heart was racing intensely with a mix of livid excitement and gut-wrenching fear. He propped himself up off the ground, turning over to look at the burning patch of concrete.

He knew he shouldn't just leave it like that. Quickly, he absorbed the lingering flames back into himself before someone stumbled onto another random fire.

He just sat on the ground for a moment afterward, reflecting on what he'd just done. He may have survived, but that was not his smartest decision. He was getting too confident, and if he continued that trend, something bad was gonna happen. He decided he needed to cool it, letting out a little chuckle at the irony of him needing to cool it.

As he approached Dylan's apartment, Sam once again had to think of the best way to present the situation to him. He practiced a few opening lines as he stood out front the entrance. "Hey, have you noticed any strange abilities? Hey, fire comes out of my hands. What comes out of yours?" Or maybe he should just show him like he had with Victor?

He pushed his hair up and off his face and made his way up the front steps, reaching for the handle of the front door. Taking out the piece of paper from his pocket, he read Dylan's apartment number, 306. The whole thing gave him déjà vu of the day of the blast, and the spiral staircase of Dylan's apartment building didn't help. The apartment was on the third floor and the higher up he went, the more he was certain he could hear a man crying coming from above him.

As he came up the final flight of stairs, he saw apartment number 306, noticing the front door was cracked open. The sound of crying was definitely coming from inside the apartment. Was it Dylan?

He could feel the pain in the cries. They made his chest tighten as each one rang in his ears. Reaching out, he slowly pushed the door open. "Dylan?" he cautiously called.

The crying stopped, replaced by sniffles and light whimpers. Sam heard a voice answer back. "Who's there?"

The door now fully open, Sam found Dylan on his knees in front of the door. He was in the center of seeming chaos; flickering lights illuminated deep scratches in the floor surrounding him, all his furnishings had been thrown back against the walls, and shards of glass and wood littered the floor.

Oddest of all was the red smoke fogging up the room.

A flicker of flames rose off Sam's shoulder. If he'd previously felt unsure about whether or not Dylan had been affected, he was certainly sure now. Taking another step forward, he felt the cold, scratched floor on his bare feet. "It's Sam ... Man, what happened?" he asked while still fixated on the room.

Without moving, Dylan spoke abruptly and with a somber tone. "She's dead."

Sam froze. "What? Who's dead?" His gut dropped. He hoped he was wrong about who he thought it was.

Dylan got a little louder. "Ashley ... I went home ... and she's dead. On the day of the blast. She went to her family's church—to pray for us." Anger welled in his chest as he began to scream. He turned to face Sam, his face caked with tears and blood running from his nose. "*You ... you said love throws things your way to make you better for it!*" Red smoke swirled around him as a low rumble filled the room. "*Well, how the fuck do I get through this!*" He roared, throwing his smoke outward and scratching the floor further. He lowered his head back onto the floor. He could no longer hold himself back from crying, releasing his sorrowful cries of anguish and loss.

Sam couldn't do anything but stand there, like a deer in headlights, each cry of his old friend a dagger stabbed into his chest. All semblance of excitement from before had vanished, replaced only by the immense guilt of talking out of his ass.

When he'd said that old line of his father's, he'd had good intentions. He'd never thought this was what Dylan would find coming home. The worst part was, Dylan was absolutely right; his father had never said anything about if the bad thing that came your way was the loss of that loved one; it was something he himself had struggled with since he was young. Sam felt tears well in his eyes. He felt horrible that he couldn't think of a single word to say back to him.

Since he couldn't think of any words, he simply took a few steps forward, sitting beside Dylan and placing his hand on his shoulder.

Dylan appreciated the gesture, knowing that there truly was nothing to be said.

The two just sat for a while, Sam feeling sorry somebody else couldn't be here with Dylan in his time of need; anybody would have been better than him. No one had ever really taken care of him in his life. How would he comfort someone else?

After some time, Dylan sat back and cleaned his face up a bit, finally clearing the phlegm from his throat. He looked around his trashed apartment, noticing the red swirls of smoke still ever apparent around them.

None of it seemed to faze him much, except one thing. He slowly turned his head toward Sam. "Where are your shoes?"

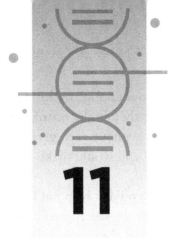

11

TEMPER TANTRUM

Hartley pulled the town car out of the midday traffic and up to the curb of Reliance's Brooklyn offices. He and Victor sat in the car for a few moments, looking out the tinted windows at the numerous reporters littered around the front of the building. It apparently hadn't taken long for word of his first visit back to Reliance to spread.

"You ready?" Hartley softly asked, glancing back at Victor, whose eyes were glued to the window.

Victor turned his head toward the front of the car. "Yeah, no time like the present."

"Attaboy," Hartley replied. He hopped out of the car and made his way around to the other side, grabbing and pulling open the matte black door for Victor.

Taking a deep breath in and out, Victor started getting out, buttoning the bottom two buttons of his suit jacket as he looked at the crowd of people, all their gazes slowly shifting toward him.

From their first glance, all semblance of reason flew out the window. The crowd of reporters roared to life as they swarmed Victor's car.

He had demanded a meeting with his board of directors, eager to get to the bottom of all this Marcus nonsense. He wouldn't allow

Marcus to even think about taking anything from him. Before he'd left his home, he'd explicitly told the board he wanted Marcus to be present for this meeting, without even giving them a chance to say no, knowing nothing he said would make any difference unless his uncle was there.

Despite his anger, he couldn't help but find himself curious as to how Marcus had fared for the last fifteen or so years. He wondered about his cousin, Avery, too, for that matter.

In Avery's case, while he hadn't seen her since the funeral, he'd loosely followed her life through the media over the years. True to the Reliance name, she'd also taken the world by storm as she grew older. News of her using large percentages of her trust fund account to finance several nonprofit organizations while she used the remaining percentage to put herself through school, pursuing a variety of degrees, had been widely spread.

Victor found it profoundly confusing how Marcus could disappear from the public eye as well as he did with his daughter being one of its beloved figures.

He shoved those distracting niceties out of his mind as best he could, determined to stand his ground as he clutched his gloved hand, hiding the armor beneath with intense animosity. As he made his way up the front steps, there wasn't a single eye that wasn't locked onto him now. This was his first official public outing since he'd come back from the dead, and it seemed like the whole world was itching for a few minutes of his time.

The group of reporters, which nearly had Victor barricaded away from the door, roared as they all rushed forward to be the first to get an interview with New York's youngest philanthropist.

He'd left his beard untouched, feeling as though this new world called for a new look. The thick black bristles made him feel a little more distinguished. His father had always worn his beard long, and something about him doing it too made him feel more confident, like his father had his back—as odd as that sounded to himself.

A young man no more than twenty-one or twenty-two years old and new to the company held the door open for Victor and Hartley with anxiety all but written on his face as he held back his fair share of reporters. Finally pulling the doors shut, the young man stammered for words until he finally was able to get out, "W-Welcome back, sir." The young man couldn't help but glance at the odd glove on Victor's hand.

Noticing his gaze, Victor placed his hand into his pocket. "An injury from the blast. Thank you. It's good to be back." He shot the guy a half smile and continued on his path, walking straight past the front desk attendant and heading toward the corporate elevator.

"Excuse me, sir. But you still have to sign in!" the attendant called, quickly interrupted by the previous young man.

"Man, what are you doing?! Don't you know who that is?! He literally runs the place," he frantically warned.

Unfazed, the attendant replied, "For now anyway." He noticed the confused look on the new recruit's face. "Let's just say there's a fair amount of people who wouldn't mind if Victor Reliance got taken down a peg or two."

• • •

The elevator dinged and opened its heavy metal doors, through which Victor hopped out before they'd even finished opening, deep in thought. He knew full well that his young age didn't sit very well with a number of powerful people within his company. Those people thought him immature and unversed with the way business was done in the world of adults, thinking him far too focused on technology, rather than their main source of income, pharmaceuticals; his father had dealt with some scrutiny on the subject in his career too, being the creator of Reliance's R & D department.

All Victor had done was continue his late father's work, believing technology to be the key to a much greater deal of development in the modern world. Where would we be without the creation of MRI scanners, X-rays, or even the common computer? Marcus's acquisition attempt wouldn't worry him as much, if not for the fact Victor felt he may succeed.

While none of his board had ever outwardly showed him how they truly felt, on numerous occasions, he'd found himself reading over company documents that had multiple instances of board members voicing their complaints toward him.

His liquid armor twitched, as if in reaction to his emotions. He'd yet again found himself unable to retract the substance and had been forced to wear a glove to cover his right hand. He hoped to find a way around that after meeting back up with Sam and Dylan later that afternoon.

Finally reaching his board's corporate office, he pulled the door open, ready to face anything Marcus had in store for him.

To his dismay, his uncle was nowhere in sight. The only people in the room were his board members, as well as the four official-looking men and women sat across from them. Then, sat at the opposite end of the table and staring back at Victor with a malicious grin, was a dark-eyed man whose presence seemed to dominate the room.

"What's going on?" Victor questioned. "I asked that Marcus be here."

The oldest of the room's inhabitants, who sat opposite the board and closest to Victor stood up, extending his wrinkled hand toward Victor's gloved one.

Cautiously, Victor took it.

"Apologies, Mr. Reliance, but I'm afraid there was some kind of mix-up regarding Marcus Reliance's appearance today. However, don't fret, we're here in the company's stead. We've been its legal team for nearly as long as you've been alive, and I trust that we'll be sufficient for today's topic of discussion," the man stated, a less than subtle hint of condescension in his voice.

Tightening his grip, Victor questioned the man. "That wasn't the agreement though! I'd think that, in the event of an attempt to take a family member's company, he'd at least have the decency to show his face." He turned to face the board. "Is this how we can expect

Marcus to conduct business were he to take over? Someone who can't be bothered to be present for important legal matters, who'd just pass the responsibility onto a proxy?" Victor released the man's hand, noticing the hint of pain on his face.

"So where is he?" Victor asked once more.

"Dead," the man at the end of the table announced with a hair-raising grin. He was incredibly young for such a position. Yet just the way he presented himself almost seemed like he'd been in it for decades.

Feeling taken aback, Victor assumed he must have heard the man wrong. "What? What are you talking about!?"

"I said he's dead. What? Are you hard of hearing or something?" he answered. Standing himself up and out of his seat, he slowly strode along the side of the table as he closed the distance between him and Victor.

"*Mr. Lawrence!*" the head of the legal team shouted. "We agreed we would find a more delicate fashion to reveal that information."

"Oh why bother?" he continued. "We all knew what a bastard he could be; even he himself did. Why sugarcoat anything?"

Victor could hardly even process what he was hearing. "Dead? When? How? Who the fuck are you?"

"Name's Anthony Lawrence, but you can call me Tony. Your uncle brought me in as his business partner a number of years ago after he'd separated from his subsidiary of Reliance Industries. And I'm now the CEO of our own ground-up company, Rebirth Pharmaceuticals."

"How old are you? You can't be more than twenty," Victor poked.

"And yet," Tony replied with a smile, "still old enough to know you're dragging this place into the dirt along with you."

Finally coming face-to-face with the object of his ire, Tony raised his hand in front of Victor as a simplistic gesture of peace. But the transparently thin grin on his face led Victor to believe he didn't intend for any semblance of peace.

Simply gritting his teeth in anger, Victor turned away from Tony and toward his board members. "Did you all know about this?"

They simply stared back at him with their dull, unblinking eyes before looking away toward a snickering Tony.

Victor continued to stare each board member in those same unblinking eyes, as if trying to gauge how they each felt individually. There were six members in total, each one a trusted confidante of his father. Some had even been part of the organization since his grandfather's days as CEO as he'd been told.

The chairman of the board and longest running member, Henry Garretson, was the one person in the room besides Hartley Victor felt he could truly trust. Henry had been named a board member before his father had even been born. Since then, he'd helped the Reliances maintain their company's image and bring up its young CEOs; he'd done it for Victor's father and for Victor himself—helping each young man to understand the ins and outs of the company, their major exports, and the political figures they'd be interacting with most.

Garretson gave Victor a look, telling him and everyone else to, "Take a seat," in his Americanized Italian accent.

The board room occupants all took their seats, tensions high and on the rise between Victor and the company's apparent potential buyer.

Beneath Victor's clothing, the armor stirred. He could feel it respond to his anger more and more. He wondered if that would end up being a recurring phenomenon.

Victor listened to the board members discuss Tony's rise through the economic ladder, how he'd been handpicked by Marcus many years prior to aid in Marcus's pharmaceutical research before he started his own company outside Reliance Industries. How the two of them had traveled throughout the states and from country to country continuing said research. How Marcus had fallen ill two years prior and, after his passing, how Tony had used everything Marcus had taught and left him to move forward and continue running their company.

Tony then went on to talk about how, after the Day of Light and Victor's presumed death, both of which caused the Reliance Industries stock price to plummet, he'd thought it may be a great opportunity to see what the board thought about a simple buyout.

Everyone in the room but Victor went on to talk about Tony's plan in the event the acquisition was accepted, how the resources and funding he would gain would aid in his research. They wouldn't go into specifics about what research he was engaged in though.

Apparently Tony had shown up one month after Victor had disappeared, with no prior warning to anybody. He'd just walked in and come straight to the board with an offer that would benefit them both.

As Victor silently sat through his meeting, doing his best to ignore the condescending looks Tony was sending his way, he circled his thoughts again and again as he slowly allowed himself to process what was happening.

Marcus was dead? Had been for over two years, no less. Had his board members known? Had they themselves just found out? And if they had known, what else were they keeping from him?

He couldn't help but wonder where Marcus's life had taken him as he slowly accepted the fact he would truly never see one of his last two remaining blood relatives again.

As far as Victor had known, for the last sixteen years, Marcus had control over only one subsidiary of Reliance. It was an obscure facility, so much so Victor had never even seen it or any documentation on it in all his time as CEO. But even that information was greatly outdated. It had been several years since he'd even heard his name. The only reason he knew about it were the vague memories he had of a phone call he'd overheard between his father and Marcus years earlier.

Whenever Edgar would have private meetings or calls in his study, Victor would always try to eavesdrop by climbing up the balcony outside. He felt determined to know what kind of work his father was doing, knowing he'd have to start sooner or later if he wanted to go into the family business.

More often than not, Edgar would always know he was out there almost as soon as Victor situated himself. Given that fact, Victor had never been able to hear anything really worth hearing, except for one time. He'd decided to try a different hiding spot this time, finding the vent that connected his father's study to the living space on the next floor up.

Silently he listened, the fan covering most of the noise, which was more than likely why his father hadn't noticed him this time. He'd overheard snippets of his father and had caught the deep anger in his voice. "Absolutely not, Marcus! We've discussed this … Stop … Your branch's funding …" Victor couldn't hear the whole sentence.

The next thing he had heard was Marcus's voice coming through the line, with no emotion behind his words, just a low bass that chilled Victor to the bone. "It's too late."

Three months later, Victor's parents had gotten into a sudden car accident. And he'd be lying if he said he'd never thought about the possibility of Marcus having something to do with it. Victor was nine when he'd heard that conversation, and it was both the first and last time he'd ever heard of whatever subsidiary Marcus was in charge of. For the last sixteen years, it'd been one of the biggest mysteries in his life.

What had his uncle's branch doing, and why had his father threatened to pull its funding?

● ● ●

After a couple hours of discussion, Victor's board voted three to three in opposition of Tony's acquisition. As per company policy, the board had to rule unanimously before a decision could be made. Given such, they scheduled a follow-up meeting three months from then after an adequate amount of time to study the trend of the company's stock price.

If it continued to trend downward like it had been, it was likely everything Victor and his father had worked for would be ripped away from him.

Victor couldn't come to terms with the fact that not just one but three of his board members had ruled against him. All it took was three more votes in Tony's favor, and everything his family had built would just be handed over to someone who, until four hours ago, Victor had never once heard of.

He exited the building in a haze, riding home with Hartley in an awkward silence, who kept glancing back at Victor as they rode through the ever busy streets.

Sam and Dylan were supposed to come back to Victor's in another hour or so, but Tony's antics had him so frustrated it was hard to get excited. The ride home blurred, with Victor completely caught up in everything that had happened since climbing out of that hole. Would his life ever go back to any semblance of normal?

As he climbed out of the car and proceeded back into his home, Victor went straight for his lab, rushing past Hartley.

The older man looked up the steps at Victor rushing inside, a growing feeling of guilt forming in his chest at the idea of not being able to do anything to help him.

As Victor burst into his lab, murky liquid spread further onto his chest. He ripped up his sleeve and looked down to see that his left arm was being covered now too. The armor shone brightly, illuminating the darkened room, and the angrier he felt, the brighter it shined.

Last time the armor had spread, he had subconsciously fought against it, preventing it from completely coating him. This time, he gave no struggle, a blinding sense of curiosity allowing the armor to take hold of him.

He ripped his button-up off, revealing that the armor had cloaked his torso in its entirety, bearing thick black tendrils that extended down onto his legs. Only his head and lower body remained uncoated. His fingertips stretched into talons, spikes poking off his back and forearms.

The grinding sensation stopped, allowing him a moment to breathe unhindered. When he felt his wits come back to him, he felt a surge of power unlike anything he'd ever felt.

Till that moment, the only tests he'd done were ones envisioned to gauge durability. He'd yet to see what the armor was capable of when attacking.

The blue glow instantly intensified. He grabbed the table closest to him and lifted it into the air. With everything on the table, he had to have been lifting at least three hundred pounds, all with one hand, and he felt he could even lift a little more.

Winding up, he threw the table across the cluttered room. The table and everything on it crashed into the wall, leaving cracks where it struck. The senseless destruction seemed to quell his resentment toward Tony, even if only for a moment.

Not wanting to lose that sense of ease he felt, he leapt at the next nearest object, slamming both his fists down into a military-grade mining laser without a second thought, easily a million-dollar piece of equipment.

Jumping around and stomping across the lab without an ounce of hesitation, he destroyed anything he saw in an almost childlike tantrum of superpowered rage. Everything that fell into his wake of destruction, he couldn't help but imagine if Tony were in its place.

Once the entirety of the room was tattered and in pieces, Victor fell still, taking deep breaths in and out in an attempt to quell his rage. He was abruptly broken from his trance by the sound of numerous clicks, the lights above him flickering on one by one.

"Holy shit, Vic?" a familiar voice called out from behind him.

Turning to see who it was, he watched as Sam slowly walked through the doorway, Dylan close behind.

Sam and Dylan entered Victor's demolished lab. And as they stepped through the shards of metal and glass, Sam was thankful they'd stopped for a new pair of shoes for him first.

"What the hell happened here?" he asked with a hint of sarcasm. Seeing Victor clad in his jet-black armor, he figured it wasn't too much of a leap to think it had something to do with that.

"How did you get in here?" Victor questioned.

"Hartley let us in. We could hear the crashing from the main hall," Sam explained. "I didn't think you'd really want him to see you from the sound of things, so I told him we'd check on you."

Victor couldn't help but feel thankful. Sam was right. Hartley was the last person he'd want to see him this way.

Dylan was still lingering in the doorway, his eyes trained on Victor. He was left speechless by the sight of the black substance laid atop Victor's torso. He had spikes protruding off his back and forearms. His fingers were clad with long talons, the tips all pulsing with that strange neon blue coloring. A large portion of the blue glow lay in the center of his chest, the blue swirling out to the rest of the armor, almost seeming to illuminate his skeletal structure. Tendrils stretched up onto his cheeks and down onto his lower body, as if to attach itself even more. Though Dylan had not been a Christian in a long time, his first thought of the armor was how demonic it looked.

Noticing Dylan's gaze, Victor quickly turned away. "Sorry ... I know I look a little odd. This just kinda ... happened."

Sam looked around once more, holding back a laugh. "All this just kinda happened?"

Victor took a good look at the room for himself. He'd gone overboard for sure. He'd just destroyed millions of dollars of equipment on an angry whim. It'd take weeks to order new materials for his tests and even longer to assemble and calibrate to his specific requirements. He could see a few intact items scattered around. *Maybe I can salvage a few things* he thought.

He touched the armor on his chest, thinking about the sensation he felt every time it came out. Just as he found that feeling, he felt a shift, followed by the slithering of his liquid armor making its way back into the hole on his chest.

It left him feeling strangely bare and exposed. It felt as though some part of him had seemed to form a connection to the armor. He was left with this new sense of discomfort he didn't understand. But he knew wearing the armor all hours of the day with his job wasn't feasible.

Dylan saw a lab coat hanging by the side of the door. Grabbing hold of it, he tossed it toward Victor. "Here," he called.

"Thanks," Victor answered, catching the coat and throwing it on.

Dylan took a few more steps into the room, rubbing his head on the way in. "This is all so much to take in. Superpowers? I don't understand how the both of you aren't mortified by all of this." It all sounded like a bad dream to him.

"How else would you describe what happened to your apartment?" Sam questioned while giving him a slight shrug.

He thought about it, and he did remember the red smoke. He remembered "blowing up" and the scratches in his flooring and his furniture in tatters. No normal person could do that. "That still doesn't change the fact it doesn't faze you two."

Sam and Victor looked at each other, both shrugging and shaking their heads. "Like I said, when mine first ... came about, I was being attacked. I guess, given the adrenaline, I skipped the shock part of it all, maybe? Then afterward, I was able to do things people only dream about, man. I was a lot more excited than I was scared honestly," Sam went on.

Victor nodded in agreement. "Once I realized what was going on, I didn't think anything could be cooler," he continued. "Disregard what you see around here."

Dylan shook his head. These two had their heads in the clouds. The only thing he could think of was being strapped down in some government lab—poked, prodded, and dissected for the rest of his life. "Was ... was it the blast?"

"That's my working theory. But unfortunately, anybody who saw anything that day, well, they aren't here anymore." A sunken look washed over Victor's face at the thought.

A brief moment of silence passed, making Victor feel a bit awkward. Thinking back to where they'd all parted, he remembered what Dylan's destination was. A smile swept across his face. "How did it go with Ashley?"

Dylan's eyes widened.

Sam looked at Victor and frantically waved his hand in front of his neck, giving him a look that almost screamed the words *shut up.*

Confused and out of the loop, Victor continued. "What's going on?"

Dylan reigned in the growing feeling in his chest, as if there was a cloud of rage within him. "She … died. On that day."

Sam's look made sense now. Victor found himself at an immediate loss for words. That was stupid of him. He should have given the possibility a thought before saying anything. He knew the death toll.

His chest tightened at the thought. While she had been Dylan's girlfriend, Victor had grown to be good friends with her over the years he'd known Dylan. "I'm so—"

Dylan cut him off before he could hear another person apologize. "It's fine." He looked around the trashed room. "You want help cleaning up?"

"Sure," Victor replied, feigning a forced sense of glee for Dylan's sake.

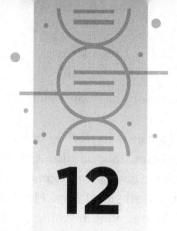

12

GATHERING OF ELITES

F ar away from the problems the trio currently faced, problems they'd yet to discover convened in the heart of a complex concrete maze—making their way through numerous ill-lit corridors, past the sections of padded cells, and around the round-the-clock laboratories, each of them finally filing into a vast stone room.

There, a powerful man greeted them with a grin of satisfaction. Seated on an eerie black throne, he overlooked a small group of men and women standing before him. Though they each may have appeared like ordinary human beings, each of them were immensely powerful in his or her own right.

Yet even so, none of them dared to challenge the godlike being who commanded them. For as harmless as he may have looked, his mere presence was enough to kill most normal men and women should he choose it.

"They're each coming along nicely," he finally said. "I can feel the residual traces of their abilities even from here."

"Can you guess any of their grades yet?" the first and foremost of the crowd called out, nearly interrupting the powerful man gazing down at them. The young man stared through the eyeholes of his black mask, the flickering light of the nearby torches slightly illuminating the fine details of the woodwork. He breathed heavily as he looked upon the man who was strong enough to lead each and every one of them with no question.

Well, almost all of them.

He intended to go higher than any of these chumps ever could. And with his innate power, he believed he could even go toe-to-toe with the boss someday. Their leader had seen his thirst for power firsthand, an event that had landed him the position of second in command of their growing force. It had proved to be a position that surely kept him on his toes, as being one of the youngest members of the organization made him the target of animosity among the others. With his abilities, though, there weren't many who could actually do much against him, and he actively welcomed the challenge.

A few days prior, he and two other of his fellow elites had been tasked with the handling and surveillance of their three newest subjects. He'd been pleasantly surprised when he'd learned that King had marked them for special treatment, meaning he saw something in them he only saw in a few select others before.

Despite his excitement, the trio had managed to shake them off before they could see what they were capable of. He was especially eager to see just how strong they'd be.

"Not yet. It's still too soon to tell. We'll let them be for the time being to allow them to develop further. After that—" their leader began to answer.

The man on the throne was cut off by a loud, raspy voice from the back of the room. "*No!*" a scarred man shouted as he shoved his way through the crowd, the very earth trembling beneath his feet. "*That's not what I was promised! I was promised a challenge by now, King!*"

He found himself cut off by thick black tendrils erupting out of the ground, wrapping its dark substance around his exposed throat. Being raised high into the air, he tried to rip away at the dark sludge, his hands simply passing through it as if only the portion physically touching his skin was solid.

The crowd all stumbled backward, feeling the powerful weight of the man on the throne's presence.

King slowly stood up from his ominous black throne. Its thick, black, and seemingly solid appearance quickly changed its shape, snaking its way beneath its wielder's feet as it raised into the air. Silence filled the room as he met the scarred man's frightened gaze, as everyone below struggled to catch their breath in the face of this beast that commanded them.

"Now, Tremor, I don't recall giving you permission to speak," King darkly told him, beginning to run his finger along a rather fresh wound on Tremor's chest. Staring at the large and only partially healed gash, the darkly clad man slowly shoved his finger into the center of the wound, giving it an aggressive twist as he did so.

Tremor tried to scream. But the tendrils grip on his throat wouldn't let him.

"I'd have hoped after your last encounter with Silver, you would have learned some semblance of respect. Yet, here we are." Giving him one last look in the eye, King slammed his hand downward, sending the black sludge and Tremor hurtling to the ground.

Everyone below quickly rolled out of harm's way, bracing for the large crash that ensued.

Coming down to ground level, King looked down upon Tremor with livid disappointment, watching his scarred body writhe in pain as he lay upon the crumbled floor. Looking around the rest of his army, he mercilessly continued, "As I was trying to say before we were rudely interrupted, *after* we gauge their ability"—he looked back down upon the slowly recovering Tremor, "then you'll get your challenge."

The young second in command nervously spoke up. "So what do you want us to do for now ... sir?" All of the bravado he'd felt before had melted away, replaced only by his quick re-realization of just how big the gap between them was.

King turned and strolled back to where his throne had previously been placed. "For the time being, I want you all to minimize the use of your abilities. I believe in the coming days, a number of our subjects may too develop the ability to sense their residuals. We don't need them finding us before we're ready." The same black substance wormed its way onto the pedestal area, reassuming its previous shape.

He took a seat on his reformed throne's cold embrace and looked at his young protégé. "Mimic, you, on the other hand, have further work to complete if you still intend to show your plan's worth to our greater endeavor."

Tony let out a big sigh. "You'll see, sir. If it works in our favor, we'll want for nothing when you're ready to give us the go order."

"For your sake, I hope you're right. Let Tremor be a reminder to everyone that we are past the point of safe return, from here on out, we cannot afford any mistakes. Remember what all this is for, strengthen your resolve, and show me you have the will to rise with me."

Accepting his leader's orders as law, Mimic nodded.

"So who're you gonna send to initially test the new subjects capabilities?" He asked his query while looking around the crowd, his eyes fixating on three especially menacing figures stood throughout the room.

With a slight grin, King said, "I thought this would be a good time to test if our returning elite has lost his touch." Turning to look at his soldiers, he found his pick at the back of the crowd. "Overcharge, step forward."

A man in his early thirties approached, with brushed-back silver hair, a bright unshaven beard to match, and a scowl on his crow's feet-riddled expression. The whole time he slowly made his way through the crowd, his eyes were fiercely trained on King. Without a word, he placed himself before the throne.

Looking down at the scowling man, King issued his order. "I charge you with performing the initial capabilities test, I want to see how well they perform under pressure. Take as much time to study them as you need. But do try not to make too big a spectacle. It's a touch too soon to have the public's attention at this moment." He waved his hand toward the door, telling the man to get to it.

The man known as Overcharge lingered for a moment, still meeting the gaze of the man ordering him around like a dog. With a swift turn, he stomped his way out the main chamber, the stone doors slamming behind him.

Their leader continued once more. "He'll come around soon enough. He's much too powerful an asset to simply let walk away."

His tone lowered as he rapidly grew more serious. He'd grown tired of speaking so long. "Final order of business, Mimic, before you leave for your assignment, I want you to coordinate with the other handlers to make sure they each know their duties. Our main subjects will be developing much more rapidly than the rest. But that's not to say a number of the secondaries won't possibly exceed initial expectations. I want to coordinate constant surveillance of our other subjects as each of them undergoes evolution."

Closing his eyes and taking a deep breath in, he continued, "I can already feel a few of them."

● ● ●

The crowd made its way out of the dark stone chamber, all going their separate paths to their own sections of the facility. An injured Tremor hobbled toward the medical bay as best he could, his face an angry, bloodied mess. He knew he'd heal within a few days, yet that didn't diminish the pain in the moment. He gripped his chest as blood leaked out his freshly reopened scar.

"Destroy that ... bastard ... someday," he forced out.

No one had ever humiliated him that way before he'd met King; even before his abilities, there were few who could ever overpower him. It was a fact he'd made great use of in his days as a military black ops agent. After his dishonorable discharge following his blatant disregard for his superior's order to stand down, he'd expertly translated the skills to his years as a hired killer.

The numerous scars tracing all along his body were a testament to his strength in his eyes, each one a memory of a time he'd brushed with death and won. Every time a new mark appeared on his body, he felt as though he'd gained newfound strength.

One day, he would grow strong enough to overthrow the old man, just like he'd always planned. "Kill … him," he muttered.

"Careful. You wouldn't want the wrong people hearing that, now would you?"

Tremor heard a familiar voice call out from behind him, turning to see Mimic making his way out of the darkened hallway and into the light.

With his hands clutched behind his back and a menacing look in his eyes beneath his mask, Mimic strolled closer.

Tremor turned back forward with a half scoff. "Piss off." He continued to hobble forward through the aches in his back.

Mimic caught up to him with ease, aggressively stepping in front of his path. "Now is that any way to talk to your superior? I suggest you take the time to learn your place here. Another outbreak like you did in there"—he leaned in closer—"And I'll take care of you myself."

With a loud grunt, Tremor swung his scarred first toward the man standing before him, a strange rumble filling the corridor as he moved.

Mimic knew, should it have connected, the punch would have done a decent amount of damage to him—that was *if* it had connected. But given his innate reflexes, it might as well have been in slow motion. Had King not given him the order to not use their abilities, he probably could have killed him in one move. Nonetheless, the order stood.

Bending his knees to duck under the attack, he pivoted around his right side, swinging his matching leg forcefully along the ground and kicking Tremor's own legs out from under him, causing the rumble that had been growing around them to quickly die out.

Before his opponent's back had even hit the ground, Mimic was launching into the air from his pivoted position, flipping forward, and bringing his left heel down into an axe kick.

Tremor found himself hammered into the ground for the second time that day.

The whole interaction was over in a split second.

Mimic brushed himself off as he chuckled, kneeling down to speak to the wheezing man below him. "I warned you to learn your place, you fuckin' fossil. Just remember, if you ever wanted to take a shot at the boss, you'd have to go through me first. You saw how that went." He stood himself up and casually hopped over Tremor's limp body, beginning to walk away from the man slowly getting his breath back.

"Just you wait ... I'll get you. You hear me, *I'll kill you!*" Tremor screamed, still making his way off the ground as spittle rocketed from his mouth.

Mimic laughed. "You know where to find me, big guy. Go ahead and try." He hopped and clicked his heels, giving the bigger man a sarcastic peace sign with his fingers as he continued down the long corridor, disappearing into the enveloping darkness.

He left his opponent alone with the fact he had been humiliated once more.

● ● ●

King finally adjourned to his quarters, taking a seat at his visibly aged mahogany desk. Clutters of papers and folders covered the desk's top; the papers were all filled with odd equations and formulas.

Three small tendrils of the black substance protruded off of his arms, reaching out across the room for the bottle of vintage whiskey and the glass positioned on the bar top. The final tendril propped open a small jar before grabbing a spherical piece of ice. The tendrils slowly retracted themselves, setting the bottle and glass atop his desk before the first two disappeared into the surface of his skin.

He took the ice sphere out of the last tendril's grasp, setting it at the bottom of his glass before pouring himself a drink over it. Grabbing a small stack of the papers cluttering the desk in his off hand, he sipped the robust, oaky flavor of the whiskey. At the corner of the stack of pages was a crest, a shield and sword bearing a crown in front of running gears.

His eyes trailed downward on the paper, gazing at an especially long equation. A number of crude sketches of a cube-shaped object sat below it. He gazed upon his creation, a wide grin of satisfaction on his face. "That marks the first phase complete."

He leaned back in his chair. "Now for phase two."

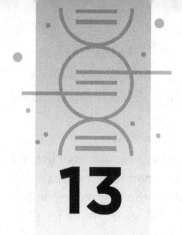

13

MEMORIES AND LIMITATIONS

The three awkward lab inhabitants grabbed a number of tools to help them clean up Victor's trashed lab. Each took care not to cut themselves on the shards of glass and metal littering the floor. They worked in utter silence, the awkwardness of Victor's question about Ashley still looming in the air.

None of them had really just made conversation for conversation's sake since before the blast. And for Sam, it had been years longer.

It hadn't always been like that. There was a time when you couldn't get Dylan or Victor to ever stop talking. Sam would sit and listen for hours, occasionally throwing his two cents here and there. He really just liked to have the company if he was being honest.

Sam thought back to the first time the three had met.

It was in Sam and Victor's junior year, Dylan's senior, as he'd skipped a grade before officially enrolling at Midtown High.

Given his troubled youth, Sam was always on the wrong side of something growing up. Constant skipping and disregard for his schooling, not to mention the multitude of altercations he found himself in with other students, consistently landed him in detention and remedial lessons.

Dylan, being the top of his classes and having skipped his junior year, was constantly asked to teach remedial lessons for other students, a task he never particularly wanted. It was bad enough being labeled Wonder Child without adding in bits of teachers' pet to that.

On the other hand, Victor had spent a great portion of his junior year beginning preparations for his new job as CEO once he graduated the following year. Given that, he'd missed a brief two-week period, landing him in a one-and-done remedial lesson to make up for what he'd missed. Being the orphan heir to such a prosperous family, Victor was swarmed by multitudes of people regularly attempting to get close and befriend him. But none of them had ever taken the time to actually get to know him as a person or what he brought to the table besides money. He often found himself surrounded by hollow words of praise and friendly expressions devoid of genuine intentions.

Through a vast number of occurrences, these three had found themselves all sitting in the same classroom that day.

● ● ●

Sam slumped forwards in his chair, surveying the room as he lightly rubbed the scar along his cheek. His thick head of hair dangled atop his forehead, a light breeze from the AC unit above him blowing through it.

It was just him and two others today, the both of them fairly new faces to him. He recognized the guy to his right. You had to live under a rock to not know who the "rich boy" of Midtown High was. His jet-black hair was combed to the side, and he was suited in a casual blazer that didn't fit the environment. He raced through the stack of assignments sitting on his desk with ease, an out-of-place smile spread across his face.

Sam raised an eyebrow in confusion. He'd never seen anyone actually look like they were enjoying their schoolwork. Turning to face the front of the class once more, he looked at the only other person in the room, a guy about his age with his face buried in a book and sat comfortably at the teacher's desk. The guy was a relatively new student to Midtown, and Sam had heard there had been some issues at his last school. But Midtown was pretty hush-hush about it.

Despite only being there a few months, Dylan had quickly caught the attention of the faculty and some prestigious colleges. He slowly turned the page of his novel, then used the same hand to fix his dark brown hair that was gelled up and styled, something he'd only recently started doing.

During his first visit to the school, he'd been given an introductory tour of the school and its campus. He was eventually taken into the drama club's space, where he'd seen the most beautiful girl he'd even seen. Determined to get to know her, he'd done some much-needed cleaning up of his act before actually starting school.

He looked over at Sam, who was just sitting there twiddling with his pen. "Did you finish?" Dylan asked.

"No," Sam bluntly replied, turning his head to look out the window.

"Have you started?" Dylan sarcastically retorted.

"No," he called back, his gaze still trained out the window.

Victor glanced up from his papers.

"Well you know I can't let you leave until you get it done, right?" Dylan leaned onto his elbows, using the desk.

Sam let out a passive-aggressive sigh. "Guess you better get comfy then."

Dylan aggressively rubbed his forehead. "No one said I asked for this, yet here I am. Look, I'm not your jailer. I'm not your parent. I'm just here to make sure you complete the things you need to."

Burying his head in his book once more, he huffed; he was ready for the day to be over.

A wave of sadness washed over Sam at the word parent, a reflex he still struggled to keep a hold of. He felt his face *quiver* slightly and quickly fought off the feeling as he did his best not to show anything else on his face. Grabbing hold of himself, he gave an unenthusiastic nod before leaning over the paper on his desk.

Blankly staring at the ridiculous equations laid out before him, Sam let out an audible groan. While he knew his way around everything that came with basic math, and few could hope to be more street smart than he was, when the math became as complicated as it was, he could feel the gears overworking in his head. He ran his fingers through his messy auburn hair, scratching his scalp with intensity.

"Do you need help?" he heard the boy beside him suddenly whisper, turning to see "rich boy" Victor Reliance looking his way.

This was a completely unexpected occurrence.

He'd never actually spoken to him, so Sam expected to see the same usual hint of sarcasm on his expression or for the daily ridicule he faced to follow his words. To his surprise, he felt like he saw genuine concern on his face.

"It's OK if you do," Victor quietly continued.

Sam was a bit hesitant, but nonetheless, he did need help. He gave in. "Um … yeah."

Victor turned his chair, leaning over to see what Sam was working on. "Oh no sweat." Going back to his desk, he pulled out a piece of paper and started writing. After he'd finished, he handed it to Sam. "Here's an easy way of remembering how to solve those, I don't know about everything, but it should help with most of what you've got."

"Thank you." Sam let the words drop out.

He looked at the paper, and to his surprise, he was able to make sense of what he saw. Using the notes, he leaned down over his papers and got to work.

Dylan glanced up from his book for a moment as he noticed Sam's pencil start scratching against the paper in front of him. With a raise of his eyebrows and a slight grin, he figured the guy must not have been as stubborn as he looked.

When six o'clock finally rolled around, the three young men grabbed their respective belongings and made their way out the classroom door. Sam watched from a distance back as Victor caught up to Dylan and sparked a conversation. When Dylan had first started here, the school had apparently asked Victor to show him around for a while. After spending some time together, the two had seemed to establish a good friendship.

Sam trailed a distance behind as he listened to the two. He never intended to eavesdrop; it was just something he did without even realizing. Another skill that had served him well in life.

Victor spoke of his brief time at Reliance Industries the week prior, how he'd met the board members for the first time since his parents passed. He went on about his excitement to graduate and take up the mantle of CEO, listing off a number of ideas he'd been brainstorming for when he did.

Sam heard him ask Dylan about the girl he'd been talking about recently, Dylan telling him it was a work in progress as his cheeks grew flush, giving a light laugh to distract from his embarrassment. Dylan told him they'd started talking more over the time Victor was gone, but he could only suppress his awkwardness so much when he'd gone over to her house for the first time.

As the three exited the main doors of the school, Sam quickly turned away from the other two and started on his own way. Now that the school day was over, it was time to start thinking about how to avoid the head of his group home tonight. He pulled out the pack of smokes he hid in the hollow lining of his backpack, lighting one up as he voiced a sigh of reluctance.

Victor and Dylan stopped as they waited for a cab to drive by, taking a few moments to plan out their night.

"You wanna grab a bite to eat?" Dylan asked.

Having skipped lunch that day, that sounded like a plan to Victor. "Hell yeah," he eagerly agreed.

Dylan started listing off a few places to go, naming a number of Chinese restaurants in the area. It seemed like his mind was made up.

Victor chuckled. He took a quick glance around the roadway as he searched for a cab, his gaze falling on Sam walking away in the opposite direction. "What do you know about that guy?" he asked, leaning his head toward Dylan.

Dylan looked over at the boy in question. "Not much, I guess. I've never really talked to him before today. Seems to stick to himself mostly. I've seen him on the rooftops during lunch periods before.

He just sits there staring off into space. Then there's the stuff people say about him outside school."

"Yeah, I've heard some of it too. But come on; he didn't look all that much like a 'beast' to me," Victor said.

He'd never heard much about Sam, only a few nasty rumors about how violent he was. But he wasn't too sure if he agreed. He thought back to the classroom, picturing the slight hint of pain on his face Sam had shown; that didn't look like the expression of some violent beast. He didn't seem like all that bad a guy, just troubled.

"Hey!" he called out without an ounce of hesitation.

Sam stopped and turned his head. Confused, he called back, "Me?"

"You see anyone else around?" Victor laughed. "You hungry?"

Sam's stomach grumbled at the mere question. Living in the group home he'd been at for the last four years, meals were never guaranteed. The guy who ran the place, "the Warden" as most called him, was a ruthless bastard in more ways than one. And Sam hadn't eaten anything in three days at that point. He nodded his head in answer to Victor's question, before seeing him motioning for Sam to come over and join the two.

Dylan shot Victor a confused look, who just shrugged his shoulders in response. "I don't know. He didn't seem that bad."

Sam caught up to them, nodding his head once more as he approached. "Hey," he awkwardly greeted.

He was hesitant for sure, no one had ever looked past his rough exterior and asked him to hang out. Everyone was too caught up in the rumors circulating about him. Was the rich kid being genuine? He felt he was. But he decided to keep his distance just in case.

"What do you like to eat?" Victor asked him.

Sam's first thought was anything at all, as his stomach was already twisting in knots at the thought. But he figured Victor for someone who'd want a more specific answer. "Tacos sound great," he decided.

Victor nodded his head in agreement, grabbing his stomach as he thought of a nice plate of steaming steak tacos, audibly voicing his excitement through hums of hunger. He glanced at Dylan with a questioning face.

Dylan shrugged, deciding it was no use arguing with Victor once he'd made up his mind. "Tacos it is," he agreed with a laugh.

As a taxi finally pulled up to the school's curb, the three of them hopped in, using the time it'd take to reach their destination to get to know one another.

For a brief time, the trio seemed to be good friends, at least on the surface. For whatever reason they each had, each one kept each other at arm's length, never really telling one another much about themselves or where they came from.

After a while, each one, unfortunately, became increasingly wrapped up in their own life affairs. Victor's outings and work trips at Reliance became more and more frequent the closer he came to graduation, making him opt for homeschooling for the remainder of his time in school.

Dylan, being a senior at the time they were juniors, graduated a year before them, at the top of his class no less. He quickly headed off to college while continuing his relationship with Ashley, the two of them lucky enough to get into the same university together.

To the best of their ability, Dylan and Victor had managed to keep in contact as they raced headlong toward the goals for the future. But then there was Sam. Shortly before his eighteenth birthday, he'd finally run away from his group home for good, having had a multitude of attempts fail in the past.

He'd experienced something even he'd call traumatic during the last few months of his junior year, after which, he had all but disappeared from the world. Knowing he'd be subjected to more torture than he'd already been if he stayed, Sam dropped out of school, taking to starting his new life on the cold streets of New York.

● ● ●

Sam had never heard much about Dylan after he left. Yet he'd periodically heard more and more about Victor as he rose up and took on the role of CEO after graduation. It all seemed like such a distant memory to him as he threw the heavy bags of trash into Victor's dumpster.

He hadn't thought of any of that in years.

He and Dylan made their way back up to Victor's lab, the both of them still engulfed by the awkwardness and unknown of everything they'd been through.

Sam looked at Dylan, who's mind seemed a million miles away. He couldn't blame him. Neither Sam nor Vic had gone through anything like he had after coming back. That wasn't quite true. Sam had lost someone too. That dog had become his best friend and was often the only being who seemed to care what he had to say. The pain he felt was just as real in his mind as Dylan's was, but he didn't dare compare their two losses.

Sam may have been attacked upon their homecoming, but he'd come out of it practically unharmed. Victor had merely walked back into his home almost like nothing had even happened. But Dylan? Dylan had come out with a scar that would never truly heal.

As they reentered Victor's lab, they saw him placing a number of objects onto a table he'd brought in from another room.

"What're all those?" Sam asked as they reentered the room.

He sighed. "This is all that survived the ordeal."

"Ordeal?" Sam asked with a chuckle.

Victor flashed him a wave of his middle finger with a sarcastic repetition of the word ordeal, giving Sam an even bigger laugh.

"Anything good?" asked Dylan in an attempt to distract himself.

"Eh … not really. Some of it'll save me some money though," Victor proclaimed, trying to look on the bright side. His stomach growled, causing his focus to drift elsewhere. "Who's hungry?"

He began making his way toward the kitchen with a sudden pep in his step at the thought of food. Sam and Dylan followed close behind as Victor went right for the fridge, pulling out a fresh box of raspberries. He leaned against the counter, picking out one at a time.

"So what can you do?" he asked, looking toward Dylan as he took a seat at the table.

He thought back to the previous night, his memories of it somewhat hazy, "I ... I'm not really sure."

Having seen his apartment, Sam interjected, "Whatever it was, it seemed like it packed a punch."

When he took a moment to think about it, Dylan could still feel that cloud of rage within him, aching to scratch its way to the surface. Raising his hand up in front of his face, he could feel it just beneath the prison of his skin. As he imagined reaching out into the heart of the pulsing red cloud, allowing it to flow throughout him, bright red smoke started billowing out of his hand.

"Smoke?" Victor questioned.

Dylan stared at the blood-red smoke leaking from himself, feeling as if there was more to it than that. His apartment hadn't come to be like it was just from simple smoke. Just as his eyes fixated upon the empty glass sat on the counter, a strange gut feeling swept over Dylan. Following the urge he felt, he extended his arm out toward it.

He felt the cloud make its way from his chest and into his arm, flowing out through the pores on his hand and slowly but surely moving across the room. The smoke wrapped itself around the glass, which started to shake back and forth. This continued for a moment until the glass slowly rose up off the counter.

Dylan watched the cup float up, moving slowly back toward him. Though he felt a slight strain between his eyes, the act was relatively easy, considering it was his first purposeful use.

As he pulled the glass closer, an image of Ashley popped into his mind, causing a wave of pain to sweep through his head almost in reaction. The smoke surrounding the glass quickly expanded and then shrunk, crushing the glass within it.

The smoke dissipated into the air immediately afterward.

Dylan let out an exasperated breath, feeling the pain between his eyes starting to recede. Catching his breath, he looked down on his hand. He could feel there was more the smoke was capable of; his breath quickened as a sharp pit of fear formed in his gut at the thought.

Victor stared at the shards of glass on the ground. "OK, maybe outside of the lab."

• • •

Victor wheeled a cart full of random objects into his lab, the squeaks of its wheels grating against everyone's ears. Sam and Dylan sat on the chairs they'd hauled in from the adjacent room, having been told to wait in the lab till Victor was ready.

Though he'd already done numerous tests on his own ability, Victor realized he'd yet to do any for the others, and there was no time like the present. He'd have to improvise the materials to do so, having destroyed the bulk of what he already had on hand. In the coming months, he planned to come up with more elaborate tests for the two and order what he needed.

Victor turned toward the two, clapping his hands before he started telling them his idea. "So, there's no getting around the fact that we've been changed. For better or for worse? We still don't know. As for the how and why, well, we don't know that either."

Sam and Dylan exchanged a look and chuckled.

"We'll get to all that in time," Victor continued. "All we can do is work with what we know for now. In my mind, that means getting an idea of what we're all capable of."

Victor waved his hand toward himself. "Sam, come here."

Sam hopped up and made his way over. "What'd ya have in mind?" He, too, was curious about what he could do; he'd already done some pretty awesome things as it was.

Victor felt the aura of heat around Sam as he approached. "Put this in your mouth," he asked, holding a glass thermometer in his hand.

"Um … what?" Sam just looked at him, unsure of whether or not he was serious.

"The first thing I've gotta do is test for a baseline. If you're able to produce flames, well it stands to reason we have to see how hot your base temperature is," Victor explained.

Given the heat he could feel coming off of Sam, he already guessed it'd be high.

Sam took the thermometer, placing it cozily beneath his tongue. The mercury quickly bubbled and shot through the tube in an instant, shattering the tip with a loud pop. Removing the broken remnants from his mouth, Sam looked at Victor. "Sorry."

Victor just stared, deep in thought. He looked over at the table he'd filled with the items that had survived his tantrum earlier. Walking over to it without a word, he shuffled through the various equipment and scraps of machinery.

He then pulled out a small metallic box with a number of cables connecting it to some sort of LED-screened panel.

"What's that?" Sam asked.

Walking back over, Victor held up the object he'd grabbed. "It's the temperature gauge for the mining laser prototype I designed; simply put, it's a defense mechanism that shuts the machine down if it overheats. I figure, in this situation, we can use it to give a more accurate reading on your ability."

He placed the screen on the cart. "OK. At first, I just want you to hold this. The thermometer wasn't that good a start, I guess," he stated before handing the box part of the contraption to Sam.

Taking the piece in hand, Sam waited a moment for Victor to tell him what the panel said the reading was.

"Incredible," Victor muttered. "Just your internal temperature is over five hundred degrees."

Sam was shocked. "What? Then how am I able to touch anything?" he questioned.

"It's hard to tell. My best guess—your skin has to be acting as a layer of heat insulation. In order for your body to house that immense heat and to not show outward signs other than a warm presence, your skin would have to be incredibly tough. *Incredibly tough,*" Victor reiterated, his face gleaming with excitement at their discovery. "This time, I want you to use your flame. Start slow, if you can, and work your way up."

Sam looked away from Victor and back at the box in his hand. Placing his other hand on it, he focused, bringing forth the warmth in his spine with a simple thought. Thick waves of heat began to cloak his hand, rising into the air above as he actively thought about starting as small as he could. Slowly, he raised the heat more and more, watching as bright orange flames gently enveloped his hands, engulfing the box in its warm embrace just as quickly.

Victor stared at the reading on the attached panel. His jaw dropped as the temperature easily passed a thousand degrees and was still continuing to climb.

Sam hadn't really tested how hot he was able to get yet. He only vaguely remembered the sensation of when he'd fought the behemoth in the alley—and the implosion he'd created.

Now was his chance to try it again, in a controlled, albeit slightly unprepared manner. But what did safety even really mean anymore?

The hotter he tried to go, the bigger his flames grew. He focused on trying to condense the flames down, but the smaller he packed the flames down, the more power Sam could feel stored within them. His concentration was disrupted by a loud crack, followed by sparks and smoke flowing out of the gauge box he held.

As they each pulled their hands away from their eyes, Victor carefully looked to see what the last reading was before it had short-circuited.

Leaning over the table, Victor let out a good belly laugh.

Sam was still shocked, he hadn't expected to break it so easily. He felt like he had barely scratched the surface of what he could do. "What does it say?"

"The last reading it gave was over 2,500 degrees. That's incredible," Victor began. "But that doesn't even make sense. With a temperature that high, the flames ..."

"The flames, what?" Sam questioned.

Victor paused as he thought for a moment. "It's nothing. Nothing will probably ever work within the laws of physics anymore." He put the now actually broken machinery back on the cart, picking up one of the six twenty-five-pound metal plates he'd brought in.

Seeing the metal plate, Dylan spoke up. "My turn I guess?"

"Yep," Victor answered. "We know the least about what your ability is capable of. All we know is your smoke seems to solidify momentarily to actually touch or move objects. So for your baseline, we need to see just how much you're capable of moving."

He placed the metal plate on the floor a few feet in front of Dylan. "Whenever you're ready."

Dylan wasn't nearly as excited about all of this as the other two; their enthusiasm about this unnatural occurrence angered a not-so-small part of him. As if the thing that had done this to them hadn't taken the person most important to him.

However, he did agree it was an unsafe idea to reintegrate into the public before knowing more. Feeling as such, he stood up out of his chair, pointing his hand out toward the plate. He stood there for a few moments, concentration apparent on his face. He then let out a ragged breath. "It's not working. I can't bring it out."

Sam walked toward him. "I don't know if our abilities work the same or similar or what. But … I've figured out that the sensation is everything. If you don't know what it feels like, how can you call on it?" He raised his hand up, cloaking it in flame. "When I use my flame, I can still feel the same initial sensation I did when it first … manifested. Now, when I think about that feeling, the flames are never far behind."

Dylan looked back down at the plate. Thinking back onto the previous night, he thought about the sensation he felt when he'd first used his ability. He remembered feeling an explosion in his chest, followed by the feeling of smoke within himself.

It was less like smoke, and more like a storming cloud of bright red rage. With that realization, prolific red smoke burst out of both his hands. He looked at Sam, who had a smile on his face.

"I guess you were right," Dylan admitted.

Looking at the metal plate once more, he extended his smoking hand out toward it. The smoke shot forth, simply smothering the plate at first. Gritting his teeth and feeling the strain between his eyes, he concentrated, almost imagining the smoke lifting the weight.

Slowly, the smoke wrapped itself around the plate, causing it to wobble back and forth. The weight was a much harder task than the glass. Finally, the smoke made its way underneath the metal plate. Yet, instead of simply elevating the object, the smoke rocketed it upward, lodging it into the ceiling.

Sam and Victor released simultaneous exclamations of excitement.

With a small line of blood trickling out of his nose, Dylan looked up at his achievement. That feeling of anger in his chest seemed to have subsided for the moment.

For as angry as the subject made him, moving something with your mind was, oddly, a good stress reliever.

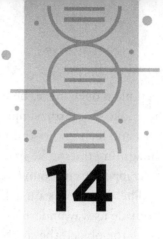

14

GUT FEELING

Victor recorded his newly taken notes on the others' abilities alongside the ones he'd already taken on his own. Being limited to the materials at hand, he unfortunately wasn't able to be as thorough as he would have normally liked.

He would have to come up with more extensive plans for further testing of the three of them in the morning. He couldn't order anything till he knew what he'd need, meaning there wasn't much more he could do at the moment.

"So," he said. "Who wants a drink?"

• • •

Victor opened the heavy wooden door to his personal bar, walking in and finding Hartley lounging on a recliner sat by the window, a book in his hand and a half-empty drink on the table next to him. He met Victor's gaze, causing a wave of embarrassment to wash over him at the thought of what Hartley was going to say to him. Had he heard the commotion he'd caused earlier?

Hartley just gave him a smile. "Hey, kiddo. You OK?"

He felt a sense of relief. He could always count on Hartley to set him at ease. "I'm better now, Harty."

Victor walked around and went behind the bar as Sam and Dylan took a seat on the stools facing the bar top, the both of them gazing around the enormous room. They wondered just how big this building actually was and what other kinds of amenities it may hold.

Victor grabbed a bottle off the rack behind the bar, setting down a twenty-year-old bottle of vintage whiskey with three glasses along with it.

It had been a long day, and a de-stressor was desperately needed. Each of them had their own multitude of questions they wanted answered, but with no way of doing so at present, there was nothing better to do than simply unwind.

Sam looked into the unlit fireplace behind them, raising his open hand out toward it. Sending out a confined blast of fire, he lit the charred logs. The sky outside had begun to grow dark, so the fire illuminated the dimming room with a flash, its gentle glow now fluttering about the space.

Hartley loudly cleared his throat and then proceeded to give Sam a dirty look. Sam saw his expression. "Uuuh ... right. Not outside the lab."

Victor laughed and poured the three glasses, passing them out. "Want one?" he asked, glancing over towards Hartley.

He smiled, grabbing his glass and finishing it off before walking over toward the trio and taking a seat next to Sam.

Sam grabbed the drink and leaned back in his stool. "I'm a bit more of an herb guy, if ya catch my drift. But I appreciate it."

The three of them each chuckled.

"So," Sam continued, his tone growing a bit more serious. "What do three guys who survived a sudden bombing and somehow came out being able to do things like that do with themselves? Do we just go back to work?" he asked, taking a large gulp of his drink as he finished.

Finishing his own sip, Dylan laughed. "What else would you have us do? Abilities or not, your rent's still gonna be there waiting in the morning."

"You're telling me," Sam said under his breath as he thought back to the eviction notice lying on his counter.

"Huh?" Dylan asked, thinking he'd heard Sam say something.

"Nothing," he said with a shake of his head, not really feeling like getting into his living situation at the moment. "You are right, though."

"Then we figure out where we stand in the world right now," Victor interjected. "We can't just act like nothing has happened. At the very least, we need to figure out what's happened to us, not to make it sound simple. I don't know about you guys, but there's no way I could let this question go unanswered. Not to mention that nobody even knows who caused it all. If we dug deep enough, I'm sure we'd be able to find something."

"If not us, then who?" he finally asked.

"The authorities. The government. Hell, the fuckin' Girl Scouts—just *anybody* more qualified than us," Dylan insisted, taking another sip. "We're not comic book characters, you two. Do you even understand what the government would actually do to people like us?"

Everyone sat in silence for a moment at the thought of that. It didn't take a genius to know that, if they were caught, the government wouldn't rest till they made an army of super soldiers—all created from their lifeless, dissected carcasses.

Victor finished his drink, pouring another immediately after. "Enough of all that. I've surprisingly had enough thinking for one day. I haven't seen Dylan for months. And you, Sam, it's been fucking years." He motioned with the bottle to ask if they wanted another too. "What have you guys been doing?"

•   •   •

Hartley watched as the three old friends took some much-needed time to catch up, filling in some of each other's blanks about one another as they downed drink after over-poured drink.

Both Sam and Dylan knew a lot more about what Victor had been doing the past few years than he knew about them or they knew about each other. It seemed like every little thing he did ended up in some form of media.

For the past year or so, he told them, he'd been working on a military contract of sorts. He said he couldn't go into specifics at the time, despite how much he might have wanted to.

Hartley joked about how he couldn't even tell him yet.

The more they all spoke, the more comfortable they all began to feel, and the more it began to feel like they were back in high school. Laughter echoed through the long hallways as they reminisced on all the times they'd stayed at their favorite pizza joint till closing, having to be kicked out by the owner all the time.

"Ralph! That was his name!" Dylan slurred.

It brought a smile to Hartley's face seeing Victor laugh. He hadn't seen him truly carefree like that in years.

Dylan talked about college, telling them about what it was like being the youngest guy around and still flying past his classmates. The pride he felt knowing the hard work he'd put in was beginning to pay off was clear.

He began to talk about Ashley, pausing momentarily as he felt his words catch in his throat, making the air feel heavy in the room.

Both feeling the drinks they had in their system, Sam and Victor placed a hand on Dylan's shoulder. Silently, each gave their friend a slight grip, as if trying to say it was all right.

He nodded his head and sniffled slightly, continuing to speak about how they'd gotten a place together as soon as she was out of high school. Right out of college, he'd gotten accepted at Moriano, and she had gone for her dream of acting even as she finished her last year.

Dylan thought about the fact that this was the first time he'd actually spoken about Ashley since finding out she was gone. What had been difficult to think about simply started to pour out around Sam and Victor.

Victor saw that the bottle was empty and turned around without a moment's hesitation to grab another. Sam and Dylan laughed as they watched him stumble over to the bottle rack. Upon his return to the bar top, they each downed another drink. Dylan and Victor then told Sam it was his turn next.

Sam talked about the number of jobs he'd had since last they'd met, joking how, if you named it, he'd done it. He mentioned how he'd almost applied at Reliance once or twice. But he didn't have any of the necessary experience, let alone the most important prerequisite—a high school diploma.

He talked about how he'd tried the dating thing a few times, but no one ever seemed to stay around that long. "I know … I don't really have a lot to offer someone," he somberly told them. He realized he was getting a little too talkative the more drunk he got.

He glanced over to his left, seeing Hartley passed out on the bar. "We lost one," he mentioned, hoping to change the subject.

"Oh shit," Victor muttered, rubbing his eyes to try and unblur his vision. He grabbed Hartley's coat off the recliner and draped it over him. "No wonder," he laughed, pointing to the pile of bottles sitting up next to Hartley. "We went through … four bottles." He couldn't stop his hiccoughs.

Dylan, wobbly, stood up, slowly walking over to the couch facing the bar. He groaned and fell onto the soft cushions before staring up at the ceiling, thinking about the bomb through the spinning that plagued his vision. He thought about how easily it had decimated that large of a portion of the city before his eyes widened as he made a startling realization.

He shot back up, ignoring the spinning he felt. "Oh my God! Moriano was in the blast zone. That means …that means it's gone. Jesus Christ, what am I gonna do?" His head fell into his hands.

"Come … work with me," Victor announced through his hiccoughs.

Dylan looked up at him. "What?"

"Yeah, why not? I know"—he quickly put a finger up, motioning for him to wait a second as he reeled the feeling of needing to vomit back in—"we could use someone with your education. Reliance is in a hole right now, as much as I hate to admit it. I need all the help I can get right now." He looked over at Sam. "I'd love to have you come work with me as well."

Both Dylan and Sam were stunned.

"What would I even do there?" Sam questioned.

"We can figure that part out later. Do you really wanna go back to being a courier?" He turned to Dylan, catching himself as he stumbled somewhat. "What else would you do?"

Giving each other a quick look, Sam and Dylan both knew it was pointless to argue with Victor once he'd made up his mind. Not to mention, neither of them were in any state of mind to argue, the both of them feeling nauseous as well.

"OK," they both agreed with a laugh.

Victor clapped. "All right, then it's settled. You'll both start tomorrow."

Just as he finished speaking, Victor started to feel the spinning again. His stomach churned as he felt a rising sensation in his throat. "Uuum ... on second thought, maybe the next day," he let out, just before bending over and hurling all over the floor.

• • •

Just outside the doorway, a silver-haired man listened to Sam and Dylan's laughter echo through the dark, empty space, his face tightening into an anger-filled scowl as he turned to look in the direction of the hallway. In a quick flash of light, he disappeared, leaving only a trail of yellow electricity bolting around the house.

• • •

Hearing some sort of crackle faintly hit his ear, Sam jerked his around toward the room's entrance as a strange warmth filled the base of his neck.

He noticed that Dylan hadn't heard, as he was preoccupied with their drunken friend. As he watched Dylan help Victor climb up from the floor and onto the sofa, Sam decided to check it out himself, almost feeling some sort of pull on the hairs of his neck.

• • •

Upon reaching Victor's lab, the electricity stopped and flashed once more. The silver-haired man emerged in its place, slowly making his way around the dim room, the only light coming from the large computer monitor nearby. He looked around the trashed space, noticing the scratches along the floors and walls.

Approaching the computer, he clicked the keyboard. The monitor turned on, showing that a password was required in order to access its files. He placed his finger onto the USB port on the desktop, firing a single jolt of electricity into it.

The screen blinked a few times, until it finally cleared up, giving him access to Victor's files on each of their abilities.

• • •

As he made his way through the maze of corridors that was Victor's home, Sam kept feeling something guide him through it all. The burn in his neck continued to grow hotter the farther he walked, and he could feel his instincts roaring at him that something was happening.

Something dangerous was roaming these halls; that much he knew for certain.

He turned a corner, seeing the entrance to Victor's lab a distance away. The cold blue light of the computer within shined into the darkened hallway.

The silver-haired man read over the files he'd accessed, paying particular attention to the files on Victor.

Hearing a creak just outside the room, he knew his surveillance period was over. He quickly looked over as much of the files as he could before whoever was coming entered the room.

• • •

Sam walked through the doorway, staring at the back of the stranger before him, his instincts screaming at him that this wasn't an ordinary person. Steam began to rise off of his shoulders, preparing him for what may come next.

"Who are you?" he gruffly asked.

As he turned his head slightly to look back at Sam, the man's cold, gray eyes pierced through him as a strange static seemed to fill the room. The man grunted slightly at the inconvenience of being caught early before turning his head back to the computer.

"*Hey!*" Sam called as flames trickled off him. "I asked you a question." He began to take a step forward.

In a quick flash of light, the man was gone.

Sam looked around, darting his head back and forth as he faintly heard that same crackling noise again. It seemed to be moving around him.

In an instant, with another bright flash, Sam felt something connect with his chest. Some kind of concussive attack launched him back, causing his hair to stand on end as he was sent barreling through the walls of Victor's home.

● ● ●

Back in the bar, Dylan and Victor jumped at the loud crashing they heard, the both of them having passed out somewhat from their inebriated state.

Both of them stumbled up to investigate once they saw that Sam was gone.

● ● ●

Sam's chest was aching, even more than that, it felt like his skin was buzzing. Yet again, he'd felt like he'd gotten hit by a train. As he attempted to stand himself up, he felt a heavy, solid object pinning him down. He moved his hands around and realized it wasn't just the piece on top of him. He'd been buried underneath several pieces of rubble.

"Shit," he whispered to himself in an irritated huff. "Hartley's gonna have my head."

He placed his arms underneath himself, pushing upward in one swift motion with all his might. The rubble burst off of him, crashing down all around him in a loud crash of dust. Sitting for a moment, he tried to catch his breath, interrupted by the sound of a footstep behind him.

Sam's attacker stood up atop the rubble, looking down onto him again with those piercing gray eyes. "Don't get up, I'm not supposed to kill you," he calmly said.

His face growing more serious, the man's gray eyes changed to a glowing golden color. As he took another step towards him, Sam felt that familiar weight pushing him down, just like he'd felt coming off of the creature in the alley. "The big guy has taken an interest, and I'm not too good with the whole holding back thing."

"*Sam!*" They both heard Dylan and Victor yell from down the hall.

They both came screeching to a stop, coming face-to-face with the intruder, feeling his glowing yellow eyes chill them to the bone.

"What do you want?" Victor questioned. His armor instinctively leaked out onto himself, sheer black overtaking his torso beneath his shirt as his heart raced with fear, the blue glow on his chest intensifying along with it.

Seeing the situation, Dylan couldn't see any alternative. He released his smoke, feeling it billow out of his hands.

With the addition of Victor and Dylan's presence, Sam began to feel something within himself, a flowing wave of energy crashing over him as he felt his excitement about having backup in a fight for once. He could feel a surge of energy pulsing beneath the surface of his skin, unsure of whether or not it was adrenaline or something else.

With a growing roar, fire cloaked his arms. He pushed harder than he ever had so far, the flames roaring off of him as the sleeves of his shirt were reduced to cinders. The air around them seemed to grow thinner the hotter it became.

The silver-haired man turned just in time to see Sam lunge at him with explosive speed, crumbling the rubble beneath where he had stood with expansive bursts of flame. He swung his flaming fist down at the strange intruder.

As his explosive attack sent all nearby debris hurtling backward with a large blast, Sam was shocked to find no one there beneath his fist.

They each looked around, frantically searching for the mysterious man.

"You can call me Overcharge," they heard from behind Sam.

They each turned to see the man standing before them, unbothered, his hands in his pockets like it was a leisurely stroll through the park. "It's nothing personal. I don't have much say in the matter. If you'd stayed down with that first attack, we wouldn't have had to do this," he told them, a strange hint of sadness in his voice.

"What are you talking about?" Dylan questioned, his heart racing at the feel of this man's presence.

"It doesn't matter, not at the moment anyway. All you need to do is defend. Like your lives depends on it," he slowly answered.

The trio felt his presence grow heavier and heavier, his eyes glowing brightly as crackles of electricity surged off of him. The bolts singed everything they touched, arcs burning long swirls into the walls and ceilings.

Sweat poured down their foreheads as they listened to his next words. "Because they do."

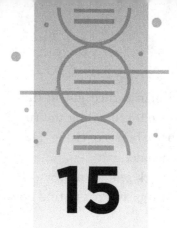

15

PERFORMING UNDER PRESSURE

With whips of golden lightning lashing off of him, each of them flailing about and singeing the space around them, Overcharge started walking towards his targets. His every step electrically burned the floor beneath him.

Sam's head raced through multiple plans of action—literally anything to get them out of harm's way. Every fight he'd ever been in, he was a normal human being. He'd never planned for a clash between superpowers. He wasn't even sure what he was really capable of yet.

He looked down at the rubble at his feet, picking up a good-sized chunk.

"What the hell are you doing?!" yelled Dylan, taking a few steps back as the electric whips grew closer, the static they held now raising the hairs on the backs of their necks.

"Improvising," Sam said with a smile, lighting the thick chunk of wood ablaze. Turning his head toward his target, he wound up and threw the flaming rubble as hard as he could.

Overcharge sidestepped, watching the fireball crash into the distant wall behind him. "That wasn't bad," he admitted.

Hearing a loud boom behind him, he turned back just fast enough to see Sam land a blazing fist into the center of his chest, sending him hurtling down the long hallway.

Sam's arm was numb just from touching this attacker who called himself Overcharge for a moment, but he just gritted his teeth and ignored it as best he could. There was no way they could hold this guy off without making contact at least a few times.

Overcharge skidded to a stop and stood himself back up. Brushing himself off, he gave a dry chuckle. "That wasn't bad, either. You have speed. I'll give you that. Now then." He disappeared from sight.

Sam felt a hand gently place itself onto his back, and before he could even turn his head, a huge blast of electricity erupted onto him. He couldn't even react as the force of the explosion launched him forward. He felt himself skid across the ground before crashing through thick wooden walls one after the other.

Finally, he burst out the side of Victor's building, feeling the less-than-gentle caress of gravity take hold of him. The fact that they had been on the third floor was something Sam hadn't remembered till he took in the sight of pavement coming his way.

He was falling headfirst at a terrifying speed; instinctively, he did the only thing he could think of and reached out. He attempted to grab onto the building to his right, feeling his fingers dragging along the bricks as he grew closer to the ground.

In a last-ditch effort, he screamed, releasing his flames with an intent to melt himself a grip in the wall. He could hear the bricks crumble as his descent began to slow.

Upon reaching the safety of the ground, he looked at his flame-clad hand. The flames had condensed down around his fingertips just tight enough that they had loosely formed into claws. They dissipated quickly before he could even start to think about what it felt like.

He looked up at the building next to him, seeing the red-hot streaks running down the wall where his fingers had just been.

• • •

Overcharge turned back to face Dylan and Victor, both frozen in fear where they stood. He gave a brief look of disappointment before turning back, zipping out of the building in the path Sam had exited.

Dylan clenched his jaw before yelling out in frustration, "*Damn it!*"

He had no idea what to do. He knew how to bring his ability out, but manipulating the smoke was another story.

Nonetheless, he couldn't leave Sam to fight alone. He dashed forward, blinded by his anger as he followed the attacker toward the gaping hole to the outside—leaving Victor behind, still frozen.

Despite his strong armor, Victor couldn't bring himself to act. The sheer force of the attacker's power had left him stunned and speechless. What could he do against that?

Overcharge came to a halt at the edge of the building, materializing himself as he looked down at the seemingly surprised Sam. He half expected the kid to be facedown on the pavement right now. But there he was, next to some strange, glowing streaks in the neighboring wall.

"You're actually pretty tough," Sam heard Overcharge calling out from above him.

He turned to see him atop the roof of Victor's building, staring down like a hunter stalking his prey. The night sky enveloped him in shadows, only illuminated by the bright yellow glow coming from his eyes. The eerie glow made Sam shudder. He quickly slapped his cheeks in an attempt to calm down.

The lightning-cloaked assailant zipped down into the alleyway, meeting Sam's gaze as he landed. He pointed his electricity-clad hand toward him, swirling his energy in the palm of his hand. A growing humming sound filled the air as Sam felt the familiar static sensation growing. The hairs on the back of his neck stood on end, his every instinct telling him the large concentration of electricity amassing before him was bad news.

He thought about the best course of action, about how he would get himself out of the way of what was to come. There were numerous paths laid out all around him; any one of them would have been an easy escape.

That's when he heard it—the murmuring of people approaching from around the alley corner a distance behind him. The loud crash of him flying out the side of Victor's building must have attracted a crowd.

The group of people turned around the corner, their hearts freezing in place at the sight of the energy charging before them. Sam watched as the mass of power began to project off of Overcharge's flexed hand. Time seemed to slow around Sam as he watched the bolt race toward him, knowing that there was a crowd of innocent civilians just behind himself.

Moving meant letting the bolt fire into them.

He threw up his hands and released as much of his flame as he could into the space before him with a deep yell; the bright orange blaze filled the alleyway between the two. He hoped to stop the attack or at least slow it before it managed to reach him.

The bolt plunged into the inferno placed before it, snaking its way through in an instant like a hot knife through butter. To Sam's dismay, his flame hadn't slowed the bolt's velocity a single bit. It burst through the wall of flame, surging into Sam's chest. A surging wave of shock spread throughout him, sending spasms coursing through his body while the bolt continued to propel him back. He flew past the growing crowd of people, now crying out in terror at the sight before them.

Dylan reached the hole in the side of the building just in time to see Sam launched back by the bolt of lightning. He felt his heart drop as Sam flew through the glass storefront across the street. "*Son of a bitch!*" he roared, feeling his smoke billowing out his arms and back, the ground beneath him now flooding with the blood-red cloud.

Overcharge turned back to face him upon noticing. "Well, look who decided to come out."

Dylan seethed with rage, his mind already filled with angry, drunken thoughts about Ashley's death and the circumstances surrounding it. Now some asshole decided to show up and attack him and his friends.

The cloud at his feet rose up around him, fueled by the anger pumping within. He looked down at the current source of his rage, throwing his hand toward him with a powerful roar. The smoke around him proceeded to form into dozens of pointed spikes, all rocketing toward Overcharge with vicious intent.

One after the other, he dodged the spikes by zipping side to side, each of Dylan's attacks puncturing the walls and ground around him.

Watching each of his attacks miss, Dylan grew more and more frustrated. He felt like, if he could land even just a single hit on the guy, it could level the playing field. Yet he hadn't been in a fight in years, let alone a fight with eerie red smoke at the center of it all.

"Hey," he heard a familiar voice call from behind him.

He was shocked to see that Overcharge had disappeared from the alleyway. He turned around to face the source of the voice.

He met Overcharge's intense gaze, seeing the yellow electricity crackling off his body in several violent, varying motions.

"First rule in a fight, stay out of your head and focus on what's in front of you," Overcharge gruffly told him, and with a wave of his hand, a blanket of electricity crumbled away Dylan's foothold.

Sent plummeting to the ground, he turned around to see the ground coming in fast. Dylan screamed out in terror at the fear of death. He couldn't think of any way to stop or even slow his fall; this was it.

Slowly, he closed his eyes and accepted what was to come. "Here I come, babe," he softly called.

He didn't know what to expect—a thud, a crunch, nothing at all? After a few moments and still nothing, he felt out around himself, his eyes still tightly shut in fear of what he may feel. He found he was surrounded by something soft, something his hand just seemed to glide through.

Opening his eyes, he looked to see that his smoke had created a large cushion around him, stopping his fall—an action that made his blood boil.

His chance to see her again had been ripped away from him by a mysterious power that had been forced upon him by someone he'd never even seen. He seethed with blood-red rage as his core filled with the desire to go berserk.

It was a feeling he'd only felt once before in his life.

• • •

Victor listened to a crash echo through the empty space around him as he stared through the holes in the walls of his home. He could see moonlight shining in at the end, a figure standing beneath its brilliant glow.

Suddenly, he heard a loud roar from outside. He recognized it as Dylan, hearing nothing but anger resonating in his cry.

Where was Sam? What was happening? Who was this person? Dozens of questions raced through his head, without a single answer for any one of them. Which was seeming to become a recurring phenomenon.

The fear Victor had felt up till that moment hadn't simply disappeared; he was a human being, and fear was an evolutionary constant in this world. But seeing and hearing some of the last people you have in this world fight by themselves was something no decent person could just walk away from.

So, as afraid as he was, he broke into a slow run, building speed the farther he ran. He felt strength in himself he hadn't ever felt before, feeling the ground crack beneath his feet with every stride.

Overcharge heard the subtle rumble growing louder behind him and turned to see a bright blue light charging toward him from the darkness. Not thinking much of it, he extended out his hand, discharging another bolt of electricity at the coming force.

Seeing the bright light coming towards him, Victor decided to trust in the armor. He threw his arms up to block his face as he ran.

The bolt collided into his arms, ricocheting into several smaller bolts that burned the structure around him. Shocked, Overcharge continued to fire at Victor as he closed in, hoping to slow him to a stop.

Victor quickly closed the distance between the two, his eyes laser focused on the obstacle in front of him. He threw his arms outward as he reached the source of the attack; causing the bolt of electricity to dissipate into nothing with a bright flash.

In that one moment of distraction, Victor used the last of his momentum to wrap his arms around their attacker's torso, tackling him out the gaping hole in the wall. Seeing the ground below, Victor closed his eyes and hoped for the best.

Struggling to wiggle his way out of Victor's tight grip, Overcharge cloaked himself in electricity. Yet, as hard as he tried, he couldn't activate his ability to move instantaneously.

"Of course your armor would be conductive," he shouted with a laugh.

Still kneeling on the ground in the alleyway, Dylan looked up at the bright source of light falling from the sky. He covered his eyes as the ball of lightning slammed into the ground in front of him, an explosion of light filling the alley.

● ● ●

With his chest burning and his head reeling, Sam stirred awake to the sound of approaching police sirens, their high-pitched wails grating against his ears. He found himself surrounded by numerous racks of clothes and a bunch of shattered glass, confused and aching.

A jolt ran through his body with no warning, causing his muscles to lightly spasm. Then came another, though slightly milder this time. He stood himself up and noticed the shattered storefront window before him as another jolt pounded through his body, dropping him back to his knees for a moment.

He quickly remembered the attack he'd been hit with. The front of his shirt had been all but destroyed. Held together only by the tops of his sleeves and the section along his back, the frayed shirt revealed beneath it a burn mark in the center of his chest, adding to the multitudes of scars already scattered around his torso.

Ripping the remnants of his shirt off of himself, he brushed the glass off his legs before leaning back to crack his neck. "Fuck that hurt," he muttered. As another light jolt hit him, he realized the effects were nearly gone. That bolt had done a number on him, though.

Running to the broken window, he leapt through.

As he reentered the dimly lit street, he could see police lights illuminating the apartment buildings around them down the road. A large cluster of squad cars was positioned just outside the street. He figured the officers were planning how to best approach the situation, given the utter unknown of it all.

He couldn't even imagine what the civilians had told them when they'd called the station.

He looked back down the alleyway, seeing a thick cloud of dust beginning to settle within. He quickly ran over, screeching to a stop. "*Guys?*" he yelled, his heart starting to race once more.

"*Sam!*" he heard from somewhere beyond the cloud of dust. "*Sam, is that you?!*" the voice called again.

He was sure it was Dylan calling out, "*Dylan? What's going—*"

Cut off by a loud grunt, Sam saw a shadow coming at him from within the dust. He braced for the worst, beginning to ignite his hands.

He quickly put them out as he realized the figure coming at him was Victor. His limp and unconscious body flew right into Sam's arms, causing him to stumble a few steps as he tried to keep his body off the ground.

He was much heavier than he looked.

The cloud of dust erupted upward in an enormous blast of electricity, quickly enveloping the whole alleyway in bright yellow light.

At the center of the blast was Overcharge, cloaked in a large electrical sphere. His scowl was even nastier than usual, and Sam wondered if it had to do with all the tears and stains in the expensive-looking suit he wore.

Overcharge looked over at Sam, surprised to see him back up so soon. Distant noise outside the alley began to turn into voices, the group in the alley quickly realizing by the sounds of their radios that police were closing in on them. Overcharge let out a grunt of frustration, knowing that King would have his head if he was caught on public news before Unveiling Day.

He extended one arm toward Sam, who still struggled to support Victor's limp body, and the other toward Dylan, whose face grew pale at the sight of the lightning around Overcharge's arms growing. Shaping itself, it formed into two large hand constructs. Before they could even react, the constructs launched at the two of them, wrapping their large electrical appendages around the trio's chests.

Once he had them in his grasp, he lowered himself to the ground, his every muscle fiber tightened as much as they could. He pushed up with every bit of strength in his legs, rocketing into the air with the trio in tow and trailing off into the distance in a flash of electricity just as the police turned around the corner.

As they trailed upward at lightning speed, Sam struggled to break the construct's grip. As hard as he tried, he couldn't focus hard enough to ignite his flame; shocks consistently ran through his body, interrupting his concentration.

He turned his head, seeing the city from above for the first time in his life—taking in all the city's lights and landmarks from a view few ever got to experience. Despite the present situation, he couldn't help but think to himself, *Beautiful.*

He was quickly broken from his distraction by the feel of gravity's touch grabbing hold of them. They had finally begun to fall back to the earth. Sam watched Overcharge's eyes dart around as he surveyed the area, seeing his eyes lock onto a distant spot a number of blocks away.

Normally, Overcharge's ability of instant movement was only able to work on himself, given that his physique was already electrical in nature. The ability consisted of converting his material body down to its basic electrical structure, choosing an end point, and closing the distance between him and that point in an instant.

Normally, that is.

Since his electrical constructs had Sam, Dylan, and Victor in their grasp, he'd created a steady electrical current within them— theoretically giving their bodies the means of instantly moving with him.

As their descent grew faster, he focused on the unique electrical current within his body. Mixing it into the current already flowing through his captives, he finished the preparations for his next move.

Feeling the electricity coursing through him, Dylan winced in pain. He could feel a strange sensation washing over him as the space around them started to glow. He could see Sam still struggling against the giant hand wrapped around them, and it looked like Victor was unconscious.

Knowing they couldn't break free, Dylan braced for what was to come yet again, that same hope that it would just end still lingering in his chest.

Quicker than they could blink, Sam and Dylan found themselves thrown against concrete flooring. The impact knocked the wind right out of them, sending both of them rolling across the roof, stopping just short of the edge.

Sam noticed Victor rolling toward them just in time to see him head straight over the edge. "*Shit!*" he screamed as he dove toward his unconscious friend. He reached out to grab onto him, the loose stones and gravel on the ground digging into his exposed chest.

He grabbed onto Victor's ankle just as he was going over, his dead weight pulling Sam over the edge too.

"*Fuck!*" Dylan screamed, crawling over to the side to look over the building's edge.

To his relief, he saw Sam dangling there, one hand gripping the edge, the other firmly gripped onto Victor's ankle. The veins in his forehead bulged from the strain of supporting both their weights.

"I've got you," Dylan told him.

He gripped Sam's forearm with both his hands, planting his feet on the steel beam to his right as he began to pull upward with all his might.

With a heavy groan from the weight of the both of them, Dylan hauled Sam's torso up over the edge, helping to pull his legs up afterward.

"I've got it from here," Sam assured him. "Where is he at?"

Dylan trusted Sam enough to know he could pull Victor up the rest of the way on his own. Like he said, they had other things to worry about.

Panicked, Dylan looked around the rooftop, not seeing their attacker anywhere. He did recognize the building they'd been thrown into though. It was the Thomas Street construction zone that had been abandoned long before the bomb had gone off. Now it just sat here, an eyesore for those around it.

Sam yanked Victor back onto the rooftop, rolling him onto his back and letting out an exasperated breath of relief as he lay down on his own back for a moment of rest.

He turned his head to look at the eerie armor Victor was clad in for a moment. It was definitely an odd sight. Then again, a man creating fire in the palms of his hands was probably just as odd. Sitting himself back up and moving toward Victor, he raised his hand up into the air. "Sorry," he let out, before smacking Victor across the face.

Right after the slap connected, Victor sprung awake. "Ow! What the hell, man?" he exclaimed, holding his cheek, ironically one of the only parts of his body that wasn't armored. His eyes quickly widened as he remembered the situation they were in.

He jumped to his feet yelling, "Where is he?"

"I don't know." Dylan sighed, still gazing around the halfway constructed building.

Sam turned and took a look for himself, feeling that same sensation he had just before finding Overcharge in the first place. "He's close," he muttered.

"How do you know? Can you see him?" Victor asked.

"You guys don't feel that?" he asked them, his eyes still glued forward, scanning the space in front of them.

"Feel what?!" Dylan questioned. He wasn't a fan of people being cryptic, preferring people to say exactly what they meant, instead of expecting him to guess.

"I can't put it into words … but I know he's close. I felt the same thing just before I first found him." If Sam focused on the warmth in the back of his neck, he could almost feel a pull of some sort.

It was the same thing before; he'd followed the pull, and it had guided him to the intruder. Maybe if he focused, he could do it again.

Closing his eyes, he let that warmth in his neck wash over him. The faint darkness that usually dwelled beneath his closed eyes began to darken as he strained to focus on the feeling.

Then he saw it, deep within the blackness. He could just barely make out a faint yellow light. As his eyes continued to adjust, the yellow flame grew until it blazed like a roaring bonfire on a dark, windy night, its light emanating out around it like a beacon.

● ● ●

Standing atop an I beam up above, Overcharge watched the trio look for him. He was ragged and out of breath. He'd never moved another person alongside himself, let alone three others.

It'll be another minute or two before I'll be up for a fight again, he thought to himself.

Looking back down, he noticed Sam standing still, his eyes closed tight. His hands were cloaked in his orange flame, and upon looking closer, he saw him shrinking the flame down into an orb of sorts.

What is he—

He was quickly cut off by the sight of Sam cranking the ball of fire straight toward him.

It blazed forward at high speed, the flames crackling filling the air. Overcharge threw his head back as the heat of the sphere raced past his face; he felt his balance tip as his head continued to fling back in response.

He groaned, whizzing down to the same level as the trio in a split second of light.

"Told ya," Sam said with a smile.

Upon seeing the enemy back in their sights, Dylan and Victor readied themselves. Both were momentarily forced to hold back their shock about Sam's intuitive guess.

Overcharge couldn't take his eyes off of Sam. *Can he really sense already?* he wondered.

His mind raced. Every ability user had the power to tell when they were close to another user. Some could even use it as a compass of sorts. But only higher-level power users had the ability to sense—to physically see the location of other advanced beings as long as you were close enough by feeling out for the innate energy that emanates from all of them to some degree.

Even then, no one had ever been able to do so only a few days after awakening.

He couldn't help but chuckle. To further develop in the heat of battle wasn't something done easily, and this kid seemed to have heaps and bounds left to grow if he could already sense this soon.

A feeling welled up in his gut, a feeling that told him, if these three were left to their own devices, they would just grow stronger each and every coming day.

A thought occurred to him. *If no one interfered in their growth … could they someday compete with even King himself?* Having only had their abilities for a few days, they each were much more developed than any other power user he'd seen this soon after awakening.

He pushed those thoughts to the back of his mind, knowing he was tasked with seeing how they did under pressure. Despite having pushed against them as he had, he hadn't truly put pressure on them yet.

When he'd been assigned this task, he'd taken it begrudgingly. It wasn't like he had an option when the big, dark bastard gave him an order, but now he found himself with a growing interest in the young men before him.

Feeling a surge in his chest, he knew his powers were back. Seeing his opponents standing ready, he could see the uneasiness in both Dylan and Victor's eyes.

Yet in Sam's, he could see something else. A fierce intensity burned into his being, one that shouldn't have been coming from the eyes of someone that young. Despite how much he'd attacked them, Sam still had a look in his eyes signifying he intended to come out on top during this confrontation. The others must have felt they didn't have much choice but to stand ready too, seeing their friend with his head still in the game and ready to move.

Human beings were a species that could grow exponentially when their backs were up against the wall, and seeing someone that you always had to protect, now standing up for himself and depending on you to have his back? Dylan and Victor didn't dare let him down.

Overcharge prepared himself, layering his body with incredible amounts of electrical energy. Despite their opposing sides, he couldn't help but respect the trio's tenacity in the face of the astronomically unknown. This was their first true interaction with the new world, and they carried themselves as if they were native to it.

Overcharge grinned. He could feel excitement curling his lips into a slight smile. He hadn't enjoyed a fight in years.

Everything up till that point had been child's play. Now the real fight began.

• • •

The only sound in the air was the wind howling through the incomplete structure they stood upon. Only the faint light of the nearby city life illuminated their surroundings.

Sam looked to his right, seeing a stack of wooden pallets and leftover wood chunks near the edge of the building. Waving his hand toward it, he set the stack aflame, giving them all more light to work with.

Now that the stage had been set, each of them stood there, waiting for the other side to make a move first.

As Overcharge's foot inched forward slightly, the others might as well have taken it as the starting gun of a track event. All three dashed forward at the powerful man in front of them.

He followed their lead, breaking into a sprint himself.

As they drew closer, Sam leapt in the air, cocking his flaming fist back in preparation to attack. He swung his powerful arm, hitting only remnants of electricity.

Overcharge had disappeared, and he was moving much faster than he had before. Now Sam couldn't even register his moving from his starting spot. Feeling the hairs on the back of his neck start to stand on end, he felt an almost static-like feeling growing behind him. Turning his head slightly, he saw Overcharge quickly charging up an attack aimed at his back.

A wall of red slammed into him, launching him backward as it dissipated his would-be attack. Dylan let out a deep breath from the strain. Somehow now, the load on his brain seemed to have diminished somewhat, making it easier to call on larger concentrations of the smoke.

Making complex shapes like he had before still felt a little out of his reach, however. Creating a clear image in his head amid the fight wasn't easily achieved.

Overcharge skittered across the ground, barely registering the black and blue fists slamming against his back. The balled fists collided with the back of his ribcage, crashing him into the ground with a shockwave that stirred up all the dust in the area. Flipping himself back up to his feet, he shot backward, placing all three of them in his sights.

Thick crackles of electric power arced off of Overcharge's chest. He threw his arms back, and the lightning was drawn from his torso and into the palms of his hands. The energy he continued to amass lit up the dim space in a pulsing, bright yellow glow.

With a roar that rumbled the metal structure around them all, he swung his arms forth into a booming clap. The energy in his palms rocketed out, enveloping the space in front of him and forming a wave of pure destructive electric energy that raced toward the trio. Composed of pure power, the wave crumbled the very flooring of the unfinished construction zone they stood on, sending tremors down to the rickety foundations it all lay on.

With nowhere to run besides off the side of the building, Sam and Dylan faced almost certain death. They watched a black figure frantically race in front of them, realizing it was Victor as he stopped and planted his lead foot down, solidifying his stance.

Having placed himself in front of the blast, Vic threw his arms up to protect his face. He mentally braced himself for the coming attack, yelling out in anticipation. Shock ran through his system as a new sensation swept over his right arm.

Sam and Dylan watched in awe as a seam along Victor's spine appeared, the majority of his jet black armor making its way along his body and onto his arm. Quickly creating a large blob around his forearm, the liquid armor smoothed itself out, forming a large shield construct—just in time to shield all three of them from the great electrical wave heading their way. It slammed into Victor's shield, splitting a line through the wave.

What was left of the electrical energy flooded out of the building, filling the night sky around them. Thousands of people looked to their windows as they watched the rubble explode out of the halfway-constructed skyscraper in a bright yellow flash.

Victor slowly opened his eyes to find the shield he had created, a large oval shape that extruded off of his arm, that same pulsing blue glow flowing throughout its form. He also noticed all his armor was gone except from his right shoulder down.

Despite his fear at the moment, he couldn't help but remark how cool that all felt. Moving his shield out from in front of him he saw the destruction that lay before them. The very ground the electric wave had traveled along had been blown away, all except the narrow pathway Victor had shielded.

Sam climbed to his feet, immediately regretting the decision. The narrow path they stood on began to crack beneath their combined weight. A large shift rang out, and they felt their footing drop out from below them and then felt themselves being sent hurtling downward and slamming into the ground of the floor below.

Overcharge walked to the edge of what was left of the flooring he stood on, staring down at Victor, who had landed on his shield construct. He grinned and then quickly disappeared in a flash of electricity.

In unison, the trio groaned in pain, shoving debris off of themselves as they climbed to their feet once more. Dylan looked over at Victor, who was staring intently at his shield.

"That's new," he remarked.

"Yeah, it was helpful at the moment, but now I have a problem," Victor announced while beginning to fiddle with and shake his arm. "I can't get it to go back onto the rest of me."

A yellow bolt raced past the three of them, quickly illuminating the space around them and then disappearing just as quickly as it had come.

They each turned around slowly, wary of being caught off guard.

The light shot between the three of them, redirecting upward and disappearing once more. Sam closed his eyes, searching for the feeling of their lightning-fast opponent. He jolted his eyes back open and threw his head back to look upward, just in time to see a light racing downward, heading straight for an unprotected Victor.

Sam dove forward as fast as he could push his body, shoving Victor from his spot. The bolt raced downward. Overcharge's torso emerging from within.

With a large crash, the two hurtled through the concrete flooring below them. They slammed down onto the lower floor, landing atop the concrete rubble with a large rumble that echoed into the empty street.

Quickly gaining their wits back, the two rolled over, leaping backward in separate directions.

As soon as he found stable footing, Sam sent his flame down into his feet, exploding him forth with amazing speed as he attempted to catch his opponent off guard. He flew toward Overcharge, who had just found stable footing atop the rubble.

Predictable, he thought. Seeing Sam perform the same windup as before, he threw up his electricity-cloaked hand in preparation.

Sam chuckled, opening his opposite fist toward his opponent as he closed in. A quick burst of flame erupted out of it, sending his body spinning up and out of the way of Overcharge's attack. As he spun, he cloaked his arm in the hottest flame he could muster, sending a flaming backfist into the back of his head.

Overcharge found himself blown forward by the force of Sam's fist, struggling to gain control of his new throbbing headache as he rolled across the floor.

Sam launched himself forward once more, this time simply increasing his running speed, staying low to the ground. If before was any indicator, Overcharge would expect Sam's usual leap / right cross. He'd have to change things up again if he was gonna have a chance of landing another hit.

As he closed in, time seemed to slow around him once more. Whether this was part of his abilities or simply adrenaline racing through his body, it didn't matter. He could use the time to improvise. He knew his opponent was worlds faster than him. He could momentarily catch him off guard maybe, but outright, the attacker was definitely faster.

He didn't know for sure, but he couldn't shake this feeling that something was off about this guy. He had to have been holding back. The sheer firepower he'd used so far was enough to kill all three of them ten times over. So, why hadn't he?

He must need us alive, Sam thought to himself.

Finally, and the truest fact of all was that only one of them wasn't a match. All three would have to attack at once to stand a chance.

The other two were still on the floor above, so for the moment, he'd have to make do alone.

Overcharge stood not ten feet from the edge of the building, watching Sam sprint toward him, keeping his body low to the ground to increase his momentum. As simple as the action sounded, it was a great tactic that few truly knew how to utilize in the heat of battle.

With incredible speed, Sam closed the distance between the two, and once he'd gotten within a few feet of him, he pivoted off his right leg, using his incredible speed to zip back around his opponent.

Feeling a great heat stop behind him, Overcharge threw his head to the side just as a fist soared through where it had just been.

Turning around as quickly as he could, he stared Sam down, who continued to advance toward him, throwing well-timed attack after attack.

If not for the electricity coursing through his body that kept him in top form nearly 100 percent of the time, Overcharge realized he probably wouldn't be able to dodge everything Sam was throwing at him. The kid was getting faster, and his coordination was only continuing to grow.

Who the fuck is this? Overcharge aggressively questioned in his head.

In the time that Overcharge had had his abilities, he'd seen dozens of people undergo awakening, a few of them even hand-chosen by King for their raw potential. None seemed to have this much innate talent for the art of fighting.

Just who had this kid been before the blast?

Watching Sam's fist race toward him, he undercut its trajectory by using his off hand's wrist to redirect it upward, simultaneously rocketing his dominant up toward his exposed gut.

Or so he thought he would.

Using his explosive speed, Sam shot his left leg upward, planting the bottom of his foot onto Overcharge's flexed fist and using its growing momentum to propel him up into the air.

Instantly racing after him with a smile hidden beneath his silver beard, Overcharge bolted up into the air, outstretching the fingers on his hand as energy flooded into the tips of them. He swung his flexed hand as if mimicking the motions of a sword swing, the energy in his fingertips launching forth in sickle shape.

Raising his palms into the air, Sam released big enough explosions to propel himself downward and out of the way. As he hurtled toward the ground, he prepared his legs for impact.

Feeling the first sign of connection to the ground, Sam used his downward momentum to seamlessly land in a squat, not even letting a moment pass before rocketing flames out of the base of his feet to propel him back upward as fast as he could.

Launching as fast as he had, even Sam struggled to see around himself. He braced his arms in front of his face as he ignited his entire top half into a flaming bullet of sorts.

Overcharge had barely had enough time to twist his body around in the air, turning with just enough time to see Sam barrel into him. The both of them crashed into the ceiling with tremendous force before falling back down to the concrete flooring. They both crashed down in a gust of dust, instantly fighting to see who regained his bearings first.

Sam flipped his torso around, planting his hands and feet down before blasting back off on all fours like an animal toward Overcharge once more. Soaring forward, he replanted his hands onto the ground, using his existing speed to roll the lower half of his body into the air before firing off two blasts from his hands to shoot him upward.

When gravity took hold of him once more, he fired off two more blasts to increase its effect, positioning his heel to come straight down onto Overcharge's head. His increasing speed left trails of flames in his wake.

Lifting his head, Overcharge blurrily saw Sam coming at him, and the fact his head was still pulsing wasn't helping him think of anything to do about it. In a last-ditch effort, he released a wave of electricity from his body as a whole, solidifying its shape around himself almost like a shield.

As Sam's foot came crashing into the electrical field, its ambient energy coursed through his body, causing every muscle in his body to spasm in response as he was shot backward in a quick flash.

His back roughly scraped across the ground as he rolled to a stop, finding himself unable to immediately get up due to the residual shocks running through his body.

Overcharge took a deep breath in, fighting to regain his composure. Sam had pushed him harder than he'd been pushed in years, and the newcomer may even have a chance of winning against him if he didn't slow down and take this seriously.

Looking forward, he watched as Sam began to pick himself off the ground, slowly hobbling to his feet. If he gave him any more time to recuperate, Overcharge knew Sam would be right back on top of him. Feeling the energy coursing through him and into the electrical field, he focused, beginning to redirect its flow.

He pointed his index finger forward, and all the energy around him began to steadily converge into its tip. With a simple flick of his finger, the energy it held bolted forward with extreme velocity.

Pulling his gaze upwards and seeing the bolt just a few inches from his face, Sam threw his head back. He dodged just fast enough to avoid serious injury but not fast enough to avoid the attack entirely. The bolt grazed across his right eye, causing him to clutch his hand over it in pain. Blood violently filled his eyes, darkening his vision in a matter of seconds.

Seeing his opportunity, Overcharge raced forward in a bolt of lightning. Reappearing just before Sam, his momentum carried him the rest of the way. In his hand, he held a long bolt—bright and yellow and charged with as much energy as he could fill it with.

As he prepared to thrust the bolt at Sam, he thought to himself, *Come on, kid, move!*

Just then, a large resounding crash came from above. This was followed by Dylan and Victor bursting through the ceiling above, heading straight down toward Overcharge as they screamed out in defense of their friend. Dylan threw his hand toward the glowing enemy, his red smoke racing forth.

A large red wall slammed into Overcharge, crushing him between it and the floor. He struggled against the smoke, surprised by how solid it actually felt.

As they got their bearings on the space around them, Dylan focused on trying to keep Overcharge restrained, visibly straining to hold his sheer strength.

Victor ran over to Sam, his usual armor placement back to as normal as it could be under the circumstances. "Sam, are you good?!" he called, quickly glancing back at the trapped lightning bolt as he dropped to his knees next to Sam.

Wiping what blood he could off of his face, Sam strained to see through his right eye. The blood continued to pool into it, running down onto his face and dripping onto his heavily scraped chest. "I can't see," Sam weakly responded, struggling to wipe the blood off himself.

"What? What do you mean?" Victor questioned.

Taking a look at the cut along his eye, he saw the electricity had arc-burned Sam's skin, leaving a lighting like pattern around the wound.

"My eye," Sam started. "I can't see out of my eye."

"What?" Victor asked once more.

He reached out and pulled Sam's eyelid up to get a look at his cornea. As Sam's bloodied eye opened up, Victor's chest tightened as he looked at his ruptured pupil, which filled the entirety of where his iris had been.

"The electricity must have torn through the small lining between the individual pieces of the eye," Victor muttered to himself.

"Is it bad?" Sam asked, still struggling to see through the damaged eye.

"Yeah … but we can't do anything about it here. We'll need to cauterize that eye to stop the bleeding once we get back to the house," Victor told him.

Sam groaned. He knew Victor was right, but he couldn't wait much longer to stop this bleeding; his head was beginning to feel light and if he passed out now, he'd be nothing but a liability. He raised his index finger, heating it up until it caught fire.

"What are you doing?!" Victor shouted.

Taking a deep breath in, Sam pressed the ignited finger against his eye. With his newfound resistance to heat, he knew it didn't hurt nearly as much as it should have, but as the flames seared into his wound and burnt his blood vessels shut, he knew it was still a pain he'd never forget.

● ● ●

Overcharge had just about had it with being pinned to the ground. He placed his hands on the concrete beneath him, pushing up with all his strength.

Dylan could feel the strain of maintaining the wall increasing, feeling his brain begin to throb in response. "*Guys!* I can't hold him much longer!" he shouted.

Overcharge finally managed to get his arms leveraged underneath him. With a quick roar, he blew a hole in the floor, dropping down and disappearing into the darkness below.

Dylan dissipated his wall, looking around with a sense of panic gnawing at the inside of his chest.

Down at the ground floor of the building, police cars hastily corralled around the entrance. Dozens of officers stepped out to see the rubble that had crashed down around the building before they and the few detectives who had shown up each followed their sergeant as he led them into the unfinished building—guns drawn.

Sam, Dylan, and Victor each darted their eyes around as they heard a quick zipping sound move around them. A bright bolt slammed into Victor's chest, knocking him to the ground. Despite his armor, he felt the wind be knocked out of him.

Again the bolt disappeared.

Sam felt a pull behind him line up with the zipping noise, and he ducked just as the bolt raced past where he'd previously stood.

Dylan watched his friend duck, wondering in his mind how on earth he knew where the bolt was coming from. "You guys don't feel that?" he remembered Sam asking.

Turning his head back forward, he felt a force slam into his back, knocking him to the ground as shocks ran through his body.

Suddenly, the zipping sound stopped, leaving nothing but the creaking of the building they were in. It sounded like any more big moves might bring the whole thing toppling down.

Dylan felt a pulling at the back of his neck, the hairs on the back of his neck standing on end as he turned around, looking up at Overcharge on the remnants of the floor above. He noticed that Sam had turned to look up at the same time. *Is this what he meant by felt?* he wondered.

Overcharge looked down at the trio from the open section above. Sam and Dylan were seemingly ready for action, while Victor was just now getting himself back up. Looking over the side of the building, Overcharge noticed the familiar red, white, and blue lights below. Knowing officers would crowd this area in the next few minutes, he decided to end this interaction with his next attack.

Raising his hand to the sky, he released a large concentration of electricity through his hand. The clear night sky above slowly faded away as thick, black clouds crowded together. Thunder abruptly filled the air, drowning out all other noise around.

The trio watched Overcharge say something, but Dylan and Victor were unable to hear it over the thunder. Sam, on the other hand, managed to get a look at his lips as he spoke, and he knew exactly what it was their attacker had said.

"This was fun."

With an exaggerated downward swing of his arm, an enormously thick bolt of lightning emerged from the dark clouds above, rocketing down toward the trio.

Sam, Dylan, and Victor looked up in horror at the godlike attack heading their way. Sam yelled out to Victor with terror in his voice, "*Shield!*"

Both Victor and Dylan dove toward Sam as fast as they could, Victor quickly throwing his arm up into the air before he'd even reached them. He didn't have time to think about the sensation of the shield. He just screamed, unsure whether it was at the lightning or at himself in the horror of possibly not being able to produce the construct.

His arm quickly expanded just as the giant bolt made contact. He thanked everything he could be thankful for that he was able to bring it out, but the battle wasn't over yet. The lightning bolt continued to rain down upon his construct; every muscle in his body ached from the strain of holding this ridiculous amount of energy back. He yelled out in pain as he heard small cracks in the shield above.

The lightning violently rattled everything around them, causing the many floors beneath them to begin to crumble away as the bolt's incredible power continued to hammer into it. If they hadn't been standing near one of the numerous support beams, the floor they stood upon would have caved and sent them plummeting down the steepening drop below.

• • •

Down at the base of the building, tremors shook the foundations of the incomplete structure, knocking the troop of NYPD officers off of their feet as they attempted to ascend the stairs despite their declining integrity.

As cracks ran down the walls around them, knocking the ceiling above them loose, their sergeant looked up in time to see a piece of debris falling in his direction. But in his ripe old age, he wasn't in any shape to roll out of the way.

Detective David Reynolds watched as his superior was crushed beneath the falling rubble, grimacing as he turned to face the other way. He knew he'd puke if he got a good look.

With Sergeant Wallace gone, he knew the responsibility of leading the rest of the officers fell to him. He radioed into dispatch. "10-999. I repeat. This is Detective Reynolds, and we have an officer down at the disturbance on Thomas Street." He looked up the rest of the steps. They still had a number of floors to go before they reached the floor where the commotion was originating. "Come on, troops. Still got a ways to go," he called out, making his way up the steps once more while doing his best not to look at the blood spilling out from beneath the piece of fallen debris.

• • •

"*I'm not gonna last much longer!*" Victor screamed, his knees beginning to buckle from the stress. He could see visible cracks forming in his shield.

Dylan panicked. He didn't know how much he could help but there was no time to think. He threw his hands up, sending his smoke out with as much force as he could. He shaped it into the thickest wall he could muster, forming it along the back of the failing shield.

Both Dylan and Victor screamed. Though the load had lessened for one, it was still a tremendous task.

Suddenly there was nothing, just the receding sounds of thunder. The trio breathed heavily, wary of taking down their defense. Slowly, Victor moved his shield to the side. Seeing the dark clouds dissipating above, he noticed Overcharge was gone from his spot on the next floor up.

"He's gone," he whispered to the other two.

Sam created another fireball, peeking his head out from behind their makeshift defenses. He didn't see him either, but he knew that didn't necessarily mean he was gone. He felt out around himself, and to his surprise, he couldn't feel their attacker's presence anywhere around them either.

Taking down their shields, the trio looked around. It seemed that Overcharge had disappeared while they had been distracted by his attack. They each fell to their knees, gasping for breath from the strain of that battle.

Sam suddenly heard an approaching sound coming from the stairwell. He bolted up and creeped over toward the stairwell. Opening the slightly ajar door, he peered over the railing.

It couldn't be compared to the panic he felt before, but he felt his heart race as he saw the approaching squad of policemen making their way up the stairs. They were only two floors below them.

"*Cops!*" he yelled as he turned. Running back to the others, he motioned for them to get off their asses and move.

They all ran over to the side of the unstable building, looking down to the ground below. It had to be at least a sixty-foot drop.

Sam chuckled. "See you guys at the bottom."

• • •

Reynolds looked upward. He could have sworn he'd just heard a voice up top. Every instinct in his body continued to tell him to turn the other direction. Whatever was going on here was above his pay grade.

Yet there he was, continuing to make his way upward.

He burst through the doors, gun drawn and ready. Darting his eyes around, he looked around the empty site, and everything he saw filled him with dread. Looking out into the city around him, he saw the rubble that had fallen to the ground and crashed into surrounding buildings, not to mention all the strange burn marks littering the ground.

What could have caused this mayhem?

• • •

A slight distance away, Mimic stood atop an empty rooftop, having snuck up there to watch the nearby lightshow. He'd been overcome with curiosity about the boss's objects of interest and wasn't keen on letting Overcharge have all the fun.

"They shook Sparky off faster than I thought," he remarked while checking his watch.

He let out a chuckle, feeling a sense of adrenaline-rushing excitement well up within him. Turning back, he began to make his way back to base. He knew that's where Overcharge would be heading, and he was eager to hear his take on them.

He leaped forward, disappearing into the night sky.

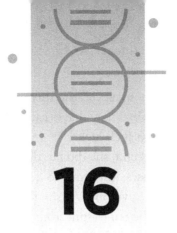

16

WHAT WOULD YOU THINK NOW?

s the morning sun crested the tops of New York's glistening skyline, every news channel in the city had camera vans lined up along the streets for blocks. Each one of their inhabitants fought to force their way to the front of the growing mass of people crowding the alleyway behind billionaire Victor Reliance's SoHo home. Dozens of channels had already gotten the first pick of witnesses to take statements from.

The surrounding streets buzzed with the sound of numerous overlapping stories of the spectacle that had taken place earlier that morning.

Olivia Ray stood in the alleyway where it was said to have all happened, taking the peculiar scene in. The story laid before her eyes was a strange one—scorch marks along the ground and surrounding building, a gaping hole in the side of Victor Reliance's home, and the storefront window across the street had been blown out. The sheer unknown and craziness of it all reminded her of the alleyway blaze a few days ago.

Having been told that her next stop was a far more damaged area, she could only imagine the sight, given the scene she already found herself surrounded by.

As she always did, she surveyed the surrounding streets, looking for any street cameras that may have caught last night's events. Unfortunately, she had no such luck.

When that was a dead end, she did her due diligence in gathering information from witnesses, listening to each and every statement from anyone who would give one. As she filled in the events of the previous night, her head began to spin from sheer disbelief. Listening to the people speak of the things they had seen—fire filling the alleyway, electricity coming from within a man—filled her with a debilitating sense of dread.

She heard a commotion abruptly start up outside the alley. Looking out to see what it was, she saw Victor Reliance making his way toward the officers stationed in the area. She recognized the first person following behind him as his acquaintance from the day of his reappearance.

She glared at Sam for a moment, watching him puff down the last few drags of his cigarette before answering the police's questions. The image of her shattered windshield in her head was still burning a hole in her bank account. She really needed to get his information at some point.

Her heart suddenly skipped a beat, catching a glimpse of Dylan trailing behind the two of them. He still had those "deep eyes" she couldn't help being intrigued by. She shook her head, knowing she was letting herself get distracted. It had been a long time since she'd felt those feelings for someone else.

We're taking a break from all that, she quickly reminded herself.

She took in the numerous scrapes and bruises on the three men, not to mention the thick gauze taped over Sam's right eye. All three of them seemed pretty banged up.

Once she had everything she thought she needed, she made her way over to Ryan.

"You ready?" he asked her, still fiddling with his camera's settings.

She gave him a nod. "Let's roll."

As she listened to Ryan's countdown, Olivia took a deep breath in and out in preparation. Hearing Ryan's voice stop, she opened her eyes to the initial red light atop the camera, meaning that Eric at the station had just handed her the broadcast.

"Thank you, Eric. Good morning New York. I'm Olivia Ray with Channel 12 news. I am currently on the scene of the disturbance outside newly reemerged tech mogul Victor Reliance's SoHo home early this morning." She did her best to present herself with an air of confidence. Yet deep down, the thought of these strange occurrences in her hometown left a growing pit in her gut.

Slowly making her way from the street into the alleyway, she continued. "Sources say that around two thirty early this morning, loud crashes could be heard coming from within Reliance's home. Numerous neighboring tenants in the buildings nearby all placed calls into their local police station reporting noise complaints. At that moment, neighbors believed Reliance to be performing another of his experiments within his laboratory—a relatively normal occurrence for him before the tragic explosion a few months ago."

She pointed up to the gaping hole in the side of Victor's building. "The next thing witnesses reported seeing was the side of Reliance's home bursting outward. The witnesses then reported seeing a man fall from the third floor of the building—landing unharmed in the alleyway below," she finished with a tone of concern.

"One witness in particular had some choice words to say on the matter," she announced. "Tenant of the neighboring building next door, Tyler Cordain, reported he went to investigate the disturbance once the noise had woken his two daughters. He and three other residents from their building all made their way to the alleyway where the noise originated. That's where they spoke of seeing some of the strangest things I've ever had the chance to report to you, New York."

She braced herself to report what she had been told. The sheer thought of it all made her feel like she was about to become a laughing stock. Yet the evidence of its validity was apparent all around her. She couldn't imagine what people at the other site had seen. "Cordain reported turning the corner of the alley to find two men facing off against each other. That wasn't the strange part, however. He stated one of the men in the alley was covered in what appeared to be lightning."

Walking back out to the street, she approached Tyler, who had been waiting where the police had told him to.

"We have Tyler with us right now, ready to tell the story in his own words." She pointed the mic toward Cordain, giving him an opportunity to speak. "Tyler?"

Cordain stared into the camera, slowly piecing his memories of the previous night together. "Well," he hesitantly began. "Just like you said, miss, I heard a loud crash, and then my daughters were screaming. They were yelling about a hole of some sorts on the side of the building nearby."

He scratched the side of his head, as if trying to figure out how to word what he wanted to say. "I obviously wanted to put them at ease, so I decided to go check out what was going on. I met up with a few friends from the building on the way down, all of them having the same idea as me. We all made our way out to the street, where we heard voices coming from Mr. Reliance's alleyway."

His face grew pale at the thought. "That's when we saw the two men confronting each other ..."

"And then what?" Olivia asked.

"One of the men, the one who stood facing us. He had ... lightning coming off of him, and his hands were pointed at the man whose back was turned to us. I don't know how else to put it, besides saying that the man held that lightning in his hands, like he was about to attack."

"That's a truly bizarre claim," she refuted.

"I know how it sounds, miss, but I know what I saw." He could still feel the fear pounding out of his chest.

"What happened after you saw the two initially?" she questioned. She could still feel her own reluctance to believe what she was hearing. Yet somewhere in her mind, she was formulating a theory on the matter. Victor and the two men with him immediately came to mind. It was too bizarre a coincidence this had happened in and near Reliance's home.

"We couldn't move … seeing something like that. I don't know who could. Then he looked at us." He could still see the image of the man's eyes meeting his own.

"The one about to attack?" She could see the apprehension all but written on his face, like he was second-guessing his decision to speak out.

"No." His look of apprehension quickly changed, instead turning into a look of determination. "The one whose back was to us. The lightning was aimed right at him, and I could see him start to move out of the way. But then he turned his head back towards us. I couldn't make out any other features with the bright light behind him, but when our eyes met, all I could see was fear."

He turned his head to look down the alley, remembering each individual moment from the previous night. "He turned back to face the bright light behind him, and with a wave of his arms, the whole alley filled with bright orange flames."

"That must have been a terrifying ordeal. You're lucky having survived the two men's attack," Olivia announced to both Cordain and the camera, turning to face the latter in order to move to the next stage of the broadcast.

Before she could get anything else out, Cordain butted himself back in. "It wasn't luck," he said a bit heatedly. "The fire guy saved us. The others can argue on what did or didn't happen, but I know what I saw. Before he knew we were behind him, he was going to move; he was gonna save himself. But then he saw us, putting him in a position of choosing us or himself. And he chose us. He stayed there. He risked his own life to throw up a wall of fire … for us!" he argued. "Then the lightning came through the flame, and even then, he didn't move. He let it hit him so we wouldn't get hurt."

Olivia couldn't help but show her shock as he made his claims.

"If that beam had hit us, we would've died. I don't understand what I saw or how those people were able to do those things. But I was able to go back to my daughters because of him. If he's watching"—he looked at the camera with tears in his eyes—"thank you."

• • •

As Olivia rode to their next stop, she thought about everything she had seen. She knew something was happening. Something dark was lurking behind closed doors, waiting for its chance to clamp its jaws down on this city's throat.

There was an obvious connection between last night's event and the bombing a few months ago—possibly even the inferno that had taken place at the End of the Line.

How could there not be?

She hadn't been given the opportunity to interview Victor Reliance or his two friends while she'd been on scene, as they'd refused to speak to anyone but the police.

That was another strange occurrence.

Her boss wouldn't be happy, but he'd have to settle for their channel being first on scene at both locations.

The area had been cordoned off by police, given the unstable state of the structure. Chunks of concrete lay at the base all around the building, and its upper sections had been reduced to a dangerously rubbled state.

Olivia and Ryan stepped out of the van, slowly making their way through the crowd formed around the police tape. They all just stared, awestruck at the thought of what had happened. Every one of them couldn't help but think that another terrorist attack had taken place.

The only witness testimonies that mattered came from the squad of police who had stormed the building last night. Every other recollection of the previous night only told of the bright lights and rubble blowing from the top of the structure.

• • •

Detective David Reynolds found himself preoccupied speaking to his late sergeant's direct superiors. Wallace's death meant changes were coming his direction—changes he'd hoped to have earned any other way.

"We'll let everything settle for a few days, but we'll have the paperwork drawn up for your promotion to the department's Sergeant. And in the meantime, we just ask that you act accordingly given your new position," his captain announced, lowering his typically aggressive tone to a simple low gruff in respect to his fallen friend. "I understand the circumstances are less than ideal, but we're down a man, and you're the first on our promotional list.

"Once you finish up here, go ahead and head home for the day," the lieutenant told him, "at least just for today. We're sending everyone else who was dispatched here last night home as well."

It was hard for Reynolds to be excited about the situation. Numerous thoughts raced through his mind—the death of his superior, hesitantly accepting a position he felt he hadn't earned, and then there was last night. While he hadn't seen what had transpired on the upper floors, he had seen the aftermath. He had also heard the stories from the crime scene a few blocks away. His gut instincts were telling him this wasn't over. All the strange occurrences in the city, starting with the bombing, were all linked.

How? He wasn't sure, but he'd sure find out.

"David," he heard someone call from behind him.

Slowly turning around, he found Olivia, looking much more hesitant than she usually did at a crime scene. For as long as he'd known her, she always carried herself with a sense of poise, always looking ready to face whatever lay ahead of her. Yet he could clearly see her apprehension to approach the building behind him. He couldn't blame her. She had to have heard the report of what happened too.

"Olivia," he said. "I take it you'll be wanting an interview?"

● ● ●

Reynolds stood in front of the crime scene, fixing his uniform's collar as he waited for Olivia to go over a few last-minute things with Ryan. Once she finished, she walked to the side of him, turning back to face the camera.

Ryan started his countdown, going silent on one.

"I'm here with Detec—" she began.

"Sergeant," David hesitantly corrected.

"Oh," she exclaimed. "That's new."

She glanced back at the body bag sitting in the ambulance a distance behind them. She'd heard that there had been a casualty last night, but she'd only just realized that it had been Wallace. David must have been reeling. The man had basically been a father figure to him for years.

Quickly adjusting herself, she hopped right back into the broadcast, needing to make up the lost few seconds. "I'm here with Sergeant David Reynolds of the New York Police Department, who was present at the disturbance's secondary location, where their team tragically lost their former sergeant last night."

She turned to face Reynolds, offering him the microphone with an empathetic expression. "What can you tell us about what you experienced?"

David's eyes glanced to his side, as if trying to think of where to start. "We'd received a number of call-ins last night, all of them reporting some kind of altercation between two men in an alley. We sent a few units to the origin of the calls. But before any of our officers could reach the scene, all present parties had already disappeared. Nothing left behind but scorch marks and a shattered glass storefront across the street."

Reynolds could feel his forehead begin to bead with sweat. He famously hated interviews, but he always ended up saying yes to Olivia. Normally, interviews were meant for sergeants or above. But now given his new promotion, he knew it would most always fall to him moving forward.

"That's when the secondary calls came in?" Olivia asked.

"Yes. The first call we received from the secondary location reported seeing a group of men on the upper floors of the Thomas Street construction site. My partner and I took the call and started making our way to the address we were given."

He dryly chuckled. "I don't think it was even five minutes before more calls began to flood in. New reports of bright lights and screams coming from the same site."

He turned back, catching a glimpse of the one lone body bag in the back of the ambulance nearby. Sadness crept throughout him at the thought of having to continue on without Wallace. His sergeant had always looked out for him, taking him under his wing after he'd first started at the department. He didn't know how he was gonna fill the shoes of the great man who lay in that thick black plastic bag.

"Sergeant Wallace called out to a few of his closest units to join us, including himself. We all convened in front of the building's main entrance. There was rubble all around us, and lights were shining from up above. It was on our way up that we lost the Sergeant …"

Reynolds fought to stay composed. That was his job now. "The building shook to the point I'm told its structural integrity quickly deteriorated around us, causing rubble to fall down and crush him. The rest of the team and I continued upward, but there was nothing. All we found at the top was wreckage of some unknown event."

"So, there are no leads on the men responsible for last night's attacks?" Olivia asked for clarification, unsure of what answer she actually wanted him to give her.

"No." He sighed. "At the moment we are still going through witness testimonies and CCTV footage looking for leads on our perpetrators. If you or anybody you know has any information that may help us identify the parties responsible, please call 9-1-1 and report it as fast as you can."

Ryan raised a hand to signal that they were clear, taking a sip of his morning coffee now that he had a chance. His eyes were intensely trained on Reynolds. His glare could have melted a hole right through him if he stared any harder.

Catching his gaze, Reynolds gave him an awkward smile and wave. He couldn't really blame him for the cold shoulder, though.

He turned to Olivia, who was beginning to gather her belongings from beside the camera, softly calling out to her after gathering himself. "Olivia?"

She looked back at him with a hint of pain in her eyes. "What?"

"Can ... can we talk?" he asked her.

"About what?" she sharply shot back, turning back and continuing to place her notepad into her purse while waiting for his reply.

"About everything," he answered, a slight quiver loosely hanging onto his words.

Olivia bit her lip as she stared into the side of her brown leather purse, immediately feeling thankful she hadn't been looking his way when David had said that. Her chest still ached when she thought of him, but the anger she felt about what he had done only continued to grow by the day.

"No," she told him. She hurriedly grabbed her bag and started to walk off toward the van. "Thanks for the interview," she called back to him before hopping into the passenger seat and slamming the door.

Ryan finished putting the last camera piece into its protective casing, loading it into the back of the van and closing its door with a huff. He turned back to look at Reynolds one last time before leaving, seeing the look of defeat painted onto his face.

"Maybe you can drown your sorrows in another homewrecker," he called out to him, hoping to add insult to injury. With a quick raise of his middle finger, he walked to the driver's seat of the van, quickly starting it up and driving off without another word.

Reynolds stared at the van until it had turned around the corner a few blocks away, knowing deep down he deserved every bit of that.

● ● ●

Victor, Sam, and Dylan waded through the sea of reporters that lay between them and the entrance to Victor's home. Each and every one of them shouted over one another, wanting to interrogate them with a barrage of questions—questions they weren't as prepared for as they would have liked to be.

Finally making their way to Victor's front door, Sam forced the door shut on the screaming reporters just outside. Holding it shut for a few moments, he caught his breath.

The trio slumped through the halls, all of them yawning from their lack of sleep, which was becoming a bit of a habit over the past few days. Between last night's fight, the swarm of reporters this morning, and every other bizarre occurrence since waking up, none of them had been able to get any real rest.

Victor half leapt onto the couch in the den, relishing its soft embrace. He let out a chuckle. "Some night."

"You're telling me," Dylan replied, moving the curtain slightly to look at the crowd outside.

Sam approached the bar. Placing his hands on it to lean on, thinking about the interviews they'd all just undergone. "You think they bought our story?" he questioned.

"I don't know," Victor started, "Saying that some kind of freak fight came crashing through my home? There's bound to be a few skeptical people, but all we can do is stick to our story. Things will die down in a few days. We just gotta wait it out. Trust me. I've dealt with my fair share of scandals."

A ding then rang out from Sam's pocket. Reaching in, he pulled his phone out and faced its cracked screen toward himself, immediately noticing the bold date stamp it showed.

February twenty-third 2020.

His mind seemed to tune out at the sight of the happy birthday message from the only social media app he had. Its emboldened letters and birthday cake emoji slammed the realization he was now twenty-five into his gut like a truck.

He glanced up at his two friends spacing out before him, wondering if he should mention it. But after a second look at their exhausted expressions, he ultimately decided now wasn't the time to care about the day you were born. They had more pressing matters at hand.

Finally taking a seat, Dylan thought about the previous night. His headache from using his ability had finally begun to clear up, yet he could still feel a pounding in his forehead. It didn't make sense to him. He'd watched Overcharge do things last night that could level buildings if he pleased, yet all three of them had escaped nearly unharmed—*nearly* being the keyword.

Sam's right eye had been blinded during last night's encounter. You could see the wound poking out from underneath his bloodied bandage.

Regardless, Dylan knew they shouldn't have survived the previous night. Why had they now survived two harrowing ordeals when thousands of people still lay crushed beneath tens of tons of debris?

Dylan knew there was much more to everything that had happened to them than met the eye. His mind raced with hundreds of questions, none of which he had the answers to. He couldn't take it anymore. He had to get out of there and clear his head. "I've gotta go," he suddenly announced.

"Go?" Victor asked. "You sure you wanna go through that crowd again?" He pointed toward the screaming gang of reporters outside the window.

Sam looked at Dylan and could see the stress gripping his expression; he didn't see a point in arguing with him. He knew that, whether they liked it or not, they'd see each other again soon.

Dylan groaned at the thought of the reporters. He'd had enough questions for one day.

Seeing the look on his face, Victor conceded. "There's a back entrance. I never use it, so there shouldn't be any reporters outside."

Dylan nodded to show his appreciation, finding himself in no mood to argue.

After agreeing to reconvene in the next few days to and discuss their shared ordeal, Dylan silently made his way out of the den. Following the path Victor told him to, he finally came across his back exit. He placed his hand on the handle, momentarily pausing to prepare himself for this strange new world they lived in.

Pushing the door open, he exited into the empty alleyway, double-checking if he was alone. He brought his hand up and let his smoke flow outward. There was no possible way to get used to the sight of it. Looking at the thick blood-red smoke, he couldn't help but feel like some kind of monster.

Demonic even.

As far as he'd pushed himself away from his faith, recent events had seemed to stir up all of those thoughts. And at the moment, he didn't know where he was going to go from here. He found himself questioning what Ashley would have thought about his new developments. Thinking of the things he had done last night, he couldn't help but feel that, were she still alive, she'd be afraid of him now.

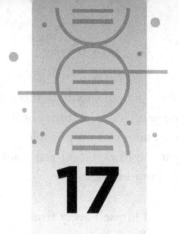

17

INSUBORDINATION

Overcharge slunk through the nearly lightless tunnel system, his only source of illumination the dim red lights strung up along the walls around him. Eventually, his familiarity with the area began to kick in; this was the usual spot. He stuck his hand out and began to slide it against the wall as he moved forward.

After a few moments, he felt an indented groove along the wall, one that was identical enough to the others along the wall that a civilian would pay it no mind. Placing his open palm on the groove, he gave it a powerful push, its force swinging open the thick stone door of King's massive, secluded complex.

He strained from the effort. Both Sam and Dylan had managed to get a few good hits on him, leaving aches throughout his torso and a continuing throb on the back of his head. Pushing the door back shut behind him, he watched as the dozens of torches along the stone walls lit up, illuminating the structure before him with their radiance. He still wasn't sure how they worked.

Down the long stretch he went, zigzagging through its maze of corridors until finally he reached two more massive doors that lead into the boss's throne room.

He stood there gritting his teeth and preparing for the worst. He knew King wouldn't be happy about how his simple scout mission had turned into the morning news biggest story. What did he expect? There isn't too much subtlety in big powerhouse abilities like his own. He'd figured out ways to make the job a lot quicker and cleaner, but that was when he was sent for a human target. No one could have expected those three to already be as powerful as they were.

"Here we go," he muttered to himself before shoving the doors ajar.

He was met with intense gazes from all of the boss's senior officers, the immense presence of every one of them attempting to weigh on him. They could try as much as they wanted. The only one whose presence had any effect on him was King.

Walking forward, they all made a line for him to head straight for the throne. Their leader stared straight at him, expressionless, which was even scarier than him being mad, in Overcharge's opinion. There was no way of knowing what he was thinking.

Suddenly, he was stopped by someone stepping in his path. He saw Mimic now standing there before him, a cocky smile on his face.

"Some job you did. Directly disobeyed the boss and his order to keep it on the downlow. You might as well have announced to the world that we're here," he told him.

"Get out of my way," Overcharge growled gruffly.

He hated Mimic. He hated the boss too, but he hated Mimic for entirely different reasons. His arrogance and the way he placed himself above everyone, stepping on whoever was necessary to get what he wanted, sickened Overcharge. You could see it in his cold black eyes laid beneath his creepy mask; Overcharge had seen that look in hundreds of people across his entire life.

"Someone's feeling tough," Mimic joked. He leaned in real close and whispered, "Why don't you make me? You know how it works around here. All you'd have to do is take me down, and my seat is all yours. You'd better hope you're up to the task, though. You know what happens when you lose a confrontation you started."

Feeling a surge of rage well up in his gut from Mimic's threat, Overcharge cocked back his fist, pumping it full of his highest-charged electricity and letting out a roar as he aimed right for the chin of Mimic's unsightly mask.

Catching Overcharge's hand in his own, Mimic grinned as crackles of electricity spread throughout his own body. He cocked his own fist back, charging electricity through it before striking Overcharge's chest and sending him forcefully rolling backward.

Overcharged skidded to his feet as he regained his footing. Looking up, he let his fear show as he saw Mimic standing there, charged with his own lightning.

"I always wondered what your ability felt like. Damn, the things I could do with this." Mimic jabbed his arm forward, sending a bolt of lightning racing toward Overcharge.

The whole crowd had begun to chant. "*Fight! Fight! Fight!*"

Disappearing from sight, a line of light quickly weaved its way behind Mimic, Overcharge erupting from within it. He swung his arm up, creating a weblike structure of electricity above them all.

With a downward swing of arm, the center of the web of lightning glowed intensely before firing a large beam of electricity down on top of Mimic. The ground trembled at its great power slamming into the ground, continuing to fire for a number of seconds.

As the rumbling settled, Overcharge breathed deeply. His body ached from the continuous use of his ability over the last number of hours. Looking at the dust floating around the room, he couldn't see Mimic anywhere, believing him to have fallen from his last attack. "You may be able to use my ability, but you don't know *how* to use it," he muttered.

A huge boom echoed throughout the room as the surrounding dust suddenly blew outward. Mimic launched forth, tackling Overcharge to the ground. He'd been heavily tattered by the beaming energy; his nice racing jacket had been reduced to nothing, bruises and scrapes lined his body from the bolt of lightning, and his mask was heavily scratched up along its wood surface.

With his hand wrapped around Overcharge's throat, Mimic seethed with rage. He slammed his head into the ground repeatedly, screaming out in a zealous rage as he did so.

Overcharge could feel his consciousness fading as everything started going black, and he was beginning to think that maybe it was actually his life that was fading. All he knew was that he didn't have the strength left to fight back anymore. His body wouldn't listen to him. This was it. After everything he had endured over the last ten years, it was all coming to an end. "I'm … sorry," he began to whisper through spurts of blood.

"*Enough!*" A hoarse voice bellowed, cutting Overcharge off before he could finish.

Thick black sludge exploded from the ground, enveloping both Overcharge and Mimic as it encased them in its cold smothering grasp. Mimic struggled against it as best he could. Overcharge, however, was still struggling to stay conscious.

Only their heads stayed exposed, as the rest of their bodies found themselves submerged in the boss's ability. He slowly strode toward them, hands clenched together behind his back.

"Sir, why are you punishing me?! He's the one who attacked!" Mimic pleaded.

"Yes, and who egged him on?" King reminded him.

Finally reaching the two pillars of black, all semblance of calm quickly disappeared from his expression, prolific anger flooding into its place.

He shot his hand up at Mimic, firmly clutching the hair atop his head with a rough jerk. His usual hoarseness turned to a low bass filled growl, and the whole room could feel the resonance of his words. "I've ordered you all not to use your abilities here or unless ordered to for that matter. Yet here you two are, my own second in command no less."

Throwing Mimic's head out of his hand, he turned to the remaining seven of his nine officers. "You all know the rules. In the world we are working to create, my word is law. None are exempt from this ruling, not even my highest-ranking soldiers," he darkly told them all.

He closed his open fist, and the black liquid containing Mimic's body slithered up and encased his head, leaving him completely submerged in the dark substance.

"What about him, sir?" one of the officers asked. With his long black hair and groomed beard accenting his casual attire suit, he looked like he belonged in a romance novel. "He knows his place here, but he still actively attacked Mimic," he finished.

"Right you are, Void," King agreed. Taking a few steps towards the other man his ability held captive, he met his gaze. He could see how hard Overcharge was struggling to stay conscious; between last night and today's debauchery, he had to be suffering from some degree of concussion.

"Now, Overcharge, I know you're well aware of our terms. I believe you're a very valuable asset, but I will not tolerate any more of this insolence." He leaned in real close and whispered something audible to him and him alone.

It was a horrific sentence promising what would happen if he acted out again. And with a closing of his hand, the substance covered his head as it had with Mimic.

Then with a single glance at the ground beneath Overcharge's prison, the thick black blob sunk down into its rocky embrace. The gazes of the remaining officers in the room trailed along the ground as they listened to the rumbling echo moving beneath their feet.

"Atom, if you'd be so kind as to repair our flooring," he asked a younger man to his left.

"Yes, sir." He excitedly obeyed. The short young man held a certain image of innocence that didn't seem to fit in with the rest of the crowd, his boyish features highlighting just how much younger he was compared to everyone else. He was dressed in what you'd expect of anyone in their early twenties—a worn-out pair of tennis shoes, jeans with holes all along the knees, and a known-brand hoodie, plus a thick, black winter coat over it all. All of it paired with his flipped-back brown hair; a thick portion of the front of it was white as snow. It was a stigma he'd had since birth.

With a casual wave of his hand, the gaping hole in the stone flooring began to slowly close itself back up, its jagged stone edges smoothing together once more until one could never even tell a crater had once been there.

"Now then," the older leader began. "In an ideal scenario, we would have waited longer to announce our presence to the current world order. But as one can guess, recent events have complicated our agenda. No matter. We'll move up our timetables to adjust to our new variable."

He paced in front of his men. "As we now know, we have three of our brothers who have developed much more quickly than the rest, and they will be an invaluable asset in pursuit of our goal. However, if they are unable to see our way, their handlers will be forced to remove them from the equation before the possibility of them becoming too powerful for the lot of you to handle becomes a reality. I'd rather not come into play just yet."

He turned toward Tremor, who had been particularly quiet during the whole interaction. Meeting his gaze, he gave him an eerie smile. "I do believe your time is coming, my friend."

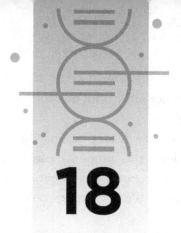

18

THE RIGHT TO
JUDGE ANOTHER

The roar of the road echoed through Victor's ears as Hartley drove him through the busy city streets. They merged onto the Brooklyn Bridge, heading toward the Brooklyn Heights area.

After Dylan and Sam had left to get some rest, Victor had done some heavy thinking. They couldn't very well do anything ability related at his home anymore, given the events of the other night. The horde of reporters still waiting outside would make it too complicated. He knew they'd eventually calm down, but in his experience, there would always be a few stragglers who decided to stick around for quite a while.

Hartley pulled up to an old run-down warehouse on the bay. It was in tatters. Evidently, no one had set foot in there for years.

"No wonder it was so cheap," Victor muttered.

Stepping out of the car, he approached the entrance. Knowing that anybody nosey enough would more than likely be keeping track of his purchases, he'd used one of his secure offshore accounts Hartley had helped him start years ago. They didn't need any reporters questioning what an eccentric billionaire and his two unknown acquaintances were doing in an abandoned warehouse on the bay.

He shoved the main doors open, letting a wave of mildew and mold smell blow out past him. "Jesus," he remarked while covering his nose.

Hartley laughed, seeming unfazed by the putrid smell. "Don't worry. I can take care of that."

They made their way inside the dark structure, looking for some kind of light source. Hartley called out to Victor after finding a switch on the wall beside the entrance. "Here we go." Numerous rows of overhead lights flicked on as he pulled the heavy switch, illuminating the large warehouse in its rusted entirety.

Victor smiled while gazing around the room. "This will work perfectly," he said aloud.

That childlike wonder almost oozing out of him was infectious, and Hartley couldn't help but smile alongside him. "Let's get to work," he told him.

● ● ●

Dylan sat in the center of his trashed apartment, a cracked photo of Ashley sitting just in front of him. He clutched his knees as he sat wondering what Ashley would've said to him to make him feel better.

The bags under his eyes had started to grow. Despite having said he needed sleep when leaving Victor's the day prior, he hadn't slept a wink since getting back.

He'd just sat in the same spot for countless hours, contemplating what to do with himself. Waves of red smoke floated throughout the space around him. He didn't understand why but using his ability seemed to calm his nerves.

Turning to look at the photo, he vented the frustrations on his mind. "What do I do, babe? Nothing seems real anymore." He wiped away a tear. "I just wish you were here."

Across the room, he heard his phone start buzzing on the countertop. He didn't feel particularly up to talking on the phone at the moment, so he just let it go to voicemail without a thought.

After a few moments, it started up again. Its buzzing echoed through the silent apartment.

Groaning in frustration, he swung his arm out toward the distant phone, the ambient smoke in the room quickly whisking it into his outstretched hand with a single thought.

"Hello?" he muttered, a low gruff hanging onto his voice from his lack of sleep.

"Dylan?" he heard a voice on the other line say. "Hey, man, it's Victor. I had something I wanted to show you guys. Think you could make it out to Brooklyn Heights? I'll send you the address."

Dylan stood there silent for a moment, thinking about whether or not he should agree to go. He sighed, knowing from past experience that Victor wouldn't stop hounding him till he agreed. "Yeah, sure. Just send me the address, and I'll make my way over," he reluctantly agreed, palming his face in irritation.

The two hung up, leaving Dylan alone once again.

He made his way into his room, quickly changing his clothes from the night previous. He picked something easy, just jeans and a sweatshirt. Once he'd gotten himself ready, he closed his door behind himself, hearing it bang on the door frame and swing back open. He'd almost forgotten he'd broken it.

Shit, he thought.

The air outside was cold and crisp, so he threw his hood up to keep what heat he had in. He walked out to the street while whistling out for a cab, hopping into it while deep in thought.

As hard as he tried, he couldn't bring himself to focus on any one thing for too long. "Maybe I should've gotten some sleep," he quietly said to himself, gazing intently out the window.

As the cab made its way through the morning traffic, he carefully swirled his smoke around in his hand, making use of its calming effect on him.

The city of New York raced past his window, all of its good and all of its bad; yet for some reason, all he could seem to see at the moment was the bad. Quick glimpses of muggings and robberies in the dark recesses of the alleyways between buildings. Cars sitting on the sides of the road with all four tires stolen from right off of them.

He decided to stop looking, feeling a strange urge within himself whenever he saw the terrible happenings of this city.

The cab pulled up to the curb next to an old, run-down warehouse that looked like it should have been condemned. He tipped the driver and hopped on out, watching the car drive off.

He was left in an empty roadway, except for the one lone town car parked nearby. He stared cautiously at the entrance to the building, second-guessing his decision to come. Suddenly he heard a loud yell, strangely seeming to come from above him.

"*Incoming!*" the voice yelled.

Dylan threw his head around, seeing Sam flying through the air, flames trailing off of his feet. He slammed down to Dylan's left, a quick flash of flames bursting out around him as he rolled to a stop on the ground upon losing his footing. He had a smile on his face, and his hair had been blown back by the air resistance of moving as fast as he had.

"Damn that never gets old," he exclaimed. He stood himself back up, brushing all the dust and pebbles off his pants.

Dylan noticed that he was barefoot and then saw that he had his shoes tied together and slung over his shoulder. "It's fifty degrees out, and you're barefoot?" Dylan couldn't help but chuckle a bit, a welcome reaction given how he'd been feeling.

"You try buying a new pair of shoes every time you use your powers," Sam remarked, throwing his shoes back on. "So, did he tell you what he wanted to show us?"

"No, he didn't tell me, just asked me to meet him here," he answered, glancing at the gauze still taped on Sam's face. "How's the eye?" he asked.

Sam placed his hand over the gauze. "It's definitely messing with my balance quite a bit. It's kinda like relearning to walk if that makes sense. There's just a lot more that goes into it now. The craziest part, though, is that it doesn't even hurt anymore."

"I know what you mean. All my aches from last night are just gone. I feel strangely good as new," Dylan agreed.

"Come on," Sam ushered. Having finished tying his shoes, he made his way to the entrance, shoving the double doors open.

As they entered, they saw Victor in front of them. He was sitting in front of one single table in a wide, empty space, typing away on his computer. Hartley sat next to him, the two of them appearing to be in mid discussion.

It was a dirty shack of a space; nearly every window had been knocked out, and the wood paneling of the walls was rotting and falling apart, not to mention the putrid smell lingering around them.

Sam closed the doors a little harder than he'd intended; he hadn't quite gotten a hang of restraining the insane strength they found themselves with.

Victor turned his head as he heard the doors slam close. "Hey!" he exclaimed. He stood up and did a quick turn. "What do you guys think?"

"I think it smells in here," Sam retorted, his hands covering his nose.

Dylan took a few steps forward. "What is this place?"

"This … is our new safe haven," Victor told them. "Can't very well meet about sensitive topics at my home, given the swarming mob still camping out front." He chuckled. "I figured if it was anything ability related, we can discuss it here." He looked at the run-down walls surrounding them, "It's a bit of a fixer-upper. But that's the point. Nobody would expect *me* to buy anything that wasn't gonna be an asset to Reliance. So, I kept this off the books, just in case of any overachieving reporters trying to find a good scoop."

"Sounds like a good plan. You do plan to fix it up though, right?" Sam asked. "At least do something about the smell?"

Victor let out a light laugh. "Yeah. We'll take care of the smell. Now onto the other reason I asked you to meet me here. We gotta address the elephant in the room. We aren't the only ones with abilities running around this city."

Sam's expression grew stern. He'd been thinking about the same thing. "If they're anything like him, that must mean there's some real monsters out there."

Dylan stayed silent as they spoke. He knew they had been attacked by someone else like them, but it hadn't really set in till that moment. What was happening to his home? He felt his heart start to pound.

"There has to be a linked cause between it all," Victor started. He slowly paced as he spoke his thoughts. "If we assume the origin of it all was the bombing, did the people responsible want this to happen? Or was it an unforeseen event on their part?"

"Who would want to cause something like this?" Hartley chimed in.

"I don't know," Victor answered, shaking his head.

"Then there's the other looming question. If someone did want this to happen, what was it for?" Sam asked, a concerned look on his face.

An ominous silence fell over them as they pondered it all. Dylan felt his heart pound a little harder at the thought of all these questions. He felt the urge to let his smoke out.

Why? Why did he have this urge inside of him? He felt like he should be a lot more cautious about using the strange smoke that lay within him. He'd only had these abilities a few days, and they already felt so natural to him.

"The thing that attacked you that first night, Sam—I'm willing to bet he was one too," Victor said suddenly, breaking Dylan out of his thoughts.

Sam thought about the possibility, knowing it made sense. There was no possible way any normal person could have been that strong. His chest ached at the thought of the brute. "It's crazy to think that there may be others who were changed that much. That guy didn't look human." Sam lit a flame in his hand. "Then again, I guess this doesn't either."

Victor motioned toward his computer. "It's not much, but I've started compiling some data on everything we've encountered so far.

If we're gonna find out how this all happened or who did this, we'll need to take a deeper look at everything that's happened since we woke up in that bunker. I've been coming up with a few ideas to help us in the days to come."

"You wanna go looking for whoever did this? Then what?" Sam laughed.

Victor shook his head. "I don't know, but wouldn't you like to know who's responsible?"

"I mean, I guess," Sam admitted.

"Dylan?" Victor asked. "You've been real quiet. You OK?"

The pounding of Dylan's chest was starting to drown out the noise around him. He couldn't be here anymore. "I've gotta go," he muttered. He turned to leave, every part of him wanting to rip the doors from their hinges with his raw strength; he knew he could.

"Whoa, what's going on? Where are you going?" Victor questioned, taken aback by the sudden development.

"Don't follow me!" Dylan yelled back, slamming the doors behind him and shattering what was left of the window.

Victor got up to go after him but was stopped by Sam's outstretched arm. "Let him go," Sam told him. "This is a whole lot to take in, and we can't just expect him to suddenly be OK with all this. As amazing as you and I may find this, I'm sure, for him, all he can think about is her."

• • •

Dylan heard the doors slam behind him, and now felt a little guilty about his outburst. He hadn't meant to snap on them, but his mind was going a million miles a minute, and he couldn't stand to hear any more about it.

He knew Victor and Sam weren't responsible for the things that had happened, but their eagerness to delve into the outcome of the blast that had taken his loved one away didn't sit right with him. Who were they to think they could even do anything if they were to ever find the people responsible? Even if they could find them, what right did they have as people to do anything to do them? They weren't a court of law or any sort of law enforcement. It would be impossible for them to be impartial.

Dark thoughts still loomed in his head about what he would do if face-to-face with the people who had caused Ashely's death. Yet despite those thoughts and how great they'd be to act upon, he'd rather everything just go back to normal.

As he walked the cold and windy streets, he thought about all the stress he was feeling. He'd accepted a job with Victor. But he knew if he went to work for him, there would be no escaping; he'd be pulled into Victor and Sam's irrational plans.

That left him jobless once again, with no idea what he was going to do with himself.

Ashley's parents couldn't pay for his apartment forever. He'd need to find some way to make money if he wanted to keep the last place he'd spent any time with Ashley. He could feel the smoke beneath the surface of his skin, his every thought egging him into using it—yearning for some kind of release for the anger welling up inside.

Shoving those urges to the darkest recesses of his mind, he pushed forward, his chest pounding alongside his racing mind.

As he walked, he looked at his city—the city where he and Ashley had met, the city where he'd gone to school to build a life with her, the city that had supported her dreams.

He looked at the concrete city that lay before him, and it disgusted him. Everywhere he looked, all he could see was trash, both figuratively and literally. The streets ran wild with waste that its citizens just tossed out their windows, filled with the forgotten people who had no choice but to call those streets home.

The streets were filled to the brim with people who had been beaten down by someone higher than them in life, whether it be from a job or the simple lack of care the city's upper class had for them.

He stopped and gave the spare change he had to the raggedy old man he saw huddled up next to a box of kittens, seeing how much more care the man was giving to the kittens than he was to himself.

They were bundled up and had a can of tuna placed next to them, but he sat there with nothing besides a thin, tattered sweatshirt.

Why in the world did a man with that much kindness end up on the streets? Why did the powerful get to sit in their ivory towers and look down on us all? Part of him knew that whoever was responsible for the bombing was definitely someone who'd looked down upon this city.

Then there was the worst trash of all, the ones who preyed upon every class they could—the robbers, the rapists, the murderers, and the hidden psychopaths.

Before the bombing, this city had seemed like the greatest place in the world to him. Now, for reasons he didn't understand, it seemed like all the filth of his home was laid bare before him, and he hated it.

He heard a slight commotion from the alley he was passing. Paying it no mind, he looked around at the street signs, trying to figure out what direction to go in order to head home.

"*Help!*" a woman's voice screamed from the alley he'd just walked past, stopping him in his tracks.

Turning around, he slowly crept back toward the alley and peered around the corner.

All the noise around him seemed to drown out, leaving him in a state of white noise as he watched what was happening. Deep within the dark alley, he saw three men cornering a younger guy and his girlfriend. The boyfriend had been beaten bloody by the men but was still giving everything he had to stay standing between them and the girl.

It didn't look like he'd last much longer though; Dylan could see bloodstains all over his clothes. He quickly noticed the knives in the men's hands.

He inched forward, ready to blast forth and knock them all out in one fell swoop. *Just slam them into the wall next to them*, he thought.

Dylan quickly stopped himself, knowing full well he'd just decided to live normally. He'd just told himself that the right to judge another wasn't his own. He went back around the corner, pulling out his phone and beginning to dial 9-1-1.

He heard the girl start to scream hysterically. Peeking around once more, his heart dropped at the sight of her boyfriend collapsing on the ground.

One of the men continued to kick him while he was down.

The other two had walked around and were inching toward the terrified young girl. Quickly looking back at his phone, a wave of nerves washed over him. He knew that, if he called 9-1-1, no one would show up in time to even do anything. The filth would get away with their crimes.

Unable to push his urges away any longer, he flipped his hood over his head. He pressed the call button on his phone, throwing it into his pocket before breaking into a sprint with such force the concrete shifted beneath his foot.

Every last drop of anger, resentment, and confusion flooded into his fist. Taking a page from Sam's playbook, he leapt upward, ready to swing his steeled fist down onto the man kicking the boyfriend.

Hearing loud stomps from behind him, the armed man turned his head. Pure terror flooded his very being at the sight of the massive red fist coming his way, originating from a man half its size.

With a loud roar, Dylan swung the hand-shaped mass of smoke into the side of his target's head. The man flew back, slamming into the wall behind the woman. Her screaming finally stopped as she saw a dissipating cloud of red. She looked over to see one of her attackers unconscious beside her and a hooded figure stood a few yards away.

The other two had already turned to see what the stomping was and were now frozen in place as they saw the man standing before them. Red smoke leaked out his whole body and had now started to fill the space around them. The attackers took a few steps back as they watched Dylan raise his hand into the air, unaware of the thicker cloud of smoke appearing above them. With a quick downward swing of his arm, the smoke slammed down on top of them, crushing them between it and the pavement.

Taking a number of deep breaths, Dylan could feel the dull pain in his head. Despite that, a feeling of clarity overcame him. All the stress he'd felt before had washed away, at least for now.

He turned and looked at the unconscious boyfriend and his girlfriend backing into the corner as she cowered in fear.

"It's OK," he told her. "They won't hurt you anymore."

She slowly took her head out of her arms and looked around. The men who had just been attacking her lay on the ground now. Standing above them was a hooded man, turning to hide his face. He walked over to what she thought was her dead boyfriend, facedown and bleeding on the pavement.

Kneeling over, he put his ear to his head and listened. "He's still breathing," she heard him say.

His head jerked around as the sound of a distant siren approached. Careful not to show his face, he turned back.

"Please don't tell them about me," he whispered before leaping up onto the fire escape above, quickly making his way up to the rooftop.

Then he disappeared as quickly as he'd come.

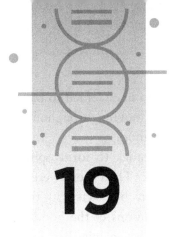

19

CAN'T COMPARE PAIN

Over the next couple months, the city of New York began to hear strange rumors popping up all over the numerous boroughs. Reports emerged of robberies, muggings, and even low-level delinquents all being stopped by a hooded figure who seemed to control smoke.

Dylan had been managing to keep under the radar as best he could. But when the urge to go out overcame him, he was powerless to resist.

If it weren't for his naturally strategic and hyper analytical mind, who knows what would have happened to him by now?

Out he'd go, parading the rooftops looking for anything to quell the rage within, doing exactly what he told Sam and Victor they shouldn't do. Part of him felt guilty about his hypocrisy, but he rationalized it in his head by telling himself he was using it for a better purpose. He told himself he was cleaning up the streets, one night at a time. But deep down, he knew it was just an excuse to cut loose.

He knew the darker parts of town were the best bet, and he'd been doing laps around the area every night.

The rumors about him were beginning to become somewhat of an urban legend around the city, as whispers about the "Hooded Guardian" could be heard everywhere. The rumors had become so heavily spoken of that no one seemed to pay any mind to the other rumors of strange figures moving throughout the city, sporting flames or some kind of black armor.

Residents were all quick to form opinions, the vast majority of them calling it a hoax. Then there were the select few, the ones who claimed to have seen these acts with their own eyes and began to advocate for the intentions of the hooded figure, attempting to convince citizens there was a guardian angel living in their city. Their belief only led to their being ostracized and ridiculed by the remainder of the population.

The nonbelievers simply couldn't fathom something like that happening in their home, all of them still reeling from the bombing that had just left countless dead.

Despite their disbelief, the truth of the matter was that something *was* changing, and the bomb was just the beginning. The night sky was lit up by the bright light emanating off of the city, every street illuminated by its unsleeping populace. The late spring air still had a bit of nip to its touch, but the warmth of the coming summer could be felt more and more with each passing day.

High above the crowds grouped along the thin streets, red footholds formed out of thin air, a pair of running shoes slamming down into them as fast as they appeared. Clad in a cheap black leather jacket that lay over the hoodie he usually wore, Dylan raced across his footholds, gallivanting across the impossibly tall skyscrapers.

Coming to the end of the tallest area of buildings, he leapt forward with nothing but an impossibly long fall below him. Soaring through the open air with growing confidence, he began his long descent. As he fell, he twisted his body, forming a thin red circle beneath his feet. Shifting the board, his speed rapidly decreased until he approached the small apartment building below him.

He hopped off and rolled to a stop, and then he looked over the side of the rooftop into the alleyway below. Within the alley, at least eleven armed men had evaded police and barricaded themselves inside with a hostage, just like the report he'd heard on his secondhand police scanner. He'd found it at a run-down thrift store near his home, and while it had hurt his pockets a bit, it came in quite handy for finding the city's filth.

At the entrance to the alley, he could see the squad of police cars rallied around each other, all of them locked out of the alley by the thin solid metal door the robbers had padlocked shut.

Works out for me, Dylan realized.

Outside the alley, one officer continued to negotiate with the hostage takers through the loud booms of his megaphone. "Release the hostage unharmed, and we can talk about a ride out of here!" new police Sergeant David Reynolds yelled.

There wouldn't be a getaway for the men inside the alley, but he couldn't risk sending his men in and harming the hostage. That left him with the single option of stalling for time until he could get sharpshooters stationed on the rooftops above.

Dylan's heart sped up at the sight of all the guns below. In the ten weeks or so since he'd parted ways with Sam and Victor, he'd been spending his nights scouring the city for any kind of crime he could find. But despite whatever lie he'd been telling himself about making the city a better place, he'd simply been leading a one-man war against the same kind of trash that had ripped Ashley away from him.

At first he hadn't been too sure how to properly use the strange red clouds that his body now produced, but the more he slowly came to use and understand its functions, the easier it became.

Despite his new skills, this situation before him was vastly different than anything he'd thrown himself into before. He'd never jumped into anything more than he thought he could handle—usually no more than four people at a time, and never more than a single sidearm. There were more than double that down on the ground, and nearly all of them were carrying a firearm, not to mention the hostage angle of it all.

If he wanted to do anything, he'd have to do it fast, before the armed men could retaliate in any way. Looking around, he roughly mapped out where each person had placed themselves in the thin space.

"Take out the two guarding the hostage first," he muttered.

He reached into his pocket, pulling out a rolled-up black bandana. Quickly taking off his hood for a moment, he wrapped the black cloth around his face and pulled the knot snug behind his head and then pulled his hood back over it, all in hopes of safeguarding his identity as best he could.

Taking a few deep breaths, he visualized the smoke lying dormant beneath his skin before vaulting over the side of the roof. Falling straight toward the furthest back of the men, he looked down at the hostage sitting on the ground between them.

The abrupt sound of his feet hitting the pavement echoed throughout the alley. *So much for surprise*, he thought.

He quickly turned around, projecting two swirling smoke plumes at the guards and slamming them into the side of the car parked farthest back in the alley.

"Two down," he remarked. Looking over at the hostage, a young man no older than eighteen, he whispered to him, "Hide."

Turning back, he met the gaze of the nine remaining men, each of them stunned by what they'd just seen. The sheer sight of what he was capable of doing had proved to be enough for most of the people he'd gone up against, most of them simply freezing up in the sight of the biologically unknown. But given the large number of people standing before him, as well as the fact they each was armed, they may end up having the courage to continue the confrontation.

Before the men could even react, Dylan had already dropped low, propelling himself off the concrete at an incredible speed. With a thick coating of smoke wrapped around his shoulder, he crashed into the closest of the remaining nine, the impact sending him flying into the two men behind him, the three of them then slamming into the alley dumpsters.

"Only six," he continued to count down.

His usual tactic of taking people out before they realized he was there had gone out the window with the first five. Now he'd have to improvise how to knock out the remaining six before they could get a shot off.

He quickly glanced at the two frightened men to his left, the both of them quivering as they stood frozen in fear. The real threat was the other four on the opposite side of the car closest to the exit who were training their sights on him.

Mimicking the motions of a punch, he shot a ball of smoke right at the head of the foremost of the crowd, knocking him to the ground. Beneath his bandana, he couldn't help but crack a smile. *It worked!* He thought to himself. All the other times he'd tried that nothing had actually happened. It wasn't the time to gawk at his achievements though, there were still five more guys to focus on.

● ● ●

Outside the alley, Reynolds could hear scuffling and the sounds of muffled yelling. His every instinct told him to charge in and show these punks how the NYPD responded to kidnappers, but he knew the procedures. He'd lose his spot as sergeant if he continued his antics from when he was a deputy.

For as much as he didn't want the job, he'd be damned if he wasn't gonna do it in a way Wallace would be proud of. "Greatness isn't chosen. It's thrust at you," he'd often say.

Over the megaphone once more, Reynolds called out, "We'll give you one more minute. Release your captive and come out with your hands up!" He knew they wouldn't comply with what they were being told. He just needed to buy time till he got the call that sharpshooters were in place.

● ● ●

Mustering the strongest wall he could, Dylan shoved the tall SUV before him toward the chain-link fence, trapping the three conscious men between the two.

All that was left were the frightened two along the wall. He whipped back, ready to take on whatever they had to give. Instead, he turned to find them swiftly dropping their guns, throwing their hands into the air.

"Hell no, man. I don't get paid enough for this," one of them exclaimed.

Giving a light chuckle, Dylan nodded toward the gate, as if telling them to turn themselves in. Before they could even move, he could see something in their eyes shift. They both started to look behind Dylan, who couldn't be more confused.

That's when he felt it; the hard, circular shape of a gun barrel pressed against the back of his head. He panicked, he must have miscounted how many people there were. Had there been someone sitting in one of the cars?

"Any last words?" a voice from behind the gun asked.

Dylan screamed inside his head. When it all boiled down, he believed himself fast enough to avoid the gunshot, but that was a rough guess at best. Then there was the risk of the bullet hitting one of the men who stood in front of him. It was just like the situation Sam had just described; he was stuck between a rock and a hard place.

Did he really want to move though? If he just stood still, he could see Ashley again or, at the very least, not be subjected to a life where he had to live without her.

Suddenly, the person behind him began to scream out in pain. The man chucked the gun away as he fell to his knees, clutching his severely burnt hand.

Dylan glanced over at the gun as it clattered on the ground, seeing that it was red-hot and had begun to melt. He felt a strain in his head, immediately recognizing the reaction from when he had fought Overcharge a few weeks ago—a slight pull that seemed to send his attention in a different direction, and upon turning to look up at the rooftop the pull led to, he saw a silhouette looking down at him and the remaining assailants.

He sighed at the sight of the figure.

"All right that's it. We're coming in!" he heard the cop scream from outside, followed by the sound of the thick padlock being fiddled with.

Seeing that the situation had been handled for the most part, Dylan figured he'd let the cops take it from here. He created a hold beneath his feet, sending it and himself soaring up toward the rooftop.

After a single gunshot echoed through the nearly silent night sky, the thin metal door swung outward, the entering cops finding themselves blocked once more by the black SUV that had somehow pinned three men between itself and the door to the alley. Looking into the thin space within, all they saw were men piled on the ground and two stragglers standing there with their hands up—like deer in headlights.

When asked by Reynolds, "What happened here?" all they could do was point up to the rooftop, further deepening the pit in Reynolds' stomach. What could have taken all these men out in a matter of minutes, without them noticing for that matter?

● ● ●

As Dylan's feet touched down on a rooftop a few blocks away, he looked over at the man standing on the edge, looking out into the city as he took his first puff of a fresh pack of smokes.

"Sam," Dylan said, addressing him directly.

Sam blew out the thick cloud of tobacco, shaking the ash off to his side as he stood beneath the darkened cloud cover. "That wasn't too shabby back there." He lightly chuckled.

Dylan took a seat on the metal venting, untying the knot of his bandana as he took a needed breather. "So, you just stood and watched instead of stepping in to help?" he asked with a huff.

"You've never struck me as the kind of guy who likes help if you didn't ask for it," Sam admitted. "And I did step in, but only when I thought it was getting a little hairy."

As Sam stepped forward into the moonlight, Dylan could see the nasty scar along his blinded right eye. A jagged gash, with strange bruise-like markings spreading out from the scar, like the photos you'd see of someone who had survived being struck by lightning. Then there was his pupil, which had burst from the trauma and expanded into the majority of where his iris once lay, leaving only small waves of blue along its border.

He puffed his cigarette once more, "So this is what you've been doing since ya left? Looks a lot like what you told us we shouldn't be doing."

There it was, the insinuation he'd been dreading.

Dylan sighed, just staring down at the sporadic grooves of the concrete roofing as he thought of what to say. "I just—"

"Relax," Sam said, cutting him off. "I'm not here to lecture, I promise. Trust me, I get it, man. This is all … Well, it's all fuckin insane, but people do worse things when they don't know how to cope with something. Knocking the right assholes around isn't the worst way to blow off some steam. Not the best, but not the worst."

Dylan clenched his jaw as a needle of anger pierced his chest, Sam's remark that he "got it" only poked at the emotions he was keeping bottled up. He knew Sam probably didn't mean anything by it. He was probably only referring to the idea of them now having abilities, but that was really only the tip of the iceberg of everything he was dealing with at the moment. "You don't fucking 'get it.' This bullshit took the only fucking person in the world I loved away from me!" Dylan started, his voice slightly rising with his emotions. "You two got to just go home, man, like nothing ever fucking happened, and you're psyched for some reason that something about what happened mutated our bodies."

"That's not fair. It's not like nothing happened. Victor and I both have had our fair share of an adjustment period. Look, man, I'm not comparing anything, but other people lost things too. Vic lost every worker he had employed in his Midtown branch when the bomb went off. Some of them he'd hired personally and had actually come to know pretty well. He even missed most of their funerals since we were gone for so long." Sam turned his head slightly as he continued. "And I ... I lost things too."

Dylan clenched his fists as his chest tightened in irritation. "Don't compare Ashley to a fucking dog! That doesn't matter!" Even as angry as he was, as soon as Dylan let the words loose from his lips, he was instantly overtaken with regret over their harshness.

Sam felt every pore of his body fill with rage. He threw his cigarette to the ground and turned back toward Dylan with an aggressive stomp, flames erupting out of his exposed skin as he shouted at him in a twistedly pained voice. "*It does fucking matter!*"

Sam pulled back as he caught his aggression taking over, lightening his expression from a violent snarl to a pained jaw clench. "I ... I wasn't comparing them," Sam solemnly clarified. "I know ... I know you lost something that can never be replaced—something you're never supposed to lose." Sam's working eye began to tear up a bit. "But my loss is just as real as yours. And it's not just you. Thousands of people all lost something that day.

"It's arrogant of you to tell me, or anyone else for that matter, that your pain overshadows their own. Everybody has their own world they're living in, willing or not. And the smallest thing can make that world come crumbling down around you."

Dylan felt the shock of Sam's outburst wearing off, his words clinging to his chest with a tight grip of truth. He wasn't used to Sam being as open about what he felt, and he couldn't blame him. In a moment of anger, he'd gone out of his way to diminish Sam's loss, and not for a single moment had Sam done anything of the sort about Ashley's death. He hung his head low as he felt a sense of shame squeeze the breath from his lungs.

Sam turned back out to the city, quickly wiping his eye before going on. "Vic's worried about you, ya know? Thinks it's a bad idea for you to be out doing all this by yourself."

"And you?" Dylan asked. "What do you think?"

"I think it's impossible to help someone who doesn't want help, and right now, you don't want help. It scares you."

He was exactly right. The thought of someone trying to help him right now scared the hell out of him. He feared that no one would understand these dark feelings he'd had brewing inside, that they'd look at him differently for being as angry as he was.

How was he so spot on?

The more he came to interact with Sam, the more evident it became that he truly had no idea who his old friend was, nor any idea of any of the reasonings behind his words.

"It'd be hypocritical of me to think it's a bad idea anyway. It's not like I haven't done my fair share of the same thing," Sam went on. "But things are so different now, Dylan. We've only scratched the surface of what's really happened, of what's going to happen from now on even."

Sam turned back to face Dylan. "Look, I'll admit, I'm not too fond of the idea of working together honestly. I've spent a really long time learning to do things on my own, and this is all really new to me. But Victor thinks that, if we're gonna have any chance of figuring out life from here on out, we need to stick together, and I don't entirely disagree.

"So will you just come back?" Sam finally asked. "Before something bad happens."

Dylan let out a heavy breath. "Come back to what? You guys? Sure, we were close once, maybe even friends, but that was years ago. Before this all started, you know I hadn't even seen Victor in almost a year? And you? You just fuckin disappeared one day. All we are now are three people thrown together by tragedy. What's the point in that?!" As he finished his blunt reply, he swiftly turned to leave, a tight grip clinging to his stomach as some small part of him told him to stay.

This was one of Sam's few attempts to bring Dylan back, again and again he found himself denied and left to watch Dylan disappear once more. Sam looked at him walking toward the building's edge. He could practically feel how mad he was.

"It's still better than being alone," he said.

"What do you know about being alone!?" Dylan turned and yelled at him, smoke rising off his shoulders.

Sam stared back at him with a strange look of understanding. "More than most." He let the admission fall out. "I know what you're doing out here. Whatever reason you tell yourself you're doing all these nightly escapades for, it's just an excuse. It's because you *want to*, you wanna cut loose, and let out all that anger inside that you don't know what to do with before it consumes you." He started to walk toward him, "I've been there. I've seen what it looks like. Trust me. It's not something you wanna go through alone. No matter how changed we are, we're still human, and there's only so much one person can do on their own. What would have happened if I hadn't shown up tonight?" he finally asked.

Dylan thought about the gun to his head. Not once since the fight with Overcharge had he come so close to feeling like he was gonna die. "I don't know," he somberly admitted.

Hopping up onto the ledge, he paused for a moment. He turned back to look at Sam once more. "Everything's so different now, man. The people we once were, the lives we once led, they're all just gone now … And I don't know what to do with that. I don't know where to go from here." With that said, he leapt off of the building, bounding off of his platforms as he slowly disappeared from sight.

Sam sighed. He'd told Vic it wouldn't work, but it seemed like he'd made some kind of breakthrough this time. That had been their longest conversation since Dylan left.

Victor had been pretty pissed off about Dylan leaving, given how good of friends they had once been, or at least he thought they had been. Yet he still continually asked Sam if he'd heard anything about or from Dylan, given how fast Sam could cover ground in the city. Victor's ability wasn't that suited for speed.

Unable to see Dylan anymore, just the lingering pull in the direction he'd disappeared in, Sam launched out of sight in a bright blast of orange, leaving a trail of flames leading into the distance.

He wasn't quite as adept as his recent lightning-clad foe, but Sam had been working on faster movements similar to what he'd seen Overcharge do that night. He'd come to the conclusion that even if he lacked the superior speed at the moment, maybe he could make up for it with quick blasting movements to keep his enemies off balance.

All he needed to do was push off the ground with all his strength and then couple that with a quick yet explosive blast of flames from whichever part of his body he was using to propel himself. Put them together and he could practically disappear from sight momentarily.

The only thing he needed to pay attention to was his aim and trajectory; he'd had some recurring issues now that he was working with only one eye. At that point, he'd already launched himself into a number of walls and objects over the last couple weeks.

He could only do one leap at a time at the moment, finding himself needing to land, even if only for an instant, to prepare himself for another burst. But having seen Overcharge dart from spot to spot in quick succession without even touching the ground that night, he knew, if he kept at it, then anyone he went up against wouldn't be able to touch him.

Over the time Dylan had been gone, Sam and Victor had worked to slowly develop their abilities further, as neither of them was able to shake this tightening paranoia that something was coming. As they each began to experiment with their powers more and more, Victor continued to pool all their research notes into his growing database. He'd been trying to think of a specific title to choose for the database, as it continued to grow more frustrating to say the words *ability database* every time he needed to bring it up. However, that still continued to be its working name.

Using Sam's strange new secondary ability to "sense," they'd also been attempting to find any other affected individuals like themselves, using the few free hours they could find each week. Each time they did, they found themselves on a long wild-goose chase. Given both their inexperience with the phenomenon, neither of them had any idea of how to properly use it. The few times it had worked, it had been a brief sensation that had withered just as quickly. And by the time they'd reach the origin of whatever they'd been looking for, they'd come across an empty space with not a soul around. Nonetheless, they continued on, neither of them knowing any better way to search for answers.

As Sam landed down on the pier, flames trailing behind him, one of his shoes started to crackle and smoke. Panicking, he yanked it off, pulling a metallic insert out of where the bottom of his shoe should have been. It had begun to shoot sparks, spewing smoke out of what looked like its battery. Victor's makeshift solution to Sam's shoe melting problem had been a bust.

Taking off his shoes, Sam entered in through the back door as Victor had suggested when coming and going from the warehouse. As he closed the door behind himself, he saw Victor at his computer, looking at different points highlighted on a map of the city.

The grime had all been cleared from the walls of the steel warehouse and the putrid smell along with it. With the worst of the property's issues taken care of, Victor had moved a number of pieces of equipment in after purchasing the place, seeing it as a perfect secluded environment to experiment with their abilities.

After he'd carted in most of the machinery he deemed most necessary for their testing going forward, he'd made up a space for Hartley to lounge around in next to the back entrance corner, figuring they may need someone with first aid skills at some points.

Unfortunately, those skills had come in handier than they'd expected. While they did heal much quicker now than they had before, pain hadn't ceased to exist. It was heavily dulled, maybe, but still just as apparent. No matter how durable they had become, one couldn't cut off a universal constant.

"Any luck?" Victor called out, having heard Sam enter.

Sam sighed and tossed his sweatshirt onto a table nearby. "Nope. He's still being stubborn. At least I actually saw him this time," he said as he approached. He set the metal shoe covers down on the desk next to Victor. "These ones were a bust, too."

Turning away from his large monitor to look at them, Victor grunted in irritation. "Damn it. I was sure I had the calibrations right this time. What did you do tonight?" he asked.

"Just a number of leaps," Sam assured him. "It was relatively quiet tonight, all things considered."

"Maybe it's the solder material on the motherboard? I'll look into a few more heat resistant alternatives. Well, your other shoes are still over there in the meantime," Victor told him while still looking at the melted covers, pointing toward the large metallic dresser along the wall. "So he's OK, though?" he asked without looking away.

Sam sighed, taking a seat as he threw his melted shoes into the full trash can near Hartley's lounge, briefly glancing at the dozen or so pairs of failed attempts stored within. "I think so, at least physically, yes, but he seems tired. He's been out nearly every night from what I hear. The media's having a field day with the whole 'Guardian of the City' bit."

Sam opened the dresser door, pulling out his pair of run-down tennis shoes, remarkably the longest lasting pair he'd had since this all started. Taking a seat in the cushioned recliner next to Victor's computer setup, Sam proceeded to stretch out. "I'll try again in the next few days. Seems to me that going to him directly is our best bet. He hasn't answered any calls or messages so far, so I don't imagine he'd start now."

"What makes you think after tonight that he's gonna come back?" Victor questioned.

"Cause I've been where he is," Sam started. "Finding an outlet's good, but it doesn't matter in the long run if the issue he's running from is still there. He's still alone, still hurting."

As Sam stared off, Victor couldn't help but notice the sad tone in his voice. He had only recently learned that Sam's parents were gone, and the way Sam worded it—*I've been where he is*—left Victor with a feeling that it was more than that. Over the two months he and Sam had been working together, he still hadn't really gotten Sam to talk about himself much at all, and the more he observed him, the more evident it became that there was a lot he kept to himself.

Then there was Dylan, who Victor couldn't even begin to understand at the moment. He knew he had lost someone dear to him, and Victor had lost people too, not anyone near as close to him as Ashley was to Dylan, but still people he cared about. He'd also lost his parents, though he was much younger, and the feelings of anger he'd had about it were all but gone. But what got him through that was Hartley's help and influence.

He wondered if he should ask Hartley for advice.

Turning back and blankly staring at his computer screen, he found himself with a strange sense of guilt for not knowing the two people who were supposed to be his friends better.

● ● ●

Dylan walked through his still-broken front door, tearing off his hoodie and bandana and tossing them on the nearby chair. Grabbing a sports drink from his frighteningly empty fridge, he took a seat on his couch.

With an easy twist of the cap, Dylan put the bottle to his lips and guzzled the electrolyte-packed drink gulp by gulp until it ran dry. He pulled the bottle away and let out a heavy breath of satisfaction before tossing the bottle toward his kitchen trash can.

As he laid his head back on the couch, he stared blankly up at the ceiling, thinking about Sam's words. *It's still better than being alone.* He could still hear the words ringing in his head.

He knew Sam was only trying to help, but he felt so lost in the vast, unfamiliar world that he didn't know if anybody could drag him back right now. He was so lost in the darkness of anger that the light of Sam's kindness was all but lost on him.

Turning his head, he looked over at his weathered police scanner, reaching out and clicking its on switch. Even though he'd just gotten back, he already needed to clear his mind once again, continually hearing Sam's pleas to let him and Victor help. There was nothing but static over the usually busy police frequency, only the occasional officer reporting they were clocking off for break echoing through his apartment.

Figuring everything seemed to have calmed for the night and that there wouldn't be anything for him to do, he decided to just go to sleep. He'd only just realized it was past midnight at that point after looking at the clock hung on the wall leading to his bedroom space, and he knew he had work in the morning. Waiting one more moment, he clicked off his scanner, leaving him with pure silence once again.

He sighed and picked himself off the couch. Making his way to his room, he thought about his new place in life, about how he'd always used to know who he was and where he belonged. And now he was left with the hollow shell of his old self, needing to be filled with something else. But that wasn't such an easy task.

As he pulled the blanket up and closed his eyes, he couldn't help but think, *Maybe I should have gone with them.*

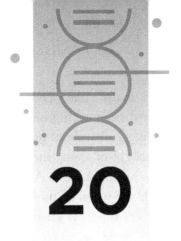

20

NOT WHAT, WHO

Dylan groaned with head-throbbing boredom. He sat at a tightly cramped desk in a small utility space that had been renovated into a records room, stuck with multiple stacks of transaction records and business contacts for the company he'd been temping at.

At his old job at Moriano, he'd have the occasional useless stack of papers to fill out and file, but that had always come after he'd finished his dealings with various other conglomerates. He had always been able to meet a wide variety of people and hear their stories in between their business proceedings. Now, he sat for four hours a day, three days a week, filing paperwork for minimum wage.

Talk about a demotion, he thought.

It wasn't all bad though. The fewer hours and shorter work weeks gave him more freedom to traverse the city at night and still have plenty of sleep before work.

Looking up from his current stack of documents, he glanced at the large analog clock above the door, hoping to see it was already five o'clock. Despite having felt like he should have been done by now, he'd only been there just over an hour. He let his head fall onto his desk, counting down the seconds till he could go out tonight.

• • •

Elliot and Maria had finally talked Dylan into coming over for dinner that night, as they'd been asking him for weeks now. It was something he'd been feeling guilty about putting off, but he couldn't help but feel sad at the thought of seeing them. He'd always said how much of the both of them he could see in Ashley, and now it was the opposite. Now all he could see when he thought of them was Ashley's face, and it crushed him every time. He knew he couldn't just drop out of their lives, though; they'd done way too much for him in his own life.

He boarded the busy train bound for Staten Island, snickering slightly at the thought that he could probably beat the train if he tried. What was the need though? He'd just be tired by the time he got there and not be up for dinner.

Laying his head against the window and plugging in his headphones, he watched the darkening city race by, randomly finding himself wondering what the guys were doing at that moment.

Part of him still felt incredibly hypocritical for the things he had said to Sam and Victor about using their abilities in this way, but he continued to tell himself he had better motives in mind when he did. While Sam and Victor were preoccupied with the mystery of their abilities and the phantom figures behind them, he was focused on the tangible—on the evil and crime he could put his hands on.

• • •

Dinner seemed to have blurred by in the blink of an eye.

After he'd first arrived, they'd all done the hugs at the front door, both Elliot and Maria promptly greeting him as he walked in. They were ecstatic to have Dylan over again, immediately rushing him over to the couch and asking him a million questions about how everything was going.

He had done his best to explain how he'd been doing without letting them in on the red smoke of it all. He talked about his new job and how he'd hopefully be able to take over the rent within the next month. They had assured him they weren't worried about it. They were just happy to have someone living there again.

None of them mentioned Ashley, trying to avoid the subject as they all knew how fresh the wound still was, for all of them.

They all managed to have a few laughs while they ate, Dylan reminiscing about some of the lighter parts of his interactions with the guys since he'd been back.

He found himself increasingly wondering how they were doing.

Once it came time for Dylan to leave, he gave them hugs and assured them he'd be back soon. Elliot and Maria waved him goodbye as he walked down the darkened street toward the nearest bus station; at least that's where he'd told them he was going.

Guilt stabbed at his chest at the thought of how little time he had put in with them lately, knowing they were hurting just as much as he was, probably more.

• • •

He grabbed at his doorknob, opening it with a simple push instead of a twist. "Fuck I need to fix that," he muttered as he walked through.

He flicked on his police scanner before heading into his room to grab his makeshift gear. Static crackled throughout the apartment as he changed. He occasionally stopped changing for a moment as he continued to hear nothing over the radio. Once he'd finished changing, he went back out to the living room, sitting down next to the scanner as he waited for something to come through.

He felt his hopes spike as an officer's voice finally came through the line. "This is Officer Marx. I'm clocking off for the night."

"All right, Marx. Get some rest. Dispatch, this is Officer Brenton, taking over Marx's post till morning."

Dylan's head dropped in disappointment.

As the minutes turned into hours, Dylan felt his eyes grow heavy and found himself nearly unable to keep them open at all after a while. For some reason, nothing seemed to be happening tonight.

Rain began to pound against his window, its consistent rhythm seeming to have a further drowsing effect on him. Feeling the weight of his eyes grow to be too much, he drifted into a deep sleep.

• • •

Dylan stirred to the sounds of voices in his apartment. Confused, he opened his eyes to find no one around. Rubbing his face, he brought his head up and realized the origin of the sound was his scanner.

"Units in the Lower Manhattan area, we have reports of a disturbance near Grand Street. Civilians have reported loud crashes and screaming moving up the roadway," a female dispatcher announced.

Another officer called back. "Isn't Brenton supposed to be covering that area?"

"He is, but I can't reach him. All we're getting from his radio is static," the dispatcher answered.

"God damn it, he probably fell asleep in his car again. Reynolds is gonna have his ass if he hears. All right, I'll head over and see what's going on, just don't tell the Sergeant about Brenton. I'll deal with him myself."

Dylan looked at the clock above his bedroom entrance. It was past 3:00 a.m. at that point. It was just a simple disturbance call. Did he really need to go?

After a few moments, he groaned, unable to resist the urge to use his ability. He quickly hopped up and grabbed his bandana off the table.

Worst-case scenario, it's just a couple kids, he thought.

Heading out his door, he made his way toward the roof, his new usual way of taking off. Opening the stairway door to the roof, he saw that the worst of the rain looked to have passed, but he found himself thankful he always took a hoodie out with him. Knowing that Grand Street was toward Victor's place, he walked to that side of the roof, stepping up to the ledge.

As he was about to leap and just create a foothold for each step between the rooftops, he started thinking. "Let's try something," he muttered.

With a deep breath, he shaped a decent-sized flat square just off the edge. Stepping forward, he made contact with the smoke's solid hold, leaning down and holding what seemed to be the front edge of the square.

When he thought of the direction he wanted to head in, the shape sprung forth, responding to his steering in his head. As he rose higher into the air, he looked out at the seemingly sinking city and couldn't help but yell out in excitement.

• • •

Dozens of blocks away, Sam sat on the edge of the dock behind Victor's waterfront warehouse, staring out at the city's glistening skyline through his good eye.

As Victor finished closing the back door behind himself, he approached Sam and handed him a beer. "Whatcha looking at?" he asked.

"Dylan's going out again," Sam told him.

"I still can't wrap my head around the idea of 'sensing.' Then again, I still haven't experienced it. So you can like … see him?" Victor asked.

"It's weird. I still haven't quite figured out how to do it on command; it kinda just happens." Sam laughed. "But yeah, I do see him, at least in a way. It's not like I can actually see him, but more like … see where he's at—like a single red flame in an endless black world."

"You think he's got this?" Victor asked, his tone unable to hide his concern.

Sam shrugged his shoulders. "Hard to say. I thought I might have felt something a few seconds ago, but it was probably just him. He's been OK by himself since he's left. Then again I just had to give him a hand the other day." He popped the top of his beer off. "I think as long as he keeps his cool, he should be OK. I hate to toot our own horns, but even without our added abilities, we're a lot faster and stronger than normal people."

"You're right. I mean it's not like he'd run into another person with powers, right?" Victor started replying, slowly regretting his words as they came out.

Both he and Sam shared a look, awkwardly chuckling as they tried to shake off the bad thought.

"No, we haven't since that night," Sam assured him. "Not to mention, we haven't heard anything about other strange stories going around. You'd think if there were more of us, we'd hear more about it, right?"

Victor gave Sam a perplexed expression. "But think about it—the three of us, that lightning guy, plus the thing that attacked you that first night. In the time we've been back, we've only encountered two others, but I have this feeling it's not because they aren't there. Not to mention all the things you've 'felt.'"

He sipped his beer as he explained. "Extenuating circumstances led us to use our abilities on a big enough scale that the city heard about it. If there wasn't anything to draw them out, then there's every possibility that they're in hiding."

Sam turned back to the skyline. "If they are out there, what do you suppose *would* bring them out?"

Victor tilted his head, scratching his neck. "I suppose the same thing as us—other people with abilities."

● ● ●

Dylan landed himself in a dark vacant alley, stumbling a few steps from coming down too fast. He blew out a deep breath as he exclaimed, "Holy shit."

Exiting out onto Grand Street, he found a disastrous scene. There was no one to be found. But shattered glass littered the road; numerous cars parked along the street had been flipped over; and huge, monstrous footprints were dug into the concrete, trailing off down the road.

Then he saw the police cruiser aways down the road that had flipped over onto its top. He sprinted over, sliding across the ground as he crouched low enough to see into the car, where he saw a bloodied and unconscious officer dangling from his seat. His name tag read, "Brenton."

Yanking the bent door open with a loud screech, he gently placed his arm beneath the officer's shoulders and then used his free hand to hit the buckle.

Dylan caught the man's dead weight as he came dropping down, carefully pulling him out and away from the cruiser. He laid him down on the sidewalk and quickly checked to see if he was breathing. Thankfully, he smelled the robust scent of potato chips on the man's breath. Dylan let out a heavy breath of relief, immediately turning his head back down the road to see where all this destruction led.

He slowly stood up and started walking down the dimly lit street, following the trail of deep footprints, keeping a close eye out for whatever had made the tracks. It was beginning to feel like he'd underestimated how much a "simple disturbance call" could throw at him.

Eventually, the tracks veered off the road and into a deserted alleyway. "What's with this city and fuckin' alleys?" he whispered to himself. The tracks were beginning to grow more difficult to see in the near pitch-black space.

Sam would be pretty useful here, he admitted.

Just as he finished his thought, a loud rumble echoed through the tight space around him, sending his heart plummeting down into his chest.

The farther down the maze of alleys he went, the louder each following rumble continued to grow, and he could have sworn he had just heard a voice coming from just up ahead. He could see light emanating from around the corner a number of feet away; he sped up to see if he could hear what was going on.

"*Get away from me!*" a male voice screamed from around the corner.

Dylan attempted to break into a sprint, before suddenly falling to his knees, crushed by a massive weight bearing down on him. Yet there was nothing around or above him. His heart raced as the feeling of hatred filled his body—but not his own hatred.

"I can't do that. I need to be stronger," a dark growling voice bellowed.

Dylan just knew, whatever this pressure was, the owner of that voice was the source of it. He inched forward as he began to get used to the weight around him. Slowly, he peered around the corner of the alley.

His face grew pale at the sight of the monstrous beast he found himself hiding from. It was enormously built like a tank, but humanlike, as if every muscle in its body had been pushed to its utmost limit. Its body was covered in some of the most severe burns he'd ever seen; the scarring even went up onto its face and head. Grime was caked all over the tankish man's torso, soaked into the scar tissue all over him.

Cowering on the ground in front of the creature was a man belligerently screaming at his attacker. Suddenly, Dylan watched as the man waved his hand at the behemoth, and a clear glass-like wall appeared between the two.

Dylan's eyes went wide; it was someone else, someone else that had been changed. That creature had to have been one too. As he came to that conclusion, he remembered Sam's story about a brutish creature that had attacked him their first night back. Was this the same thing?

"Sam fought that thing?" he whispered to himself.

He looked back around the corner, just as the beast thrust his arm forward, shattering through the glass-like wall. He grabbed the man by his throat, raising him up into the air with the simplest of ease.

Strange waves of white energy began to flow out of the man's skin as he tried to scream out, the entirety of the white substance then flowing toward and being swallowed up by the beast that held his throat. Dylan watched in horror as the man writhed in pain, until he suddenly went limp.

The beast tossed him aside with minimal effort, his body rolling on the ground until he came to a stop just before the corner of the alley, his cold, lifeless eyes pointed directly at Dylan.

There was no doubt about it. He was dead.

Dylan instinctively felt he had no way of beating the thing that stood before him, leading him to worm his way backward.

Swinging his leg right back, he felt it connect into a trash bag full of old bottles.

With a confused groan, the beast turned its head toward the sound. It lunged forward, crumbling the ground beneath his feet as it came to a stop and quickly looked around the corner, seeing a figure hightailing it out of the alley. It let an eerie grin sweep across its face before taking a heavy step forward and stepping right onto its previous lifeless victim, his unthinkable weight crunching through his ribcage like a anvil dropped on a bundle of sticks.

With a powerful movement of its leg, the creature burst forward toward its new target, stomping its feet with enough force to leave distinct footprints in the concrete. As it moved with considerable speed, the creature swung its mighty arm down, grabbing chunks of the ground and flinging the rocks Dylan's way.

Though he evaded the majority of the debris as he turned the corner, Dylan still felt multiple blunt impacts against his back. He ignored the pain, running into the middle of the road, thinking he'd have a better chance against this thing in a wide open space—be it chances in a fight or chances of quickly getting away.

Bursting out of the alley in a cloud of dust and debris, the creature darted its head over to look at him with its intensely red eyes, the thick red veins in them extending out onto his face. Dylan couldn't help but feel a sudden shudder run through his body at the sight.

He threw his hands up into the air, and a thick red wall appeared above the creature. Dylan shouted as he brought his arms down, the wall following suit. "*Stay back!*" he screamed, the sight of the poor man's lifeless expression burnt into his eyes.

With a simple gesture, the beast stopped the wall's momentum, holding back the enigmatic force with only one hand.

Dylan maintained his hold, focusing on shoving his construct down with everything he had. He could feel the beast's resistance with every push he gave, a slightly worse headache accompanying it every time.

The beast let out a chilling laugh before it effortlessly shoved the wall upward, shattering Dylan's concentration and sending him stumbling. The brute dropped down, springing forth at an alarming speed for its size, bracing its shoulder for a head-on collision with its prey.

Dylan threw up as thick a wall as he could muster on short notice, placing it between him and his fast approaching attacker. It made little difference as the beast's massive shoulder seemed to shatter the smoke structure as if it were thick glass.

Barreling through, he smashed into Dylan's chest, hurtling him back as he crashed over the tops of a number of parked cars. Landing on the sidewalk nearby, Dylan leaned against the car behind himself as he gained his wits back. His head spun profusely as he clutched his aching chest that surely housed a broken rib or two, clamoring to catch his breath all the while.

Given no time to rest, he felt the car he was leaning up against lift up from behind him. He turned over, looking up as the behemoth held the car above its large, grotesquely-defined body. Like a rogue wave crashing down and capsizing a boat, fear crashed over Dylan as he watched the beast wind up, as if about to slam the car down on top of him. He sent every last drop of energy he could find in his body's depths into his palms as he swung them together, aiming directly at the creature's chest. Smoke billowed out of him, beginning to violently swirl around his hands and arms.

"Not enough," he said to himself.

Dylan screamed as he pushed his body even further than he already had, circulating his power into one enormous swirling sphere of energy, a kind of energy he'd yet to see out of his ability so far.

With a thought, he created an opening in the sphere's structure, releasing the immensely powerful energy he'd built up. The red energy shot forth, enveloped in a vortex of swirling red smoke.

It connected with the creature's chest, bombarding the beast with everything Dylan had.

The monster stumbled a few steps, dropping the car off to its side as it struggled to maintain its footing against Dylan's attack. Still, it continued to push back against him, loving the thrill of a real challenge after having had such a dull previous encounter

After a number of seconds, Dylan could feel his strength begin to wane. He felt blood trickle down his lip as he was slowly forced to his knees by the beast's resistance, his attack quickly dissipating as he lost his focus. "Damn it," he muttered.

While his new attack had seemed to briefly slow the creature, it still wasn't enough. It shrugged off the vortex's effect, resetting its sights on Dylan. It lunged forth at him and started throwing a flurry of massive fists. It took almost everything Dylan had to evade them. Each fist he dodged either landed in the ground or the cars parked around them, barreling through like a hot knife through butter. He could feel his heart skip a beat at the thought of being hit with one of those.

As they moved farther up the street, Dylan couldn't help but notice the lights turning on in the building windows along the street. He hoped no one would be stupid enough to actually come out here right now.

The more the creature missed, the angrier it got. Beginning to lash out even more wildly, it screamed with every movement—like a wild animal intent on one thing, Dylan's life.

Finally getting out of the beast's reach, Dylan broke into a sprint up the street, knowing he needed space to think of a proper counterattack. As he ran, he spotted a parked car coming up. Knowing his attacker was still racing after him, he mustered his resolve and created one of the thickest walls he had yet underneath the car.

Quickly looking back at the beast, its eyes trained on him, he flung his arm back. The wall launched the car up into the air and toward the thing behind him.

Instead of hearing a large crash like he had expected, all he heard was the slight crinkling of the car's aluminum exterior. Whipping backward as he came to an abrupt halt, he watched as the creature held his improvised projectile above his head, grinning as it tossed the car through the wall of the apartment building on its side—as easily as one would a baseball.

Dylan felt his heart skip a beat once again, immediate guilt creeping through him as the sound of a young girl screaming emanated from the hole in the building. "*Mommy!*" the girl screamed prolifically, filling Dylan with blood-red rage.

No more running, he thought. The farther away from the creature he got, the more destructive it became, and he'd had plenty of death in his life already. He shrugged off whatever pain he felt at the moment, bursting toward the beast faster than he had before. As he ran, another thick, red vortex began to rotate around his whole body this time. It grew stronger the farther he ran.

The creature could see what Dylan was going for, and it broke into its own sprint toward him. They approached each other at inhuman speed, Dylan sending all the violently circulating energy into his one fist as he cocked it back, seeing the creature do the same with its own massive hand.

Both jetted their arms forward, and their powerful hands collided in a prolific explosion of red. A shock wave followed in its wake, blowing everything in its path back with incredible force.

After the dust began to settle, Dylan groaned as he propped himself up from the ground, a piercing ringing running through his ears. Every car parked on the street that was at least somewhat still intact screamed out through its alarm, the ringing echoing out across the empty, sleeping city.

"Ow," he let out as he attempted to put weight on his right arm, a searing pain shooting up to his shoulder as he did. Looking at it, he could see the severe bruising on his lower arm. "That's definitely broken," he muttered through pained breathing, slowly hobbling to his feet.

He felt drained, like his last attack had taken much more than he'd expected out of him.

If the residents of the street hadn't been awake before Dylan showed up, they definitely were now. He could see at least a dozen people peeking through their shattered windows up above. In a nearby third floor window, a young man in awe of what he was seeing decided to take out his phone to record what was happening.

Dylan's eyes widened as the ground quickly shook, darting up to look for the beast. Terror flooded his heart when he couldn't find him—only a small empty crater … just about the size of the creature's large feet.

A whistle filled the air as he looked around for it, growing louder and louder until Dylan realized it was coming from above him. Looking up, he leapt out of the way just before the beast crashed down where he'd once stood. Its feet caved in the ground beneath it, causing it to plummet into the sewer system below and giving Dylan a moment to stand back up.

Before he could even think to run, a hand shot up from the ground, clutching Dylan's chest with its monstrous size. The rest of the creature slowly climbed its way out of the hole its hand had made. Dylan rose into the air as it climbed to its feet, struggling with everything he had to break its grip. He struck at his attacker again and again with his one good arm, using his smoke to harden his blows, but no matter. The creature just grinned at him, content now having finally gotten its hands on his prey.

Its teeth were caked with grime, a collage of yellow and brown staining each and every tooth like an abstract painting. "Got you," it gleamed.

Continuing to struggle, Dylan shouted at the beast. "*What the hell are you?!*"

"Not what, who," the creature growled. "Mikhael. Not that it matters anymore."

Suddenly, Dylan felt his strength begin to leave his body, an intense fatigue taking him over. He couldn't even muster the energy to react when the white light began to leak out of his body, just like it had with the man from the alley.

Dylan knew what came next. There wasn't a doubt in his mind that the man from before was not this beast's first victim; nor would he be its last. Was he really just gonna be another lifeless body tossed aside by this creature and left to rot?

He looked at the beast he now knew as Mikhael once more as his grip tightened, seeing the satisfaction in his eyes as Dylan's body began to feel heavy. All he could hear in his head were Sam's pleas for him to come back. "Just come back before something bad happens," he had said.

If Dylan had had the energy, he would have chuckled as he thought about that. He had known Sam was right all along. It had just been these dark and twisted feelings he'd been having telling him that he was better off alone—that he should just avoid connection from here on out, because without it, there was no risk of feeling the way he did.

He knew that was where he'd gone wrong. Connection was what brought out the best in people. Ashley had always helped Dylan to see his potential, showing him he was always more capable than he had believed. If it hadn't been for his connection with her, who knows how the trajectory of his life could have changed?

Feeling blackness creep in around the edges of his vision, he thought of every time Sam and Victor had reached out and of himself ignoring it every time. With no one but himself to hear his last words, he whispered what may have been the last sentence he'd ever speak. "I'm sorry, guys," he let out, resigning himself to whatever came next.

"*Back off!*" Dylan heard a familiar voice roar from behind him. Suddenly, he felt the subtle knock back of a small, contained explosion a few feet from his face.

The hand grasped around his chest instantly let go.

He opened his eyes as he fell to the ground, watching the creature skid across the concrete and come to a stop nearby, a figure now standing between the two. The figure held intensely burning infernos in each of his hands, their bright whipping motions swaying in the windy dead of night.

"Sam?" Dylan weakly asked.

Half turning his head back, still cautious of taking his eyes off whatever lay before him, Sam gave Dylan a kind smile before whipping his head back toward the creature. It was a smile that seemed to bring time to a standstill, quelling the fear burrowing in the pit of Dylan's stomach.

A cold, armored hand placed itself on Dylan's shoulder as someone else stepped in front of him. Victor looked down at him, his own hood on, the tendrils of his liquid armor trailing onto his cheeks slightly illuminating the edges of his face. "You catch your breath. We'll cover you," he told him.

Victor could hear Dylan's ragged breathing, not to mention the numerous spots of blood peeking through his dark clothing. The lighthearted expression he'd shown Dylan vanished as he turned to look at the creature crawling to its feet, replaced by a piercing look of anger. He grinded his teeth as he approached Sam, whose own mood-lightening smile had been replaced by flames frothing from the corners of his mouth as he nearly shook with rage. Waves of heat rose up off of his back as he lowered himself into a fighting position.

The two of them watched as the creature reached its feet, scratching at its jaw and feeling a sharp wince of pain at its touch. It growled as it eyed Sam with its blood-red gaze, seething with rage as it roared out, signaling that it was time to go.

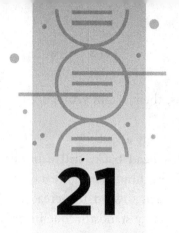

21

NOT A COMIC BOOK

S am glared at the hulking behemoth, watching it violently scream into the air as it poked at its aching jaw, when suddenly he realized something. Even though it was much bigger, and much more monstrous feeling than before, he could tell one thing for sure from the burn scarring covering its body.

"That's the thing that attacked me all those weeks ago," he said in Victor's direction, speaking in a dark tone that Victor wasn't used to hearing out of him, a tone that left him with a strange uneasiness.

He glanced over at Sam with a look of surprise, yet still maintaining that feeling of animosity he felt before, feeling like it would give him the edge he needed at the moment. "I knew you said it was a beast, but man did you ever undersell it," he shot back.

"It's a lot bigger than before, nastier-looking too," Sam explained. "We can figure out why later. We have other things to think about," he said while turning to see the beast set its sights on them. Tensing his legs up, he felt the familiar warm feeling travel down his bones, followed by an explosive burst of flames out of the soles of his feet— immediately reducing his shoes to ashes.

He shot toward the beast, hoping to close the distance before it had time to react. Sticking his shoulder out like a battering ram, he slammed forward and rammed into its chest, toppling the beast back to the ground as he rolled over the top of it, instantly springing off his hands and back to his feet with a slight skid along the pavement.

This left the beast surrounded with him ready on one side and Victor on the other.

• • •

Up above, families and neighbors murmured among each other about what they were seeing. For the most part, they all found themselves trapped in their homes, either from fear of leaving into the battlefield below or due to the entrances of their apartments having been blocked off.

They all watched with their wide, unblinking eyes as these strange beings geared up to fight the monster that lay between them, having just come to the rescue of the one who had just been fighting him alone.

Several frantic calls had already been placed into the police station from homes all over the block, all of them screaming belligerent nonsense into the dispatcher's ears until they were told that mass units were on their way. Now, all they could do was watch and hope these three intended less harm than this creature did.

• • •

Victor took off with incredible speed toward the monster, seeing it picking itself up to face Sam, who glanced past the beast to see Victor sprinting over with something in mind.

Just as the beast reached its feet, Victor swung his armored arm up into the base of its spine, causing it to bend backward and exclaim in pain. "*Topple him!*" Victor screamed.

Sam caught his friend's drift. He burst forward again with his blazing right knee cocked back. Swinging it forward at the creature's forehead with all he had, he sent it toppling backward right on top of Victor.

Victor placed his arms up, catching the creature by its back. He squatted down, the ground cracking beneath their combined weight, and sprang himself and the creature up. Throwing it into the air, he sent it flying and watched it land on top of a few cars a distance away.

Sam couldn't help but laugh. He knew he was strong, but Victor's strength was on another level.

The beast ripped its way out of the metal surrounding it like thin wet paper, rage practically leaking out its thick skin. It growled like a wild animal after having its meal stolen.

"What do you say you give me a little ammo?" Sam asked as he approached Victor.

Victor nodded, sending his armor quickly slithering its way down to his leg. He stomped at the ground, crumbling into a few dozen small chunks. "I'll take the close game," Victor announced, beckoning his armor back into its usual place and taking off toward the creature.

Sam grabbed a few of the chunks with his left hand, placing a good sized one in his right and setting it ablaze. He looked at the beast as it prepared for the incoming tank that was Victor. *Here's some cover,* he thought to himself. Winding up, he chucked the flaming ball of concrete straight at the beast, the flame's intense heat melting it into molten rock as it connected into the beast's shoulder.

It grunted as it stumbled back, screaming out as the glowing red liquid singed its skin.

Seeing its momentary distraction, Victor focused on his fists, watching as his armor thickened up his knuckles. Taking his chance, he began to hammer a few armored punches into its gut. He pummeled at its belly one hit after the other, stunning the creature for just a brief few seconds longer.

Quickly shaking it off, the creature swung its massive arm with exponential speed toward Victor, who was barely able to produce his shield in time. The creature's blow rocketed him back, sending him crashing through yet another parked car.

"Shit," Sam exclaimed. He threw flaming stone after stone, each one pelting the beast's chest and splattering molten liquid all over it.

Which only proceeded to piss it off more.

As the creature started to run at him, he reached down to grab another stone only to find he'd run out. He sighed. "Here we go."

Just before the attacker reached him, Sam darted to the left, simultaneously firing off a simple fireball toward it. He aimed at the beast's hair, setting it on fire like he'd hoped. "You're a lot creepier when you don't talk," he told him.

The beast waved at the flames atop its head, distracted by the two men surrounding it.

Victor finally ripped himself from the parked car, bending its thick aluminum with ease after bringing his shield back in. Looking over to Sam, he saw the beast swatting at itself. Using the free moment, he thought back to everything Sam had told him about this creature.

"Yeah it was insanely strong, but that wasn't the scariest part. It was how inhumanly fast it was, despite its huge size. Like you could close your eyes with it far away and open them back up to see it right in front of you."

Brushing off the glass and dust on him, Victor reentered the fray, his mind racing for a plan of attack. *Just can't give it time to attack*, he told himself. Breaking into a sprint, Victor did some more quick thinking. The best way to keep it from attacking was to keep it off balance and to work in tandem. They couldn't very well plan out an attack in front of the beast, so they'd have to improvise.

Luckily for them, they'd been practicing just that.

He whistled loudly for Sam to hear, shouting out, *"Low!"*

Hearing Victor's call, Sam dropped down, tightening every muscle in his legs. Normally when he used burst movement, he had to gauge his surroundings and modify his power output accordingly, but right now all he needed to do was knock this thing over. He shot forth with as much power as he could pack into his explosions, twisting his body so his feet were pointed forward just before his outstretched legs slammed into the beast's shin.

The creature's legs shot out from under it as Sam raced below, screeching to a stop on the street. He looked up in time to see Victor leap into the air over him, clasping his hands together above him as he twisted his own body midair. He swung his arms down with all his might onto the back of the creature's head, sending its face crashing into the road.

Sam figured that wouldn't do the trick. He extended his arm out and superheated the ground beneath the creature with a carefully aimed blast of flames. The pavement began to liquify, sucking the beast into its boiling embrace and quickly cooling itself back down under the cold night air before the creature could shake off Victor's blow.

The beast shook its head as its senses came back, feeling the solid rock that now encased its mighty physique. It struggled against the makeshift prison; despite its great strength, it couldn't do much without the momentum of swinging its massive arms.

Dylan watched in shock as the beast lay still beneath the concrete. With all he was capable of, all his great new abilities, he hadn't been able to make a scratch on the creature. Yet the two of them, using various code words and limited communication, had managed to beat the beast back.

It seemed like maybe things had ended.

Unfortunately for them, though the beast was trapped in one spot and unable to generate any momentum, all that had done was further aggravate it. It groaned as it flexed every muscle in its brutish body, slowly but surely cracking the newly hardened pavement around itself. Agitatedly wiggling and worming its log-sized biceps, one of its monstrous arms burst free from the ground. It then slammed that free fist against the ground again and again.

"Shit," Dylan said softly.

Sam and Victor alone were enough to momentarily immobilize the monster, but they'd need him too if they wanted to actually stop it. The question was how? Would they have to kill it in order to stop it? He shoved those worries to the back of his mind, pulling himself up with his good arm.

Looking down at his limp, bruised, and broken right arm, he knew he wouldn't be too much help if he couldn't even move around without writhing in pain. He thought deep about how to best work around his current handicap and did the only thing he could think of at the moment. Smoke flooded across his arm, coating it in its entirety. He felt its solid grasp squeeze down around the broken bone, causing him to wince in pain for a moment. When he realized the pain was receding, he knew his idea had worked. He'd created a sling of sorts, applying constant pressure to dull the pain and keeping the sections of his bone properly placed so it could heal correctly.

He just hoped he'd set the bone right, but that was something he'd have to deal with later.

Dylan figured things out just in time to see Mikhael burst out of his temporary containment, flinging large chunks of road every which way. The trio jumped together, readying for what he still had in store for them.

Turning to face the three of them, the beast didn't even bother screaming this time. It simply shoved all of its fingers into the thick pavement below and started to pull upward, groaning from the seemingly impossible task. The ground on which they stood started to rumble, suddenly breaking free from the rest of the roadway.

The behemoth threw the patch of pavement up into the air, the trio still standing atop it as it began to slowly flip over. It was now evident the creature intended to crush them with the school bus-sized chunk of rock.

As Victor and Dylan promptly leapt away to safety, they turned back to see Sam still holding onto the huge flipping boulder.

"*What are you doing!*" Dylan screamed.

Gripping the flying object with all his might, Sam took a deep breath inward, feeling as though time around him had begun to slow once again.

The basic principle of his burst movement was the quick stockpiling of his firepower into a designated spot on his body and then just as quickly discharging the energy in the desired direction he wanted to be propelled. He'd already slightly altered that same principle to create his mildly explosive punches.

He thought to himself, *If I use the same idea, but up the firepower and widen the range, then maybe* ... Exhaling his deep breath, he summoned every bit of flame he could find in himself, channeling it into his palms. After a moment, his roughly flexed hands began to brighten with their rapidly increasing temperature, until they glowed so brightly their sheer heat started to melt into the stone chunk.

With a sudden roaring shout, the energy stored within Sam's palms exploded forth in the form of a high-powered, forward-expanding shock wave of flames that hurtled him backward from the sheer force.

It had been just powerful enough to completely alter the boulder's trajectory, even giving it a bit of a boost as it instead started racing right back to its origin. The boulder crashed down onto the brute, an eruption of dust and rubble following suit and filling the street with its deafening echo.

Sam pulled himself up from the concrete, knowing his back was gonna ache in the morning. As he approached Dylan and Victor, the trio waited for something to happen, each of their hearts beating out of their raggedly breathing chests. A feeling of pure bloodlust suddenly weighed them down as they felt the beast's killer presence once more.

A loud boom rang out through the street, sending another wave of dust and debris rushing out from the rubble. Through the dust they began to see a silhouette peeking through, standing atop all the destruction.

"What does it take to bring this thing down?" Sam questioned through heavy breathing.

Dylan strained his eyes as the creature began to emerge from the smokescreen. "Wait," he told them. He pointed at the creature's labored breathing. "I think he's finally tiring out."

They all watched as the creature wheezed its way forward, eyes locked on the three of them. It stayed at a steady walk instead of its usual blitzing, further verifying Dylan's words.

Sam glanced at Dylan's smoke-clad arm. "That arm still up for a fight?"

"I won't be much use up close," Dylan admitted, just before shooting him a quick grin. "But I can sure as hell give you two some cover."

Victor chuckled. "Wouldn't have it any other way."

They all faced the creature once more, bracing for the endgame of this destructive confrontation.

"One last push guys," Victor announced as he outstretched his balled fists to his sides, leaving them hovering in the air in front of Sam and Dylan.

They both smirked, extending out their own fists to tap Victor's before they entered this battle's endgame.

Victor and Sam shot forth, turning to take opposite sides of their target, leaving Dylan open to attack from the center. This was a simple divide and conquer technique, easy enough for Dylan to pick up on despite having not trained with the two of them.

Victor shot in low, sinking his armored fists deep into its ribs. He kept a close eye on the movements of the beast's arms this time, wary of being blown back again.

Sam, on the other hand, had always done his best maneuvering between close-quarter and long-distance attacking, even before getting his abilities. His years of fighting in the alleys of New York had honed his natural fighting skills higher than most, as if readying him for the ability he would one day gain. Now he could shoot back forth between the two as fast as he wanted. Using his burst movement, he unloaded chunks of flaming debris at the beast, quickly blasting forward to pummel at the creature as he guarded himself against the rubble.

Dylan watched the two go toe-to-toe with the beast, keeping it locked in one spot. He needed to think of the best way to cover their blind spots, but he needed something that wouldn't catch Sam and Victor in the crossfire—something pinpoint accurate.

His eyes widened as he had an idea. The night that Overcharge had attacked them, Dylan had managed to shape his smoke into a barrage of arrows hundreds strong. If he could recreate that image, could he sacrifice its shot count to up their individual damage?

"Worth a shot," he told himself, swinging his good hand up to face the beast as it fought off the attackers at its sides. Smoke flooded out around him, creating a thick cloud at his back. He tried to aim using his palm, finding it hard to see exactly where he'd be shooting. He changed how he held his hand, mimicking as if he held a gun now

"There we go," he muttered, now having a good line of sight. He aimed the tip of his finger right at the creature's shoulder, still slightly struggling to keep it in sight as the beast moved around.

Mimicking the kickback of the gun, a harpoon-sized arrow blasted out of the patch of smoke above him and rocketed straight toward the brute.

The arrow shot through its bicep, lodging itself halfway through. Its arm fell limp before it screamed out in pain, beginning to swing its other arm around wildly, an increasingly frantic look on its wide-jawed face.

Sam could see that the monster was on its last legs. He knew they needed to act now and end this battle before it could recover. He squatted down and placed his hands on the ground; a towering inferno erupted upward around the creature, trapping it in its blazing confinement. Sam wasn't done though. He launched himself up into the air with a trailing blaze, flipping over and descending into the eye of the blaze.

As he fell, he brought the flames of the inferno into himself and packed them into his readied fist. Its intense blaze grew the farther down he fell, the dwindling vortex adding to its power. As he closed in, he roared out and threw his empowered fist right into the beast's jaw once more. An eruption of heat exploded from the place of impact, actually seeming to rid the block of the cold winter air.

Sam fell to his butt once he'd climbed off the behemoth, lying down on the now warm ground and taking a moment to breathe finally. He glanced up to see Victor and Dylan approaching him, the both of them breathing heavy too.

"Did we do it?" Sam asked.

Dylan looked over at the creature, lying still atop the pavement. He could clearly see the beast still breathing, simply having been sucker punched into unconsciousness. He slowly strode up to it, taking a moment to look at its incredibly structured physique before he raised his hand up, locking an arrow onto the back of its head.

"What are you doing?!" Sam yelled as he shot up from the ground.

"We can't just leave it to do all this again," Dylan announced. "It was trying to do the same to us."

"*That doesn't matter!*" Sam shouted. "That's not how we do things!"

"*What do you mean, 'how we do things'?*" Dylan aggressively replied, looking back at the other two with his finger still trained on the creature.

Dylan's yelling muddled through the creature's unconscious state. Hearing arguing over what to do with him, it slowly came to. It continued to listen, waiting for its chance. The beast knew it was too weak to go against them any longer than it already had. These three were worlds stronger than the meals he'd had so far.

"We don't *do* anything," Dylan went on. "We're not superheroes; we're just people whose bodies were changed, violated even. We're not bound by some moral code like the guys dressed in spandex in comic books. This is a literal monster, and monsters need to be put down."

"Dylan, please," Sam pleaded. "You don't know what kind of path this will pull you down. It will take a piece of you that you will *never* get back, and you'll become just as much a monster as he is."

All three of their heads bolted around as they heard sirens fast approaching, a fleet of police cars racing their way.

The beast saw its chance as they turned away; it slammed its fists into the ground with the last of its strength, creating a hole in the street. It dropped down into the sewers and disappeared into the pitch-black tunnels below.

"*Damn it!*" Dylan exclaimed. "*It got away!*"

"You were still going to do it!?" Sam shot back at him.

"*Guys! Now is not the time!*" Victor screamed, pointing to the rally of police cars pulling up around them. "*We gotta go!*" he aggressively insisted.

Dozens of officers jumped out of their cars with their guns trained on the trio, each of their eyes filled with dread. They'd all seen the roadway as they approached and had no idea of what could have that much destructive power.

The last car skirted to a stop, and Sergeant Reynolds shot out the cruiser with his megaphone in hand. "*Get down on the ground with your hands behind your head!*" he told the trio. A sense of uneasiness filled him as he looked upon the faceless, hooded figures before him.

Sam gripped the back of both of Dylan and Victor's coats, squatting down real low as flames built up under his feet. "*Sorry Officers,*" he screamed out as he burst into the air in a blast of flames, dragging the other two behind him.

The force of his blast blew all the loose dust up into the air. Surprised by the freak occurrence that they'd seen, the officers immediately opened fire, letting their fear drive their aim rather than their years of trained practice.

Dylan reflexively threw up a half sphere around the three of them, letting out a sigh of relief as he watched two or three of their rounds actually bounce off of the shield he'd made.

Each of the officers' guns trailed into the air until the threat of their bullets falling from the sky increased.

It was no use; the three men had disappeared into the night.

"*Shit!*" one of them shouted, pounding on the hood of his car. "What do we do now, Sarge?" he asked as he turned over to look at Reynolds, who now stood a few yards away. The officer's eyes widened as he got a good look at the landscape Reynolds was fixated on.

It looked as if the street had been carpet-bombed. Numerous holes led to the sewer system below, and nearly every car on the block had been totaled, not to mention the damage to the buildings surrounding it.

The officer met up with Reynolds, who stared expressionless at the scene. "What the hell is going on here, sir?" he asked feebly.

The sergeant took a few moments to respond, thinking about every strange rumor that had gone around since the Day of Light. "I don't know," he admitted. "But we're gonna find out."

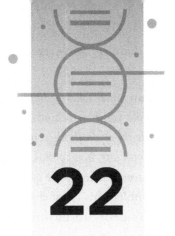

22

HOW MANY DEATHS?

As Sam bounded across the rooftops with his reluctant occupants in tow, Dylan waited for a good chance as they touched down on a rooftop between leaps before angrily yanking his arm off his jacket. "Get the fuck off me!" he shouted.

The trio put some space themselves, each of them filled with vastly different trains of thought. Victor looked over at the two of them, seeing the prolific anger boiling over in both their eyes.

Sam's face was red with rage. "I can't believe you were gonna do it!" he yelled through his struggling restraint, motioning toward the direction they had come from.

"*Of course I was gonna do it!*" Dylan exclaimed as he ripped off his hood and bandana. "*It is a monster!* Now it's free to attack someone else!"

"Guys, stop," Victor attempted to chime in, not really knowing how to diffuse the situation.

"*That still doesn't give you the right to take a life!*" Sam screamed, restraining his arms at his sides as he felt the familiar heat of rage creeping its way into his mind. "What? Do you think having these abilities makes us judge, jury, and executioner now? We're not gods!"

Dylan shook with anger, getting up in Sam's face and pushing him repeatedly, each time a little harder. "*What would you have me do!? Let*

the damn thing just walk away after what it did!? You always spout off this
holier-than-thou bullshit while you hide behind this fucking veil of mystery,
like you know better than us, like you think you're somehow better than us!
You talk about how to deal with loss, how to shake off someone following you,
saying me killing a monster would take a piece of me!"

"Back off," Sam grumbled, his chest shaking in anticipation. He
could almost taste Dylan's desire to hit him, and it was beginning
to seep into him, stirring something nasty that Sam had worked for
years to submerge.

Dylan shoved Sam's chest as he kept going, *"Well, how do you know,*
huh? What makes you the expert on all of it?!"

"I said stop," he urged, his voice lowering as he tensed his fists
in preparation.

"No, damn it!" Dylan continued with another more forceful shove.
"Who the hell are you to tell me what the right decision is!? More than that,
who the fuck are you, man!?"

Sam just stood there, silent as he reigned in his anger, both at
Dylan for what Sam knew he was about to do and at himself for
driving someone he truly thought of as a friend to such a point of
anger with him. And even further, he was angry at himself for half
wishing Dylan would strike out against him in hopes of appeasing
the side of him that yearned for combat.

Victor stood and watched his two friends face each other with intense
ferocity, his gut twisting in knots at his own inability to even bring
himself to speak and break it up. He didn't think killing was the way, but
he couldn't help but side with Dylan in his point about Sam's consistent
avoidance of revealing the basis behind his line of thinking and strange
set of skills even before abilities had become part of the equation.

"That's it?" Dylan fumed. "You're not even gonna say anything?"

Sam sighed a forceful breath. "What do you *want* me to say?"

Just as he finished his half-assed response, Sam felt a sudden
impact across his right cheek that sent him stumbling a few steps. He
immediately knew he'd pushed Dylan over the edge, forcing him to
do exactly what Sam had secretly hoped he would.

"H-Hey," Victor started to weakly call. "That's enough."

Sam stared at the rooftop for a moment before turning back, bursting forward at inhuman speed as he slammed his hand against Dylan's throat, gripping it and shoving him up against the brick chimney behind him. Dylan had struck first, it was only fair he defended himself, that was how he'd always rationalized it before. Why should it be different now?

No! Sam screamed at himself in his head, his eyes widening as he seemed to rip control of himself back from wherever it had just gone.

He quickly released his grip on Dylan, taking a few steps back while raising his arms in surrender. "We don't have to do this," he called out to Dylan as he regained his bearings, coughing to clear his throat.

It was no use, Dylan's anger toward Sam had come to a boiling point, and his functioning arm was already positioned and in motion for another strike. His balled fist landed against Sam's cheek once more.

Victor stood in shock at the situation unfolding.

"*We do, actually!*" Dylan shouted. "Until you wanna answer the simple question of who you are, how am I supposed to be able to trust you and whatever bullshit you spew out?"

Gearing up for another blow while Sam stumbled back, Dylan broke into a run while cocking his fist back.

Gritting his teeth, Sam glanced back at the fist darting straight toward him before gently tilting his head back and out of its trajectory. Now on the outside of Dylan's arm, Sam lifted his own arms up and planted them on Dylan's back and then gave it a good push into his knee racing the opposite direction. Throwing his hands up again, Sam clenched his jaw in restraint. "We can end this now."

"Guys! That's enough!" Victor shouted more loudly this time, subtly looking for a good opening to jump in and end it.

Looking back to face Sam, Dylan charged forward once more, throwing a wide left hook as he approached. The state of Sam's very being shook with anger as it took everything he had to restrain the beast within, doing his best not to hurt Dylan in the process of the admittedly deserved outburst directed at him.

But as always, his restraint thinned quickly. Seeing Dylan quickly closing the distance between the two, Sam jetted his fist at Dylan's in-use shoulder, knocking all the momentum out of his left hook.

Just as Dylan was shaking off the impact to his shoulder, he glanced over to see another fist racing toward the side of his cheek.

"This is what you want?!" Sam shouted. "*Huh!?*"

After shaking off the connection to his cheek, Dylan bolted off his planted foot, slamming his opposite shoulder into Sam's gut like a battering ram as he tackled him to the ground. The moment Sam's back thudded against the rooftop, Dylan took the opportunity to pin his neck with his broken, aching arm while throwing a few strikes into Sam's unguarded cheek.

"*God damn it!*" Victor exclaimed, his booming voice echoing through the once-silent dead of night. He started to march forward, intent on doing what he should have done before it had gone this far and pull the two of them apart.

Yet before he could make his way over, he watched as Sam managed to get his foot positioned onto Dylan's gut amid his one-sided barrage. With a heaving shove of his leg and a forceful shout of his growling tone, Sam shoved Dylan up into the air and sent him crashing down onto the hard stone rooftop.

Sam sprung to his feet, lunging toward Dylan as he hobbled his way off the ground. "*This is what you wanted!*" Sam gruffly screamed. Grabbing Dylan's collar, Sam lifted him from the ground slightly and slammed his balled fist into his already bruising cheek. "*This is it!*" he told him.

Victor finally wrapped his armored hands around Sam's cocked fist as he attempted to stop him or Dylan from hurting one another anymore. "*Sam, that's enough!*" he urged while continuing to hold his readied fist.

"*This is what taking a life turns you into!*" Sam finally finished, his word's abrupt end stunning every person present, even himself.

Feeling his clear mind once more, Sam looked forward at the bruised and bewildered Dylan in his grasp and back at the loosening grip of an expressionless Victor. Feeling an immediate crashing wave of regret slamming into his chest, Sam let go of Dylan's collar as he shook his way out of Victor's loose grip.

Putting some distance between himself and the two of them, Sam clenched his guilt-riddled fists as he sat himself down and up against a wooden garden near the edge of the building. "I'm so sorry," he whispered. "I ... I shouldn't have snapped like that."

Victor quickly looked back at Dylan to see if he was all right, feeling relief at the sight of him wiping the blood from his lips as he gave him a slight nod. Victor sighed, his every muscle fiber was telling him it was time to go home and sleep in the bed he loved, but here he was forced to act as an intermediary between two of his friends because one of them wouldn't just open up to them.

And he'd be lying if he said he didn't at least partially agree with Dylan lashing out at Sam for it. But there was only one thing his mind could really think about at that moment. What had Sam meant by what he'd just said to them?

"Dylan does have a point, ya know?" he finally said with a hesitant clench of his jaw without turning to face him. "He shouldn't have thrown the first punch. You shouldn't have continued to escalate it. And I ... I should've stepped in sooner, before it got this out of hand. But nonetheless, Dylan's motivations for coming at you like that were justified, because as much as I hate to admit it, the truth is we *don't* know you. You've always seemed to stop talking once we shift the focus onto you or the past. You've been like that since we were in high school too. It's always felt like you know a lot more about us than we've ever known about you, like you've always kept this wall up around you." Victor turned to face him directly, "Why?"

Sam sat in silence, staring back at Dylan and Victor as they both kept their gazes trained directly at his eyes, all the while carefully pondering his next words. There was much about himself he wasn't really ready to talk about with people yet, but at the moment, and given everything that had just happened, it seemed only fair he answered their questions.

With an expression they'd never seen him give, one of deep sorrow from memories long since buried, he turned his head out to the glistening city skyline. "I've ... had to kill people before—a long time ago."

As the space around them grew deathly quiet, Dylan and Victor, awestruck by what Sam had just said, stood in silence as they found themselves momentarily unable to react.

"My parents didn't just pass." He spoke softly as he gazed at the lights shining around them. "They were killed when I was really young, and I was there when it happened."

Dylan and Victor looked at each other in shock, neither of them knowing what to say. They both slowly took a few steps forward and took a seat on the ground next to him. Surprised that someone as closed off as Sam had finally decided to share, they both figured that maybe now wasn't the time to talk but, rather, a time to just listen.

All the anger from before seemed to just melt away.

"I was six, and after experiencing that ... something in me changed." Sam continued, "I've never really tried to put it into words but ... it was like my sun disappeared, and the longer I spent without its light, the darker and angrier I could feel myself become."

Dylan felt the weight of Sam's words sit heavily on his shoulders. He knew exactly what he meant by the sudden lack of light. *Six?* he thought to himself.

"Ever since then, I've felt ... something dark, always creeping in around the corners of my eyes, always scratching beneath my skin to get out. And the only thing that ever calmed it, was to lose myself in anything that got my blood pumping, that made me feel any bit more alive than I already did. It always led me to pick fights when I was young."

Sam leaned his head back and stared into the night sky as he fell deeper into his story. "For a really long time, I told myself I was doing what I needed to do to survive, and that was partially true at least. But the truth of the matter was, I came to love it."

He clenched his fists till they turned white as he spoke. "I loved the feel of my heart pounding in my chest, the tingle of adrenaline on my face. I loved the look of fear people gave me when they realized they'd fucked with the wrong guy. I loved when the darkness would creep into my eyes and the next thing I knew, I'd wake up next to numerous unconscious pieces of shit.

With a scratch of his neck, he hesitantly talked himself up, feeling a strange pit in his gut about bragging about something that had led to such a dark occurrence. "I've always been a pretty good fighter if I had to say so myself. I'm definitely not a world champion or anything of the sort, but I was always able to handle the occasional two or three against one. Eventually though … Well, nobody wins forever."

Sam pulled out his pack of smokes, putting one to his lips and lighting it with his opposite finger. "It happened sometime after we'd all first met and after we'd all drifted apart. During the time I knew you guys, I'd calmed down quite a bit. I guess being around you finally helped me learn other ways of coping. But all that did was give the wrong people the push they were looking for."

Dylan and Victor glanced toward one another, confused as to what he meant.

"One day I found myself hopelessly outmatched, surrounded by a bunch of familiar faces, old and young. Looking back, I guess they thought that since I'd seemed to mellow out over the recent weeks, that was their best opportunity for some payback." He thought of the image of the small, pissed-off mob of people cornering him in a darkening alleyway as he blew out another puff. "I remember them cornering me in an alley close to home, most of them pulling some kind of knife or bat from who knows where," he started while giving the bridge of his nose a squeeze in response to his light headache.

"I'm not honestly sure how long it went on, but it felt like hours—fighting, running, bleeding. There's a lot of it I don't actually remember. Like I said, I have a tendency to black out in really intense situations. All I know is … I came back to my senses to the sound of a snap and the feeling of someone's head falling out of my grasp."

His voice fell low at the image in his mind. He could still feel the texture of the man's hair, his final breath running through the hairs on his arm, the loud snap that echoed through both the alley and his ears despite the downpour of rain. It was a noise he would never forget.

"After I came back to myself, I looked down at the ground in front of me, and there were more people on the ground than just the one who'd fallen out of my hands. Two more lay still at the feet of the rest of the assholes who attacked me, who all just stared down at me with a look I'll never forget—fear. That was the first time I had ever not enjoyed that look. They all took off, leaving me alone with the men that I … had …" Sam had started to choke up, stifling back the onset of tears beginning to form in his good eye.

"It's OK." Victor spoke up, placing his hand on Sam's shoulder.

Unable to bring himself to meet either of their eyes yet, Sam just nodded.

"So what did you do?" Dylan asked. All hints of his anger from before had dissipated, replaced by confusion and a familiar feeling of guilt. He'd always had a way of saying the wrong things at the wrong time, without knowing the right things about the person he was talking to.

"I mean what does any scared seventeen-year-old do in that situation? I just ran—from everything." Sam dragged the butt of his finished smoke along the ground. "Dropped out of school, left my group home. Even if I didn't have much, I left it all behind." He looked at Dylan and Victor. "Including the two of you."

The other two stared forward, absorbing everything they had just been told. They had gone from knowing next to nothing about the man they had called friend to knowing what could only be one of the biggest secrets of his life. And what a secret it was.

Victor looked at Sam, his face flush with a colliding force of anger and sadness as he confusedly pieced together his emotions on what he'd been told. "Why didn't you just ask us for help? Did you assume we wouldn't help you just because you … what? *Defended yourself*? Friends are supposed to help each other, man, through fucking thick and thin. I mean, I thought that we were friends. I guess I can't deny that we all kept our distance, but ... we were friends, weren't we?"

"I don't know honestly," Sam admitted. "We were young, ya know. We didn't even know ourselves; at least I didn't. Not that I necessarily do now though, either. But you two were working to better your lives; Dylan had gone off to college and was working on his masters, and you had started the process of taking over your family company and everything that came with it. You had both seemed to move onto different paths than myself. Knowing that I wasn't meant to go near as far in life as the two of you, I found myself ... not wanting to drag the two of you down with me."

Both Dylan and Victor felt their chests constrict, left speechless by Sam's outlook on himself.

Sam turned over to Dylan, who was still processing everything, continuing to think back to his decision to kill the creature and Sam's pleas for him to stop. "After I ... did what I did that night, a piece of me died, quite a few of them if I'm honest. Pieces of me I've tried everything to bring back. I've done everything I can over the last number of years to change myself, to try and fill that gaping void, but they're gone."

Sam's face tightened as memories flooded his head. "I couldn't let you do that to yourself, not when I knew the cost. Monster or not, if you rationalize it once, it only gets easier every time from then on out, and not everybody we may face down the line will look as much like a monster as that thing did."

Looking out towards the city, he finally finished. "After how many rationalized deaths do you become just as much a monster yourself?"

Dylan looked back forward, overtaken by Sam's question. He couldn't help but start rethinking everything Sam had ever said to the two of them, both recent and not so recent. He had once thought Sam had been giving them advice out of his ass; now he understood he'd actually been trying to steer them away from the things that had plagued him in life.

He had been telling them without telling them about who he was.

"It's because you want to, you wanna cut loose and let out all that anger inside that you don't know what to do with, before it consumes you." Dylan thought back to when Sam had told him that on the rooftop the other night, knowing now that it must have been how he'd felt when he was young.

Both Dylan and Victor had multitudes of questions they wanted to ask. But judging from the strained expression on Sam's face, it looked like it had been hard enough for him to share what he had as it was.

Murdered parents? Blackouts? Having taken a life? He'd told them so much but so little at the same time. But as much as they wanted to dive deeper into the enigmatic man sitting beside them, they both decided to leave it for another time.

"Thank you," Dylan whispered. "I … I was too ready to make that decision. It wasn't our decision who lived and who died before all of this, and that doesn't mean it is now."

"That still begs the question though," Victor said. "If we'll have to do this from time to time now, what do we do about the other people with abilities we might have to take down. I doubt the police could do anything to hold that thing from tonight."

"I don't know," Sam admitted. "That's the problem now. Everything's different; the rules, the repercussions, but we have to figure out something. You guys realize, right? Everything is about to get a whole lot more complicated. We were seen tonight, by the cops no less."

All of them let that fact sink in. They'd had stories of their exploits surface on the news and some other obscure sources, but never have there been any eyewitness testimonies that really mattered.

"I mean, what are the chances people even believe what they'll say though?" Dylan asked.

Sam scratched his head as he thought about it, "I don't know. I mean if the roles were reversed, would you believe it?"

"No, I don't think I would," he answered.

"It could be interpreted in other ways too," Victor added.

"What do you mean?" Sam questioned.

"I mean, if you think about it, they only really caught the tail end of everything. They saw, what? Us launching into the sky in a blast of flames? There's every chance I would hear them describe what they'd seen, and it could just sound like an innovative piece of tech," Victor shrugged.

"Maybe," Sam hoped. "Nonetheless, I think it's important, now more than ever, that we stick together and watch our backs."

They all looked out upon their home, the three of them wondering when next they'd come in contact with another person with abilities and whether or not they'd be friend or foe.

● ● ●

Thick black tendrils receded from Overcharge's sunken face, stirring him from his long slumber while his first glimpse of light in over a month greeted him with its blinding embrace. He struggled to force his eyes to adjust as his vision slowly came back to him.

He looked up the steps in front of him, seeing that familiar powerful presence sitting upon the throne at the top.

"Welcome back, Overcharge," King called out.

Though his body was still encased in the solid grasp of the black substance, he found he now had slight mobility and was able to move his face a bit, allowing him to slowly peer around the room. He could see another black coffin structure beside him, slowly creeping off of its captive.

Mimic emerged from the substance, his physique devoid of the size it once held, now left atrophied and weak. His face flushed red with rage as he stared back at him.

"Leave us, Mimic," King boomed.

Staring at Overcharge a moment longer, Mimic finally turned and limped out of Overcharge's view, heading toward the door with an all but silent huff. Overcharge cautiously turned his head back to the boss, his head still a bit fuzzy.

"Now then," King said. "Let's discuss the matter of your outburst."

Overcharge couldn't bring himself to speak; no food, water or sunlight for the last number of months, or however long he'd been in there, had left him atrophied and weak, and simply turning his head had taken most of the energy he had. A normal human would have succumbed to base needs and died weeks ago, but one of the upsides to having abilities was the upgrade to your body's natural survival defenses.

It was a phenomenon King had researched thoroughly.

Those with these powers could go extended periods without any outside nourishment by living off the strange energy within themselves that manifested as their individual abilities. No matter how torturous the process may be.

Using what strength he had, Overcharge nodded in agreement.

Standing up from his throne, King slowly strode down the steps as he spoke. "I believe the scale of your abilities and your rate of growth are vital to our plans going forward, but make no mistake. Your place here has been made abundantly clear. You are to do as you are ordered, and everything will work out for you."

Overcharge could feel his ability tighten around him as King grew closer.

"I will not tolerate another outburst like that, no matter the cause. I know Mimic's ego is a dastardly trait, but you will respect him like the superior he is to you. If we have to have this discussion again, you know what will happen, don't you?"

Coming in scarily close to his face, King's tone grew deadly serious. "Do not force my hand, Overcharge. I know you would do anything to prevent that, wouldn't you?"

Overcharge felt all strength leave his body with the sound of his threat. His eyes fell low as he summoned what stamina he had left. "Yes ... sir."

A smirk swept across King's face. "Good." He turned back to return to his throne, giving a wave of his hand.

With that wave, the black liquid around Overcharge snaked its way off and back into the ground below. He immediately crumbled to his knees from his fatigue, realizing quickly that the coffin had been the only thing holding him upright.

King groaned as he heard the thud of his atrophied prisoner hitting the ground. He looked down to see Overcharge's extremely thinned physique struggling to support its own weight. "Void?"

From out of a thin shadow along the walls, thick black smoke began to flutter about, allowing a man to slip through and into the room. In his casual suit attire, he looked as though he came from a sophisticated background. His elegantly long and soft black hair tied up in a ponytail revealed his chiseled jawline beneath his groomed stubble. He announced himself on approach. "You called me, sir?"

"Escort our pardoned guest to your infirmary. I'm sure he'll be needing some medical attention."

Giving his leader a proud nod, as if implying the command was his pleasure, he strode forth. Void knelt and placed his hand on Overcharge's shoulder, and in the blink of an eye, a plume of black smoke enveloped them both before quickly dissipating—leaving no trace of either of them in the main hall.

● ● ●

Overcharge gasped as the smoke around them disappeared, revealing a new scene before him. "The infirmary," he remembered King saying.

The man who brought him here gently helped him to his feet, carefully laying him back on a soft cot before walking over to the sink nearby and pouring a glass of water.

This was his first interaction with the man known as Void, having only seen him throughout the complex and in elite gatherings a few times. King was adamant that each of them keep their abilities and histories to themselves as much as possible—a rule he and Mimic had both broken.

So, his ability was something along the lines of copying. He wondered if he could keep the abilities permanently or if there was a time limit of some sort.

Overcharge watched as Void rummaged through the cabinets above the sink, pulling out a variety of bottles. "What did you just do?" he asked, disorientation flowing throughout him from whatever that black smoke was.

Void turned back with a smile. "Now, I thought you'd have learned the rules by now. Then again, I know what you're feeling; it's a little odd the first few times. The nausea will pass though." He turned back and opened a few of the bottles, pouring a number of different-looking pills into his palm before he walked over to Overcharge with his hand outstretched.

"Take these," he told him, saying it in such a way that, on the surface, it had seemed like a request, but within the resonance of his voice, Overcharge could feel that it was an order.

Looking at the bright multicolored pills in front of him, he opened his mouth and threw them in, taking a glass of water from Void to wash them down. Almost immediately after swallowing, he began to feel energy welling up within him, almost like his body was revitalizing itself faster than it already had before.

"Are you a doctor?" he heard himself asking.

"Of sorts," Void chuckled.

"What does that mean?" he asked, raising an eyebrow in his confusion.

"It just means I'm familiar with the subject matter. In this case, the subject matter being the physiology of powered individuals." After setting each and every bottle back into the exact location he'd grabbed them from, even so far as to rotate each bottle's label the same direction, he walked over to the door, looking back to his brief patient before he left.

"Word of advice—I'd heed the boss's warnings. No one gets on his bad side and doesn't lose something in return."

On that ominous note, Void exited the room.

Overcharge stared forward as he felt his strength slowly but steadily returning, riding the wave of his thoughts as he sat by his lonesome.

A solemn look washed over his low hung head. "I know."

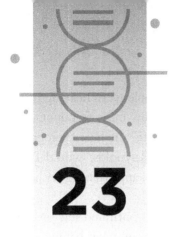

23

STILL ADAPTING

O livia stood in shocked disbelief as she stared at the chaotic scene of last night's attack. It looked as if the street had been turned into a war zone of some sort, littered with trails of destruction stretching out across multiple blocks.

Hearing the words she'd reported during her broadcast had left her reeling from the information overload.

She blankly listened to the clamoring crowd of people that was approaching mob status, hearing them all aggressively fighting to speak over one another as they hammered their questions at Sergeant Reynolds.

He and the other officers had their hands full keeping the crowd as calm as they could.

"*There's monsters running around the city?*"

"*Why weren't the police here faster!?*"

"*What the fuck are we doing about this!?*"

"*Are they gonna attack again!?*"

Olivia stood on what almost seemed to be the last bit of intact roadway, continually rereading the witness statements from the previous night. She was going off the theory that last night and the construction site attack were linked. What once had been mere rumors spoken by the slim few eyewitnesses had begun to spread, now more and more people were hearing of the strange happenings in their city as attacks grew more frequent.

"Unbelievable, isn't it?" she heard someone call from behind her. She jerked back to see Reynolds, who'd finally tore himself away from the mass of civilians, approaching with his hands clasped behind his back.

She turned back and continued staring at the reports she held in her hands. "You actually saw what happened?"

He sighed as he reached her side, momentarily leaning on the nearby lamppost to lessen the strain on his feet. "Contrary to some of the reports, my squad and I only caught the very end of everything. Our questioning of the nearby tenants about what happened before has yet to yield any new tangible information, just numerous stories of men shooting flames and smoke from their hands."

"And?" she pushed. "What did you see?"

He looked out onto the destruction. "I don't know, but I know we haven't seen the last of it." As he finished, he turned to look at her, catching the smell of the familiar lavender-scented shampoo she always used.

"So, how have you been?" he asked, the tone in his voice rising.

Olivia immediately knew what his tone meant. "Stop, David. It's been months now ... You made your bed; now lie in it."

She quickly walked off to meet back up with Ryan, eyeing him near the van as he filmed background footage for the broadcast, leaving Reynolds regretting having even thought of them getting back together.

A number of months before the Day of Light, he'd made one of the biggest mistakes of his life. After a night of drinking with his fellow officers at their regular spot along the water, Reynolds had met a young woman who had seemed to make him forget all about the girlfriend he claimed to love lying asleep in their shared bedroom back home.

Suffice it to say, when he returned home the next morning instead of the night before like he had told her he would, it didn't take a reporter's mind to surmise something wasn't right. It had just taken one to get to the bottom of it, given his lack of honesty in the situation.

• • •

Olivia hightailed it back to her news van, finding Ryan beginning to neatly place all of his equipment back in its predetermined spot.

"Hey, Ray," he called to her once he noticed her approach.

"Hey," she shot back, her mind a million miles away.

"You OK?" he asked.

"Yeah, it's just hard to wrap my head around all of this, and then there's David," she admitted as she took a seat in the back of the van.

"He's still trying?" Ryan laughed.

"It's not funny. You know I still …" She slowly stopped before finishing her sentence, as if keeping herself from actually admitting that she too missed him.

Ryan sighed, walking over to take a seat next to her as he placed his arm around her. "I'm sorry, hon. Why don't you come out with Jason and me tonight. We'll get your mind off of David and onto someone a little more … sophisticated."

Olivia let out a smile despite her reluctance. Ryan had always been great at breaking her out of her moods. "With my luck, you two lovebirds will end up ditching me for the coat room again," she said with a laugh.

"One time, and I've apologized over and over," he defended, holding back a smile.

"I know, I know. I'm kidding. That sounds good. I could use a good night out."

"Excuse me?" they heard a man ask as he knocked on the door of the van. Turning, they saw a young man in his twenties standing there with his phone in hand. "You're Olivia Ray, right?"

"Yes I am. How can I help you?" she asked, sounding confused.

"I … have something. My girlfriend told me I should have given it to the police, but …" He paused.

"But what?" she pushed, her interest now slightly piqued.

"But I don't think they'd do the right thing with it. I think they'd spin it against them." He clutched his phone tighter at the thought.

"Against whom? What is it you have?" She could feel her excitement rising within her, always eager for a good story.

The man looked up from the phone in his hand, an eager yet worried look on his face. "I have a video of what happened last night."

Olivia's eyes went wide. She nearly leapt forward at the man amid her zealous journalistic outburst. "*You do*? That's amazing, how much do you want for it? It's not much, but I can give you all the cash in my purse!"

He put his hand up. "I don't need anything. Just … tell the truth, no matter how the public reacts." He placed the phone in her hands and turned around to leave without another word.

"*Wait*! You realize how much some people would pay for this, right? Don't you at least want your phone?!" she called out.

"Thanks to them, I can just buy another," he said without turning back, continuing forward until he disappeared into the crowd.

Looking down at the mysterious phone in her hand, Olivia's mind raced about what the contents it held could possibly show her. She turned back to Ryan, who had a smile on his face.

"Rain check?" he asked.

She gave him a smile back. "Sorry. Looks like I have my night cut out for me."

● ● ●

In the alleyway just outside the crime scene, a man observed the aftermath of last night's battle. As he peered around the corner, the light in the street revealed his features to anyone close enough to see.

Void stared as a female reporter clutched her newest scoop in her white-knuckled hand, having somewhat overheard the young man from before giving her footage of last night's event. King had tasked him with seeing what the masses knew about the incident, wanting to regulate their knowledge of anything ability related until they'd put all their pieces in place.

As the reporter and her cameraman drove off, Void turned around, quickly disappearing into a thick cloud of black smoke.

● ● ●

"Your arm is gonna need some time to heal," Hartley told Dylan. "How much time? I couldn't tell you. As you can probably guess, this whole ability fiasco doesn't seem to follow the basic rules of medicine. But from what the boys have shown me so far, I'd say the bruises on your face should disappear in a day or so."

Dylan looked at the sling work Hartley had done for him, just in the nick of time too. Consistently holding his smoke over his arm was beginning to take its toll. "Thank you, Hartley."

Dylan hopped off the table, throwing his jacket over his fresh sling. He made his way to the other end of the warehouse, eager to see what Sam and Victor were fiddling with at the computer. In the short time that he had been gone, it seemed that the two of them had done numerous renovations to the warehouse. It almost looked like a simple office space now, as compared to the molded shack it once had been.

As he approached, Dylan couldn't help but take a look at Sam, thinking about how much more he had to learn about him. From the outside, he'd have figured him for a kind person, not that he wasn't, but to know that he'd taken a life before … Dylan couldn't even imagine what must go through his mind on a daily basis. Did he think about it often? Or did he push it to the back of his mind trying to forget about it?

"Feeling better?" Dylan heard Sam ask, breaking him from his thoughts.

"Yeah, a bit. Still a little sore," he told him. "What are you guys working on?"

Victor swiveled out of the way of the screen, allowing Dylan to see the project he was working on. At first glance, he couldn't tell what it was he was looking at, but after a few seconds, he realized what it was.

"Is that a mask?" he asked.

"Well," Victor replied, "more of a helmet, but yes. Among other things."

"Other things like what?" Dylan asked.

"You've been gone for a while, so there's a lot for you to catch up on. I've been developing some countermeasures to help regulate the drawbacks of our abilities," he explained.

Dylan just stared at him with a confused brow raise. "Drawbacks?"

Victor explained further, "In Sam's case, you can imagine the effect his ability has on matter that isn't made of his skin; only his own cells are impervious to the destructive nature of fire—natural or otherwise. So given that, I've been trying to develop a material that's resistant to his flames effects, hopefully at some point, solving his issue with going through clothing as fast as he does. Unfortunately with no luck so far."

"And in my case?" Dylan questioned.

"Yours is a different story," Victor answered abruptly. "Unfortunately, I've seen your ability firsthand the least out of the three of us. The most I could think of in terms of drawbacks for you were the nosebleeds you get after prolonged use."

Dylan thought about the few times he had overexerted himself to the point of his brain feeling like it was melting, followed by heavy nosebleeds that didn't seem to stop until he deactivated his ability. "Yeah … that's definitely a pain in the ass. It puts me out for a while if I go that far. Were you able to come up with anything?"

"Not a whole lot," Victor admitted. "It's a lot more of a challenge trying to stop something happening on the inside rather than on the outside. I *have* come up with a few possible ideas for a de-stressor of sorts, though."

"A de-stressor?" Dylan repeated, confused.

"Well, if we assume the nosebleeds happen due to overexertion, maybe we can't stop it completely, but maybe we can focus our efforts on a remedy that reduces its overall effect," he clarified. "And on that matter, I've made a little progress. I have some friends in my pharmaceutical R&D lab doing some testing."

"Do you trust them?" Sam asked.

"Not with everything, no." He elaborated. "I trust them with the project but not the reasoning behind it. For all they know, they're working on a simple new migraine remedy prototype."

"Huh, so how would it work?" Dylan questioned.

"Well, theoretically, I believe the reason your nose bleeds is because your ability is putting strain on the process of blood flow in your body. So, in order to cope with the strain of pumping your blood through those narrow passageways, your medulla is thinning your blood to the point that it's easier to pump, in turn making it easier for you to bleed at a much higher rate from even the thinnest of cuts."

Victor explained his thought process in tandem with showing a variety of human brain diagrams. "For as superhuman as we are, it's as though our bodies are still in the process of adapting to the changes."

Dylan stood there staring at Victor, having no idea what half of what he said meant. "Medulla?" he asked, sounding confused.

"The part of your brain that's in charge of body functions. It's what tells your heart to pump," Sam chimed in.

Dylan and Victor turned toward Sam with a confused look on their faces.

Sam was taken aback. "What? I do read, ya know," he sarcastically replied.

Victor laughed. "In other words, your brain is making your body pump too much blood, much too fast, and the excess is exiting through the thin, easily torn blood vessels on the inside of your nose," Victor explained, trying to word it more simply.

"I figured you woulda known that, Mr. Too-Good-to-Be Valedictorian." Sam chuckled.

"Hardy-har-har," Dylan retorted. "Even in high school, all my classes were business and economics related. I never studied anything regarding medicine."

Victor switched back to the helmet schematic. "All jokes aside, I believe we may be close to a possible solution. My guys are supposed to have a test sample tomorrow. We can stop by my Brooklyn location in the morning and pick it up."

Dylan took a seat next to the two of them. "Whatever you say. I do appreciate the help."

"So, what's our next move?" Sam asked, leaning back in his chair as he stared up at the ceiling.

"I'm not necessarily sure. I've been winging it all since we came back." Dylan laughed.

"We prepare," Victor told them. "Think about it. Last night was the third attack since we woke up. It's fair to say it won't be the last either. Something is happening out there."

Sam and Dylan both looked over to meet Victor's eyes, seeing the serious expression lain across his face.

"Look at Sam," he continued. "You can literally melt concrete into molten liquid. You can create blasts that propel you dozens of feet into the air. And who knows what else you may be capable of in time? All of us for that matter. If there're powerhouses like you simply walking the streets, hiding in plain sight, one can only imagine what someone with a less than stable personality could do if pushed too far."

The trio stared off, letting the gravity of Victor's words sink in for a moment. There was every possibility their city could turn into a war zone at any moment. It was honestly surprising that it hadn't already.

They could all feel in their guts that, if it ever came to that, they may just be the city's only line of defense.

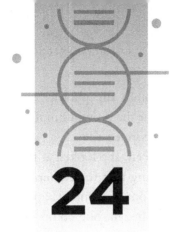

24

TOO CLOSE FOR COMFORT

Hooking the phone to her laptop, Olivia took a seat at the desk in her somewhat recently acquired high-rise corner office. It was a perk of her on air reporting promotion she was still getting used to.

As she waited for the phone to finish synching to her computer, she looked out her glass walls and into the raging bullpen. Dozens of reporters, new and old, were all parading around each other as they competed for both written and on-air stories. Everyone here made any attempt to snake your scoop the moment you relaxed, something she wouldn't miss going forward.

A ding ringed out from the computer as a notification popped up that the sync was complete. She clicked on the pop-up, finding herself being directed to the phone's files.

"OK, photos," she murmured to herself as she scrolled through the list of folders, finally finding the file listed as "photo/video."

She was presented with a vast collage of memories spanned across the screen in front of her, numerous photos of the young man with a woman she assumed was the girlfriend he'd mentioned. "Cute couple," she commented.

As she scanned through the photos, she saw the most recent addition time-stamped for the previous night. "That must be it," she surmised, clicking on the video file.

Switching to full screen, she looked at the starting image of the video as it loaded, noticing that the camera view showed the scene from what seemed to be out of a third-floor window.

Suddenly, the video began. She could immediately hear a man and woman begin to argue. "Get away from the window," a woman's voice aggressively whispered.

"Hang on. I just want to get a look," the man told her, angling his camera downward more and bringing a strange scene into view.

Olivia gasped as she watched a hand shoot up from the ground, clutching a man in his one monstrously sized hand. Olivia couldn't look away as a strange white light flowed out of the man and into the creature's body.

She nearly jumped as she watched another male figure burst onto the scene in a blast of flames, knocking the creature back and knocking his captive out of his grasp.

A final figure approached the chaos, him and the other new guy sprinting forth in tandem as they seemed to cover their recovering comrade. She watched in awe as the battle continued to unfold before her, hearing the occasional gasp from the man and woman recording.

To her dismay, between the couple's ramblings and the destruction occurring outside, she couldn't make out any dialogue from the battle below. Though she could swear she'd seen them speak to one another a few times.

As the video came to a close, she watched the creature disappear into the sewer system, leaving the three men frantically looking around. She watched as two of them seemed to bicker a bit. Then the fleet of squad cars whipped in front of them not too long after, and she watched as David's familiar figure popped out of one of them.

It didn't matter. The three mystery men launched into the air, escaping before anyone could do anything about it.

Leaning back in her chair, Olivia's mind ran through everything she'd just seen, all of it only confirming every strange story the city had thrown at her recently. It was one thing having simply heard of these occurrences, but to see it for yourself was an entirely different ballgame.

The idea that there were … "advanced beings" living among the unknowing population, and they'd only heard of a small handful of sightings. As a respected journalist, she had to consider the possibility the video could have been faked. But considering that she'd been given the video not even six hours after the incident, she didn't find it likely someone could have done that good of a job on such short notice—especially given how well it lined up with every statement she'd taken that morning.

"For the moment, let's assume everything has been true," she said to herself, walking over to the whiteboard she had stationed behind her and rotating it around so the crowd outside couldn't weasel her story out from under her.

She sketched out a loose timeline of events, noting all the various information she had about the individual incidents. Starting with the vague reports of the altercation that had led to a blaze in the End of Line alleyway nearly two months ago, there were five other incidents that all seemed to be similar in nature—from testimonies of flaming men or red smoke saving people, to random absolute destruction.

All seemed to be incurring increasing damage to the city each time.

She looked at the information written in front of her, thinking about any possible linking factors. If she assumed everything was connected, there had to be a reason these occurrences had only just begun to happen.

There was the possibility they'd been around for some time but had managed to stay out of the public eye, but with the degree of destruction the ones she'd seen were capable of, it seemed impossible for every single one of the anomalies to hide that well.

She pondered. She knew that, if these people hadn't been around before, there had to have been something that made them that way—something that could have the potential to create a new kind of being.

An odd look washed over her, and slowly, she reached forward and wrote a new event at the start of the timeline.

Stepping back, she looked at the newly written words, "Day of Light." Sure it may have been a stretch, but without any other information, it was her best working theory at the moment.

As her eyes darted from event to event on the whiteboard, she thought of something. Walking back to the desk and replaying the video, she looked at the three distinct figures fighting the creature. A perplexed look shot across her face as she walked back to the board, marker in hand.

The event that had involved the "lightning man" had taken place just outside Victor Reliance's home in Lower Manhattan and had *then* moved to another spot nearby. The next day, she remembered seeing Reliance show up for the interviews with two other men. All three of them had been pretty banged up too.

It was the same trio she had seen coming out of the Day of Light's crater site a few months ago.

She shot up and over to her purse, snatching out her own phone. She zoomed through her photos till she came across the pictures she'd taken of her damaged windshield. "They're the same day," she told herself as she looked at the timestamp of the photo, dated the same day the first alleyway blaze occurred.

She added to her collage of information on the whiteboard, writing Victor's name in bold writing and then adding in "Bedhead" and "Deep Eyes" below in place of the other two's names.

Finally, she added a big question mark next to all three.

She couldn't help but picture Deep Eye's face in her head. Even if she didn't know his name, she hadn't been able to shake the feeling she'd had when she'd first seen him out of the back of her mind. "I sure hope you're not a terrorist," she mumbled.

She knew all of this was much more of a leap than she was usually comfortable taking, but somewhere in her gut she had a feeling these three were somehow involved.

She knew her mind wouldn't stop racing without the other two's names. Grabbing her phone once more, she found David's number still saved in her contacts, something Ryan had begged her to delete multiple times—something she still couldn't bring herself to actually go through with.

She stared at the number for a while as she thought about the years they had spent together, the both of them pursuing interacting careers. They'd figured the two of them would be an unstoppable team, a cop to stop the crime and a reporter to tell the story, and for a long time they really had been.

But some things don't last forever.

Then came the recurring anger that bubbled up every time she thought of him walking through the front door, reeking of booze and perfume. She groaned in frustration as she tried to push the anger back once more, clicking the text icon for David's number.

It's for the story, she told herself.

"Hello, Sergeant Reynolds"—she started typing—"I was hoping you'd be willing to share some information with me again. I'm working on a story, and I need to access the witness interviews from the incident outside Victor Reliance's home a few months ago."

She clicked send while letting out a sigh, not knowing if it was from anxiety or disappointment that was all she was talking to David about. She still didn't know exactly what she wanted to do about everything.

She hated feeling as indecisive as she did lately.

As she threw her phone back into her bag, she hopped back onto her computer and replayed the footage. With nothing else to go on at the moment, she wouldn't be satisfied till she'd analyzed every single frame of the video.

Replay after replay, she stared wide-eyed and alert, jotting down anything she found of interest.

● ● ●

After a while, Olivia finally unglued her strained eyes from the screen, seeing the dark night sky outside her skyline window.

"Shit," she muttered, turning to look at the empty bullpen outside her office.

Looking at the clock, she realized that not only was it past midnight, but everyone else in the bullpen had wrapped up some time ago and left, leaving her to her lonesome after hours—something her boss wasn't too big on.

It wasn't that he didn't appreciate the enthusiasm of a reporter working a good story, but he was the kind of man who was off the clock by 10:30 p.m. and on his way home to his wife and kids. He always said, "If I'm not here, you're not here."

He'd had issues with employees ransacking other coworkers' desks for scoops after hours, so he'd made a rule for no after-hours work. Of course, Olivia was pretty bad at abiding by the new rule.

She placed her notes and the man's phone in her desk drawer, locking it shut before she tidied up the rest of her work space. After she grabbed her bag, she walked out of her office and locked it behind her—her usual routine.

Olivia strode through the silent bullpen, and finally got into the elevator, leaving the empty floor behind for the night.

• • •

A thick plume of black smoke appeared in the center of Olivia's now empty office, allowing Void easy access to the reporter's carefully locked workspace. He quickly took a look around for anyone before muttering to himself with a smirk. "While I admire a hardworking woman, that took much longer than expected."

He strode through the room, taking a glance at the makings of Olivia's office, finally coming across the locked drawer in her desk. From his viewpoint atop the building across the street, he had watched her place the phone into this drawer.

He ripped the lock open with his bare hands, smirking as the phone slid into sight. "Bingo."

He slid up on the screen, luckily finding that the password had been removed. The first thing he found was the video in question. Quickly giving it a watch, he studied the boss's top picks for recruitment.

He stuck the phone in his coat pocket, turning to look at the whiteboard behind him. The room and whiteboard had been filled with small notes and ideas about the recent ability sightings, and it looked like she was much closer than he knew the boss would be comfortable with.

With a deep breath inwards, black smoke filled the room in its entirety. The smoke pressed up against the glass, making the room appear to be a pitch-black void from outside while it swallowed up everything in its infinite emptiness.

And just as quickly as the smoke had appeared, it instantly collapsed in on itself, leaving nothing behind—no Void, no desk, no notes.

Nothing.

25

COUNTDOWN

1:20 a.m.

Dark. Numb. Empty.

These were the sensations that ran through Void's body while he moved throughout the space his ability took him through, until the gate opened, letting light shine into the darkness. And it allowed him to slip from one point to another with but a thought.

He stepped out from within the smoke, finding himself faced with multiple powerful presences before him. King sat atop his throne, his elite soldiers lined up at his sides, ready for any order.

"Welcome back, Void," their leader rang out. "I trust you have good news?"

Void reached into his pocket, quickly shooting the phone toward the boss with a strong whipping motion.

With a simple gesture, King caught the phone despite its incredibly strong velocity.

"No matter what she may know, it doesn't make a shred of a difference without any evidence. Now she has none," Void started. "But the issue is, she does know much more than we intended for anyone to at this stage. Should I send someone to 'make sure she forgets'?"

"All these new variables … It seems one cannot truly account for every possibility. No matter, it doesn't matter what knowledge one human may have. We are ready. I believe we have amassed enough power to announce our presence to the populace.

"It is time the world knew FEAR."

King stood up from his throne, ready to address his army. "You all know your roles, where you're needed, and when. The time has come to show the masses a world of our making!" He turned to face Tremor, who was lined up silently along with the other soldiers. "Your time is finally nigh, friend."

Tremor's scarred lips curled into a sinister smile. Finally, he'd be able to get out of this hellhole. If he performed his assigned task to the big guy's liking, he'd be almost guaranteed a promotion.

As the powerhouses exited the main hall, ready to enact their leader's ambition, Void stayed behind.

"Was there something else?" King asked.

"I think you should give that video a watch. I saw something that may pique your interest," Void ominously suggested with an excited smirk.

With a grunt, his leader opened the phone, finding the video ready for him to play. He watched as the video began, immediately noticing the young man within the creature's grasp. His lip curled into an eerie grin as he watched the phenomenon that occurred next.

09:34 a.m.

"This is your big break you talked about?" Olivia's boss, Carter Bellingdale, asked with a tone of condescension.

Olivia couldn't even muster any words.

She'd made a big deal to Carter about the story she was working on and had asked him to come take a look—only to find her office had been ransacked clean, with nothing to show for all the work she'd done, not to mention years' worth of stories and articles she'd had published. Every major story she had written in her entire career had been stored in that office.

"I … I don't know what happened. Everything was here when I left last night."

Carter just looked at her. "Is this your way of telling me you're quitting?"

Olivia's eyes went wide, "*What? No!* Carter I swear. I might have stumbled onto the story of the century last night."

"And let me guess," Carter interjected. "Some phantom figure came and took all of your files?" He shook his head. "I have bigger fish to fry, Ray. There's still no word on the numerous deaths or missing persons in the End of the Line's alleys, and you waste my time with boogeymen and conspiracies with no actual proof of what you're implying. You know how things work around here. I never figured you for a wolf crier."

Olivia watched silently as he walked off with a scoff, leaving her standing alone, surrounded by the stares of the many who would toss her off her metaphorical high horse for their own gain without a second thought. She could feel the weight of their gazes crushing her from without, each and every one of them scrutinizing her in their heads, doing so in such a way she could practically read every one of their thoughts.

She shot around, nearly stomping her way out of the bullpen as she felt that familiar pressure build up behind her eyes.

As she hopped onto the elevator, she waited for the doors to close before quickly breaking down for a moment. She hadn't been embarrassed like that since college, and she knew her coworkers would be gunning for her position even harder now that she seemed to be on thin ice.

She thought about the sheer craziness of the last few months, about how she had only stumbled onto her scoop yesterday and how it had taken less than twelve hours for someone to come and take it.

Was she right? She could only surmise that she had to have been close to something if someone had found it appropriate to disrupt her story. The only person she could think of as the culprit, the only name she knew in the whole case, was Victor Reliance.

The elevator let out a ding, signaling it had reached the ground floor. She quickly wiped her tears away, putting on her game face. Rushing forward, she shoved her way through the sea of people in the lobby, doing her best to hold back the tears remaining in her eyes.

She searched her thoughts. Without anything else to go on, she had nothing at her disposal that would help her in her endeavor to uncover whatever was going on. So, what would she do?

As she pushed open the thick glass doors, she aggressively bumped into someone on their way in.

"I'm so sorry!" the man shouted, quickly looking down at the shaken-up women who had bumped into him.

"Olivia?" she heard his familiar voice say next.

She looked up from her haze, realizing it had been Reynolds she'd bumped into. "David? What are you doing here?"

Reynold's took a step back, immediately noticing the severity of her expression. "Hey, what's going on? Are you OK?"

This was the last thing she needed. She had already gotten worked up enough without seeing David's face and all the negative emotions that came with it. "What do you want, David?" she asked aggressively, uneager for a drawn-out conversation.

David reached into the bag at his side, pulling out a couple of filing folders. "I brought the witness statements from the alleyway incident like you asked." He extended his arm forward, offering her the folders.

Olivia went silent, feeling the tears well up behind her eyes once more. She leapt forward, grasping David in a tight hug. She had thought she'd lost everything, leading her to completely forget the favor she'd asked of him the night before. "Thank you so much," she said as she let him go, feeling the awkwardness rise between them.

Grabbing the files, she turned around sharply and headed down the street toward her car. "I'll explain everything soon!" she called out to David, leaving him confused and out of the loop.

As she made her way to her car, Olivia opened up the files he'd given her. There were about two dozen or so statements. And somewhere in them was the name of Victor's cohorts and, quite possibly, another clue as to what was happening.

She unlocked her car, hopping into the driver's seat as she tossed the pile onto her passenger side. "Here we go," she told herself as she merged into the morning traffic, not noticing the two familiar names now visible in the pile.

12:27 p.m.

"I said I'm sorry," Victor exclaimed. "It's not like I have any say when Anthony and his legal team decide to drop new negotiations on us. Hell, I was told we wouldn't even be meeting again till after they'd evaluated the stock trend for at least another week. Unfortunately, I have to adhere to standard takeover policy in this situation, and that means I have to be there whenever negotiations take place.

"I'm already under enough fire missing as many days as I have. I can't afford to force any more board members over to the other side right now."

Tony's legal team had finally scheduled the next meeting regarding his hostile takeover of Victor's company, putting a stop to Victor and Dylan's plan of stopping by his pharma lab together for the time being.

"No. I got that part, but why do you want me to go to your lab by myself?" Dylan asked.

"Well we still need to test the product's effects, don't we?" Victor asked him as he threw his overcoat on.

"I mean, there's no guarantee it'll even work, right?" Dylan insisted.

"No," Victor admitted. "But it's a stepping stone to stopping the negative effects. It won't be forever. Like I said, I believe our bodies are still adapting to our abilities. Why else would we continue to evolve like we are?"

Dylan couldn't help but sulk a bit, he had never even been to Reliance *with* Victor, let alone by himself. Still, he knew it was pointless to argue with the man.

"OK, fine." He finally folded.

"Relax," Victor told him. "I've already let my buddies know you're coming. Just ask for Alex. On the other hand, Sam," Victor started as he turned to face him, "while I'm gone, I need you to stick around here. Project A should be finished sometime today, and Hartley will need a second set of hands while doing the final assembly." He pointed over to the machine whirring in the corner of the room.

"Oh shit, I figured it would have taken longer than that," Sam exclaimed.

"I had to jump through some hoops, but I was able to get us a pretty nifty toy," Victor joked. "With the new 3-D printer, we should be able to produce necessities for ourselves way easier and with way less risk of being questioned about any weird purchases."

Hartley called out from his lounge area, "Are you sure you don't want me to drive you, kiddo?"

"No, it's OK. Sounds like both the Brooklyn and the Manhattan bridges are blocked up all the way across. I'm just gonna take the train. Plus, you need some rest, Harty. You've been staying up all hours of the night with us," Victor said, his tone reassuring.

"Now how come the meeting can't just be at your Brooklyn location?" Sam asked. "Isn't that where the first one was?"

Victor shook his head. "I don't know honestly. His lawyers said he'd requested to meet at their offices in Chelsea."

As Victor and Dylan made their way to the door, Sam stood up to walk them out. The three of them said their goodbyes for now out in front of the warehouse, Dylan and Victor leaving for their individual destinations, Sam heading back in to relax for the afternoon.

None of them had any clue what the day had in store for them. Nor were they aware of the watchful eyes fixed upon them.

● ● ●

A few blocks away, three figures stood atop an apartment building rooftop watching the two men leave the warehouse, a familiar chuckle ringing out of the forefront of the three. Mimic couldn't help but feel the excitement well up within him.

He turned to face Overcharge and Tremor standing behind him. "You guys know your jobs?"

The two of them gave a nod without a word, making Mimic chuckle once more. It seemed like King had finally broken their tenacious spirits, a surprisingly difficult task to do.

"Remember, extend the invitation and get their answer as soon as possible," Mimic instructed. "If they accept, escort them to the boss. If not … well, show them how foolish a choice it was.

"Tremor, do you remember when to make your move?"

"Three o'clock," he answered. A thrilling chill ran up his spine at the thought of what was happening today, a feeling that brought a grin to his face beneath his hooded trench coat.

"Good, that leaves everyone two hours to complete their orders." Mimic said, highlighting their time constraints. He gave Tremor a more serious look. "There's a great deal riding on your success today. You know what will happen if you don't succeed, right?"

"I know," he told him, wiping his grin from his face as he glared back at his direct superior, the memory of the humiliation he'd made him feel still fresh in his mind.

Mimic gave Overcharge a look. "Nothing to say?"

Looking up from the ground, Overcharge stared him in the eye. "Nothing to say."

Mimic scoffed, turning back to face the road and watching Dylan make his way toward the Brooklyn area. "No matter. It's time to go." Leaping forward with haste, he stuck to the rooftops as he began to tail him.

Tremor caught sight of Victor going the opposite direction, giving a confused expression as he saw a woman trailing a distance behind him. He stepped over the edge of the rooftop, plummeting downward until he smashed into the ground, the concrete seeming to warp beneath him and cushion his landing. He sprinted off, maintaining a safe distance between him and his target.

All that was left on the rooftop was Overcharge, left in silence as he thought about what was about to happen today. Closing his eyes, he could see the familiar energy of Sam, who sat inside the warehouse.

He sighed as he took a seat on the ledge, feeling doubt creep into his heart about going through with this. He knew what was on the line, what the boss would do if he disobeyed again. Yet he knew fully well that siding with these people would bring about the death of the modern world.

"What do I do, Gracie?" he whispered to himself.

1:13 p.m., Victor's location

Victor walked down the street, thankful he'd grabbed his overcoat before leaving. "Fuckin' cold," he told himself.

As he made his way to the nearest train station, he couldn't help but feel a tingle in the back of his neck—as if he was being watched. He slyly turned his head back for a second, taking in the faces of the people behind him.

Right off the bat he didn't see anyone he knew, but he couldn't shake the eerie feeling following him around.

He could see the entrance to the Court Street station a few blocks ahead, but he decided to take a small detour first and turned around the corner to his right. Taking a lesson from Sam on being followed, Victor took the next three consecutive rights, forming a circle. Anyone still there after that was definitely following you.

Finally getting back to where he had started, he casually took another glance behind himself. This time, he noticed one familiar female face in the crowd. "Shit," he whispered.

● ● ●

A distance behind Victor, Olivia slipped in and out of passing crowds as she worked to tail him. She had been following him since the morning, having sat outside his home and followed him to the strange warehouse where he met up with the two other suspects on her list—who she now knew as Sam Newman and Dylan McMaster.

Her multitude of questions only grew after seeing where he had met up with them. When she had gone through his property listings, there hadn't been anything about the waterfront location.

Her low-key pursuit had been going relatively easy, till he randomly decided to take a couple consecutive turns.

"Damn," she whispered.

She tried to blend into the crowd a little better, wondering if she'd been made. She thought it safe to assume she had, considering Victor had seemed to pick up his pace. It looked like he was heading for the Court Street station. *Looks like we're going for a ride.*

● ● ●

Victor made his way through the station—buying his ticket, going through the loose security, all the way till he took his seat at the end of the traincar. All while feeling the same hunch he was being watched.

He carefully looked around the train car, seeing the same woman from before sitting on the opposite end, appearing to hide her face as much as possible.

He'd only met the woman a handful of times, back during the simpler days of just being a company CEO, but he recognized her from the mob of reporters he always ran into. More recently, he remembered her being the first person they'd met when the three of them had first come back to life. He even remembered seeing her outside his building the morning after Overcharge's attack.

That's not good, he told himself.

As aware as he was of being followed, he failed to notice the true source of the tingle in his neck. Quietly placing himself in the center of the metal box between Victor and Olivia, a hooded figure grinned in anticipation.

2:01 p.m. Dylan's location.

Dylan held a normal looking pill between his fingers. "So this is it?" he asked.

"That's it," Victor's colleague Alex confirmed sarcastically. "One quote-unquote coagulation pill, modified to Victor's specific parameters. I have no idea why someone would want a pill to make blood thicker, but he's the boss. Do you know what he's working on?"

Dylan panicked slightly. What was he supposed to say? *Hey, my abilities make my blood too thin, and I'm at risk of bleeding out, so I need this pill to make my blood thicker.* There was no way he could say that. "I'm not sure. I'm just the guy he asked to pick it up."

"Fair enough. But, man, he's been requesting some weird things lately. I'd love to get a look at what he needs all that machinery for," Alex remarked.

"You and me both." Dylan laughed.

What machinery was he talking about? It sounded like Victor had been making plans for more than just helmets.

Saying his thanks to the lab workers, Dylan made his way toward the exit and walked out onto the busy street. The moment he stopped, he felt a strange sensation, the familiar pull of his gaze. Following it, he turned to look to his left and saw a distant figure standing atop a rooftop, creepily staring down on him.

He felt chills as he met the figure's eyeline, the same sort of chills he'd felt when he'd looked at Overcharge that night. The strange mask the figure wore only added to his suspense.

The masked figure suddenly turned around, seeming to drop down into the alleyways behind the building. Dylan gritted his teeth. He'd just been reunited with Sam and Victor and had promised them he wouldn't go out on his own anymore.

Yet, what was he supposed to do?

It seemed like the person was intent on getting Dylan's attention. Could he ignore the possibility of another monster's rampage?

Looking down at the pill in his hand, he gripped it tightly as he quickly made his way toward the alleys.

2:28 p.m., Sam's location

Sam sat forward in his chair, a cigarette lit between his lips as he stared at the chess pieces before him.

He'd been asked to help Hartley assemble Victor's newest project, but with Hartley's efficient touch, they'd finished that in less than an hour. Now all that was left was the calibration program Victor had asked Hartley to run. Easy enough.

Yet, Victor hadn't seemed to think of something for Sam to do while he waited for everyone to get back. His apparent boredom had made Hartley laugh, taking out the travel chess kit he always kept in his bag.

For as street smart as Sam was, he couldn't hold a candle to Hartley's strangely good sense of strategy. The older man repeatedly checkmated him within a matter of thirty minutes.

Despite the repeated losses, Sam appreciated the company, already beginning to understand how much of a positive influence Hartley had on people. He couldn't help but feel jealous Victor had had someone like him throughout everything he had been through, despite knowing that it was petty and he should be thankful his friend had a support system.

"You really should think your moves out more," Hartley told him as he set up for another game. "You're only looking at the first available move, and it's narrowing your focus. Try playing out the first two moves for each piece in your head—the first being your own, the second being mine. Think about how each move will affect the both of us, whether or not the sequence of moves will benefit you or come back to bite you. You can't just gun for the king either. Strategically cripple my army first, and when the king and his forces are weak, then you attack."

Sam did his best to take those words in, knowing Victor wouldn't be where he was today if he'd ignored this man's teachings. He stared down at the pieces, beginning with the left side and slowly started to play out his options beforehand.

● ● ●

A few blocks away, Overcharge stood up from his ledge seat, a calm expression on his face—as if he'd finally made a decision on what to do. In a flash, an emission of electricity blanketed over him.

• • •

Sam's eyes went wide. Aggressively, he jumped up from his seat and tackled Hartley out of harm's way, sending his chess pieces scattering across the floor. In an explosion of sparks, Overcharge landed before Sam, the air crackling with his raw power as he looked up to face him.

"*Get back!*" Sam screamed at Hartley as they regained their footing, waving the older man away as he turned back to face the crackling center of the room.

"Hey," Overcharge said. "It's been awhile."

Without any hesitation, Sam leapt forth in a blaze, cocking his fist back as he pumped it full of firepower. He let out a roar as he approached his eerily calm target.

2:43 p.m., Victor's location

Victor hopped off the train, trying to hurry past the crowd before the reporter could catch up to him. He found himself trapped behind a sea of people in the main area of the station, hundreds of people trying to file out a two-at-a-time door.

What the hell is going on? he asked himself.

As the minutes began to slip past, and the crowd seemed to be at standstill, Victor sighed. It was looking like he was gonna be late for his three o'clock meeting with Anthony. He looked around slowly, trying to see if he could find the woman he'd seen standing somewhere in the growing crowd.

Since she didn't seem to be anywhere in sight, he turned his head back, only to find himself jumping at the sight of a man standing in front of him, motionless. The small bit of his face that Victor could see was covered in nasty scars, making Victor's skin crawl at the thought of how the man had happened to get them.

"Can I help you?" he cautiously questioned.

Meeting his eyes, Tremor finally spoke in his familiar raspy voice. "Victor Reliance, it's good to finally meet you. Too bad the other two couldn't be here too. I would have loved a chance to go against the three of you together."

Victor's heart immediately started pounding. He was dead positive the man before him was someone with abilities, just like him. Why else would he mention Sam and Dylan too?

"I've been asked to offer you a chance at salvation," Tremor ominously said.

• • •

Olivia watched from behind a large group of college students, all clamoring about their much-needed days off. She watched as Victor talked to someone she didn't recognize, and strangely enough, he seemed to be pretty shaken up about something. She decided to try and get closer to hear what they were talking about.

She weaved through the crowd, careful not to be seen.

2:54 p.m., Dylan's location

Dylan slowly strode the seemingly empty alleys, keeping an eye out, as well as trying to feel around himself for the man's presence. Hearing the air howl around himself, he darted his head around.

"Hey," he heard a man call from a distance behind him.

Dylan jerked around to face the possible foe. "Who are you!?" he aggressively called back. Another seeming gust of air filled the space around them. Dylan blinked a few times as he noticed the man disappear from his sight.

"Someone with an offer," Mimic said as he placed the tip of his finger on the base of Dylan's neck.

Dylan quickly rolled out of the way, stunned at the man's sheer speed. Not even Sam was that fast. He may have even been faster than Overcharge.

"You can call me Mimic," he told him. "And I've come to extend you an offer—one you would be smart to take."

"Mimic?" Dylan whispered. "So I take it it's not far off to say you know that Overcharge guy?"

"Another one of the family, so to speak." Mimic chuckled. "We sent him to gauge how fast you three had developed."

Dylan gritted his teeth. Gauge their ability? What did that mean? Could that possibly mean that Victor was right? Had someone done all this for the purpose of giving people abilities? Was this man standing before him one of the people who had taken Ashley away from him?

"Who the fuck is we?!" he questioned, slyly letting his smoke loose from behind in case of emergency.

"Not so fast, new blood. All in good time, provided you make the right choice today." Mimic threw his hands outward, boldly making his invitation. "Will you stick to the side of the weak, decaying bags of flesh that is humanity? Or will you rise up and fight with your new brothers and sisters to create a world of our own making?!"

The air grew thick around them as Dylan let those words take hold in his head. "What the hell are you talking about?! Are you … are you asking me to turn on humanity? To turn on who I once was? You're kidding, right?"

Popping the pill he held into his mouth, Dylan released his smoke, letting it flow out violently all around him. He had no idea what the pill would do to him, but it didn't seem like he had much of a choice. He felt the smoke wrap around his injured arm. It didn't feel broken anymore, but he knew it was definitely a handicap.

Somehow he just knew that this man was much different than Overcharge. Whereas Overcharge had given off more of a mysterious presence, Mimic's overall being just extruded a sensation of danger. The eerily demonic black mask he wore didn't help either.

"I don't know who the hell you *think* you are, but you chose the wrong guy to mess with," Dylan yelled out.

Mimic just chuckled. "That it?"

As soon as he finished his question, an eruption of red emanated out of Mimic. That familiar red smoke circled around him, just like it was Dylan, only seeming to be multitudes more dense.

Dylan's eyes went wide. "What the fuck?"

2:56 p.m., Sam's location

Overcharge dashed from spot to spot in quick lightning leaps, barely dodging each of Sam's flurry of flame-enhanced attacks.

He's faster, he thought to himself as he pivoted his head out of the way of his fists again and again.

Sam continued to push forward, hoping not to give his opponent a chance to strike back. Yet, something kept bugging him. His opponent hadn't even tried to retaliate yet.

Overcharge could feel his irritation grow the more he darted around, finally coming to a powerful stop as he released a wave of electricity from himself. "*Enough!*" he screamed.

Sam found himself blown back by the electrical wave, skirting to a stop as his attacker shouted at him.

"I didn't come here to fight you!" he told him.

"What else would you be here for?" Sam questioned, keeping his flames ready for anything.

"I came here … to tell you about FEAR," Overcharge boldly stated.

Sam couldn't help but be intrigued. One moment, the guy says less than ten words during an encounter. Next, he's openly sparking conversation.

Carefully, Sam agreed to listen. "Talk."

2:58 p.m., Victor's location

"A chance at salvation?" Victor repeated. "What the hell does that mean?"

Tremor just stared back at him. "A certain collective has deemed you and your friends fit to join our cause and create a world where our kind thrive."

There was no mistake now; the phrase *our kind* could only mean one thing. Victor's calm demeanor shifted, he was positive the man before him had abilities like his own. His instincts told him to take the opportunity to put him down before he knew what happened. But with the vast crowd around the two of them, there was no way he could do anything quickly enough for no one to notice.

Speed was Sam's forte, not his own.

• • •

Olivia wormed her way just close enough to hear the tail end of the conversation between Victor and the mystery man. She only managed to hear Victor tell him, "Find someone else. I'm not going anywhere with you." She then watched as Victor walked past the man, attempting to hurry out of the building.

Tremor just stood there, a growing grin on his face. He turned his head to look at the large clock on the stone wall above, reading the clear three o'clock from the clock's hands.

Raising his open hands up into the air, he reached out, feeling all traces of earth in the ground and walls surrounding everyone. He felt the stone, dirt, and minerals that comprised the train station and the ground it laid upon. Once he'd grabbed hold of all earthly materials, he violently closed his fists.

Every exit of the building simultaneously caved in, and the ground beneath everybody's feet shook as cracks ran along the ground blocks down the road and then up the foundations of the whole structure. In one fell swoop, nearly a hundred people lost their lives being crushed by the falling rubble. That left the remaining few hundred trapped inside the station with Tremor—and no possible way of escape.

Victor panicked. Frantically, he darted his eyes around the room. Men and women screamed all around him as families clung to one another, shielding their loved ones as best as possible. Victor's heart raced as he thought about what to do. Any move he made against the man would no doubt reveal him and his abilities to the public. He turned and looked at the man, who proceeded to take off his large overcoat, revealing him for all his scarred entirety.

Tremor took a spin around. *"Relax, everybody!* Today you all shall become sacrifices for the greater world to come. While none of you will live to see it, it will be thanks to all of you that we will achieve the first step to our new world." Casually glancing toward Victor, he finally finished. "For our time ... has come."

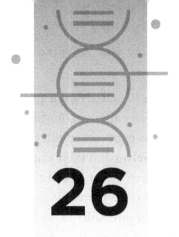

26

A PLACE TO DIRECT
THE RAGE

"Talk!" Sam ordered once more. "What the hell is FEAR, Overcharge?"

"For starters, I'd rather not be called that if it's OK," he told him. "My name ... is James, James Conway once upon a time, and I am ... owned by an organization made up of many people like us—many people who are much more powerful than myself. Our leader calls us FEAR."

Sam slowly put out his flames, standing himself upright to listen to what he had to say. "And who is this leader?" Sam questioned.

"There's a lot I need to tell you and not a lot of time," James explained. "Our boss wanted me to offer you an invitation to join his cause, same with the other two. I imagine they're both being asked the same thing right about now, along with the several other potential recruits scattered across the city. But I didn't come here to recruit you. I came to warn you."

Sam quickly glanced over to the lounge area, seeing Hartley cautiously peek his head around. Being as unsure about the situation as he was, Sam discreetly motioned for him to stay where he was at. "Warn me about what?" he asked.

James's face fell pale as he stared down at the ground. "As changed as you three think your lives are now, nothing will ever be the same after today. FEAR and its eight other elites are finally making their move, announcing themselves and their cause to the world."

"And what cause is that?" Sam hesitantly pushed.

James met Sam's gaze once more, his face revealing him for how scared he was. "The end of humanity as we know it—a world broken down to its foundations and rebuilt the way he sees fit. He'll kill every last normal person on this planet to get what he wants."

"Who is he!?" Sam frantically pushed again, a deepening pit of fear forming just below his chest.

"Despite his and my own shared history … he never told me his real name, he'd already given it up when I met him all those years ago. He'd already rebranded himself … as King."

Sam stayed silent, the gravity of those words continuing to pound in his head. He and the others had figured something bigger than anybody realized must have been happening. But the end of the world?

A number of months ago, they were just regular people, only focused on their next meal and getting to the next day. Now, there was the chance they'd have to fight off someone hell-bent on killing off the non-powered population?

"Why tell me all this? Won't it put you at risk?" Sam asked.

James gave a look of vulnerability, turning to take a seat in the chair closest to him. Sam carefully followed his lead, sitting in the seat next to him. "There may have been a time … when I believed in the cause. But time and everything it brings you changes people." James told him all this with an expression of regret, before turning to look him in the eyes. "It's too late for me to get out or retaliate. His claws are in me too deep. But you three … You're still so young, still a blank canvas, undyed by anyone's colors. You could be or do anything you wanted."

James scratched his head. "When you and I fought, I'll admit, it felt like I was looking at a younger me. You still had hope in your eyes and a fire in your chest, like you hadn't let anyone truly take it from you yet … And I can't let myself help you lose it."

Sam's face sunk at the word *hope*. What did James mean he seemed like he hadn't lost hope. What was he talking about?

Before he could ask him, a sensation ran through the back of his neck. Simultaneously, the two of them jerked their heads around, both of them consumed by the same pull in that direction.

"It's begun," James whispered, his regretful clench of his jaw seeming to highlight his feeling of uselessness.

He stood himself up, slowly walking to the center of the room. Stopping one last time, he turned back to Sam. "If you're smart, you'll take your friends and run while you still have the chance."

In a flash of light, James was gone, leaving Sam to process all the absurdity he'd just heard. Though he tried to make sense of it all, he couldn't bring himself to sit still long enough to do so. He could feel some tremendous power at work across the water.

Hopping up to race over, he heard a loud ding from the machine in the corner, meaning the frequency calibration program had finished uploading.

Coming out from behind the corner, Hartley spoke up. "They're finished."

With a few quick strides, Hartley opened up the machine, reaching in and removing the three objects within one by one before taking a moment to look at a few key points along all three.

As he finished his last second check, Hartley let his head fall for a moment before looking over to Sam. In that one moment, his mind flashed back to years prior, to the much less complicated era of three young boys who were free to live how they saw fit.

But standing before him now was a man whose being extruded a sense of preparedness in the face of the destructively unknown, he knew those young boys were long gone, replaced now by young men beginning to pave their own way in the world even if it meant combatting the predominant force worming its chilling grip around the world's throat.

Giving a quick smile, he placed the helmet's into a bag along the nearby table, extending out his hand as he offered them to Sam.

"Just … be careful, kid," he hesitantly called to him.

"Don't worry," Sam responded with a grin. "I won't be alone."

● ● ●

Victor watched, petrified in terror, as Tremor slammed his hands onto the ground, which was followed by a loud, low rumbling. The next thing he knew, the very ground beneath them, as well as the walls and ceiling around them all began to shift.

The building's normal solid state found itself reduced to a near liquid consistency—moving and morphing around the crowd trapped inside. Victor found himself hurled against a pile of people as the ground violently changed shape, opening his eyes just in time to see another large group of people being flung right at them all. The large ball of people screamed in horror as they felt themselves continue to be thrown around while whatever was happening happened.

He could feel only the low rumble and the tight shifting of the structure surrounding them, leading to dozens feeling their airways tighten as the crowds grouped together even closer. They all desperately gasped for air, writhing in slow agony as they tried to move in the large cluster of victims.

Then there was nothing, just the unraveling of the large ball of flesh. Victor landed on the hard ground with a loud thud, pulling himself up to his knees to see what was going on.

His jaw nearly dropped when he saw what had once been Penn Station, now a completely altered space, made up of what looked to be remnants of the building and the street outside. All the exits had been covered up except for the lone hole in the roof that was allowing a small sliver of light to enter.

Looking around to see how everyone else was, Victor noticed the familiar female propping herself against the wall nearby. *Shit*, he thought with an irritated expression. *She's only here because of me.*

The sound of Tremor's voice rattled him back. "*Here we go!*" he shouted.

A block of stone beneath his feet cracked itself loose, slowly rising up into the air with Tremor in tow. The block rose up higher and higher, until it finally went through the hole at the top, perfectly sealing everyone inside in the pitch black.

● ● ●

Tremor looked out onto the vast crowd forming around his creation. The once beautifully crafted architectural design was now reduced to a large lump of earth sat atop its surface. He could see the growing number of law enforcement vehicles making their way down the busy streets from this height.

"Aaaah, this is a good view." He chuckled.

The first of the police officers skirted to a stop down on the ground, quickly leaping out of his car and aiming his gun up at Tremor as he stood atop his giant stone dome.

"*Come down with your hands above your head now!*" the young man screamed, boasting as powerful a voice as he could, despite how tightly he had to hold his bladder at the moment.

Tremor slowly glanced down at him, raising his hand to his ear with a sarcastic expression. "*What?*"

The officer heard skidding on all sides of him. Looking back down to see dozens of his fellow officers pull up alongside him, he felt his fear lighten a little. With determination filling his chest, the officer looked back up at the perp. He gave one final look of pure fear before a pillar of stone smashed down on him and his cruiser.

"*Hughie!*" the other officers screamed, immediately opening fire on the man above.

Their each and every shot was blocked by a thick sheet of concrete that peeled off the dome and began to zip around Tremor with a simple thought. One by one, pillars of stone followed the sheet's suit, erupting out of the dome, extending out, and shooting downward to flatten the officers below.

"Finally," Tremor said after letting out a deep breath, shaking with pure excitement.

He shouted for everyone below to hear, reverberating his voice through the soil and stone he stood on to cast his voice out even farther than he could ever hope to with just his vocal chords. *"Bring me every news camera in this city!"* His voice echoed out, reaching the ears of the hundreds of people who hadn't followed the crowds as they ran away, left frozen in fear below.

Victor listened to the rumbling outside, screaming so loud inside his mind that his face twisted in agony. *What do I do!?*

●　●　●

Dylan skidded across the ground till his back slammed up against the alley's dumpster, knocking the wind out of him on top of the momentarily blurring vision from hitting his head. Mimic was continuously pushing him back, cornering him against the dead end.

He wasn't giving him any room to counterattack, hammering him with his very own smoke again and again.

"How … are you doing that?" Dylan asked through ragged breathing, leaning against the dumpster as he began to slowly pick himself up.

Mimic swirled the smoke around in his hands. "Oh this? It just didn't seem like you were using your 'ace in the hole' of an ability to its full potential. I just thought I'd give you some pointers." Motioning a circle with his off hand, a sharp and violently spinning cone of red formed in front of him, launched forth at high speed by a punching motion of his dominant hand.

The cone ripped through the air with a loud boom, moving so fast the construct struggled to maintain its form, leaving swirls of smoke following behind it.

Panicking with almost nowhere to dodge, Dylan threw his hands up in front of him, projecting as much smoke as he could muster into the space before himself. He hoped he could solidify his own smoke enough to stop its raw power.

Was he capable of creating things like that too?

He watched the two constructs collide in a concussive blast of red, knocking up all the dust and debris into the air.

As the dust slowly settled, allowing light to creep its way back into the alley, Mimic uncovered his eyes to see if Dylan had gone down with that example of the power difference between them.

He gave a light chuckle as he saw Dylan's figure visible through the smoke, still standing and ready for more, judging from the look in his eye. He couldn't help but admit, "That was pretty good."

Mimic raised his hand up again, the smoke trailing along with it.

But in the next instant, his eyes widened. He looked at his hand, watching the smoke fizzle out and dissipate from his palm. "Shit," he whispered.

Confused by his remark, Dylan remained ready to counterattack once more.

Mimic looked up to face Dylan one last time, his expression of disbelief quickly being replaced by a feigned air of confidence. "Oh well, I guess it's for the best really, I don't know if I can bring myself to kill someone who looks so pitiful. Though I have to say, I'm a little disappointed. Hard to believe he actually thought you guys would prove to be a challenge." He scoffed. "Do try and make the best of the decision you made today. You'll come to regret it very soon." Giving a sarcastic half bow, Mimic launched out of view too quickly for Dylan to track.

Falling to his butt, Dylan finally breathed deeply, now no longer physically suppressing his anxiety. The encounter had lasted only a few minutes, but that man was stronger than Overcharge in almost every way—his presence, his power, his speed, and the way he'd used Dylan's own smoke against him.

"Was that his power? Copying?" Dylan thought to himself aloud.

He picked himself back up, releasing the smoke laid over his arm. Walking back out onto the street, he expected to see a crowd wondering what the commotion had been. Instead, he found a number of people gathered around a storefront a few blocks down the street. All of them were intently watching something inside.

Feeling curious, he slunk down the street, moving past the crowd to get a look for himself. Shock filled him from within as he saw the scene on the screen.

• • •

In the Garment District across the water, every form of law enforcement had formed two perimeters around a large stone structure that stood where Penn Station had once been—one just below the dome itself, and one five blocks out, preventing any more civilians from entering the area.

Standing atop the stone dome, a man shouted for every camera in the vicinity to hear. "Primitive beings of this doomed world! You all have the honor of witnessing a turning point in history! No longer will the weak manipulate the narrative to be falsely designated as strong! No longer will we be divided on trivial matters such as race or origin! No longer will the truly strong be held down by the weak masses grouping together!

"Our organization, FEAR, will create a world where the truly strong thrive. *And we will root out and dispose of the filth that holds us back!* Many of you may not even know of the power you hold, but our leader can see potential, and those of you with it will see a paradise unlike anything you could ever imagine."

He gleamed with a smile on his scarred mouth. *"Will you join us in the next step of evolution!?"*

• • •

Dylan couldn't believe his eyes; to see two other ability users in one day was absolutely insane.

"Penn station?" he whispered to himself. His eyes widened as he slowly pulled himself from the crowd, breaking into a sprint down the street. *That's where Victor was heading,* he thought to himself.

As he raced down the long straights and sharp corners, feeling the adrenaline pumping through his veins, he watched the scenery begin to slightly blur past him from his speed. He quickly hit Sam's number, frantically waiting for the tone to go through.

"*Dylan*!?" Sam screamed as soon as the line connected, sounding like he was talking through deep breaths. "We have a huge problem!"

"I know. I saw," Dylan shot back. "Have you heard anything from Victor!? He was heading to Chelsea and would have had to go through Penn Station."

"Shit," Sam swore. "No, I haven't. I'm almost across the bridge. Meet me across the street at Moynihan Station as soon as you can."

The two agreed to a spot and hung up, both of their minds distracted with everything they had experienced today. And to top it all off, the day wasn't over yet.

So forward they continued, knowing they may be the only thing capable of protecting the city at this time.

● ● ●

Sam looked over the railing of the roof at the huge concrete dome across the way. The streets were filled with the pounding of its builder's ability as he crushed the law enforcement below.

"Oh my god." Sam let the words out unwillingly as he saw stone pillar after pillar crash down on top of police cruisers.

Hearing a whooshing overhead, Sam jerked his head up to see Dylan, coming in fast from above on a floor of smoke. Leaping off his platform, Dylan rolled to a stop next to Sam. The both of them now ducked below cover together.

"What the hell is that?" Dylan questioned, panic apparent in his voice.

"I don't know, but there's its source," Sam gruffly told him, motioning to the figure maniacally laughing atop the dome as he snuffed out countless numbers of the civilians on the ground.

Sam could feel blistering heat emanating from within himself, his chest beginning to burn with rage at the sight of the lost below.

"Sam ... you're smoking," Dylan pointed out, waving his hand through the heat waves and smoke rising off of Sam's back.

Sam looked down at his hand. Waves of heat poured out from the pores of his skin and, with them, the sensation of a surge of power. He clenched his fist, keeping the image of the dead ingrained in his mind. He'd never really had a reason to carry the anger he did. He'd been hurt in this life, yes. But even in good times, the anger had held its hooks in him. At least now he had somewhere to direct it this time. He wouldn't dare let this rage subside until he'd brought the maniac down at least.

"Good," he remarked.

"So, what's the plan?" Dylan asked, brushing off Sam's ominous reply.

Sam looked back over to the dome, straining his eye to sense. Two distinct lights shone across the street, a tannish brown one on top and one more familiar blue energy inside. "Victor's definitely in the dome."

"What's he doing? Why hasn't he fought back?" Dylan pointed out aggressively.

"I bet he can't," Sam started. "Just based on the fact that was once Penn Station, I think it's safe to say there's more than just Victor in there. He makes a move, then even if he won, life's over. The secret's out."

"So it's just us." Dylan scoffed. "Look at the size of that thing. Whatever his ability is, do you think we even stand a chance?"

Sam thought of all their options in his head. With a furrow of his brow, he handed Dylan one of the objects from the bag he carried at his side and then took a second one out of his pocket. "Not alone, we wouldn't."

● ● ●

Olivia shuddered, finding herself stuck in a tightly cramped space with no light whatsoever. All the while some psycho was going nuts with the very earth around them. Everyone around her all seemed to have the same idea, each of them taking out their phones in an attempt to illuminate the dark space.

Everyone inside could hear the screams from outside. They could all feel the ground shake again and again with no idea what was happening. Olivia could hear dozens of people crying out, and she couldn't blame them. They'd all been told they wouldn't live to see the next day.

She found herself tearing up too, knowing she had willingly followed someone she believed to have abilities into this mess. *How stupid could I be?* she asked herself.

She wondered where in the structure Victor was. And was he as scared as her? If he really had abilities, wouldn't he have done something already? She pounded on her head as she felt her chest growing tight. Had she really walked into her own death for no reason?

Yet, she could also argue, he wouldn't have used his abilities if he didn't want to be discovered. "Damn it," she whispered.

"Are you OK?" she heard a familiar voice call out, assuming it was directed at her.

No freaking way, she thought to herself. She had heard the voice numerous times on TV and in interviews.

"Victor Reliance?" she softly called back.

He waited a few moments to respond, as if processing who it was he had checked on. Suddenly, a light shined, being pointed at her face. She closed her eyes from the sudden blinding. "Of course, it's you," Victor muttered. "Did you really follow me all the way here?"

It was pointless to deny it. She had been caught red-handed. "Yes," she admitted.

"Why?" he questioned.

"You know why," she said ominously.

Victor made sure to keep the light off his face, worried his expression would give it all away. There was almost nothing else she could have been talking about besides the obvious answer. He chose his words carefully, "What are you talking about?"

"You know damn well what I'm talking about!" she replied aggressively. "You robbed my office of everything, all to stop me from writing the story. I know you took the phone."

Now Victor really was confused. "What fuckin' phone?"

Suddenly, the roof above opened up, the thick circular stone lowering to the ground with Tremor riding on top. Light filled the space, blinding those inside momentarily.

Tremor breathed out as he spoke. "Ah, what a rush. I haven't been able to cut loose like that in years. A little time to charge up, and the main act is soon to come." He walked to the emptiest section along the wall, squatting himself down into a criss cross position and closing his eyes.

The crowd leapt upward, quick to move out of his way and to the other end of the dome. Everyone huddled together, whispering among themselves.

"What do we do?"

"He's just sitting with his eyes closed."

"I wanna go home, Mom."

"We should attack while he's distracted," one man finally suggested. "This might be our only chance now that he's not paying attention."

Multiple others seemed to be on board with his half-cocked plan, pulled along like a stringed puppet by their urge to survive. "He's right," a number of them agreed.

"I wouldn't do that," Victor whispered, sitting against the wall, eyes trained on Tremor across the way. "We'll all die. You saw what he did to the station."

"We're all gonna die anyway if we don't do something!" the man half shouted back. "I ... I don't know what he is, but this isn't just rumors anymore, man. At least like this, even if it's the worst-case scenario, we can go out on our own terms." The man turned to face as much of the crowd as he could. "If we all rush him at once, there's no way he can take on all of us at once. Who's with me?" he finally asked.

"Don't do this," Victor pleaded.

The vast majority of the crowd nodded their heads in response, all of them turning toward the scarred man on the other side of the dome. They stood themselves up, readying for a fight.

All at once, the multitude of the adults from the crowd raced forward, leaving the children they hoped to protect behind. All of them screamed out with every ounce of bravery they could muster. They ran with their fists cocked toward their currently blind captor.

Just as they were about to reach him, a thick wave of the ground shot upward, curving back down and swallowing almost half the crowd.

What was left of their makeshift battalion screamed out in terror this time, watching the ground reset to its original shape with a liquid-esque ripple, the ones swallowed up nowhere to be found.

Tremor sat still in his same spot, his eyes still closed. "Keep in mind, I only need a few of you. Another act like that, and I'll slaughter the lot of you till there's only one left." He shot Victor a quick glance as he said that, closing his eyes once more afterward.

Victor fell to his knees, gritting his teeth as he cursed himself for his lack of resolve. How many had died today because he wasn't ready to lose his life as a human being? Because he cared about his own life more than someone else's? *What would Dad say right now?* he wondered.

Finally standing up from his spot, Tremor grinned. "Now, for the final act." He rose his hands up into the air, and everyone within a mile could feel the rumbling deep within the ground—as if something more was about to happen.

● ● ●

In a huge blast of flames, the ceiling burst open. The eyes of everyone inside darted upward to see rubble bursting inward as Sam flew through, his fist still outstretched from his entry.

Falling through his makeshift entrance, Sam looked through the lenses of the helmets Victor had designed. Their slick red and black design was perfect for hiding their faces during a fight.

Sam looked down at the crowd, seeing Tremor stood a distance in front of them all. Feeling rage flooding through him once again, he tensed his body and prepared for battle.

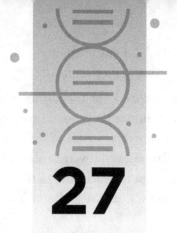

27

MAKE ME FIGHT FOR IT

S am came crashing through the top of the dome, shattered rubble falling all around him and heading straight for the crowd below. *"Now!"* Sam yelled out, his voice garbled courtesy of Victor's helmets.

He flipped himself over in the air to look upward, eyeing the smoking red rope shooting towards him. Reaching out and grabbing it, he yanked hard and twisted himself around again.

On the other end of the rope was Dylan, shooting downward at incredible speed thanks to Sam's throw. He quickly maneuvered through the rubble through careful wall placements before slamming down into the ground, shooting his hands into the air without a moment's hesitation. He winced in pain after stretching out his not-quite-broken but incredibly sore, smoke-enveloped arm.

Heaps of red smoke erupted out of his palms, shaping itself into a dense enough shield to protect all the civilians. He audibly groaned as he felt the backlash of the rubble hitting the hastily made construct.

Victor sighed in relief at the sight of the two of them.

Sam landed just outside the field of debris, trusting in Dylan to handle the rubble. He stood not ten feet from Tremor, who just grinned at the situation. "What the hell do you have to smile at!?"

Sam shouted, smoke rising off his shoulders from the rage he held in his chest.

"Who doesn't love a flashy entrance?" Tremor cackled. "Plus, I was beginning to think this was gonna be smooth sailing the whole way through. No achievement means anything unless it's fought for." He squatted himself low, his arms outstretched at his sides as he readied himself. "So? *Make me fight for it!*"

The two of them bolted toward each other, catching the other's respective attack with an aggressive growl. They traded blow after blow, shock waves erupting outward from the sheer force of their collisions. The crowd watched from within the red orb as the two men shot around the dome at inhuman speeds.

Neither Sam nor Tremor had yet resorted to using their abilities, the both of them still gauging their enemy's capabilities one step at a time.

Bring his off arm up to block Tremor's right-hook, Sam jetted his right fist forward towards his exposed jaw, finding himself forced to adjust his actions based on the sight of Tremor's leg curling up in front of him and preparing to straight kick and place some distance between the two of them.

Bringing his own leg up, Sam found himself agreeing some distance would be best for the moment, so after planting his foot onto Tremor's own, Sam pushed off at the same time as him, their combined strength sending each other skidding away from one another.

As soon as he found his footing, Sam sent his flames into the tips of his toes, bursting him forward in an attempt to catch his opponent off guard.

Twisting his body around, he angled his shin to come down onto the back of his opponent's neck as he soared over him.

With a chuckle, Tremor reached up and grabbed onto Sam's ankle as he closed in, thrashing him to the side and hurling him toward the wall of the dome, where he smashed in with a large crash of crumbled stone.

Shit, he's strong, Sam thought to himself, shaking his grogginess off as quickly as possible. *He's almost on par with Victor.*

Pulling himself from the groove in the wall, Sam crouched down, tensing his legs with all the strength he could send their way. Without even using burst movement, Sam launched forward with enough power to dig up the ground below him.

Flying toward Tremor, he watched his opponent tense his torso in preparation. Improvising in the moment, Sam threw his legs forward and stuck his hands into the air, releasing two simultaneous blasts to propel him into the ground and using his existing momentum to skim across the ground and slide right between Tremor's legs.

Coming to a quick halt just behind him, Sam prepped to launch his fist upward into his opponent's back, instead looking up to feel an elbow swinging into the blind spot of his right eye.

The solid point connected into the side of his helmet's cheek, shattering some of the metallic materials that made up its surface and sending him spinning from the sheer force; it almost felt like he'd been hit by solid stone. Using the momentum of the spin Tremor had sent him into, Sam planted his hands on the ground and let loose a quickly stockpiled force of flames from the tip of his foot as he pivoted his left leg around into a boosted roundhouse to his foe's unguarded chin.

Tremor stumbled a few steps before looking back at Sam with a bloody grin. Wiping the blood from his lip, he threw his arms out to his sides. The stone he stood on liquified and slid up his legs, eventually making its way onto his fists before solidifying once again around them.

With that same maniacal grin that only added to Sam's growing rage, Tremor began to walk toward him with readied fists.

Sam stood back up and met him halfway, jetting his right arm in the hopes of landing the first blow of the trade.

With a swift duck of the head and pivot of the body, Tremor evaded the fist and threw his own stoned one upward into Sam's gut.

Clenching his jaw and reeling the oncoming stomach ache in as best as possible, Sam twisted his torso and sent his elbow down into Tremor's collarbone.

Buckling from the pressure somewhat, Tremor felt his body shake with excitement. Finally, a worthy opponent who could trade blows back and forth with him. He looked up to Sam's torso twisting back to normal and waited till the moment his head reached its usual spot to stomp his foot down and force his solid head upward into his already damaged helmet.

Staggering from another impact to the head, Sam felt his chest warm with festering anger that continued to push him forward. He swung his head back down to look at Tremor before tucking his balled fists close to his chest and ducking low, pivoting from side to side as he inched closer. As he closed the distance, Sam lit his ready hands ablaze, packing the power as tightly into his hands as he could.

Tremor raised his hand up flat before Sam could reach him, pulling dozens of small stones free from the ground and rocketing them toward Sam from all directions.

From foot to foot, leaping from side to side, back and forth and every which way in between, Sam burst around with everything he had to avoid the hailstorm of stone.

Finally, he burst forth with such force the stones around him began to sizzle, coming to an abrupt stop just before Tremor with a look of power lain across his face that Tremor had only ever seen on King.

Sam couldn't help but think back to Hartley's words. "You're only seeing the first available move, and it's narrowing your focus."

For some reason, the words now clicked in Sam's head. In every fight he'd ever been in, he'd gone for the finishing shot right from the get-go, without even thinking out what would happen if it didn't work.

Well, here was his chance.

Thinking as fast as he could, he planned out his next few moves, also allowing himself time to imagine a retaliation. Bursting an erupting plume of controlled flames from his elbows one after the other, Sam rocketed his condensed, flame-cloaked fists up into

Tremor with a powerful roar to signal the start of his planned course of attack.

First, a one-two-three combo into his gut starting from his lead hand, the impact of which forced Tremor to lean over in pain.

Next, a boosted knee upward into his nose since the last attack had nearly hunched him to his knees—an action that sent Tremor's head flinging back into an exaggerated stumble.

Finally, starting into a sprint, Sam leapt upward and swung his cloaked fist back, only racing it forward once again when he knew he had a clear shot on Tremor's chest.

Finishing his planned barrage, Sam watched as Tremor skidded across the ground, coming to an abrupt stop, letting loose chilling cackles as he brought himself back to his feet.

"I can't get enough of this." Tremor cackled. "That's not all you've got, right?"

It felt like flames filled the inside of his chest as Sam looked the lunatic standing before him in the eyes. And when he did, it was just like that first night back, when he'd gone against Mikhael. His soul seemed to leak out of him and reveal his true nature to him, and this man before him was just as much a monster as that creature was.

Maybe even more.

Sending his flames down into his feet, Sam burst forward with a growling roar that echoed within the dome. As he raced forth, approaching Tremor with incredible velocity, he stuck his rigid elbow out.

An eruption of dust scattered within the dome, the crowd straining to see through the thick cloud irritating their eyes.

Slowly, they could see the silhouettes of the two appear.

Sam had crashed into Tremor with enough force to continue into the wall behind them, crumbling several layers of the stone. He held his elbow rigid in place, until his eyes went wide at the sight of the sheet of stone stuck between the two of them.

Another boom then echoed out, causing Tremor to look over and see that Dylan had burst through the side of the dome, leading the rest of the hostages out.

"*Go!*" he shouted with an aggressive wave.

Victor stood in the crowd as it raced out of the new hole, staring at Dylan. Dylan returned his look, knowing what Victor was thinking. He nodded toward the hole, urging Victor to get out.

There was nothing he could do that wouldn't give everything away.

With a loud shout, a fist of stone shot through the sheet and slammed into Sam's chest, rocketing him backward. Bouncing off the ground skip after skip, Sam found himself landing on a less solid surface than he expected. He looked back to find that Dylan had raced over to catch him.

"You OK?" Dylan asked.

Tremor slammed his hands down onto the ground, quickly closing back up the exit Dylan had created, trapping the unlucky few who weren't fast enough to make it out.

• • •

Olivia burst out of the dome, racing to the huge perimeter of law enforcement stationed nearby. She couldn't help but look back. She'd just seen something she knew was going to change everything the whole world knew. Through the crowd, she could see Victor running out with them all, looking back at the dome himself.

Had she been wrong? Had she really gotten herself into a life-or-death situation for no reason at all?

• • •

Victor finally made his way past the police barrier and was quickly taken to a fleet of ambulances for medical care. Not that he needed it—he'd had his armor ready underneath his clothes the whole time.

Yet, he hadn't done anything. He'd resigned himself to let everyone in that dome die as long as his secret was safe. He'd … fallen. Was his life as a human so important it should cost other people their own?

As he sat in the back of the ambulance, he stared at the dome. "Did I do the right thing?" he quietly asked himself.

• • •

Sam and Dylan stood side by side as they faced down Tremor, who's expression had shifted to a twisted portrayal of anger. The ground beneath his feet rippled in an almost liquid-like fashion as he groaned in frustration.

"Now you've done it," he muttered. Faster than the both of them could see, the ground beneath Tremor exploded. And before they could even finish their blink, Tremor appeared in front of the two of them with his leg cocked back. As a thick layer of stone wrapped itself around his shin, he shot his leg forward with all his might.

With almost no time to spare, Dylan reflexively shoved Sam out of the way just as the thick stone leg planted itself into his chest. He burst backward, slamming into the wall behind them.

Pulling himself out of the wall, Dylan thanked his lucky stars he'd had enough time to put up a thin shield along his chest, or he would have been looking at a much different outcome.

Sam and Dylan's initial goal upon coming in was to free the hostages as quickly as possible. With that many people waiting to be collateral damage, Sam couldn't cut loose as much as he needed. Picking himself back up from the ground, Sam burst forth in a highly condensed blast of flame, careful not to burn any of the remaining civilians.

Tremor steeled his front side, readying himself to grab Sam out of the air again once he was close enough. With Sam in midair and no foreseeable way to evade, it seemed to Tremor this was a checkmate for one of the two.

Sam grinned, releasing two smaller explosions out of his hands to propel him up and over Tremor. Flipping over the top of his head, Sam extended his leg outward, wrapping it in a cloak of flames before propelling it forward with a quick blast.

"*Here's this back!*" he yelled out as he hammered his shin into the back of Tremor's neck, rocketing him forward.

Letting out grunts of pain as he skidded across the ground, Tremor nearly gasped as he rolled right into position of Dylan's smoke-clad fist. Clobbering him right into the ground, the impact sent out another shock wave that shook the foundation of the structure.

Dylan leapt back over to Sam's side. "Think that'll do it?" he asked.

"Doubtful," Sam remarked as he pointed out the shifting of the ground around Tremor.

As it liquified in nature once more, the ground wormed its way onto his body, lifting him back up to his feet as it hardened itself back to normal around him. With only his head visible from within his armor of stone, Tremor thought back, back to when he'd first been told about these three.

● ● ●

"I'll now be assigning your individual target," King announced. "And I want to stress, absolutely no contact is to be made until the day of unveiling."

Tremor stood in the crowd of elites, each one handpicked by King over the last decade or so. Tremor himself had only been recruited less than two years ago, making him the newest besides Atom.

Including himself, there were nine elites gathered.

They all looked at the folder full of information on their targets. Every one of them was hypothesized to soon undergo full awakening if they hadn't already in the two months since the Day of Light.

"I want every subject monitored day in and day out, every choice they make analyzed, and every action recorded and relayed back to me," King continued.

After listening to him finish his brain-numbing spiel, his officers proceeded to exit the main hall.

"Tremor, Overcharge, stay and chat with Mimic and I," he boomed.

The two gave one another a look of confusion, before slowly strolling back into the great room.

"You're telling them?" Mimic questioned in his usual snarky tone.

"I believe the insight is crucial for what's to come for them. The three of you will have a slightly different mission than the rest. The rest of the soldier's subjects have already left the incubation chamber, secretly reintegrating themselves back into society. Yet ... each of your subjects still lies there to this day, a full month longer than the previous ones," he told them.

Tremor and James gave their leader a perplexed look.

"But even the longest incubation period of the elites was less than two months. What does that mean?" James blurted out.

"I believe these three will be of a different caliber than we've yet to see, which is why you three who have been assigned to them will be given a secondary objective depending on the outcome." King waited a moment before continuing, adamant he had their attention. "Whereas most of the others have been ordered to let their subjects rot with the humans with what time they have left should they refuse, a few candidates, including yours, if they should happen to deny salvation, will need to be disposed of. Before they mature enough to hinder our plans."

"Whoa," Tremor said. "I thought we were trying to recruit people, not get rid of good candidates. Why these three specifically?"

"Call it intuition. I can feel their power growing even from here, and they haven't even awoken yet. Plus ..." King then began to fill the two of them in on an exclusive secret only known by himself, Mimic, and two others before that day.

"No fucking way," Tremor shouted.

"How do you know that though!? How is it even possible?" James shouted.

"It matters not how I know. The point is, these are the facts. When they were recovered from the ruins, I myself had no idea the blast would have this effect on them. I'll admit, the three of them were a miscalculation on my part," King explained. "But ... science doesn't scare. It analyzes and adapts. And I've incorporated their presences into our plans."

"You really think they'll be that much of a threat to us?" Mimic questioned, almost feeling insulted.

"I do," King assured. "For at the very least, these three are ..."

28

BLACKOUT

"**A**-class," Tremor murmured, finishing his memory.

"What?" Sam questioned.

"That's what he said you'd be. I just didn't expect him to be right."

Sam and Dylan gave each other a look of confusion, neither of them having any idea what A-class meant.

"When you say he … do you mean this King guy?" Sam asked.

Tremor's eyes went wide, quickly turning into another look of anger. "Seems like Overcharge did more than just fail his objective."

Dylan looked at Sam in shock. "You saw Overcharge!?"

"It's a long story. Let's wrap things up here, and then we can talk about that, and about your own encounter," Sam told him. He glanced over at the group of civilians huddled on the other end of the dome; them being in here was gonna be a pretty big handicap.

Tremor's anger seemed to leak out of him, the ground around him rumbling in tune with his heart. "You think … you can just 'wrap things up,' just like that?"

In a matter of seconds, his stone armor flowed up and over his head, leaving him encased in its solidly thick humanoid shape.

He released a deep exhale, and the stone around him thinned out, increasing its flexibility as it lightened its protection around his joints and added that extra material to the stone armor plates all over his body. After a few seconds, he cracked his neck from side to side, crouching down into his battle position.

"Well, just fuckin try it!"

Seeing Tremor inch forward and dig his heavy foot into the stone below, Sam and Dylan burst toward him in unison. Every step they took left imprints in the ground, whipping dust up into the air.

As they closed in on one another, Tremor leapt upward, coming back down to slam his stone fists into the ground, his insane strength sending thick, widening cracks beneath Sam and Dylan's footing.

Seeing the ground open up below them, revealing the growing pieces of crushed bodies that had been buried underneath, Dylan focused on the large opening. Quickly, he halted his movement and threw his hands out, flooding his smoke into the large crags and slowly creating a sheer surface across the now altered flooring; both for their benefit in this altercation, but also because he didn't know well he could fight with the urge to purge his stomach bearing down on him.

He then turned to Sam's back, creating a thick wall behind him. *"Here's a boost!"*

Dylan shoved the wall forward, sending Sam shooting forth with the combined speed of his own and the walls.

Moving as fast as he was, Sam had no time to think of his next attack. He simply ignited his hand and swung it back as he prepared for impact.

Sam fist collided with Tremor's chest before he could raise his defenses, sending out a shock wave from the sheer force of the destructive impact. Sam couldn't help but think how natural this all felt at that moment, like this was what he was meant to do with himself, with all that anger he kept bottled up inside that just sat and waited for its chance to claw its way to the surface.

Jumping back, Sam patted around his arm to put out his burning sleeve. He peered through the dust to see if they'd managed to do any serious damage.

"Damn," he muttered, seeing Tremor picking himself back up through the dust. The parts of his armor that Sam had collided with had simply thickened themselves to increase his defense.

Tremor shouted out, clapping his thick armored hands together with an ear-ringing boom. Thick stone pillars shot out of the inside of the dome, racing downward at Sam and Dylan from all sides.

Side to side, they dodged, feeling the impacts of each pillar resonating and echoing in the tight space. They did their best to weave around to the opposite side of the dome and away from the civilians.

On the outside of the dome, the ground surrounding the structure began to dip inward, forming a moatlike gap around the perimeter.

Sam burst around the room, nearly being crushed every time he had to stop and redirect himself. It seemed like the pillars were beginning to speed up. Glancing over at Tremor, he could see him straining despite the armor surrounding him.

He's pushing himself, Sam thought. *Guess I gotta do the same.*

Stopping quickly to change direction, Sam attempted to increase his speed through faster stockpiling of flame, unable to stop thinking about everyone counting on the two of them to get them home. He could feel his innately high temperature rise within him as he kept his growing anger clutched tightly in his chest.

Dylan shot out wall after wall, pushing himself out of the way just quickly enough to avoid Tremor's barrage.

This isn't working," he told himself. He thought about his options, knowing they needed to actually get an attack in if they were gonna have any hope of stopping the attacker.

As he continued to form construct after construct, he thought to himself, *This is quite a bit of smoke, I've never been able to put out this much before. Does it have to do with the pill? If I can put more smoke out than before, shouldn't I be able to put more power into my individual attacks?*

Straining more than before, Dylan tried to add more smoke to each wall he created, shoving it outward with more force than before. Extending his hand out, he sent a wall up at an incoming pillar, shattering it before it could get too far off the ceiling of the dome.

He grinned. "There we go."

Around and around they moved, dodging and destroying the pillars as they came at them, slowly but surely moving closer to the source of the attack—all the while trying to keep the crowd out of harm's way.

Dylan glanced over at Sam, who seemed to be working on something himself. He'd been bouncing around from spot to spot, when he suddenly halted his movement, right below a pillar heading for him at incredible speed.

"*Sam!*" Dylan screamed, stuck blocking his own share of attacks and unable to get to him.

The pillar raced down, seeming to suddenly screech to a halt just above Sam's head.

Straining his eyes, Dylan couldn't help but chuckle. As worried as he was, Dylan remembered just how much Sam could improve in the middle of battle. The pillar hadn't simply stopped; Sam had stopped it and was continuing to melt it just before it reached him.

Without even moving a finger.

Tremor gritted his teeth, sending every pillar hurtling towards Sam.

With a gesture of his hand, the air around Sam began to ripple, and waves of steam and smoke rose off his body as a whole. One by one, the pillars came to abrupt stops, Sam's aura of heat melting them into molten liquid at his feet.

"Don't worry," he called out to Dylan, who was still staring in disbelief. "I'm on the verge of figuring something out."

Dylan figured Sam had thought of some way to use his abilities without risk to the people around them. The barrage of pillars finally came to a close, and the constant outpour of energy finally caught up to Tremor, winding him momentarily.

They both watched as Tremor fell to his knee, letting out ragged, skipping breaths as he tried to recover from his fatigue.

He hadn't ever used his ability this consecutively before.

Dylan looked back at Sam. "Follow my lead?"

"You got it," Sam said gruffly, not taking his eye off their opponent for even a moment.

The two of them faced Tremor together, preparing to finally put an end to this horrible day. They both looked on as Tremor reached his feet, and despite his heavy labored breathing, he looked as though he had steeled himself to continue on regardless. He'd never experienced a fight like this in his life, and he wasn't about to let it slip away because he was a little out of breath.

This was the challenge he'd been craving.

As Tremor glanced at the state of his armor, Dylan saw his chance. He bolted forward with a little help from a foothold meant to propel him forward faster. Wrapping smoke along his forehead, Dylan swung his solid head down and headbutted Tremor.

Staggering from the impact, Tremor struggled to place his focus back onto Dylan. He felt his body shudder from another impact in the base of his chest and yet another in the side of his ribs. Finally forcing his eyes open, he helplessly watched as Dylan landed enhanced blow after blow, coating his every attack in an increasingly thicker layer of smoke.

Almost hardening the smoke into a pure solid.

What was left of Tremor's stone armor began to crack and chip. He felt pieces of it stripped away under the barrage of Dylan's consecutive attacks.

"Now!" Dylan yelled out, immediately leaping out of the space between Sam and Tremor.

"On it!" Sam remarked.

Already crouched low, Sam felt his aura of heat in the space around himself. Metaphorically grabbing ahold of it, he pulled the waves of heat in and cloaked himself in its energy, feeling a surge of power coursing through him.

Exactly how Tremor had at the beginning of the encounter, Sam burst forward with such speed and power that the ground he stood on crunched upward. His body raced forward so fast the flames propelling him forward seemed to burn like jet engines.

Appearing before a dazed Tremor in the blink of an eye, Sam looked down upon the crazed maniac responsible for the deaths of hundreds in only a matter of hours. He threw his arms outward, igniting his open palms as quickly as he could. With another wave of his blazing hands, the air around Tremor burst into an intensely rotating sphere of flames, swirling around him as it attempted to hold him in place.

"*Switch!*" he screamed.

Seeing a pathway into the inferno slowly start to open up at the base, Dylan pointed his hands forward, flooding them with the vast amounts of smoke he was still able to produce.

With but a thought, the smoke immediately started spinning around his flexed hands, speeding up until it reached a violent swirling motion. Dylan kept the image of the beam he'd produced during their altercation with Mikhael a few days ago vivid and fresh in his mind, doing his utmost to properly reproduce its results.

Watching the red glow in his hands intensify, Dylan subtly pushed his hands forward, releasing the heaping amounts of energy he held as easily as one would blink. The beam raced forward just in time to meet the fully opened entrance into the inferno Sam had conjured, heading straight for an unsuspecting Tremor, who still had his hands full constantly recoating the stone armor before it melted onto him.

Pure hateful anger plowed into Tremor's armored torso, forcing him back into the dome wall from its consistently powerful onslaught. If he hadn't been in direct contact with as much earthen material as he was, he knew this attack would have instantly rubbled his armor to bits. Yet luckily for him, despite its challenge, he was able to keep a constant influx of stone running into the armor, repairing it just as quickly as Dylan's attack could damage it.

Though he'd found a way around it this time, its toll was beginning to take effect. He could feel his armor's repairing slowing bit by bit.

As the barrage finally came to a close, and the intense red light finally dwindled, Dylan fell to his own knees in exhaustion.

He felt something drip onto his arms. Reaching up, he felt the blood pouring out of his nose. "Guess I still overdid it a bit," he muttered.

Breathing deep as he slowly stepped away from the wall, Tremor's skin trembled with excitement. He stared straight into Sam and then Dylan's eyes before giving them a smile they'd never forget. With a quick, powerful motion, he outstretched his arm toward the awestruck civilians.

Before that day, the craziest thing the collection of variously aged individuals had ever experienced were drunken bar fights; over-the-top high school drama; and for a select few, the baffling realization that there was no Santa Claus.

With a loud grunt from Tremor, dozens of tire sized chunks of concrete erupted out of the ground, all rocketing at the dozens of people experiencing the worst day of their lives. Each one of them was overwhelmingly gripped by fear at the thought that now it was going to be their last.

Sam and Dylan screamed out, the both of them launching forward with everything they had. As time seemed to slow around them both, they watched as the large stones moved in slow motion toward their targets.

Sam shot as big a burst of flame as he could muster on short notice, grabbing Dylan's arm as he rocketed forward. He flung the both of them as close as he could as fast as he could. But even as fast as he was, and as powerful as they both were, it made no difference.

Sam looked into the eyes of a young boy staring back at his own, watching as a single tear flowed down his cheek just before everything went black for him.

Neither of them would ever forget the screams they heard the first time they ever truly failed.

Screeching to a stop and falling to the ground just before the bloody mess of their failure, they both just stared forward. Neither of them was able to look away from the sight of the people they had let down, dozens of innocent people who would never see the light of day again.

Dylan shifted his helmet up, unable to hold back the urge to empty his churning stomach. He had never seen such an intensely horrific scene. It was even worse than when they'd made their way through Light Valley. The image and severity of it would remain engraved in his eyes for the rest of his life.

Sam sat deathly still, deep warming breaths running out of his mouth. He stared at the scene before him, a bloody gruesome mess, the likes of which he'd only seen once before. Flashes of images ran through his mind, of a young boy's arm pushing open closet doors— only to find the mangled mess that was his parents' bodies.

Thick waves of heat rose off of his back as he let out a deep breath of air so hot it was visible to the naked eye.

"I told them they were unnecessary," Tremor cackled raggedly. "Hostages were nothing more than an insurance policy to buy me some time. They were little better than trash as it was."

Sam's body jolted, a burning feeling filling his lungs as he slammed his head into the ground with such force it dug into the solid earth. He groaned as he felt something taking place within himself.

"Sam? What's going on!?" Dylan frantically asked, wiping the vomit from his lips.

Swinging his head back upward with a powerful roar that rumbled the foundation of the structure, Sam let loose the biggest dose of firepower he'd ever created before, releasing it from his mouth in the form of a raging beam of pure destructive force that raced toward the top of the dome.

Dylan screamed out as he threw up a shield, immediately blinded by the intense blaze that only continued to grow.

In all the time he'd had his abilities, he'd never held back such a destructive force. It was taking everything he still had in the tank to keep his defenses up. He could feel the sheer force moving him back, his toes digging into the earth as he held on.

When he finally felt the force of the blaze die down, Dylan slowly looked forward, finding Sam now standing with his hands out at his sides as he faced Tremor. Most of his shirt had been singed off, leaving only tattered remains held together by fraying threads. He crouched low as he growled out in anger toward Tremor's direction.

His helmet had been blown clean off his head, revealing that both his eyes had turned to a bright, white-hued orange, further accentuated by fluttering flames billowing from them both. Even the scar along his eye had begun to glow faintly.

His every breath was so hot it began to heat the tight space around them.

Glowing orange veins glistened through the remains of his clothing, their sheer heat starting to slowly burn away what remained of his shirt. They traced his body all the way down to his forearms, where they and his hands had begun to glow bright white with blistering heat.

Dylan's face twisted into a look of pained realization. The more he found out about Sam, the more he learned about what he'd had to go through in this life. But as he witnessed the sight of Sam's heavily scarred torso, he realized that they still hadn't even scratched the surface.

Slowly, waves of heat started to float around the entirety of the small area, until Dylan could feel sweat dripping from his forehead like a faucet.

"Sam?" Dylan quietly reached out.

Letting out another loud roar, Sam burst forth faster than Dylan had ever seen him go, erupting up a boulder-sized chunk free from the ground from where he had stood.

Dylan was stunned. What the hell was happening?

He thought back onto everything Sam had ever told him about himself, remembering one key phrase he had said. *"I have a tendency to black out somewhat in really intense situations."*

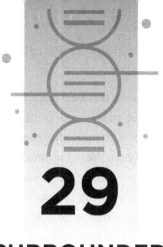

29

SURROUNDED

A few minutes earlier

Victor couldn't peel his eyes off the dome, his mind racing as he thought about what could possibly be happening in there. He'd already refused medical attention from EMTs, keeping his armor at the ready if he might be needed. But even now, he questioned if he could bring himself to do it.

He glanced at the hundreds of people still within the first layer of the police barricade, their own eyes glued to the testament of how little they knew about the world.

This was it. No more rumors on social media, no more whispers heard along the streets; the whole world would hear about what had happened today.

He could see that the reporter had managed to make it out all right. Olivia, as he heard what looked to be her cameraman call her. The both of them had exchanged intensely teary hugs when they'd first found each other, quickly wiping their tears and beginning to unload a few cases out of his van—no doubt preparing to be the first ones to tell the world.

They'd have to work fast. Between the civilians with their camera phones and the dozens of news vans pulling to a stop outside the blockade, they were in for a struggle for the first word.

With no warning, Victor heard several loud, screeching noises ring out on all sides of the dome. He jerked his head around to see dozens of military vehicles coming to a stop within the cordoned-off area, dumping out hundreds of armed soldiers, who fell into a circle unit formation around the entirety of the stone structure. All of their guns rose up and trained themselves on their target in unison, as if connected to one another by a hive mind.

As a final truck pulled up to the scene, it turned itself around, reversing its back end toward the dome. The truck's landing pad slowly rolled open, setting itself on the ground and creating an exit for the tall brute of a man who emerged from within.

"Oh fuck," Victor muttered to himself.

He'd heard that the military had pulled its presence out of the city relatively quickly after the bombing, an ultimately strange occurrence, given that the bomb could have been the work of any number of terrorist organizations.

But now it was beginning to make sense. It wasn't that they had left the city. They must have been lying wait in hiding, waiting to see if there would be a secondary attack.

And just how right they were.

"Fucking Starsk," Victor said gruffly through a frantic expression. He recognized the man from his numerous dealings with Reliance Industries and its technological patents the government was currently working on procuring.

Colonel Garret Starsk of the United States Army offloaded the landing pad, coming to a halt as he stared intently at the earthen structure.

"And the bureaucrats said it was over, huh?" He spoke gruffly through his thick, graying mustache, its fine tapered lines sitting just above his lips and extending no farther than the sides of his mouth.

"All right, soldiers," he began.

Yet before he could even finish his sentence, an ear-deafening roar rang out from within the dome, followed by a raging plume of flames ripping through the outer extremities of the dome and rising high into the once clear blue sky. The force of the blast cracked several large chunks of the stone free from its greater whole and dropped them to ground with numerous large gusts of rubble and dust.

The crowd below uncovered their eyes as they stared up in horror, watching the flames finally die down and wither into smolders. They could all feel immense heat radiating out from whatever was inside.

Victor's face sunk at the realization that had been Sam's voice, and this heat filling the air couldn't have been coming from anybody else.

"Come on, guys," he whispered, feeling his eyes begin to tear up from his own lack of resolve to stand up and help.

● ● ●

Sam's enormously dense fist of flame connected into Tremor's jaw, instantly dislodging it from its usual connection point. The stone armor around his head shattered like glass as he rocketed back into the wall of the dome with such force he found himself lodged in its gripping embrace.

Before he even had a chance to regain his wits, he felt a scalding hot hand grip the stone armor over his shoulder, yanking him free from the wall and tossing him at the ground like a softball.

Sam roared out with such force that shock waves bounded off the innards of the dome. His flames finally finished burning through the exceptionally tattered remains of his shirt as he bellowed out, revealing him in his current monstrous entirety. Orange glow emanated out of the several enlarged veins running around his chest and arms, converging within the center of his chest and illuminating the numerous scars and burns across his torso.

He reset his sights onto his target as he exhaled another deep, visible breath.

Tremor blinked over and over, trying to unblur his vision, turning back to face the beast-like thing behind him as he crudely crunched his jaw back into place. "What ... the hell?" he rasped out slowly.

Shooting up into the air in a streak of flames, Sam shattered the space beneath his feet as he impacted on the top of the dome above Tremor. Immediately crouching down, he tensed his legs once more, kicking off and shooting downward at an almost untraceable velocity. Wrapping both his lower legs with an intense cloak of flame, he twisted his body around and aimed his heels for where Tremor knelt.

Unable to shake the sight's reminiscence of a racing meteorite, Dylan watched his friend plummeting toward the earth in a blazing light. He noticed that the glow of his once gentle orange flame seemed to brighten the farther he dropped. Dylan couldn't believe what he was seeing. Was this really Sam? Was the incredibly kind person he had known capable of turning into such a feral being, as if he was an animal?

Tremor just barely managed to get out of the way by using the ground beneath himself to throw himself clear.

Sam hit the ground with his powerful legs, the incredible heat he held beneath the surface of his skin making deep divots in the ground with his landing.

Dylan seemed to watch in slow motion as Sam leapt out of the crater he'd made, the lower half of his pants sizzling as he continued to make his way toward Tremor. The air in the dome had gotten so hot it had actually become somewhat hard to breathe, making it even harder for Dylan, who already found himself frozen in shock, to move.

Sam's feet had started to melt the ground beneath him with every step as he walked toward his opponent, watching him slowly recoat the stone armor on his face.

They both exploded forward, gearing up to trade blows.

Just before they connected, Sam seamlessly burst to the side and then immediately reappeared a distance behind Tremor. Holding his clenched fists high above his head, he packed them full of a massive amount of energy, and with a roar, he slammed them down into the ground.

Hearing a quick rumble beneath his feet, Tremor looked down just in time to see a geyser of magmatic stone and flames bursting out of the stone flooring, scorching him and his armor as it propelled him upward.

He screamed out as he felt the volcano-like eruption begin to melt through the armor he'd once believed invincible. Feeling the eruption die down after a few moments, he found himself grabbed once more by gravity's hold and beginning to fall back downward.

He couldn't believe what was happening. This couldn't have been the same inexperienced pup he'd fought not even ten minutes ago. He was being overpowered—and by only one of them.

Where had all this power suddenly come from?

Just before hitting the ground, Sam burst forward and cranked his flaming fist right into Tremor's gut, rocketing him back with a blazing shock wave. He dragged up chunks of the earth as he skidded across the ground before finally crashing to a halt on the wall of the dome.

Tremor found himself brushing with unconsciousness as he felt the impact of himself falling to the floor.

Sam breathed deeply. The hot, visible breaths freely flowing from his mouth began to ignite themselves and now to shift to bright orange flames frothing out the sides.

He looked down at his hand, and after a moment of concentration, set it ablaze.

Yet, unlike anything he'd done before, he struggled with the properties of his flame. Until finally, the flame stretched out, forming a solid, almost bladelike structure around his lower arm. Its intense heat sizzled the dust floating around them.

With a swift downward motion of his arm, the blazing blade swiftly sliced through the ground like a knife through butter, leaving a red-hot slash mark in its wake.

Dylan's eyes went wide, he knew just from the looks of the attack Sam had brought out that it wasn't one intended to incapacitate. He sprung up from his knees, seeing Sam begin to race forward. He ran with all he had and placed himself between the two.

"*Sam, stop!*" he screamed while grabbing onto his shoulders and attempting to hold him back. He shouted out in aggravation as he felt the flesh on his palms begin to boil.

Shrugging it off as best he could, he tightened his grip, determined not to let his friend do something he'd regret.

With his unlit hand, Sam shoved Dylan to the ground before continuing to walk forward. He snarled as he looked upon his enemy, who was still reeling from his last attack.

With another swift motion, Dylan placed himself before Sam once more. "*Sam! Look at me!* Come on, man," he began. "You know this isn't you. What you're about to do … isn't you. Don't let whatever's happening change who you are, man."

Sam stood in front of him, blazing weapon still in hand, staring intently down at Dylan with his vicious, flaming eyes. His every muscle was tensed and ready for anything, and his expression was soaked with long-since-buried rage.

Dylan stared back, his arms falling down to his sides. "Would this be what your parents' wanted for you? For you to truly lose yourself?" he softly asked.

Sam's expression lightened. He seemed taken aback. Flashes of a man and a woman smiling at him appeared in his mind's eye, their mere presence bringing him unhindered peace.

Dylan watched as a single tear dropped from his working eye, hoping it was a sign he'd managed to get through to him somehow.

But then, the mental images of Sam's carefree, smiling times with his loving parents found themselves engulfed in raging flames, replaced by bloody images that flashed again and again in his head.

He saw the hundreds of people who'd lost their life to this cruel, unforgiving hellscape, either by the untold tragedies this world brought or even by his very own hand.

His parents.

Folks who'd protected him on the streets.

The three men he'd killed when he was younger.

His dog.

Everybody lost in Light Valley.

And now all these countless dozens of innocent bystanders.

Sam's lightened expression quickly found itself soaked with fierce anger once more. With an aggravated swing of his off hand, he made sure Dylan couldn't stop him again.

As he watched Dylan skid across the ground through the seeming passenger seat of his own eyes, Sam turned back forward, propelling himself toward Tremor with every ounce of power he had.

Forward he soared, the insurmountable heat he produced almost bending the air around them.

As Tremor secured his balance once more, he couldn't help but give a light smile as he watched a quick thrusting motion of Sam's flame-clad arm.

● ● ●

Dylan groggily pushed himself up off the ground, feeling intense aches course through both his head and body from the impact he'd had with it.

Shaking the last of his confusion off, his expression grew deathly serious before he jerked his head around. His eyes widened as he saw the heartbreaking scene before him.

● ● ●

The blackness Sam experienced gradually began to fade out, allowing him to slowly see the light through his own eye once more. Starting from a hazy pinhole, his vision subtly clearing up as a few more seconds passed.

He suddenly heard a wet cough of some kind, coming from somewhere incredibly close to him.

Slowly, the flames billowing from his mouth and eyes reduced to dying smolders, and the enlarged glowing veins across his arms and chest reduced themselves to their usual size, their eerie glow following close behind as they finally faded away.

As his body finally returned to its normal state, his blurred vision finally cleared, revealing to him what he had done.

His eye instantly began to flood with tears as he let out light trembling quivers, looking down to see his flame-cloaked arm plunged through Tremor's armored chest. The wet cough he'd heard had been him choking on the blood pumping through his mouth.

"Well ... this isn't how I saw today going," Tremor suddenly rasped through the blood oozing out the sides of his lips.

Sam couldn't even bring himself to muster any words. He just took in numerous breaths that caught in his mouth as tears continued to flood down the side of his pained expression.

As quickly as he could, he put out the flaming structure on his arm, immediately coming to regret the decision as all the blood held at bay by the flame began to smother his skin. "Fuck ... fuck ... fuck," he managed to mutter, feeling his body begin to shake with shock.

Being as gentle as he could, he started to pull his arm out the man's torso bit by excruciating bit. Light whimpers loosed themselves from his lips as he watched Tremor jolt in pain in response to the movement of Sam's arm.

Finally, the tip of his fingers slipped out of the gaping hole he'd created.

Sam grabbed onto Tremor's shoulders as he started to lose his balance. Gently, he lay him down on the ground with trembling hands as he thought about how to stop the bleeding.

"No, no, no, no, no," Sam cried. "Please not again."

Dylan continued to watch his friend lose what little remained of his humanity, his own tears swelling up as he watched Sam slam his fists into his head again and again, hearing his heart-wrenching cries of regret ringing out and echoing through his ears.

"*Fuuuuck! Please no! Not again!*" He screamed so forcefully his throat ran raw.

Dylan felt his tears leave the crest of his eyelid and begin to pour down his own face as he picked himself up, hobbling over to his pained friend as quickly as he could.

Every cry Sam let out panged Dylan—hitting him in the center of his chest. He thought back to Sam's words. "It will take a piece of you that you will never get back."

Dylan came to a halt as he finally reached his belligerent friend, who just slowly looked up to meet his eyes, revealing the pain and regret searing into his expression. Dylan then looked down on Tremor, who still seemed to be struggling through his blood-soaked breaths.

Judging by the hole through his chest, there was no possible way he was going to make it through the day. It was astounding enough as it was that he was still able to cling to life with his organs plunged through.

"Sam ... we need to go," Dylan softly told him.

Sam looked back at him with his tear stained expression, "But ... I can't just ... leave him here."

All the anger Sam had felt had been blown away by burning regret at what he'd done. He hadn't forgotten what Tremor had done, but he knew now that he'd brought himself closer to being just as much a monster as Tremor was.

"There's nothing we can do," Dylan told him. "I guarantee you we're already gonna have our hands full trying to get out of here and past whatever is waiting outside. It's not like we can walk up and hand his body to the police. They will lock you up, whether or not you ki—"

He immediately cut himself off as he watched Sam's face grimace in anticipation of the word *kill*.

"They'll lock us up for what we are, Sam," he corrected.

Sam's head fell low. "I know."

Dylan grabbed Sam's shoulder, noticing that, despite the fact he wasn't scalding to the touch anymore, his body still seemed a great deal hotter than before. He pulled him up to his feet, beginning to lead him to the center of the dome below the small entrance they'd made in the top.

"Not … so fucking fast," they heard a weak voice rasp behind them.

Turning back, they saw Tremor inch his way back and prop himself up against the dome wall. His stone armor had completely chipped itself off of him, almost like he no longer had the energy to keep it in place. "You aren't leaving here … that easy."

Clapping his hands together once more, he forced out a maniacal cackle through his blood stained lips that echoed through the dome.

Tremor had already failed both his assigned tasks, having been unable to take his target out of the picture, and letting what would have been FEAR's second stronghold be taken back. The least he could do before he finally bit the dust was take these two down with his final breath.

"Let's all go to hell together now." He forced the words out with the last of his strength, and as they slipped through his curled smile, the light of life slowly faded from his eyes.

Suddenly, the dome shifted, followed by a thick rumbling running throughout its structure. All the holes in the dome's exterior quickly closed themselves off, sealing the remaining two in the pitch black.

• • •

The crowd formed along the police barricade all watched in horror as the dome started to lower itself into the ground.

Victor burst out of the ambulance, shoving his way through the crowd. He slammed his hands down onto the barricade, staring fearfully at the sinking structure.

Come on, guys, he pleaded in his head.

• • •

Dozens of thick cracks ran up the solid stone walls, slightly letting slips of light into the space. The whole structure jerked downward, continuing to slowly make its way lower.

"Are we sinking!?" Dylan blurted out.

Chunks of the top of the dome began to break loose, falling straight for them. Before they knew it, the dome in its entirety had begun to come crumbling down as its base sank lower and lower into the earth.

Dylan instinctually threw his arms up, projecting as thick a shield as he could muster. Unlucky for him, his countermeasure for overexertion had fizzled out of his system a while ago, and he could feel the blood drip from his nose down his front side. He screamed out in pain as the rubble piled up atop his slowly faltering shield construct.

Sam panicked. Their brief moment of light was quickly receding the farther down they sank, and before they knew it, darkness was closing in around them. He looked at Dylan as he stood as firm as he could beneath the rubble. If they couldn't get the debris off the top of Dylan's shield, there was no possible way they were gonna get out of here.

Dylan started to kneel, struggling with the large weight. He screamed out as he felt pops all throughout his body. *"I can't hold it much longer!"*

The already tight space was now forcing the both of them down to their knees as the rubble continued to settle downward.

Sam stepped in closer to Dylan with the only idea he could think of. *"This is gonna burn! Just hold on!"*

He threw his own arms up, and an engulfing wave of flames erupted within the rubble, continuing to grow in size and temperature at an alarming rate. The shrinking space around them quickly lit up as Sam steadily increased the flames' power.

● ● ●

The city braced as a bright inferno burst forth from the top of the seemingly sunken structure, its strange white hue brightening the slowly darkening sky.

Slowly, rubble started to flatten out, drips of molten liquid dripping off the crumbled stone and pooling up atop Dylan's shield. Even as much progress as that seemed to be, it made little difference.

Sam could see Dylan growing weaker by the second as he strained to keep hold of his construct. *It's not enough*, he told himself.

Keeping a consistent hold on his inferno above, Sam concentrated, reaching out for that strange power he'd felt earlier, needing as much of a boost in this moment as he could get. He felt that feeling of heat that innately enveloped the space around him. Pulling it in tightly, he felt its power course through his veins. Bright orange energy began to glow throughout the veins on his arms as he held the surge of energy within himself, sending every ounce of firepower he had upward.

His flame's sensation and its very appearance had now changed, shifting from its once bright orange to now sporting a strange whitish hue with it.

Ever since they'd woken up in that bunker, Sam had somewhat noticed his core temperature rising each day. He wondered how long it would be before he wouldn't be able to touch people anymore.

The inferno raged violently, rising high enough up into the sky that it could be seen from miles away. The rubble started to melt at an accelerated rate, turning to a lavalike substance before the crowd outside's eyes. Its heat quickly spread out, drastically raising the temperature of the surrounding area. Sweat poured down the faces of the civilians closest, as if they stood within throwing distance of an erupting volcano.

Dylan screamed as the heat scorched the palms of his hands even more than they already had been. It was taking everything he had to keep the shield intact.

Before he knew it, Sam looked up to see a vast pool of melted stone, its source material now completely depleted. "*OK, it's done*," Sam shouted. "*Open it from the center!*"

Dylan strained with every muscle he had in his body, slowly moving his hands away from each other. The shield up top began to open up from its center, dragging the molten rock along with it. Once it all had been pushed to their sides, they found themselves surrounded by a pool of red-hot liquid quickly closing in around them. Dylan fell to his knees, knocking his head on the ground as he went down.

"Dylan!" Sam shouted.

He dove over to him. Putting his ear to his mouth, he felt a wave of relief as he heard a ragged breath make its way out.

Sam could hear voices from outside the structure. Lucky for them, even though the top of the dome was gone, they had still sunk low enough that no one could see them.

That gave him a moment to prepare.

He could see Dylan's helmet and what remained of his own being submerged in the molten liquid, meaning he'd need some other way to hide their faces on their way out.

Throwing Dylan's hood over his unconscious head, he then ripped off one of his sleeves and tied it around his own face and head as a last ditch effort. He slung Dylan over his shoulder and crouched himself low in preparation. When he felt a sudden warmth at his feet, he looked down to see the magma had engulfed him up to his shins.

Yet, he didn't feel an ounce of pain.

He glanced back and took one last look at the man known as Tremor, watching as his lifeless body was slowly submerged in the molten lava.

Gathering every bit of energy he'd stored up, he sent it all down into his feet, launching the two of them up and onto the mound of earth along the sunken dome.

As his flame-engulfed bare feet gently touched down, he felt every organ in his body drop at the sight of the countless automatic firearms pointed directly at him.

Every one of the soldiers holding them screamed for him to get down on the ground and surrender himself. Their eyes strained with terror as they looked upon the seeming monster before them.

Sam caught sight of Victor through the crowd. He saw the same frantic fear in his expression as he watched his friend's face down the barrel of a gun.

Guilt constricted Victor's chest as he looked upon Sam's heavily scarred physique. Just how much had he been through even before life got as crazy as it had been lately?

"*Hold!*" the crowd heard a bass filled voice boom.

Colonel Starsk stepped through his ready and waiting line of soldiers. He took a few more steps before coming to a halt below the mound Sam stood upon, looking up at him in an effort to see his somewhat hidden face.

Sam did his best to keep it hidden by keeping his head low and turned toward Dylan's unconscious body. He could only hope his face was hidden as well.

"I'm Colonel Garret Starsk of the United States Army," he said, introducing himself. "Would you like to identify yourself?"

Sam just stayed silent, wondering what direction would be best to leap in when he found a moment.

"OK then. Neither of you seem to be the individual reported to have concocted this enormous structure," Starsk pointed out. "So where might he be?"

Sam felt a jolt in his chest, clenching his jaw tightly as he continued his silence.

"Can I take that as an answer then?" Starsk asked, pointing to the coating of blood on Sam's right arm.

Victor's heart dropped. He hadn't noticed the blood himself at first. *What the fuck happened in there!?* he screamed in his head, gripping the barricade till his knuckles were white.

Sam jerked his arm behind his back, his heart racing a million miles a minute as he faced down the might of an entire country. As his heartbeat continued to thump faster and faster, he suddenly felt an intense ache in his blinded eye. Some kind of warm feeling began to flutter through it, causing his vision to go haywire as it flashed between his normal vision and flickering flames amid an endless black space.

Two scenes overlapped again and again as he looked out on the crowd, one of numerous random people he'd never met before and the other three unmistakable multicolored flames of an ability-wielding individual.

A bright neon blue he seemed to recognize as Victor.

A dim magenta.

And a purplish-pink.

Between the vast crowd of people and the continuing aches in his right eye, though, he couldn't distinguish which ones they were.

He brought his free hand up, trying to put pressure on the ache, an action that only stoked the fires raging in the eager soldiers' hearts.

"*Don't fucking move!*" the collection of them shouted, readying a direct shot on his exposed chest.

"Settle down, settle down," Starsk ordered. "Let's not make this any worse than it has to be, all right?"

He glanced back at the crowd of rescued hostages huddled behind the police barricades.

"I've heard a few of the folks back there whispering about how you two got them out. Now in light of that, I will give you this one-time option to stand down now, and we can end this as peacefully as possible.

"How about it?" he offered.

Though he remained quiet even still, Sam's answer was a resounding no. He darted his head around, looking for the closest yet tallest building he could make the jump up.

"Hey," Starsk started, his voice rising. "Don't do anything stupid now, you hear? *Men! If he moves from that spot, you are free to open fire!*"

Victor's chest repeatedly pounded like a meteor strike, his fight or flight warring for control of his body. Jump in now and fight to save his injured friends, maybe losing his life in the process? Or stay right where he stood and retain the legacy he and his whole family had worked their whole lives to build?

"Shit. Shit. Shit," he forcefully whispered through tightly clenched teeth.

"So?" Starsk questioned. "What'll it be?"

Sam gave the colonel a quick glance after spotting a building he felt confident he could reach even with Dylan's added weight. Crouching down and mustering the biggest clusters of flames he could on short notice, Sam launched into the air slower than his usual expertise.

"*Fire!*" the colonel screamed out.

The large circle formation of soldiers all opened fire at once, the air above them becoming a frenzy of ricocheting metal that pelted the neighboring buildings relentlessly.

Sam felt three warm impacts along his right shoulder, their intense stinging immediately coursing through him.

Their force knocked him off his trajectory and sent them heading toward a nearby balcony. He pulled Dylan off his shoulder and turned his own body around as they came crashing down onto the apartment's wooden table.

Falling on the bullet wounds in his shoulder felt almost as bad as Overcharge's lightning coursing through your body. His vision continued to flash between the two scenes, sending pulsing throbs through his right eye every few seconds.

Sam kept him and Dylan low as the gunfire below continued to shred into the stone balcony. If he was gonna have any chance of getting the two of them out of here, he'd need to find another way out of the city.

"*Bravo squad! Enter and locate! Alpha, surround the building and secure exit points,*" Starsk ordered with a wave of the hand.

His soldiers effortlessly split into two perfectly decided groups, the two forefronts of which led them forward to their assigned duties.

Sam could hear the loud crash of the building's entrance being breached down below by Bravo.

"Fuck, fuck," he muttered, trying to thinking of their next move.

He figured his only option was to get to the opposite end of the building and out onto another before Alpha could surround the place. Throwing a piece of the wooden table, he shattered the sliding glass door of the apartment and instantly threw Dylan back over his shoulder as he started to sprint into the building.

Using his momentum, he barged through the door, knocking it clean off its hinges and lodging it in the wall outside. He winced in pain from the still pulsing holes in his shoulder.

Everything they'd gone through in the last hour was finally starting to catch up with him—lacerations, head trauma, and now blood was continuously spilling out of him. His head felt light as his good eye started to haze over slightly, and the constant switching between his normal vision and whatever was happening in his right eye only worsened its effect on his sight.

He gave himself a good slap across his own face in an effort to wake his aching body and mind up.

Coming through the open door, he looked around and found himself with no path directly to the other side of the building unless he wanted to barrel through more people's apartments.

That meant he needed to go up.

He shot his head around again to see which direction the stairwell was in. He found its entrance at the end of the long hallway. His heart pounded in his chest as his mind raced with millions of thoughts, and he wouldn't have any chance of calming himself until he got the two of them somewhere safe.

With fear's claws clutching into his expression, he bolted forward, ramming the next door down as he entered the stairwell. His speed nearly took him over the edge of the railing, having to grip it and bring both his and Dylan's weight back over.

"*Target spotted! You up above, do not move!*" he heard someone from below shout out assertively.

Bravo squad had already made it up to what looked like the fifth floor, only four below where he stood. He began to book it up the stairs with everything he had in his dwindling energy reserves, bounding up several steps at a time to cut as much time to the top as possible.

He heard a loud pop ring from below and saw a collision of something in the stairs above him.

"*Final warning! Stay where you are!*"

Sam couldn't even hear his words over the white noise deafening his ears. His heart raced so fast he had trouble processing what was even happening outside the pain he felt at the moment.

Up he continued, clinging to the wall as much as possible as he did. He could see the roof entrance two more floors up, giving him all the incentive he needed to keep his ass in gear.

He finally burst through the rooftop access door, panting for breath as he darted around looking for his next jump direction.

As much as he may have wanted to head straight back to Victor's warehouse, he couldn't until he made sure no one was able to follow him back. His face sunk as he realized his pursuit had probably only just begun. He had no way of knowing what kind of numbers the army had stationed in the city.

He could hear the thudding of footsteps growing closer behind him, meaning he didn't have all day to sit up here and sulk. He picked the first rooftop he laid his eyes on, immediately bursting forth and blasting toward it in a trailing blaze of flames.

The soldiers filed out onto the rooftop with their guns drawn and ready, fanning their gazes around in search of their target. Bravo squad's leader lowered his weapon, making his way toward the roof's edge as he watched the flaming figure bound its way across the building tops.

"Shit," he whispered. He holstered his weapon and walked over toward the opposite end of the rooftop, looking down to catch sight of Colonel Starsk.

As he met his superior's fierce gaze, he gave him a light shake of his head, pointing in the direction the target had escaped toward.

Starsk groaned, shouting out for as many of his soldiers to hear as possible, "*Regroup!*"

They all took the next few minutes to fall in line in front of their direct superior, placing their automatic weapons in their specially designed back holsters before every trained individual belted out in unison, "*Ready for orders, sir!*"

Starsk viewed his surroundings, his innate ferocity leaking through the frown plastered on his face. "Alpha squad, I want you following the Evo's trail through the city! Contact Charlie squad for backup! Bravo, you're splitting into Bravo and Delta! Bravo handles getting the civilians out of the local law enforcement's evacuation perimeter! Delta's in charge of beginning to properly cordon off the area!"

With an exaggerated wave of his hand, Starsk's soldiers howled in response, bringing their hands up for routinely practiced salutes as they did. "*Sir, yes, sir!*"

Off the three teams went, leaving Starsk to continue to stare at the remains of the earthen dome, the knowledge that the figures hiding in the shadows had finally made their move pounding in his head.

Now, they responded to this declaration of war.

●　●　●

Victor slunk away from the awestruck crowd, each too distracted by racing thoughts on what they'd all experienced to see the tears building in his eyes as he walked behind the large group of ambulances crowding the street.

He slid his back down the side of the large red vehicle as he struggled to come to grips with the immense pit burrowing in his stomach, his growing guilt gnawing at him from within.

"I'm so sorry, guys." He sobbed to himself, his face flush red beneath the floodgates of tears staining his face. "I was fucking useless."

30

WE FIGHT

D ylan felt the warm light creep into his slowly opening eyes. He looked up to see the run-down ceiling of Victor's warehouse above him, the pattern giving him a strange sense of déjà vu. Turning his head to the side, he spotted Hartley and Victor sitting around a few monitors, both of them looking to be discussing whatever it was they were watching.

"All manner of local and state law enforcement are thoroughly investigating today's terrorist attack alongside the on-scene military personnel." A reporter's voice boomed from the TV.

He slowly began to lift himself up, but didn't get very far before feeling searing pain shoot throughout his arms and head. "Ow," he groaned.

Both Victor and Hartley jerked their heads at the sound, bolting over to Dylan's makeshift bed. "He's up!" Victor exclaimed. "Started to worry us for a minute there."

Hartley immediately made his way to check on Dylan's bandages, taking a look at the heaps of bloody gauze around his hands specifically. "Don't flex those hands too much for the next few days. You'll interrupt the healing process."

Dylan stood himself up, lightly touching his head as he shook off the grogginess. "Worried for a minute? I don't understand. How long have I been out?"

"Only a few hours," Victor told him.

Dylan's brow furrowed in confusion. "What happened? I remember everything was coming down—" His eyes went wide as he began to remember what he'd been through, seeing flashes of a crazed flaming animal. "*Where's Sam?*" he shouted.

Victor's smile quickly faded with the question. "He's OK. He's out on the deck, but ..."

Dylan started to pick himself up so he could go out to check on him. He could only imagine what he was feeling right now.

"Wait," Victor told him. "He doesn't want to see anyone right now. When he came hobbling through the door ... covered in blood, he wouldn't tell me what happened, either in the dome or afterward. He just laid you down, grabbed his smokes, and asked to be alone for a while. He wouldn't even let Hartley treat his wounds."

Dylan's eyes moistened, and he dropped his head low as everything finally came back to him. "Fuck," he muttered.

Victor couldn't be angrier with himself. Judging by the looks of it, he'd sat by safely while his friends had laid their lives on the line for hundreds of people they'd never even met. His face tightened as he looked at his traumatized friend. Dropping to his knees before him, he started to voice his apology through catching breaths of guilt. "Dylan ... I ... I'm so sorry. I just ... I just watched as it happened. I was too scared to reveal myself and to lose what my parents left to me ... And so many people died because of it," he forced himself to say. "And I just sat and watched as you both were forced to fight in my place ... and Sam ... Dylan, I have to know. What happened in there?"

Tears dripped from Dylan's ducts as he thought back to the gruesome sight of the civilians they'd let die. "We failed."

He looked back up at Victor with his flooding face and began to recount to him what had transpired during their altercation with the man known as Tremor.

As Victor and Hartley listened to the harrowing story Dylan proceeded to tell, Victor's own eyes began to widen, their shine becoming more prominent as they filled with his regret over not having stepped in. Before he knew it, there was no holding back the salty, guilt-riddled flood behind his eyes.

He turned his head, looking out the small window to the back deck, seeing Sam leaned up against a wooden post as he stared out into the bay's night view.

• • •

Sam kept his right eye shut tightly as he looked at the glistening lights of the usual scene laid out in front of him, clutching his aching, bloodstained shoulder all the while.

Quickly, he clasped his left eye shut as he opened his right, causing both his damaged pupil and iris to begin to glow a bright, white-hued orange as the scene before him switched to a pure black expanse, the occasional flickering fire popping through the darkness.

Somehow, whatever had happened to him earlier today had done something to his eye, bringing back its vision in a sense of the word. Now it was like his right eye singularly held his ability to sense other powered individuals, or Evos as he'd heard the soldiers chasing him today say.

He switched back to his working eye, groaning from the strain of keeping one eye shut at all times. It was gonna take some getting used to, but it'd be worth it to be able to see one scene at a time.

Glancing down, he looked at the bits of dried blood still clinging to his right arm, feeling the pulsing pain in his chest they brought. He wiped a tear away, trying to justify to himself that he'd stopped Tremor from killing anyone else, but only at the cost of dozens of innocent people and at the cost of another piece of his hollowing self-worth.

Or was it his humanity?

He couldn't help but think about James's warning, saying that nothing would ever be the same after today, meaning this wouldn't be their last fight against FEAR. He wondered if he should have listened to him? If he should have taken Victor and Dylan and just run before any of them could be hurt any worse?

But even through his pain, he knew he wasn't one to run away from a fight.

He looked back through the window into the warehouse, watching as Victor helped Dylan to his feet. Thinking about how Dylan had seen what he'd done, he wondered what his friend now thought about him.

• • •

Victor helped Dylan hobble over to his monitors, setting him down in one of the nearby chairs as he showed him what had been happening since he'd been out. Every monitor was tuned to a different news station, multiple reporters' voices overlapping all at once.

"… Followed by the structure suddenly sinking into the ground as the reports state. Witness testimony states that two enhanced individuals evaded the army's efforts to capture them, leaving no trace of the third who revealed himself a member of the phantom organization, FEAR, as the structure sank below ground level," Olivia finished, motioning to the now empty lot behind her.

"Where Penn station once stood is now replaced by a large crater, similar in fashion to the Day of Light's devastation. The military has begun to erect mobile labs over the remainder of the scene, but whether it's for our protection or for their gain is still unknown.

"It appears," she quickly began again, finding herself cutting her sentence short as she reacted to something happening off camera. "New York, this is not a drill! It seems the military is vacating several city blocks around the site. Everyone is being asked to leave the area immediately."

Dylan, Victor, and Hartley all gasped as they watched dozens of new high-tech trucks roll on scene through the TV, all of them unloading numerous people clad in the same hazmat suits they'd seen people wearing when they first exited Light Valley.

"The soldiers are even ordering the police and medical teams to vacate the scene immediately!" Another reporter screamed on a different screen. "It seems like they're claiming the section of the city for their own investigation into the incident."

"What's that?" the reporter asked someone off camera.

"Hey, that's expensive equipment! You can't just ... New York, we're being forcibly removed from the area! Hey, I'm going!" the reporter yelled at the soldiers shoving them out.

Hearing a loud roar overheard the warehouse, the three of them threw their heads back, almost immediately jerking them back down toward the door as they heard it slam open.

"Guys, get out here, now!" Sam screamed.

The three met Sam outside, looking up to see a gut-plummeting sight moving above them. Dozens of military helicopters flew overhead, all making their way across the water to the incident site. Their combined horsepower filled the air around the city with a low rumbling.

"Holy shit." Sam let the words fall out.

"I say we get back inside," Victor urged them all.

Reentering the warehouse, Victor shut the door behind them, keeping his hands placed on the door as he rested his forehead on it as well.

"It's the government's logical response to what happened," Hartley announced. "Unknown entities with extra human abilities? Of course they'd claim the scene ... They'll have national-level geniuses showing up any day to investigate the incident."

"Not only that, but an organization of extra human individuals just declared war on the non-powered populace," Sam added.

"FEAR," Victor muttered.

"This is what James warned me about," Sam said as he took a seat again, thinking back to everything he'd been told.

"James?" Dylan questioned.

"I guess that's Overcharge's real name. He came to me just before that guy's attack, told me he'd been sent to invite me to join some organization that was gonna create a world where the strong thrived or something," Sam explained. "Instead, he chose to warn me that something was coming. He told me they're led by a guy who calls himself King.

"And he said to run now while we have the chance."

"King?" Dylan asked with an irked look. "I don't like this guy already. That's not all, though. If we've been going on the assumption it was the blast that did this to us, and we've now been told what's happened was planned by this King guy, does that mean we've already come in contact with the people responsible?" He felt his chest tighten at the thought of the man whose idea it'd been to blast a hole in New York, ripping Ashley away from him and her parents.

The three of them all gave each other a look; neither Sam nor Victor had thought to make that connection yet.

"It's possible," Victor answered.

"Well that's the closest we've gotten to an answer in months. What else do we know about them? Did ... James tell you anything else?" Dylan asked Sam.

"He told me their leader's name and that, including James himself, there's nine elites under King's command," Sam answered.

"I feel like we can assume the guy from today was one of them, which would make it eight now, right?" Dylan clarified, feeling an instant grip of regret at the words. He glanced over at Sam to see if he could figure out what he was thinking.

Sam clenched his jaw for a moment before sighing. "And now the military has entered the equation."

"I guess so." Dylan chuckled dryly.

"Eight of them and three of us," Victor stated ominously.

Hartley loudly cleared his throat behind them, giving a slightly irritated look as they turned to look at him.

They all couldn't help but chuckle.

"I'm sorry ... Four of us," he restated.

Feeling the mood lighten, they all thanked Hartley internally, finding themselves thankful for his way of breaking the tension. They all took a moment to let everything sink in.

"So?" Dylan asked, breaking the silence. "What do we do?"

"I guess," Sam answered, "we start to prepare. It doesn't really seem like there's a choice in all of this. Whatever FEAR is, it's made its intentions clear. It's declared war on everything in its way."

"Where do we start, though?" Dylan asked as he looked down at his hands. "It's not like there's a guide on fighting a war fought by people with abilities. Look what's happened to us just going up against one of them."

Victor looked at the state of both of them. Sam had definitely taken the worst of it, but Dylan hadn't escaped unscathed; he could see spots where the blood was seeping through the bandages around his hands and head.

They both had put their lives on the line, not only for him but also for hundreds of strangers as well, and he'd just run away. How could he ever hope to help them if he couldn't even bring himself to fight for anyone but himself? He knew, if he ever wanted to stand beside them as an equal, he'd need to make a change within himself.

As scared of the thought of losing what he'd built in this life, what his family had built in this life, the thought of watching his friends die in front of him because he was too much of a coward to move scared him more than anything.

"We train." He stood and spoke powerfully, sparking a reaction in Dylan and Sam. "We've seen how far we've already come, and we know we can go even farther. If we're not enough, then we'll find others. If one thing's been confirmed in the last few days, it's that we're not alone. Who knows how many others are out there right now, hiding in fear of what's happened to them? They might not have had people to help them through it like we did."

Sam looked at his friend, seeing the drive building behind his eyes. He could almost physically feel his fear, but still he stood before them trying to encourage them. And he was a hell of a motivational speaker.

Yet, though Sam tried to be as well put together as possible, knowing he had the definitive support of his friends behind him, beneath it all, he could still feel his mind in a vortex of emotional turmoil. He wondered how long before the support of these incredibly kind people wouldn't cut it anymore, how long until he was so far gone nobody could help him.

And when that time came, would they continue to be there for him or would they look at him like everyone else when they realized how broken he was? Monstrous, even?

He decided to leave those fears for another time.

Knowing that Victor was right, they all nodded in agreement. They may not have asked for this fight, but they sure as hell weren't gonna lie down and submit without at least making it difficult for those who would try to destroy the world. If there were others out there, undyed by FEAR's colors, they'd find them.

Sam lit his hand ablaze. "If FEAR, or whatever it's called, really did plan that blast and the effects it would cause, they're sure as hell gonna regret letting us leave that bunker."

EPILOGUE

"It appears Tremor has failed his objective," King bellowed at his soldiers. He looked down upon his eight elites, all symmetrically lined up in front of him.

Yet now there were more. Standing behind a few of them were a number of newcomers, young and old, all gawking at the huge stone complex they found themselves in.

James and Mimic stood alone in their line, keeping their eyes low as they waited for their inevitable punishment.

"The two of you as well," he boomed at them. "You were instructed to eliminate the threat given the circumstances, yet they still walk this earth. At least Tremor attempted to take two of them down with him. What do you have to say for yourselves?"

"Opportunity wasn't there," Mimic immediately called back. "We were instructed to keep out of the public eye until Tremor made the reveal."

"*And?*" King growled.

"Well, he hadn't made the reveal yet." Mimic sneered.

A weight fell over everyone's shoulders, dropping them all to their knees with a thud. Sweat dripped down each and every one of their terror-stricken faces, elite and newcomer alike. Mimic did his best to look upward and face King, who just sat atop his throne glaring down at him.

"*Would you like to reword your response?*" he asked slowly.

"I ... I'm sorry, sir." Mimic forced this out through the weight crushing him to the ground. "I ... got careless. I ... thought I had more time. His ... ability was hard to keep a hold of. I didn't know if ... I could do it within my time limit."

The weight finally lifted off of everyone's shoulders, all of them gasping to catch their breath, all except James, who still continued to be crushed.

"So they are A-class then?" King asked Mimic as he stood himself up, slowly walking over to meet his eyeline.

Mimic rubbed his chest. "I think so. But it was strange. Given I lost my grip, it has to mean at least one of their abilities is A-class level, but their usage is weirdly limited. It's almost like they aren't even aware of what they're capable of yet."

"Hmm." He pondered. "A worthwhile discovery."

Placing his hand onto Mimic's shoulder, King gave him a sudden otherworldly grip that forced pops and cracks to echo through the liquid layers of his body and into the open space. He shoved him back down to his knees while still intensely gripping his collar bone, allowing him to force out his pained breaths before continuing. "But one successful task does not negate the failure of another."

With a thought, King's strange black substance oozed out from the insides of his coat sleeves, enveloping Mimic in its icy touch once again. "If the pit didn't fix that nauseating attitude, perhaps Silver can come up with something that will teach you to hold that conceited tongue of yours."

Glancing to the right side of the room, King laid eyes on a middle-aged man who had already fixated his obsessive gaze on the man who had been his direct superior up until that moment, now seeing him gasping for what little breath he could bring in with fear in his young eyes.

"I finally get some playtime?" he asked with an odd tilt of his head as he let loose a crazed giggle, already beginning to make his way over to meet King's order.

"In moderation, yes. I don't want to lose any more high-tier soldiers before we can see what the newly recruited crop is capable of. So as long as he survives to fight for us in the end, you have my permission to employ level-two methods."

Silver's wide grin almost seemed to curl at the ends when he heard that. Not since the induction of Overcharge had he been able to use anything higher than level one.

"You got it, boss." He giggled.

With a forceful outward thrust of his hand, the surface of his skin liquified, its bright peach hue lightening into a metallic color as his arm lengthened and sharpened itself. Finally, a long silver blade formed at the end of his left arm.

"Tremor would have loved to see how pathetic you look now," he quickly whispered towards Mimic's black casing.

Swinging the blade forward, he plunged its sharp tip through the black substance coating Mimic's body, seeming to narrowly miss any vitals. He lifted the black blob into the air and slung it over his shoulder, proceeding to half skip out of the large stone throne room, whistling an eerily creepy tune on his way out.

King finally looked down on James, his piercing black eyes almost seeming to plunge through him without moving a finger.

"And you? What excuse might you have for your failure to complete your task yet again?" he shot at him, his very words rumbling the stone space around them all.

James hesitated, not only in response to the still active weight pushing down but also because he knew he had to be very careful about his next few words. "He managed … to get away … by escaping into the bay." He forced the words out. "I can't make pinpoint use … of my ability … in the water."

King sighed. "Now see, I don't know if I can believe that. You heard it yourself. My own second in command tried to lie to me. Now why would I believe you and not him?"

James felt the weight growing heavier and heavier by the second, coupled with the look of animosity growing in his superior's eyes above him. "I … I don't know."

He watched as King leaned in close to his ear. "I hope you haven't decided to step back on your side of the agreement, now have you?"

James's face went pale at the accusation.

"Perhaps I'll have to pay a visit to—" King started.

"*No!*" he screamed through heavy, panicked breaths. "Your task was failed by me—no one else. Whatever it is you're gonna do, you do it to me, you fucking hear me?!"

James's outburst brought a smile to King's face. "I do love that protective instinct of yours—makes you incredibly easy to manipulate. I think you and I should take some time to reacquaint ourselves with one another, to relearn exactly what the other is capable of if unnecessarily pushed by dying devotion to a doomed species."

He pointed his finger upward, and a sheet of his liquid ability rocketed from the ground and wrapped itself tightly around James's solid physique, pulling him down into the ground to disappear into the black.

"I'll be by soon, my obstinate companion," King whispered. "Atom?" he then asked to his left while still pointing at the gaping hole in the ground.

The young man gave King a quick laugh before waving his hand toward the requested fix spot, instantly mending the shredded stone back into its former whole.

"Thank you, my friend," King said with a smile.

He waved his arms outward in a welcoming manner, taking a few steps forward before addressing the beginnings of his army. "Newcomers! You have made the correct decision in where you place your allegiance. We seek to create a world where none can hurt you, where anyone who would wish you harm is squashed beneath your foot. We'll create an ascended society that will live on for thousands of years.

"Many of you have been subjected to the current society's ideals of what strong and weak truly mean, confusing it with the rich or the poor, the educated or the illiterate, the haves ... or the have-nots.

"But I stand before you today to reteach the true hierarchy of this world and to show you how much strength you actually possess.

"In the world we will go on to create after today, you all will realize how much the modern world has brainwashed you, confined you, even plotted against you. You will all come to realize that true power in this misguided world is the strength to bend that very same world to your own will and build it into anything you could imagine.

"In a few months' time, we will hold a rank reevaluation for the sake of all you fresh faces. This means that, after you've all taken the time to familiarize yourselves with your abilities and the potential they hold, we'll hold specialized screenings for advancements in ranks, for only a select few of you will have what it takes to be fit for the role of one of my elites. Now, this is not an insult to any of you, even to my existing elites, as we've already discussed what true power in this world is, and they've accepted what may happen when we give you all a chance to show us what you're capable of. Regardless of rank, though, rest assured there is a place for each and every one of you here. Every one of you has something to offer the world we will create.

"And now that you've all taken the first step toward the top of the food chain, this is my promise to each and every one of you," King went on. "No longer will you cower in fear of a corrupt politician's greed-laced agenda! Never again will you wonder if you'll have enough money to decide between food or housing! Never again will you wonder where your place in this world is! *For if you follow me, the world itself will be yours!*"

Despite their reservations given what had happened only moments ago, none could deny the feeling of power they felt flow into them when they heard King speak of the future they would create.

The foremost crowd broke into roars of agreement, all the front rowed elites beginning to chant together.

"*We are FEAR!*

"*We are FEAR!*

"*We are FEAR!*"

Slowly the newcomers began to follow along with the men or women who had brought them there, feeling the power many of them had only recently developed coursing through their enhanced bodies.

"We are FEAR!
"We are FEAR!
"We are FEAR!"

King looked upon his army with a smile, knowing this was only the beginning. "So, shall we begin Phase Three?"

Printed in the United States
by Baker & Taylor Publisher Services